This book
MALICE MASTERPIECES 5
contains novellas
Twenty-One through
Twenty-Five
including:
MEANDERING MALICE
MANIACAL MALICE
MONITORING MALICE
MARKED MALICE
MANDATING MALICE

A K'Anne Meinel novel

Book 21 MEANDERING MALICE

She's cold, she's tired, and she just wants to go home to her family. Those preventing Alice from reaching her goals are about to learn there is a steep price to pay when you get in her way. With two civilians to protect from their enemies, will the horror she is about to unleash repel them or will they help her overcome the obstacles keeping her from her goals?

Alice is about to unleash the beast within. Come along and watch as she makes decisions that may affect the rest of her life...they will most definitely affect others' lives!

Book 22 MANIACAL MALICE

Alice is just finishing up a few minor details that have kept her from returning to her family—killing a few people that kept her away, blowing up a few things, taking revenge on the heartless...Can Alice FINALLY go home?

Book 23 MONITORING MALICE

Alice is home and must explain to Kathy why she watched her family go on with their lives and didn't show herself.

While she watches her wife being set up by thugs in positions of authority and is forced to witness Kathy's first foray into dating since being widowed, Alice struggles to control her murderous temper! She must learn to be patient...very patient.

Come along for the ride as we see things from Alice's distinct point of view.

Book 24 MARKED MALICE

Would you know how to bring someone back to life? Well, Alice is not just a killer...she once brought her wife back to life. And now, her wife has an opportunity to repay her. But can Alice keep fact and fiction straight while trying to avoid sharing the gruesome details of her recent adventures with her teenage children? What happens when one of the children learns some of what Alice has been through? And what happens when Alice and Kathy realize their children aren't the only ones aware of Alice's deeds during her time away? Join Kathy and Alice as they answer two vitally important questions: 'Who believes they have damning evidence that gives them the power to control Alice Weaver?' and 'Can these two women salvage their marriage...do they even want to?'

Book 25 MANDATING MALICE

Who is Alice Weaver? The CIA believes they are about to find out...but are they? Do they really want to meet the real Alice Weaver? Perhaps, some things are better left hidden. Some agents think they already know who Alice is. After all, they have a file on her and so does the FBI. But what they know is only what Alice wants them to know. When Alice Weaver shares information with those in authority, they will be left scrambling for cover!

Also by K'Anne Meinel:

Novels in Paperback:

SHIPS *CompanionSHIP, FriendSHIP,*
RelationSHIP
Long Distance Romance
Children of Another Mother
Erotica
The Claim
Bikini's Are Dangerous
The Complete Series
Germanic
Malice Masterpieces 1
The First Five Books
Represented
Timed Romance
Malice Masterpieces 2
Books Six through Ten
The Journey Home
Out at the Inn
Shorts
Anthology Volume 1
Lawyered
Malice Masterpieces 3
Books Eleven through Fifteen
Blown Away
Blown Away
The Alternate Cover

Small Town Angel
Pirated Love
Doctored
Veil of Silence
Malice Masterpieces 4
Books Sixteen through Twenty
The Outsider
Pirated Heart
Recombinant Love
Survivors
Inn the Dog House
Flight
An Island Between Us
Malice Masterpieces 5
Books Twenty-One through Twenty-Five
Beauty and the Beast

Vetted Series:
Vetted
Cavalcade (Prequel)
Pioneering (Prequel)
Vetted Further
Vetted Again

Novellas in Paperback:

Sapphic Surfer
Sapphic Cowgirl
Sapphic Cowboi
Mysterious Malice (Book 1)
Meticulous Malice (Book 2)
Mistaken Malice (Book 3)
Malicious Malice (Book 4)
Masterful Malice (Book 5)
Matrimonial Malice (Book 6)
Mourning Malice (Book 7)
Murderous Malice (Book 8)
Mental Malice (Book 9)
Menacing Malice (Book 10)
Minor Malice (Book 11)
Morally Malice (Book 12)
Morose Malice (Book 13)
Melancholy Malice (Book 14)
Mad Malice (Book 15)

Macabre Malice (Book 16)
Marinating Malice (Book 17)
Macerating Malice (Book 18)
Minacious Malice (Book 19)
Meddlesome Malice (Book 20)
Meandering Malice (Book 21)
Maniacal Malice (Book 22)
Sayyida
The Northwood Lodge
Monitoring Malice (Book 23)
Marked Malice (Book 24)
Shanghaied (Prequel)
Outback Born
Outback Bred
Outback Heritage
Outback Native
Outback Splendor

Novellas in E-book:

Outback Escape (Prequel)
Mandating Malice (Book 25)
Methodical Malice (Book 26)
Malevolent Malice (Book 27)
Militarial Malice (Book 28)
Machiavellian Malice (Book 29)

Malefic Malice (Book 30)
Religious Experience
Lied

Pocket Paperbacks:

Mysterious Malice (Book 1)
Sapphic Surfer
Sapphic Cowgirl
Meticulous Malice (Book 2)
Mistaken Malice (Book 3)
Malicious Malice (Book 4)
Masterful Malice (Book 5)
Matrimonial Malice (Book 6)
Mourning Malice (Book 7)
Murderous Malice (Book 8)

Mental Malice (Book 9)
Menacing Malice (Book 10)
Minor Malice (Book 11)
Morally Malice (Book 12)
Morose Malice (Book 13)
Melancholy Malice (Book 14)
Mad Malice (Book 15)
Macabre Malice (Book 16)
Marinating Malice (Book 17)

In E-Book Format:
Short Stories

Fantasy
Wet & Wet Again
Family Night
Quickie ~ Against the Car
Quickie ~ Against the Wall
Quickie ~ Over the Couch
Mile High Club
Quickie ~ Under the Pier
Heel or Heal
Kiss
Family Night 2
Beach Dreams
Internet Dreamers
Snoggered

On the Parkway
Stable Affair
Kept
Stolen
Agitated
Love of my LIFE
Quickie in an Elevator,
GOING DOWN?
Into the Garden
The Book Case
The Other Women
Menage a WHAT?

Audiobooks

Doctored
Sapphic Surfer
The Rockhound
Cavalcade
Pioneering
To Love A Shooting Star
Mysterious Malice
Ghostly Love

Stable Affair
Sapphic Cowgirl
Love of my LIFE
The Book Case
Flight
Sayyida
Vetted

Videos

Biography of Books
Ships
Sapphic Surfer
Ghostly Love
Long Distance Romance
Germanic
Sensual Sapphic
Sapphic Cowgirl
Couples
Lie Next To Me

Sapphic Cowboi
Timed Romance
Readings (SHIPS)
Doctored
Veil of Silence
She's Coming (The Outsider short)
It's Coming (The Outsider short)
The Outsider
Vetted

Novels/Novellas in other Languages:

Sapphic Cowboi: Vaquera Safica (Spanish)
Sapphic Surfer: Surfista Safica (Spanish)
Sapphic Surfer: ケーアンヌ・マイネル (Japanese)
Doctored: A Doutora (Portuguese)
Doctored: La Doctora (Spanish)

LARGE Print Novels

SHIPS CompanionSHIP, FriendSHIP,
RelationSHIP
Erotica Volume 1
Long Distance Romance
Children of Another Mother
Bikini's Are Dangerous
The Complete Series

Malice Masterpieces
The First Five Books
To Love a Shooting Star
The Claim
Represented
Timed Romance

K'ANNE MEINEL

Malice Masterpieces

5

Books Twenty-One through

Twenty-Five

ISBN-13: 978-1959436089

K'Anne Meinel is available for comments at KAnneMeinel@aim.com as well as on Facebook, Google +, or her blog @ http://kannemeinel.wordpress.com/ or on Twitter @ kannemeinelaim.com, or on her website @ www.kannemeinel.com if you would like to follow her to find out about stories and book's releases.

www.shadoepublishing.com

ShadoePublishing@gmail.com

Shadoe Publishing is a United States of America company

Cover by: K'Anne Meinel @ Shadoe Publishing
Edited by: Deb Amia, Grammar Queen

MALICE MASTERPIECES

5

Table of Contents:

MEANDERING MALICE

BOOK 21

She's cold, she's tired, and she just wants to go home to her family. Those preventing Alice from reaching her goals are about to learn there is a steep price to pay when you get in her way. With two civilians to protect from their enemies, will the horror she is about to unleash repel them or will they help her overcome the obstacles keeping her from her goals?

Alice is about to unleash the beast within. Come along and watch as she makes decisions that may affect the rest of her life...they will most definitely affect others' lives!

"Who is helping these women?" he demanded angrily.

"You don't think they could..." began the man he was talking to.

"No, I don't. No one woman or even two could be doing all this. I want names. I want faces. I want deaths!" He was nearly foaming at the mouth he was so angry. "I want that money back! With interest!" he demanded.

The third person in the room, a woman, smiled evilly. That was the command she had been waiting for...

"What is this place?" Alice asked Sasha, unable to read the Russian script. They had flown on many airplanes in the last twenty-four hours and she was tired and irritable. She was also looking for a hotel.

Sasha peered through the rain, barely able to make out the sign next to the door. "It is a piano manufacturer," she answered, wondering at the grin that appeared on Alice's face.

Alice thought rapidly and quickly tried the door, making sure her glove was in place so no fingerprints would be left behind. "Stay here," she breathed in an undertone to Sasha. "Do not touch anything...not the door, not *anything*," she stressed. Quickly she disappeared inside. The door, although locked before Alice played with it, was not armed.

Sasha stared in consternation as the blonde disappeared inside. It was not the first time she had wondered at the woman's skills. Who exactly was Alice Weaver? The wait wasn't long, perhaps half an hour, but the rain made the air cold and Sasha was tempted to go after Alice, however, remembering other times she had disobeyed Alice, she had second thoughts about that idea.

"Here, put these in the bags," Alice handed her coils of what Sasha assumed was piano wire.

"Wha–?" she started to ask as she unzipped one of their bags and started stuffing.

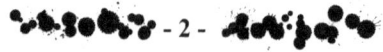

"We may need this," Alice told her as she relocked the door and made sure everything was left as they found it.

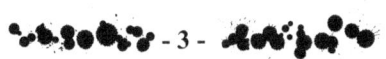

As they had come over that last rise, the walk seemed endless. They stopped to survey the view. Alice could tell that Sasha didn't stay physically fit from hiking or jogging. If her bitchin' was any indication, she didn't exercise normally, but what lay before them made the journey worthwhile. The valley itself looked lush after the high desert they had been traversing.

"Oh, my God," Sasha breathed as she looked at the valley. Alice echoed her sentiments.

Someone had invested a lot of money at one time and had built out here in the middle of nowhere. They'd used local stone to create a palace of sorts in the muted shades of brown that were prevalent in this part of the world. Long, sweeping paths led up to the main structure, something from the days of Maharajah's when elephants would have ponderously brought them home. The structure wasn't in the Mideastern or Oriental style. It was unlike anything either of them had seen before. There were turrets and even what looked like some sort of medieval moat. It was almost reminiscent of Russian architecture with a taste of St. Petersburg and the Grand Duchess about it.

"Where's the binoculars?" Alice mumbled and then her arm shot out to keep Sasha from walking farther down the road. "Wait! Let's see what we are up against." She found her binoculars and, checking the position of the sun so there would be no glare off the lenses, she began to scan the buildings and surroundings. She spotted armed guards, dogs, and then power lines. Following the lines, she saw they came in from the mountains to the south of the structures. Some of the mountains even had a dusting of snow on them.

"What do you see?" Sasha asked, worriedly. They'd traveled so far to find this man. He had been very wily and had lots of hiding places. "Do you think he is there?"

Alice handed her the binoculars silently while she thought about their options. She was sure it was a trap. The Assemblage couldn't afford to take any more losses. Alice and Sasha had killed some of the upper echelon of their membership before they scattered. From what she had read, they were all going to hide; they would transact business from afar. In this age of the internet, electronic transactions were easy. They were also easy to divert and Alice had several under her own belt, accumulating wealth they had stolen from Sasha in addition to removing any, and all funds she could from their coffers. She felt it was only fair as they had stolen time from her life away from her own family. Compensation in the form of money and their lives wasn't too much to ask, was it? Apparently, they didn't agree. The bounty on the two 'blondes' was enough to have every underworld person in Russia hounding their trail. Fortunately for them, they weren't in Russia. They also weren't blonde anymore; their hair was decidedly black.

Kazakhstan was a huge nation and she wished she knew more about it. It was unfortunate their purpose for traveling in Kazakhstan was to kill one of its citizens—a Russian by the name of Konstantinov which, Sasha informed her, meant that he was a descendant of Konstantin. So far, Alice was not impressed, and then she had come over that last rise and seen this monolith that was the man's home. She guessed his billions weren't enough for him. He had coveted Sasha's and now he was in a bit of a pickle…They were on his trail. He fled Moscow in such a hurry that when Alice and Sasha had gotten there, they'd been able to get on his computer, get beyond his sophisticated firewall, and find out where all his homes were. This was the second home they had come to and Alice was getting angry at the waste of time he had caused her. She wasn't happy.

"You think he's down there?" Sasha asked after looking throughout the valley and at the palace.

"I don't know," she sighed honestly. "I really would hate to have to travel to Kyrgyzstann or China to find this guy."

"But he didn't have homes in…" Sasha began before she realized Alice was teasing. Some days she wasn't always sure the woman was kidding. She had thought after being with Alice constantly for all these months, she would get used to the American. She hadn't. "Vhat do you tink ve should do?" she asked instead, deferring to Alice. The woman was uncanny in her knowledge of how to take these guys down.

"It's obviously a trap," Alice told her conversationally, taking up the binoculars again and perusing the palace. The various levels and walls made it a fortress to be reckoned with. Why would anyone need such a castle out here in the middle of nowhere?

"Do we give up?" she asked, almost hopefully. She was tired. They'd been after these people for a long time. They'd killed many, and yet some had managed to elude them. They still didn't know who all the members of The Assemblage were. A few they hadn't been able to label on their charts due to missing pictures, as they slowly eliminated them.

"I won't be inconvenienced," Alice said tightly. She wanted to end this as much as Sasha did. She wanted to go home. She wanted to make up with Kathy and go on with her life. She missed her children! She even missed her dog, Coco!

The barking of dogs could be heard across the valley. They had to have known the two women were there. Alice wasn't surprised when she heard from behind them, "Put your hands up!" She'd sensed them long before they spoke, the hairs on the back of her neck standing up. She could have escaped. She had thought about it. But there was Sasha, and it was Sasha they'd been after all along. Alice had just been an afterthought. She didn't think they knew what they had caught when they'd ordered the blonde woman's capture…Sasha's capture. Alice too was blonde and they hadn't known what to do with her. If they had been smart, they would have killed her. Originally, they hadn't known which woman was which, and this worked against them until it was too late. Alice had been killing them ever since.

Alice put her hands up over head. She understood their coarse Russian commands. Her own Russian was imperfect, but passable. Sasha had put her hands up immediately and turned to see their captors, but she couldn't see a thing as the sun shone right in her eyes, just as the man had intended. It was intimidating.

"What are you doing here?"

"We're hiking," Sasha told him immediately. It was what Alice and she had agreed upon if anyone stopped them on the long hike from the nearest town. They'd gotten a ride from Almaty, but the rest of the trip was hit or miss as they made their way here. They'd walked a long way and they were tired and hungry.

"Oh, yeah? What's in these bags?" he sneered as two of his men grabbed each of the women's arms. He patted them down himself, removing a long knife from inside the boot of the woman with the short, spikey hair. "What would you need with a knife like that?" he asked as he looked at the huge blade. It had a stout handle with a compass on it. He unscrewed the compass and found fishhooks, line,

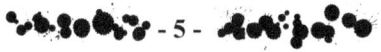

waterproof matches, and other objects in the handle. "Clever," he breathed as he looked at the survival knife. "Hiking, eh?" he asked as he flicked the blade back and forth in front of both women. Even their army didn't issue such a fine blade to its men.

"We got lost and found the road," Sasha asserted. "We hoped to find shelter."

It was obvious he didn't believe them, but he *was* interested in the pretty, black-haired woman. Two women out here alone was a novelty. He made sure he patted Sasha down a second time, hitting all the areas he was interested in. She cringed from his touch. The two men holding her watched and laughed, anticipating what their leader might do. When he reached for her breast a second time, she wrenched her hand from one of the men holding it. Her own hand came across and slapped him upside the face.

It was the distraction Alice was waiting for and she bent over quickly, pulling her own captors off balance and sending first one, then the other tripping forward. It gave her just enough time to grab one of the bags which wasn't zipped shut. Her hand reached inside just as the leader grabbed her. Her thumb slid aside the safety and her finger pulled the trigger. A nail shot out of the bag, through the fabric, and lodged in the man's thigh. He screamed in pain and bent over. In quick fashion, Alice shot the two men holding Sasha and then turned the nail gun on the men who had accosted her and were just getting up from the ground. What the nails did to the men wasn't pretty. The first one, she put out of his misery; he wouldn't stop screaming and it echoed across the valley. The next sound she heard was Sasha vomiting the contents of her stomach at the sight of what Alice had done to the men.

Alice put the safety on the gun and retrieved her knife. She also searched through the men's pockets, taking their identification, money, and weapons. "Come on," she told Sasha, who had recovered enough to help search the men at the end.

"Vere are ve going?" she asked, swallowing to keep from throwing up again. She seemed to do that a lot, swallow that is. She wiped her lips on the back of her sleeve.

"They have to have some sort of transport around here," Alice responded. "That means there is a back way into that place. I want to find it and these should help," she held up a couple of plastic cards she had taken off the bodies, the kind that were used in electronic locks.

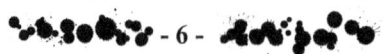

"Don't you think we should hide or bury…" Sasha asked.

Alice hesitated. It was a good point and they were in sight of the palace. She nodded and put their booty in one of the bags. She pulled out her knife and began cutting branches to cover up the bodies. Sasha hurried to carry them when she realized what Alice was doing. She made sure the cuts were out of direct sight of anyone on the road and she even used dirt to hide the fresh cuts. They soon had a natural-looking mound covering the five bodies. Alice staked it down farther by rolling a couple of rocks onto the edges.

"That should hold them for now." They started off, carrying their now marginally heavier bags and looking for the transport.

"Do you tink dey vill be missed?" Sasha asked, looking back and then looking around, attempting to be of some help. She often felt if she didn't make herself useful that Alice would dispose of her just as easily.

Alice shrugged. Of course, they would be missed. How soon was really the question. That palace looked like it was well guarded and not all the guards would be taken in by a pretty face or be distracted so easily. She relished the unexpectedness of her actions. It worked in her favor as they didn't expect a petite woman to attack, always attack. They expected her to cower in submissiveness, but Alice couldn't be called submissive…ever.

They found the ATVs parked back a ways from where they had been standing. The men must have followed them up the path. They were spotted a lot sooner than Alice had realized and this bothered her. In her mind, that meant electronic surveillance of some sort. As she inspected the ATVs, she was surprised to find they were electric, a lot quieter than a gas-powered vehicle. The range would be a lot shorter though. It must be difficult to get a gas tanker out here to fill their vehicles so this made sense. Electricity could be wired in and she'd seen the wires across the valley.

"Do you know how to drive one of these things?" she asked Sasha as she stowed her bags in one of the pack saddles up front in a basket that was tied to the vehicle.

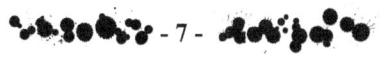

"No, I've never driven one," Sasha answered, looking at the ATV as though it was from another planet.

Alice mentally sighed. For such a brilliant businesswoman, Sasha had few, if any outside interests. Her life had been spent making money and she didn't enjoy herself at all. Alice showed her how to start the electric vehicle and maneuver it. More importantly, she showed her what and where the brake was. She was right. The electronic vehicles were nearly silent as they set out, following the tracks on the desert that led to their location. The loop cut wide and she saw where rocks had been strategically placed to hide the cameras that must have shot Sasha and Alice's arrival on their land. She knew the palace would be alerted to their arrival and there wasn't about to be any surprise. She mentally swore about that, but decided she would worry about it when the time came. She was eager to meet her host as they rode the long way around the valley to the palace.

The AK-47s were impressively new. The sunlight bounced off their barrels in the sunlight. They were also pointed at the two women so they would give no argument. Alice had no problem surrendering. Only Sasha seemed surprised that their good luck, made possible by Alice's skills in the past, had given out. Alice pondered the fact that the guns were Russian and not from Kazakhstan. They went willingly, especially with the barrel of one of the guns pressed up against their temples and then later, pushed against their spines, prodding them. They were led inside. The bottom floor of the palace was what one would expect in a medieval castle...dungeons and all. These were, however, modern in design with electronics and surveillance equipment. The two women were led to a chamber and pushed inside. There were two bunks attached to the wall and they turned to look as their captors clanged the metal door shut.

"Vat are–" began Sasha, but Alice shushed her, a finger to her lips as she pointed at the surveillance equipment in the corners of their cell. Sasha watched as Alice walked over to one of the cameras and hopping up, ripped it from the wall. A shout could be heard from down the corridor and someone came running, yelling in Russian.

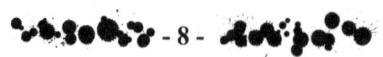

"Don't touch..." a voice beyond their metal door said in Russian. Then eyes peered through the small glass at the top of the door.

Alice threw the camera at the eyes and they disappeared for a second, then a loud yell was heard as the camera crashed against the door. She headed to the second camera and jumping up—it was higher than the other—soon ripped that down as well. The door whipped opened and she was slugged in the gut with the butt of one of the guns.

"Leave the equipment alone!" someone ordered. She was slugged again and this time she went down, only to be kicked.

"Halt!" another voice ordered. "Move them to other cells, separately!"

Alice was hauled up, still clutching her gut and unceremoniously taken across to another cell. She saw that Sasha was taken to a cell beside their old one and thrown inside. She braced herself and felt the floor as it rose to meet her as she was deposited in her own cell. She carefully got up again and looked around the room for the cameras, deciding she didn't want any more kicks to her abdomen as they hadn't broken her ribs...yet. She left the cameras alone after giving them the finger and sticking out her tongue childishly, then went to sit on her bunk and consider her options.

Sasha wasn't sure what to do. Of course, they had spoken about the possibility of them being incarcerated again. She fought down her panic, trying not to compare this to when they were in the jungle. This prison was newer, cleaner and had no bugs in evidence...but it was still a prison and they were captured.

"You, Ms. Weaver, have caused me and my organization quite a bit of problem," he told her in his imperfect English. Sasha and Alice had been brought upstairs by elevator into the main palace. It was quite impressive. The library they were brought to was a smaller version of the Wren Library in Cambridge, England, allowing the architecture of the room itself to be seen above the book shelves.

Alice blinked, a little surprised that he knew her name. But after all this time, it was probably reasonable that they knew who she was. Did they know where her family was? Did they really know WHO she was?

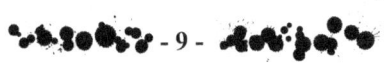

"Are you also the one who put a key logger program on my compatriots' computers?" he asked with a sardonic grin. It was a simple program and yet it had done so much damage.

Alice didn't answer. She kept herself calm, her breathing steady, and her wits about her, looking for an opportunity to use them. There would come a time….

He watched her curiously. She wasn't a beautiful woman. She was attractive in her own way, but beautiful…no. She looked at him curiously and he supposed that would make some people uncomfortable. Her eyes were odd. He couldn't put his finger on the reason why, but they were a bit…odd.

"So, tell me, who did you hire to kill my business partners?"

Alice didn't even bother to blink at that. He obviously wouldn't believe her if she told him. Instead, she glanced around the room and, using her peripheral vision, watched as Sasha sagged against her ties. She wasn't holding up well and Alice thought she knew why. She was remembering how hopeless it had felt when they were captured and imprisoned in Honduras. She only hoped the Russian woman would remember all they had accomplished together and not give into this questioning.

Alice was bored. She knew this type of man. He was hoping to trip her up by getting her to speak. Instead, she began to survey the room, taking in the immense size to match the house…it was a palace after all. She wondered if she should mention that he was compensating for other shortcomings? No, that would put him on the defensive, so she kept that one to herself, but it did amuse her. She noticed he liked to collect things. On the upper walls were scimitars, swords, and even a set of Japanese swords called daishō. The large sword was a katana and its companion, the smaller sword, a wakizashi. She wondered if he knew that daishō literally translated as 'big-little'? Again, he was compensating and she nearly smiled. When worn, the combination was the official sign that the wearer was a swordsman of Japan during their feudal times…a samurai. He probably had it because it looked pretty.

"You see something you like, Ms. Weaver?" he asked, realizing her attention was not on him.

She smiled and nodded, "Yes, I notice you have a fine collection of swords and knives. Do you collect to collect, or do you know how…?" she left off, hoping to pin prick his pride.

"Ah, yes. I have authentic swords from all over. This was our hunting cabin at one time," he boasted pridefully as his hands swept out to show off the room. He rose magnificently to her baiting. "Do you practice?"

"I did at one time. I was quite good, but it's been years," she led him on further. "I don't suppose you know how to use them?"

"Of course, I do!" he denied hotly, rising to the occasion. "I'm sure I'm much better..." and then he realized what she had been doing. "You think you're so clever?"

"Why, whatever do you mean?" she tried, and failed, to sound innocent. Her eyes were wide, but they didn't hide the telltale yellow-orange of them or their distinctive cat-like quality.

He gave a couple of orders in what sounded like Russian, but...not. Alice watched Sasha's head come up and she looked at him speculatively. She wondered at the significance of that.

"This is Abram Berinski," he introduced the bespeckled young man who looked myopically through his glasses at the two bound women.

"And this is Evgeni Konstantinov," he said with a bit of pride, "my niece."

A very pretty-looking Eurasian woman walked in and looked at the two bound women. She glanced from Alice to Sasha and then quickly back at Alice. Alice stiffened slightly, recognizing the signs of attraction on the young woman's face.

"Evgeni is a computer expert," he continued with a grin. "She has found your accounts!" he finished with relish.

Alice didn't bat an eye. She saw out of the corner of her eye that Sasha looked devastated. All their hard work!

"She has transferred all those millions, those *billions*, back to The Assemblage accounts!" he boasted.

"Uncle..." the woman tried to interrupt.

"So, now we find out how you..." he began, still boastful.

"Uncle..." she grabbed his arm to get his attention.

He continued to ignore the woman. "Abram! How much was the total she found?"

The amount the accountant stated had Alice's eyes changing slightly. They started to look more cat-like, almost yellow. She saw Sasha slump even farther in her ties as she heard the amount.

"Uncle!" Evgeni finally got through. Then, in rapid-fire Russian, in a dialect that Alice did not understand, she spoke to him. Sasha began

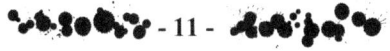

to sit up straighter. The tone, the pleading, even a word here and there told Alice more than the actual words. She watched Konstantinov and his reaction. First, he flushed. Then, he became angry.

He turned to Alice. Her expression hadn't changed. "You think you are so clever! We will find it! We are on the trail! Evgeni will defeat you!" he roared at the end. "Take them away," he ordered the guards and the two on each side of the prisoners hustled Sasha and Alice unceremoniously away. Alice turned her eyes on Evgeni as she went by and just looked at the young woman. Evgeni flushed, but didn't turn away from the prisoner.

Alice was bored. It had been many, many days without human contact. She knew it wasn't a good state to be in.

She tried to do her stretches, tried staying in shape, but with cameras—and she knew there were several watching her—she was careful not to show them what, or how much, she was capable of. This room she had been thrown in had smooth, metal walls. The cameras were deep-set and she was unable to get to them as she had in the other room. Her gut was still bruised from being hit over that.

She wondered what Konstantinov would do with them now. He hadn't gotten the money he thought he had. Alice had set a false set of trails that any good hack, and she was sure Evgeni Konstantinov was a good computer hacker, could have found. She'd made it marginally difficult so they would think they were on the right trail. The real money, the money they thought they would find, would never be found. Those billions had been transferred so many times, and into so many accounts and currencies, it was long lost. Sasha and Alice had made a lot off the exchange rates alone. Their investments had really paid off. If The Assemblage had really gotten the funds, they wouldn't have recognized the amounts. The amount Abram Berinski had quoted them told Alice they had found the fake accounts, the ghost accounts. And now, somewhere in Europe, Alice and Sasha's computer was finding computers they hadn't found before, finding funds that would slowly dwindle away and eat at the last of The Assemblage's holdouts. Alice knew that, Sasha didn't.

She sighed. Time alone like this was not good for her psyche. She thought about Kathy and the kids, missing them horribly. She had been away a long time…too long. They would have moved on. And she was worried that the last of The Assemblage would go after them. She couldn't do much about that here.

The cell door rattled; they did this twice a day to feed her. This time a package was sent under the door. "Shower and change into this," a voice commanded in Russian.

"And if I don't?" she challenged in the same language.

Alice didn't even get to finish her question before she felt the crackling and saw an arc in her room. The metal in the bed and the walls became electrified. If not for the blanket that Alice was laying on, she would have felt that, and the pain would have been excruciating. She got the message, and when she was sure the electricity had been turned off, she got up. She headed for the shower and without looking at the cameras, began to strip off her clothing. She took a long shower. The water wasn't very hot, but there was plenty of it and she enjoyed it. Her short hair had turned blonde. The last dye job hadn't lasted long and she hated how short her hair was; she missed the long mass of it. She shrugged and, wrapping a towel around herself, opened the package. Inside was a beautiful dress, matching shoes, and her cosmetics and perfume. She was surprised they would let her have anything of her own. Carefully, she applied the lotion that was with her cosmetics. Next, she applied makeup until she didn't recognize herself anymore. It had been a long time since she wore a 'face.' After drying her hair a little more with the towel, she styled it in a becoming spiked style before she started dressing. Unselfconsciously, aware of the cameras that were probably taking stills of her naked visage, she put on the bra and panties, matching of course, as well as the dress. The pantyhose was a nuisance, but she managed and then she slipped on the shoes. She hadn't dressed this formal in a long time and wondered at the occasion. She could see the entire combination in the small reflection of the stainless-steel wall. She shrugged and waited. They were watching her so they knew she was ready. Finally, she carefully applied perfume to her neck. Just a dab on both sides. She washed the perfume and lotion from her hands carefully.

"Ms. Weaver?" the door opened and a man stood there, dressed formally in a tuxedo. "I am Xander Baltizar," he introduced himself in

English. At her startled look, he smiled. "I'm his son," he clarified. "Xander Baltizar *the second*," he emphasized. Then with a little grin of mischief he added, "I believe you knew my brothers, Vashti and Leonid?"

Alice could appreciate morbid humor. She did indeed remember Vashti and Leonid. She'd killed them on the Filipov farm back in Russia. She wondered if this Xander Baltizar knew where his father was…where Alice and Sasha had *left* him? She wasn't about to enlighten him. She smiled instead and took his proffered arm. "What's the occasion?" she asked.

"Oh, we of The Assemblage have decided to celebrate. You wouldn't happen to know where my father is, would you? He would so enjoy this party. My mother wouldn't come, but I decided for the sake of my family that I would attend," he informed her.

Alice didn't move a muscle at the mention of Xander Baltizar. He might still be somewhere on the plains outside the mine, wandering forever, for all she knew. After these many weeks, she hoped, for his sake, he was dead.

They opened the cell across from her own and Sasha walked out. Her gown, what there was of it, was equally as beautiful. The only thing marring its beauty was the gunshot wound on her shoulder. The scar was nasty, but at least it was mostly healed. Time might heal or fade that scar, but for now it was horrible, dark, and detracted from Sasha's beauty. Sasha looked up, startled at seeing the second Xander Baltizar standing there.

"Ah, Sasha my darling, you look exquisite," he bowed slightly, releasing Alice's arm from his as he reached for the other woman's hand.

Sasha was struck dumb for a moment as she pulled her hand away before he could kiss the back. Alice sent her a warning look…Play along, they had to see where this was going to lead. Sasha saw the look and understood. Swallowing her ire at one of the Baltizars standing before her, she allowed him to reach out and recapture her hand, turn it, and gallantly kiss the back. "Xander, this is a surprise," she managed to say in Russian.

"I hope it is a good one?" he asked her with a sardonic smile as he pulled her hand onto his arm and offered the other elbow to Alice once again.

"We shall see," she answered noncommittally.

He laughed as though she had told a very funny joke. "Ah, yes. You two have been very, very naughty, haven't you?" he glanced back and forth between the two women he was escorting up the hallway. "Well, this isn't over, but tonight should be interesting. *Very* interesting."

Neither woman missed the insinuation. Alice leaned back in time to catch a look from Sasha before they continued into an elevator. The fourth-floor button was pushed and they rose within the gleaming box.

"So, what is planned?" Sasha asked, resuming the conversation as though she were the Sasha of old. She remembered such witty repartee when she had once been courted by this family.

"Ah, that is a surprise and entirely up to the two of you," he said mysteriously. Neither woman asked him what he meant, which seemed to disappoint him.

He showed them into what was obviously a ballroom. There weren't many people there. Alice immediately realized this was the last four of The Assemblage as well as their spouses or employees. All of them were involved in some way, somehow. What she wouldn't have given for an explosion to take them out at this moment.

Konstantinov watched his two captives arrive. He was still angry that they had somehow out-maneuvered him on the trail of the funds they had stolen from The Assemblage. Evgeni was still working on that on his orders, but even she had told him admiringly how beautiful and simple they had made it so they couldn't find the monies. He chastised himself many times for calling the remaining members and bragging that they not only had the two women in custody, but had found the monies. To have to tell them that it had been a carefully calculated trick to make him think they had, had been galling. Even now, more monies were being diverted or siphoned off, but he didn't know about that yet.

He had to admit that both women looked beautiful in the gowns Evgeni had chosen for them. He winced at the horrible scar on Sasha's shoulder. Her beauty was marred because of that. However she had gotten that scar, he hoped one of the men of The Assemblage had given it to her. His eyes narrowed at Alice Weaver. They had critically misjudged her and her involvement. He was still convinced that she had hired someone to kill the members of The Assemblage. She didn't look like she would harm a flea. Evidence supporting the theory that she and Sasha had acted alone had been accumulating and still he wasn't convinced.

Once their guests arrived, he signaled and one of his servants began the music. He had wanted an orchestra, but was cautioned about having too many witnesses. It was thought if they treated the two women with refined tastes and class, they would be more amenable to the possibility of giving them information. Still, they had the two in custody so they could always torture it out of them.

A couple of the guests began to dance. Alice and Sasha were escorted over to Konstantinov. "This is our host," Baltizar began.

"We've met," Alice said dryly.

Baltizar smiled in delight at her humor. "Ah, Ms. Weaver, may I have this dance?" he asked smoothly. Before she could say yes or no, he whisked her off onto the dance floor and into a waltz.

"Ah, they look like a beautiful couple," Konstantinov mentioned to Sasha. He glanced down at the woman to see her reaction. She had been close to this family at one time. They had intended for her and her wealth to come into their family. The woman didn't even react.

Sasha couldn't have cared less if Baltizar danced with Alice. She hadn't cared for him or his family for a long time. She realized why they were here. The remaining members of The Assemblage wanted to gloat, they wanted something to show the women. She wondered when they would just get to it. Why dress them up and parade them about like this? She watched as Baltizar tried to put his moves on Alice, nuzzling into her hair and then her neck.

"Ah, Ms. Weaver, what is this scent you are wearing?" Baltizar asked as he held her close for the waltz…too close.

Alice, trying to let him lead, further relaxed into his arms at his question. He took that as encouragement. Thinking she was enjoying his hold on her, he pulled her closer and started to nuzzle her short hair. Next, he rubbed his nose into her neck, inhaling deeply of her scent. Alice tried not to smile when his lips began to kiss along her neck, becoming wetter as he licked his lips and then slightly tasted her. Alice waited, then waited some more. She was starting to worry slightly.

"Um, do you mind if we sit this one out?" he asked shortly. "I'm not feeling…well," he finished and Alice led him to a plush chair that didn't face the dance floor.

"Of course not," she said kindly, feigning concern. "Here, let me help you," she offered solicitously.

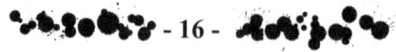

Alice left him, snagging a water from a waiter and opening it. "Here, drink this," she offered, watching as the effects of her perfume, the one she had bought in Greece, took effect. The water dribbled from his mouth as he stared at her, horrified. She smiled into his eyes as she left him and returned to Sasha.

"Didn't you like dancing?" Konstantinov asked her as he looked beyond her to where Baltizar was sitting, gazing into the fireplace. He wondered what the man had said to her that she had left him sitting there.

"Yes, he's a good dancer, but I prefer to dance with–" she began and was interrupted.

"Ms. Weaver, would you dance with me?" another voice was asking. Konstantinov and Alice both turned to see Evgeni Konstantinov standing there.

"Evgeni," her uncle hissed. "Behave yourself!"

"I'd be delighted, Ms. Konstantinov," Alice told her before her uncle could ruin this opportunity. She saw the attraction the younger woman could not hide.

"Evgeni, please," the woman insisted, pulling her jacket down slightly, emphasizing the fact that she was wearing a tuxedo, the cummerbund pulling her waist tight.

She took the arm the tuxedo-wearing young woman offered and allowed herself to be led onto the dance floor. Alice wondered if she could pull this off twice in one night, but Evgeni wasn't holding her as close as Baltizar had.

"You are a brilliant woman, Ms. Weaver," began Evgeni in a heavily-accented voice. It reminded Alice immediately of how Sasha had sounded when they first met. Her English had improved a lot since then.

"Please, call me Alice," she told her with a seductive smile. Her eyes held the woman, drawing her in. "That is very nice of you to say."

"Ah, I can see the beauty in what you have done to my uncle and his friends. That was very clever of you to make those ghost accounts. Is it your program that haunts them now?"

Alice neither confirmed nor denied that. She tried to look innocent and still seduce the woman. After all, she was part of the 'enemy camp', and as much as Alice hated the idea of killing her, she didn't know how much the woman was in on this. "I don't know what you mean?" she asked instead.

Evgeni just smiled, pulling Alice a fraction closer. "You are, like Sasha, a woman who loves women, yes?" she asked next.

"What makes you think that?" Alice asked in return, wondering if they knew about Kathy or their children. She would give nothing away.

"Are you and Sasha lovers?" she asked instead, pulling her just a tiny bit closer, as though Alice wouldn't notice.

"No, why would we be?" Alice almost mentioned Sasha's partner. She had been about to say, 'Sasha has Lexi.' She didn't, however, want to remind 'them' about the existence of her either. No need to give them further ammunition against the two of them.

"Ah, I thought perhaps, being a passionate woman, you would need a woman by now," she smiled down into Alice's face, enjoying the view as they twirled around on the dance floor. A couple of people had left the floor, disgusted to see two women dancing together like this. Others couldn't have cared less and continued dancing with their wives or partners, not paying attention at all.

Alice glanced over Evgeni's shoulder. Baltizar was sitting in the chair as though he were gazing into the fire. She wondered if he was dead yet and when someone might notice. They would, of course, figure out quickly that Alice had something to do with it. She looked around the ballroom. It was styled after something she had seen in France once. Or, maybe, after something that Catherine the Great and her era had built. The stylish wood was all painted white with gold trim. It was garish, it was expensive, and it was par for the course with what she had seen of this overdone palace that Konstantinov had built.

"Do you really think I cannot go without?" Alice teased, looking up at the woman with a glint in her eye.

Evgeni didn't recognize the predatory glint. Instead, she saw what she wanted to see, what she hoped to see...desire. She moved closer. Alice was now letting her lead the entire dance. Her strong legs led the smaller blonde around on the dance floor effortlessly, thigh to thigh. They were a good match. "I saw Xander trying to seduce you," she virtually whispered, her lips near Alice's ear.

Alice smiled, her cheekbone rising and hitting Evgeni's cheek. "Not with my permission, I assure you," she said dryly.

"You didn't like his attentions?" she asked, her hand on Alice's back slipping down to the small of her back, inching towards the

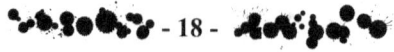

blonde's buttocks so elegantly and enticingly displayed in the gown she had chosen for her.

"I didn't ask for them."

"Do you like your dress? I chose it for you," Evgeni bragged.

"Do you watch me through the cameras too?" Alice whispered in return, hearing the woman's breathing accelerating slightly. She knew it wasn't from their dancing. She saw as someone began to look closer at Xander Baltizar sitting in the chair by himself, staring into the fire with vacant eyes.

"I do. You have a magnificent body," she said admiringly.

"Thank you," Alice returned, turning her cheek slightly against the taller woman's.

Evgeni didn't miss the slight move. She desperately wanted to put her leg between Alice's and have the woman grind against her. That thought alone was making her horny. She put her lips against Alice's ear to judge the smaller woman's reaction.

Alice gasped slightly, for effect. She knew that Evgeni wanted her…wanted her bad. For a second, the taller woman faltered in their dance.

"Do you want me?" Evgeni managed to ask, echoing Alice's thoughts as she kissed below the ear, her tongue swiping along the ridge, kissing lower. The woman was wearing the most delightful of scents. She must find out where she bought her perfume. Evgeni would keep her and…her tongue started to feel funny and so did her lips. Almost a burning sensation and yet… She didn't feel very well.

"Yes, I want you…" Alice began, then when Evgeni pulled back, Alice saw the effects of the perfume. She smiled in a friendly manner. "Are you okay?" she asked, as she would have asked anyone, almost as though she…cared.

Evgeni frowned, wondering at the spreading sensation on her lips and tongue. She licked her lips again and then she swallowed.

"Maybe, we should go sit down?" Alice offered considerately.

Evgeni allowed herself to be led to a chair adjacent to Xander's. She saw Alice turn her back to someone who had been about to speak to Xander. "Isn't this cozy?" Alice asked brightly, this time in Russian so the person would hear her, as though she were including Xander in the conversation. They wandered away. Alice looked at Evgeni and then glanced at Xander. She smiled and then said, low, "Since this probably won't work a third time tonight, I'll tell you. It was the

perfume. You all watched me through the cameras as I applied it to my person. It protects me from absorbing the deadly perfume into my body." She smiled into Evgeni's alarmed eyes, and when the woman made to rise, Alice held her firmly to the plush upright chair by leaning on her hands that covered Evgeni's arms. "Oh, no. In a moment, you won't be able to move, but I assure you, it isn't a bad way to go," she said conversationally in English. She lowered her voice again so only the two of them could hear. "Your family and their friends," her glance took in the people dancing, "have a lot to pay for. You chose to come into the family business and for this you must pay," she actually sounded regretful. "Goodbye," she said as she saw the concoction had paralyzed the other woman. She got up and left her in the chair next to Xander, who Evgeni could now see was quite dead. She tried to rise, but found herself unable to move. Whatever had been in that perfume worked fast. She looked around the room, but found she couldn't see far. Faintly, she saw as Alice moved away towards her uncle.

"You have tired another dancer, have you, Ms. Weaver?" he asked congenially.

"Ah, well, they all think they can handle me," she answered, her Russian better than when she had begun so long ago. "Perhaps I could entice you?" she asked hopefully. Sasha stared at her in alarm, wondering how she could be so friendly with the enemy.

"Oh no, I leave the dancing for those who know how. I'm afraid I have two left feet," he joked.

"Perhaps I could teach you," she offered generously, being sure to spread her arms wide and show off her charms. The dress had been intended to do that very thing and it wasn't lost on her or him.

"Many have tried," he bragged with much bravado, "but alas, no one has succeeded."

"Would you consider me?" she said with such innuendo she could hear Sasha gasp. She didn't dare look at her Russian friend.

He smiled down at her, sure he understood her double entendre. "I don't think that would be a wise move. There is something about you, Ms. Weaver that intrigues me. There is also something about you that tells me not to trust you."

"Then perhaps we should try swords sometime. That is another dance," she dared him.

"You are good with swords?"

"That and a few other things?"

"Are you any good with guns?"

"Maybe," she shrugged, showing off the dress again with that elegant shrug. The fabric raised enough that it tightened across her breasts.

"What, you think you are John Wayne?" he asked with a swagger.

Alice rolled her eyes. How he could compare her to that man, that six foot plus man of Hollywood hero status, she didn't know. Her own petite frame would look ludicrous next to such a man. She shook her head, "No, I prefer to think of myself as more of a Robin Hood."

"Who is this Robin Hood?"

"You learn American cinema and you know who the great John Wayne was, but you don't know who Robin Hood was?" She shook her head regretfully, using the opportunity to look around the room and assess her enemy's capabilities. She shrugged, "I guess he was more English than Hollywood."

"So, who is this Robin Hood?" he asked, genuinely interested.

"He was a knight of the English court who went kind of rogue when his king was off on the crusades. He began to rob from the rich and give to the poor," she answered, quoting one of the many movies out about the man.

"Ah yes, I can understand this rogue," he answered. "But why rob from the rich when the poor keep on giving?" he smiled and then laughed at his own joke.

Alice was burning at his jibe, but smiled politely. Just then someone noticed that Baltizar wasn't staring into the fire and went to check on him. She wondered how far along Evgeni was or if she was already dead? It had been long enough, but the poison affected everyone differently; that was the beauty of it.

"Konstantinov!" shouted the man who discovered Baltizar. He was shaking the man, his limp body like a rag doll.

"What the hell?" the older man took long strides and was soon beside his business partner and niece. It was then someone noticed Evgeni. A woman screamed.

Two guards behind Alice and Sasha took a step closer to them both, cutting off any exit they may have been planning. Alice was very aware they were there.

"Vhat's going on?" Sasha hissed.

"Wait and see," Alice murmured, watching intently as they realized not one, but two of their own had been killed right before them. They

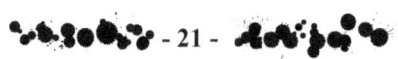

wouldn't be able to figure out how. The only common factor was Alice.

They shook both the now cooling bodies trying to 'wake' them, only to find them limp and lifeless. Both fell to the floor and their pulses were checked.

Alice took a glass of champagne from a passing waiter. She was thirsty after all that dancing.

"They're dead!" a voice rang out in Russian.

Konstantinov looked up at his two prisoners. Sasha was looking appropriately horrified. Alice however, was looking merely…interested. She took a sip of the long flute of champagne, nearly finishing it before her eyes met his over it. She lowered it and looked at him wide-eyed. He supposed she was trying to look innocent. "You!" he bellowed, signaling to the two men standing behind the women. He got up slowly from the two dead on the floor and began to walk purposely across the floor towards them. "You!" he said again, pointing at Alice so no one would be confused about whom he was addressing.

Someone turned off the music and everyone stared, those unaware of the discovery coming over to find out that two of their own were now dead.

"You had something to do with this, didn't you?" he bellowed into Alice's face.

"With what?" she asked, bored. She thought of taking another sip of her champagne, but eyeing the glass, decided to keep it as a weapon instead.

"How did you manage to kill them both under our very noses?" he asked, angrily. He glanced at Sasha, who was now looking curiously at Alice.

"How had Alice killed two members of The Assemblage?" Sasha was wondering. She'd cheer, but knew they wouldn't be alive long if she did.

"I don't know what you are talking about. You supplied me with this dress. I have nothing," she spread her hands wide to show she had no weapon, nearly sloshing the remaining champagne out of her flute.

"You did something!" he accused, pointing a finger. "You did something!" he repeated.

Her arms still wide, Alice brought her hand down, spilling the rest of the champagne in the glass. The liquid combined with the glass as it

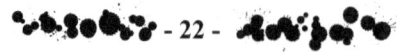

shattered against a table. She swiftly brought it back up, intending to cut out Konstantinov's neck, but he jerked back slightly at the sound of the broken flute and this saved his life. Alice's reach wasn't long enough and the tall man was only marginally sliced.

"Seize her!" he roared as his other hand went to his cut neck. Pulling out a handkerchief, he blotted and then held it to his neck as he saw the amount of blood.

Alice had expected that and elbowed the man trying to grab her. Expecting little resistance from the petite blonde—her appearance had distracted him—he never expected what he got. Alice, feeling the elbow strike his mid-section, quickly shot her fist holding the shattered flute up and into the face of her attacker. The glass, initially intended for Konstantinov, did its job as it sliced into the face of the man. As he was bending over, her hand came up with the glass, shooting it deep into his brain and through his face. She let go of the glass. Another one down.

Sasha wasn't about to go quietly. She too had fought off her attacker. When he grabbed at her arms, she had crouched down. Losing his balance, he went flying over her head. Having no weapon, she quickly kneeled across his throat. Having lost his breath and surprised at her defense, he immediately tried to inhale, but it was cut off by her knee. He pushed at her and, being stronger than her, Sasha found herself falling backward.

Alice caught her before she landed. "Whoa, there," she said as she helped the woman to regain her balance.

Sasha looked down and nearly threw up. The man Alice had killed was a bloody mess. The one Sasha had tried to kill was rubbing his now bruised neck and slowly sitting up, glaring at her.

"Ah, you two have skills," Konstantinov commented, calming down as he saw the violence acted out before him. His guests were murmuring behind them. "Perhaps we should bring in the present I've been saving," he said conversationally, gesturing to someone out of sight. He was still holding a handkerchief to his bleeding neck.

Alice and Sasha turned to see them bringing someone into the ballroom, someone unwilling, struggling, and then…"Lexi!" Sasha cried, hurrying forward as she recognized her girlfriend. "What in the world are you doing here?" she asked, concerned.

Alice and the others watched as the two women embraced. Lexi was no longer struggling. Instead, she was holding the blonde tightly.

"Sasha!" she cried, tears starting to flow. "They told me you were dead!"

"Ah, she was, and will be again," Konstantinov commented quietly, keeping his distance from Alice, who eyed him.

Alice was trying to determine if she could take out another of The Assemblage. She glanced at the other two who had always remained blank on her screen. Few pictures, rarely seen names, but she and Sasha had both known they rounded out the twelve. She knew who they were now. She also knew if she took out Konstantinov here and now, her life would be forfeit and the other two would carry on, expanding The Assemblage to its former glory.

Alice turned back to watch Sasha and Alexis, known as Lexi, as they reunited and wondered how it might be, if ever, for her and Kathy. She blinked back tears as her heart swelled for her friend at being reunited with her lover. She held it in check, knowing Konstantinov and the other two were watching. Any weakness would be exploited. She'd dealt them a shock tonight. One of their own and a second had been taken out in a matter of a half hour and they didn't know how.

"Do you think this is wise?" a voice from Konstantinov's right asked him. Alice turned slightly to bring the man into her view. She studied his face, memorizing it.

"Give her a little joy before I take it away," he grinned evilly. He saw that Alice was watching and gestured. "Have you met our other...guest," he said to his friend.

"No, but I've read the dossier on her," he said in a snide manner. "Perhaps I should see how good she is, eh?" he leered.

"What? You think you could take me?" she answered in the same tone as his. She looked him up and down and then fixed her gaze as though he was a worm. "I don't *think* so."

Konstantinov grabbed the man's arm before he could lunge at the woman. "Perhaps we could have a little entertainment," he said louder so the rest of their guests could hear. "You want her," he turned to the man who lit up at the invitation, "you have to best her," he nodded to one of his hirelings who ran out of the ballroom. In the ensuing silence, Lexi and Sasha became aware of the quiet and looked around. Lexi looked terrified. Then she recognized Alice and she began to look angry as she looked from Alice to Sasha and back again.

The hireling came running in carrying two of the swords. They looked medieval, from England, and Alice looked at them in surprise.

If she had guessed which sword Konstantinov would pick, she would have thought his ego would make him choose the Japanese swords, the daishō. Still, the choice wasn't hers and she didn't react to seeing what was brought. The other man did, however.

"What? You expect me to fight her with that?" he asked incredulously.

"After what you made me go through to buy that from your esteemed family, I thought you would like it," Konstantinov said reasonably.

"I never said I knew…" he began blustering, starting to sweat.

"Ah, but you bragged how your family were master swordsmen."

Cornered, the man began to take off his tuxedo coat and then his vest and tie. Alice gazed on with an amused look on her face.

"You aren't going to fight him, are you?" Sasha hissed in her ear.

Alice turned, surprised that Sasha had been able to get this close without her hearing. She saw that Lexi was holding her girlfriend's hand as though she wouldn't let go. She also saw the anger in the other woman's eyes and wondered at it. As the woman's eyes darted between Sasha and Alice, she thought she knew why Lexi was angry. "Yes, I think I shall," she said in a snobbish voice, almost laughing.

"You could get killed," Sasha said unnecessarily.

"Yes, I could," Alice answered and then looked at the dress she was wearing. It was tight-fitting and didn't allow for much in the way of leg movement. She kicked off her shoes and considered cutting the skirt.

"I believe I'll take…" began her challenger arrogantly as the hireling brought forth the swords.

"As the challenged, *I* get to choose," Alice interrupted haughtily.

Glancing at Konstantinov, their host answered for him, "She's right."

Alice looked at both swords. They were exquisitely crafted with long, sharp, metal blades. The handles were encrusted with precious stones. One of them though, was missing a stone and her eyes narrowed in on it. "I'll use that one," she said, pointing to the sword. She saw both her host and her challenger looking delighted with her choice. She knew they thought she would choose the better-looking of the two swords, but she also knew something they didn't…the one she had chosen had been *used*. That was probably why the stone was missing. It had been used and the other one had never been tested. She waited while they cleared the dance floor, everyone standing back before she was handed her weapon of choice.

"On guard," the man said to her, taking a stance that was absolutely unbalanced in addition to mispronouncing the word. She recognized him from her dossier on the twelve men responsible for The Assemblage…always behind the scenes, always collecting a full share. He was as nasty as his companions and deserved what she was about to serve him.

"En garde," Alice returned, giving it the correct French inflection; his English had been atrocious. "Préparez-vous à mourir," she added in French for effect, and then in Russian as well, "Prigotov'sya umeret." She could hear the gasps around her as both men and women understood her, but it was her opponent she was watching. She could see that telling him to 'prepare to die' had psychologically affected him. He had already started sweating at this challenge his host had manipulated. Just because she was a woman, he thought he could defeat her, but he didn't know Alice Weaver.

His first attempt to strike her with the sword was a failure because Alice simply slipped under it and danced away, but her nylons were making the slippery floor of the ballroom even more slippery. She quickly bent down, pulled at the edge of her dress, and putting the point through the seam, slit the dress up to her hip, exposing her muscular thighs. She grabbed for the nylons to do the same, but by then the man had recovered his balance from the fruitless swing and was slicing at her again. She parried it, following the blade down its entire length and had him yelping as he backed away from the nasty cut she could have given him. She quickly cut at her nylons, but he was back before she got to the second leg. The hold her one bare foot gave her on the wooden dance floor helped immeasurably as she ducked under his slice again then spanked him with the flat of her blade, making him look the fool and sending him flying. It gave her just enough time to slice through her other nylon and have two bare feet on the slippery floor. She gripped her sword tightly.

"Come on, you coward," she hissed, egging him on, trying to make him angry. She repeated it in French and Russian for her audience.

"Coward? You call *me* a coward?" he asked angrily.

She nodded and smiled, waiting for him to come to her as she made come hither motions with her free hand. Then she put her free hand behind her in a classic stance and waited.

He was angry: first, that he hadn't ended this quickly and second, that she had dared to disparage him so easily. She should be frightened of him. "I'll get you yet, and your girlfriend too," he verbally poked at her as he brought his sword up again and made to slice at her.

Alice easily parried and laughed at him as she countered. "She's a woman," she pointed out. She hoped he meant Sasha and not Kathy. She prayed they knew nothing about Kathy.

"Okay, your *woman* friend," he said in a nasty-sounding voice. He slashed at her again and quickly tried to come back across her body.

Alice took one step and then another to the side, easily out-maneuvering the inept fool. Not only was he a poor swordsman, but he couldn't insult very well. "She is a woman and she is a friend, however, she is merely *a friend* and nothing more to me than that." She hoped Lexi got the hint in that statement and she hoped they were still talking about Sasha. "Unlike *your* friends that hope you die now," she glanced at the two remaining members of the original Assemblage when she said it.

He glanced where she had looked and while he was distracted for that instant, Alice took the initiative and sliced across his chest. The white of his tuxedo shirt immediately turned crimson. He yelped and jumped back, but Alice didn't let him get away. She pressed her advantage, knowing the pain would distract the inept fool. She took another swipe at him across his belly and that too turned crimson. He looked at her incredulously, unable to get away and amazed at her speed. She wasn't even breaking a sweat or breathing hard. Her other arm was on her hip as she sliced him to ribbons. With a battle cry, he went after her, smacking her blade out of his way and earning a cut on the back of his arm as he did so.

Alice saw him coming like a bull in a china shop and stepped aside, went into a slight crouch, and tripped him. He fell face-first on the floor and slid across the wooden floor. "Ohhh, that's gonna hurt," she said aloud in a humorous tone, not bothering to translate it this time. Enough murmurs did it for her.

Enraged, he got up off the floor, not noticing that he had slid across the dance floor on his own blood. His face was a mess from sliding along the wood and her humor was not appreciated. "You bitch," he said, the word coming in clearly despite the language barrier.

Alice narrowed her eyes slightly as she decided to end this. She was no longer amused and didn't want to give him the opportunity to get lucky. She let him stand up before she began to slash her sword back and forth in front of him in some highly complex and beautiful moves, showing she was not a novice at sword play. As it mesmerized him and her audience, she quickly took advantage and sliced halfway into his neck, severing the artery and causing it to spurt across the floor, flecking guests with his blood.

"You've killed me," he said unnecessarily as he dropped his sword and put his hands up to his neck to stem the flow. No one went to his aid as they watched him drop to his knees and slowly fall into a pool of his own blood.

Alice turned and dropped her own sword. There was no point in continuing or trying to get to the last two members of The Assemblage. There were AK-47s trained on her at that moment. She marveled once again at how shiny and new they looked and wondered if any of the morons holding them knew how to clean a gun, much less fire it.

"Well, well, well, someone has taken lessons," Konstantinov clapped as she dropped her sword.

Alice smiled and made a mock bow. Her smile didn't quite meet up with her eyes, which were an odd shade of...yellow. Konstantinov nearly took a step back.

"But how good would you be against another?" he mused as he tried to hide his fear of this woman. No, it wasn't fear. She simply made him uncomfortable. He did wonder if perhaps she was responsible for more of the killings than they had realized.

Alice shrugged, "Bring me another."

He smiled as he tapped his mouth. "Return them to the cells," he ordered. He needed to think. He knew planning without first thinking it out carefully would be foolish.

His men took the three women and led them away. This time they did not put them in the elevator, but made them climb down the steps. Alice was fine in her bare feet, but Sasha was wearing heels and Lexi wore some sort of flat shoes. Lexi looked the roughest of them all despite Alice's fight. Without thinking about it, the soldiers threw the three of them in a cell together.

Alice listened at the door until she heard them step away and walk down the corridor. They might think with the women locked up they were safe, but putting them in the cell together hadn't been very bright.

"Are you all right?" Lexi asked Alice, concerned.

"Yeah, I'm fine. How are you?" she asked with a grin, pleased to see her.

"I don't know. They grabbed me a couple weeks ago. I don't know how long I've been here."

Alice glanced at Sasha. "You think they grabbed her before or after the mine?"

Sasha shrugged and held Lexi in her arms protectively. She couldn't believe she was here. She felt so good. She smelled so good. She was...alive. At that moment, she didn't care when they grabbed Lexi, she just wanted her to be safe. "We have to get her out of here," she said unnecessarily.

"We will," Alice promised and looked around the cell with interest. The cameras were there as well as the steel walls, protecting them from unnecessary digging. She'd finally figured out why they put the walls up that way—they could, at will, fry them with electricity.

"How did you two come to be here?" Lexi asked.

"Now is not the time to tell our story," Alice said in a warning voice to Sasha who had been about to tell her girlfriend everything. "The walls have ears," she said meaningfully and glanced up at the cameras. Then she pointed to be sure they understood her.

Sasha nodded. "I'll tell you everything vhen I can," she promised. "For now, let's just zit," she encouraged Lexi to join her on the bottom bunk and then realized there were only two beds. "Vhere arc ve all going to sleep?" she wondered aloud.

"If you two can't share a bunk, I'll sleep on the floor," Alice told them, which led to an argument about who would sleep where. Finally, they agreed to switch off, depending on how long they were kept in this cell.

"How long do you think we will be in here?" Lexi asked as she held Sasha's hand protectively.

Alice shrugged. "Could be a day, could be a week. We are at their mercy."

"How can you be so flip?"

"How can you not?"

Sasha squeezed Lexi's hand to shush her and they sat back on the bunk, just touching along the length of their bodies. Alice envied them the warmth, the companionship, and simply finding each other. It did, however, present another problem: how to get one more person out of the situation they found themselves in.

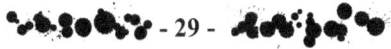

They kept them there for three days and nights. Each day they took one of them out of the cell to ask them questions. Sasha was the second. They spoke little in the cell itself except in murmurs and even then, kept the information informal. They didn't want to give their captors any information they could use against them.

As they led Sasha away, Lexi turned to Alice, "Thank you for keeping her alive."

Alice nodded, but didn't say anything.

"She told me nothing happened between the two of you."

Alice glanced meaningfully up at the cameras and then back at Lexi, "No, nothing would. She is a friend and that is all. Is that what worries you?"

Lexi shook her head, glancing up the cameras too and wishing they could talk...*really* talk. She could see that Alice understood though. The woman frightened her after what she saw in the ballroom. Alice had no problem killing people. After what Konstantinov had told her Alice and Sasha had done, she had to wonder how much of it was true. She had thought he told her lies to frighten her into giving him more information or signing over properties. She hadn't believed anything she had been told. Konstantinov kept saying to his companion that the two women had to have hired someone, and yet they argued that the two women were doing the killings themselves. Lexi wondered. Sasha, the woman she had known, would never kill anyone; however, she hadn't seen her in over a year. She looked a lot different than the sophisticated Russian she had known. Even their conversations were different. Finding Sasha here had been a revelation. She had been convinced she was dead.

She remembered that night when she was taken out of her cell and brought up to their ballroom...She had wondered why? What for this time? She fought them, struggled with them, and then she had seen her..."Lexi!" Sasha cried, hurrying forward as she recognized her girlfriend, pulling her into her welcoming arms. "What in the world are you doing here?" she asked, concerned.

Lexi glanced over Sasha's shoulder and recognized Alice Weaver. She too was thought to have died on that fateful night when Sasha's beautiful yacht had blown up. She hadn't believed The Assemblage when they, unwilling to take no for an answer on the sale of the things Lexi had inherited from Sasha, had finally kidnapped her, beaten her, and held her hostage. They tried to force her to sell properties at their prices, but she had refused. The more they threw against her, the more stubborn she became. It wasn't only because of the price, it was also the principal of the matter. Sasha had owned these businesses, these properties, and some of them had sentimental value to Lexi.

Lexi had stopped struggling and welcomed Sasha into her arms. Feeling her alive and being held in her arms had nearly broken her. At first, she thought it was a look-alike, someone to mess with her mind further. "Sasha!" she exclaimed, starting to cry. "They told me you were dead!"

They both heard that vile man say, "Ah, she was, and she will be again."

Lexi had watched in horror as Alice accepted that sword fight. It was obvious to anyone watching that Alice knew what she was doing. The other man was inept. He had frightened her when they questioned her, he and the other one who stood silent along with the albino brother. What was his name…Baltizar? She saw a body, no, two bodies lying near the fireplace…a man and a woman. She wondered what had happened to them.

Being taken back to the cells and put in the one cell together had been a bittersweet torture. She wanted desperately to rip off Sasha's clothes and see that she was real…that she was the *real* Sasha. It was agony to be this close and not be able to consummate the love they had for each other. They couldn't talk freely. And then, there was Alice as their chaperone and of course, the cameras. She didn't want to put on a show for whoever was watching.

"Notting happened between us," Sasha whispered reassuringly to Lexi as she glanced at the striking woman that was Alice. "She has taught me a great deal," she understated, not wishing to alarm her beautiful Lexi.

Lexi closed her eyes for a moment, feeling the seductive accent go through her like an arrow and then wash over her. She had missed this woman, missed her in so many ways. Finding out that Sasha had left her enormous fortune to her had been a shock. Her family had been excited upon finding out their dear old mom was a billionaire, but Lexi would have given it all back to have Sasha return instead. Finding out

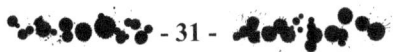

she didn't intend to use it to their benefit had estranged her from some of her greedy relatives. Instead, Lexi began setting up a foundation in Sasha's name. She sold off some of the properties that seemed less relevant, but those were bought up too quickly and there was an odd sense about the buyers. She'd stopped selling and found pressure mounting from certain factions regarding the immense and extensive properties that Sasha owned. She became suspicious and stubborn about it all.

When she was kidnapped and beaten, she become only more determined. They could kill her and not get a cent of Sasha's or her money. She'd been smart and had drawn up a will immediately. She'd even used the same attorney Sasha had hired on Alice's recommendation. Nia Toyomoto had been pleased to help her sort out the various investments and properties, then create the foundation where the funds would go. In the event of her own death, her family would receive an income from the foundation in perpetuity, but the properties, the enormous investments, the incredible sums of money were all tied up in the foundation and only Lexi could untangle it if she wished. Knowing an irrevocable trust would further tangle things, she had considered setting up a revocable one.

Coming back to the present, to Alice sitting there looking at her and waiting for an answer, she shook her head, "I know her and she isn't a cheater."

Alice shook her own head to the negative, "No, she is faithful. She has missed you a lot." She smiled slightly, ruefully, reflecting on her own situation, but she wouldn't mention Kathy, not here, not now, not knowing who was listening and watching. Alice came and sat beside her on the cot. "She's a surprise and she's helped me a lot, but she stayed mostly in the background," she lied cheerfully.

"No, she didn't," Lexi countered and looked directly at Alice, then glanced up at the cameras. She shook her head. This conversation would have to wait for another time.

Alice smiled and then looked away as they waited for Sasha to be returned to the room. The Assemblage was questioning all of them to see if they could get any information that would help them retrieve the billions stolen from them before they killed the women. None of the women had any delusions otherwise. Alice knew Sasha and Lexi's whispered conversations as they tried to keep things between them had probably been picked up by whatever microphone was in this cell. She smiled to herself wondering if they had realized their aborted lovemaking had been heard, and not just by the microphones. Alice didn't sleep that soundly and it was obvious by the heavy breathing and the fumbling just what was going on between the two lovers. She knew they would both be mortified if she mentioned it. Only a clanging noise from the hall had stopped their attempts. Alice had rolled over and gone to sleep, smiling and wishing she could go home to Kathy.

Alice's turn with The Assemblage finally came. She laughed at their attempts to get information from her. She outright laughed aloud in their faces at their threats of intimidation, rape, and blackmail.

"You hold nothing over me," she told them succinctly, "nothing more."

"We could..." blustered the man behind Konstantinov. Alice still wondered at his involvement since she didn't have much on him.

She glanced around the library and it was then she realized there was more to it than a resemblance to another, more famous library. Something didn't add up here. The walls, covered in books, didn't match the size of the room. To her, that meant there was a secret room or chamber within this room. She didn't let on that she had noticed, but she scrutinized the area rather than listen to their constant questions. She wasn't going to answer anyway, so why bother. She thought, or rather imagined, that a book on a shelf behind her inquisitive enemies moved of its own accord.

"Perhaps we could share?" they offered generously.

Alice laughed at that. "Share? You mean the things you stole and no longer have?"

"We could come to some sort of an agreement?"

Alice stopped answering.

Konstantinov finally had had enough. They'd been going at her for hours and she hadn't broken. They'd gotten more out of Lexi, and that was nearly nothing. Sasha had despised them and spat at them. Her Russian heritage had come out in so many ways and she told them nothing. This...this *American,* he despised on so many levels. "She's been playing games with us," he finally said dismissively. "I think it is time we played games with her," he smiled evilly and Alice felt a little

prickling up her spine. He turned and pushed a button on his desk.
Two guards came in. Using his chin to point to her, he ordered, "Shave
her and give her back the gear we found on them. We hunt this
afternoon," he told the two men who smiled and high-fived each other
before they took Alice back into custody. She could have fought them,
seriously thought about it, but then two more arrived, and two more
after that, and then she saw the palace had military types at every exit,
standing at attention and waiting.

It took more than those two men to hold her down as they shaved
her head again. Alice knew it was done to demoralize her, but it
merely pissed her off. They all sported new bruises by the time she
was done with them, but they had also gotten in their fair share of
punches, kicks, and smacks. One had even punched her between her
legs to get her to submit, for which he had earned her enmity for all
time. "You will pay for that someday, comrade," she threatened him in
Russian, promising him with the finality of what she said. He had just
laughed. She was helpless, at their mercy, and having heard what she
might have done to others, they had no mercy for the bitch. He relished
the idea of hunting her as their employer had promised. It was going to
be a good hunt and killing her would be quite satisfying. The hunt had
been planned before the bitches were questioned. It had been hoped
that one of them would reveal something, anything, but they would find
her computer, they would find her hiding places, and she would pay.
There was no one to say what could and couldn't be done on the hunt
and he intended to rape this pretty woman, teach her what a real man
was all about. The intent was in his eyes and Alice read it accurately.
He was feral, he was a plague on humanity, and she knew from what
she had gleaned that it was going to be a fight to the death. It would be
no loss if she killed him and his kind, and the other three weren't much
better. They enjoyed feeling her up as they held her down so they
could shave her head. They'd debated about shaving her pubic area
too—speaking freely in Russian, not realizing she understood them—
but finally one of them had been the voice of reason. If they were
caught diddling before they were allowed, it would mean their heads.
This was an interesting bit of information for Alice. They returned her
to the cell she shared with Sasha and Lexi. They were holding each
other when she was thrown inside.

"What happened?" Lexi asked, aghast at Alice's appearance. The
cuts and bruises were nothing in comparison to the shaved head.

"Oh no, not *again*," Sasha said, horrified at seeing the shaven head and Alice's appearance.

"Again?" Lexi asked, looking at Sasha for confirmation.

"Yes, they did this to her in Central America too. Right after they blew up the boat and took us to a prison there."

"Why didn't you *tell* me?" she frowned.

Sasha pointed at the cameras and then went to help Alice up from the floor. "Are you all right, my friend?"

"We need to get ready. They have decided what they are going to do with us," she told her through a swelling mouth (they'd punched her there for good measure.) She felt her teeth with her tongue, both real and fake, to see if any were loose.

"What?" both women asked.

"They are going to start hunting us. I don't know the details, so don't ask," she mouthed, feeling the blood in her mouth and heading for the sink to spit it out.

Lexi and Sasha looked at each other in shocked horror.

"They're going to *hunt* us?" Lexi finally asked.

Alice nodded and immediately regretted it. Her head was cold, but she also had a headache from the beating she had just endured. She turned on the faucet and ran cold water over her tongue, splashing it onto her face. Her hand continued over her bald pate and she grimaced at the feeling. Closing her eyes for a moment, she gathered her thoughts, feeling the old anger at such unfair treatment coming into her core. She was about to unleash a part of herself that she normally kept tightly tethered. Sasha had seen parts of it, but this...*this* was a beast that Alice didn't like letting out. She'd kept it suppressed a long time, but at the word *hunt,* and after what she'd heard those men discuss, she knew it was time to unleash her inner beast and take no prisoners.

"Ve have to get out of here," Sasha stated in English.

"How?" Lexi asked, the fear obvious in her voice.

Alice glanced up at her fellow prisoners, her eyes beginning to swell shut. She looked back down at the water and rinsed her face with it. The cool water felt good against her skin.

"Alice," Sasha hissed, Lexi's fear becoming her own, "You have to get us out of here!"

Alice turned as the door opened again. "You three. Change into these clothes or we will toss you out in what you are wearing," one of the guards said as he threw piles of clothing to the floor. He leered at

them and then closed the door again. Since Alice and Sasha were still wearing the dresses they had on at the ball, they both knew a change was a good idea. They picked up the clothing and found it was all army issue fatigues. Sorting out each other's sizes, they handed out the clothes. Alice felt decidedly weird wearing frilly underwear under the rough clothing of the army; the thong was really riding up her ass. She was grateful to be wearing socks and boots again. They fit particularly well and she wondered at that as she dressed. She looked in the camera, speculating who was watching, always watching.

Not long after they were fully dressed, their meals arrived. Alice looked at her own tray suspiciously. Now would be a good time to drug them. She watched as Sasha and Lexi both ate, saw nothing out of the ordinary in their actions, and began to eat her own food. She knew the camera was watching them, it had moved. The lens caught the light, proving it was moving. She'd learned to ignore it, but she was aware of it, ever aware they were being watched.

One by one they used the facilities, trying to look everywhere but at their companions as they used the toilet that was in the room without even a modest wall to hide it or them. Everyone averted their eyes when any one of them had to use it, but it was still awkward, especially when noises or smells ensued. Still, they had learned to use it as they had no choice. It was late in the afternoon when the soldiers came for them…two for each of them.

Alice was the last summoned from the room. She knew that was because she was the most dangerous, or they had finally realized that Sasha and Lexi could be subjugated easier. She saw that all three of them were tied with thick and long zip ties, the ties behind their backs wrenching their shoulders. She wanted to fight, but looking in Sasha and Lexi's frightened eyes, she thought she would wait and see exactly what these men had in mind. She also saw that all six men were prepared to fight her if she started anything. She recognized the stances; she knew they were ready. She saw the cameras in the hall were trailing them, moving as they walked by. They were led to a room where a higher-ranking officer met with them. He was dressed in full battle fatigues and obviously ready to go to war. He stood up from the table where he was sitting as they were brought into the room. A chair stood across from him at the table.

They were made to stand at attention across from him. The guards were on both sides of each woman and a pace behind. "We are giving you all a chance," he began brightly.

Alice nearly rolled her eyes as he began what she thought of as a pep talk.

"You see, you three have been a royal pain in our asses."

"What is he saying?" Lexi hissed at Sasha, her Russian not as good as the rest of them—it hadn't been needed before in business dealings where English or French was the presiding language.

"I'll tell you later," Sasha answered, her anger over how they were being treated making her snap the answer. She immediately regretted taking it out on her girlfriend.

"We thought we would make it fun for our men since you refuse to cooperate with us. We will find your computer," he looked directly at Alice and nearly flinched at the orange eyes looking coldly back at him. He blinked, trying to remember if they were that ungodly color the last time he had seen her at the party. He switched his look to Lexi, "We will get all of your properties and if your heirs won't sell them, they will pay."

Lexi looked so horror-stricken at his threats, she nearly cried. She knew the foundation would hold if she was declared dead. She also knew these men didn't care about any of the legalities.

"You have nothing...not anymore," he spat at Sasha. In his mind, she had betrayed her country by leaving her inheritance to *that* woman—he glanced again at Lexi for a second, thinking 'to an *American*.' "I personally want you dead," he continued, looking at Sasha. "All you had to do was cooperate and you would have made money, money for all of us."

He glanced at Alice again and nearly did a double take. Her eyes were yellow now. Maybe it was a trick of the light. Still, it made him uneasy as he took in the scratches and abrasions visible on her person. Her eyes were swollen, the skin around them making the colors change, at least that was what he had convinced himself. The bald head was a nice touch and he was glad that Konstantinov had ordered it.

"Do any of you have anything to say before we continue?" he offered generously, taking in all three.

"Vhat do you vant us to say?" Sasha asked with contempt in her voice.

"How about you tell us what we want to know?" he tried a little joke.

"There is nothing to say," she clipped this out decisively.

"Ah, that is where you are wrong. We could have tortured it out of you...out of your girlfriend," he glanced lasciviously at Lexi and smiled when Sasha bristled. "We are tired of the games you people have played on us. Whoever you hired will die for working for you," he finished.

"What if I told you we didn't hire anyone?" she asked and Alice wanted to shut her up. It didn't pay to let your enemy know what you were capable of.

"You? Sasha Brenhov? Capable of murder? Capable of executing the men in The Assemblage?" he started to laugh. It was a genuine laugh of mirth. He continued laughing and it echoed in the small room. It took a while for it to die down.

Alice looked at Sasha, catching her eye. She looked ready to deny what he was laughing about, to give him examples of what she had done. Alice shook her head slightly and Sasha got the message.

They waited patiently until he wiped the tears from his eyes. "You are nothing more than a bloated billionairess. Your father made money in Mother Russia off the backs of people like me. He made his mistake when he decided to get all patriotic and renege on deals!"

Sasha leaned forward to correct him, but remembering Alice's look, she kept her mouth shut. She had been the one to move their businesses on the more legitimate side, to get them away from the element that made them dirty. Yes, her father had made a lot of money off such endeavors, but she hadn't. She'd inherited vast wealth and made it bigger. Legitimately. It was just the greed of people that were associated with The Assemblage that couldn't fathom that she wouldn't want more. They couldn't understand that she wouldn't join their illegal endeavors or let them into her legitimate ones. She stood and took his insults.

"And you...obviously, you have funds that allow you to get into bed with this one," he directed his comments at Alice. "Those business deals out on Long Island will be really profitable for us," he smiled, but it didn't reach his eyes. He was still alarmed at the yellow color of her eyes. They also appeared to be narrowing. They reminded him of something familiar, but he couldn't put his finger on it. "Perhaps we should investigate you more," he put in, "investigate your family and see what we can find there."

Alice nearly rose to the bait. Instead, she answered, "As you probably already know, my wife and I were divorcing. There is nothing to find there since it was already worked out before you took me." She knew it was a bluff, but she had to protect Kathy, had to somehow divert attention away from her and the children. Why they hadn't already investigated her or found out more, she didn't know. She was certain they hadn't known who she was for a long time and this had hindered their search for information on her. She wondered exactly how much they even bothered to learn before their members began to die.

"You have a wife?" he asked as though this was new information.

"No," Alice shook her head. "In case you weren't listening, we were divorcing. So no, I don't have a wife."

"Ah, but you must have loved her at one time or you wouldn't have married her!" The man sounded pleased to have gotten some information out of her, even unintentionally.

Alice smiled, a smile that normally sent chills down people's backs. She'd been slightly out-maneuvered and she didn't intend to let that happen again. Without warning, she jumped on the table, using the chair as a step between her and the man, then jumping on him, using her legs to wrap around his neck and wrench it. The unexpectedness of her move alarmed them all. He went down from the onslaught, further strangling himself as her legs wrapped and the muscles squeezed. Feebly, he tried to get her off, but the combination of her muscled legs, gravity, and his fall worked to his detriment. The surprise was complete and she had strangled him with her legs before the six guards managed to pull her off him. He hadn't stood a chance and they looked at each other in alarm as first one, then another, used the fact that Alice's hands were tied behind her back to punch her repeatedly. As she went down, she was pleased that they didn't see her hands behind her back as she pocketed something from the man's person. The blows were nothing as she became used to the pain, her mind going elsewhere so she didn't feel it.

"Stop it, stop it," an authoritative voice called as they came into the room, several other soldiers pulling the men off Alice. "What is the meaning of this?" he demanded. Alice recognized the voice of the man who had stood behind Konstantinov. She still wondered at his anonymity, but it didn't matter. She'd killed one of The Assemblage without knowing his name, she'd kill another. For now, she'd see where this led. Her body was aching and she was bleeding badly. "Pick her up," he ordered and Alice was set on her feet, weaving badly. "What is the meaning of this?" he demanded again and then he saw the officer on the floor, obviously dead.

"She killed him, sir," one of the six guards reported, standing at attention.

"How? I thought her hands..." he began and then saw for himself that Alice's hands were still tied behind her back. That meant they had been beating her while she was unable to defend herself.

"She strangled him with her legs, sir," another answered.

He looked at the situation speculatively. He glanced at Alice. "Tie her feet and take her to the infirmary," he ordered some of the men who had piled in behind him. "You, take them back to their cell and you'd better hope the game isn't off!" he threatened.

Sasha and Lexi were hustled to their cell, looking back as Alice was dragged in another direction. The infirmary they called it, but it was really another cell manned by someone with medical experience. They watched until they were thrown into their own cell, still with the ties binding their hands behind them.

"What the hell?" the man on duty said as they brought Alice into his infirmary. He could see she had been beaten, and badly.

"She killed Kirkarov," one of them stated as they put her on the table without releasing her hands or feet.

"Kirkarov?" he asked incredulously. "How in the hell?"

"She strangled him with her legs," he reported and they all looked at the small, bald-headed woman on the table with alarm. She didn't look deadly with her hands and feet banded together, but after what they had been told and all the deaths in The Assemblage, they had to wonder.

"Let's get these off her," he went to clip one of the bands holding her hands behind her back.

"I wouldn't do that, sir," one of the guards warned him.

He looked up, debating whether to listen to him or not. If she had killed Kirkarov, then perhaps it was better to keep her bound. He did the best he could to examine her. She was going to look horrible shortly with all the bruises he could see on her face. Her gut was a mass of red marks and that was going to bruise as well. Still, he didn't detect any broken bones, and while she flinched at some of the probing with his fingers, she managed to hide most of her pain from him. This woman must very tough to take punishment like that, but he kept that thought to himself. He thought about taking a scan, but knew that his superiors wouldn't like that. She was, after all, a prisoner and they planned on hunting her and her comrades rather than just outright killing them. He didn't know what the women had done, but the men were all excited at the prospect of hunting humans.

"Okay, she can go," he said after he had patched up some of the bleeding abrasions. He looked in the yellow-orange eyes and shuddered. He knew what was there; he knew death when he saw it. As he helped her up, he whispered, "Good luck." He could see she was startled, but hid it well, and he turned away as though he didn't care.

They dragged her down the corridor to an overly large SUV that reminded Alice of a Hummer, only it seemed blockier. It must be the Russian version of that vehicle, or whoever made Hummers copied this and made them friendlier. They waited as Sasha and Lexi were brought out. Two guards got in the back of the vehicle with guns drawn. One drove and one rode in the passenger seat with his gun drawn, facing backward toward the prisoners. A familiar set of bags were thrown at the women's feet and Alice peered through her swelling eyes meaningfully at Sasha, who looked surprised they had given their 'supplies' back.

They drove a ways from the palace, many miles out into the wilderness. It reminded Alice of the Pacific Northwest and she had a flashback to what happened to Kathy those many years ago, and how she had handled that. She took a deep breath, suppressing those terrible memories, but keeping the beast she had unleashed back then alive in her psyche. She'd need it. When they stopped in the middle of an enormous field, she brought herself back to the present.

"You three *out*," the guard in the front gestured with his gun as one of the guards in the back got out and opened the door for the three women. Alice scooted over, but with her feet and hands tied it wasn't easy to slide out gracefully. She nearly fell as she penguin hopped to the side of the road. One of the guards threw the two bags at their feet. The other guard from the back, his gun drawn, spoke up, "You three have two days to get yourself hidden or start to escape." He laughed at what he thought was a joke as they looked around. The white-capped mountains in the distance were a deterrent if the pine-encrusted hills and slopes around them weren't enough. "Here, let me remove those," he offered as he snapped the ties with a wire cutter. Pausing momentarily, he gave the wire cutter to Sasha to cut Alice's bindings. He didn't notice as she slipped it into her pocket when she was finished. "I can give you another bag with guns, or some food and a few supplies. You choose," he offered generously. "We will give you only two days and then we *hunt* for you." He slapped a rifle he had strapped to his back to emphasize the word 'hunt.' "I don't give you much time beyond those two days," he laughed again evilly and the other guard laughed with him.

Alice let Sasha and Lexi choose whatever they wanted from what the man had offered and filled another gear bag with their choices. Lexi tried to reason with them, but they pretended not to understand her English or her French, and they totally ignored her attempts at Russian. Even Alice, who now had a basic understanding of Russian, knew that Lexi's Russian was worse than her own.

"You have two days," he repeated and gestured that they should move away from the vehicle.

Sasha went to lift the bag of things they had chosen and found it too heavy.

"Here, let me help," Lexi said with a tremulous smile. She hadn't liked the way those men looked at them. Their smiles had been...predatory. She too found the bag to be too heavy. She put it back down and looked at the other two bags.

Alice sorted her gear and took a few cans of food. She put the one bag on her shoulder, wincing at the pain in her ribs and stomach, and gestured to the other one. "You can divide that up," she indicated the first bag and then the one she'd sorted, "and between you, you might be able to carry it all." She knew they had too much and the soldiers had made sure that they had very little ammunition for the few guns they had chosen.

"You didn't take a gun?" Sasha asked as they divided the food and weapons.

"I don't like guns," Alice said as she adjusted the knives she had brought into the various pockets of her outfit. Already the harsh fabric the military used was chafing her. The thong was very uncomfortable at this moment.

"I thought you were some sort of expert!"

"Naw, I don't like guns!" she repeated.

Alice looked at the road from where the guards had dropped them off. It formed a V and ran in two different directions. She looked down both. She knew she could go back to the palace and kill every one of those motherf'rs, or she could stay and wait for the fight she knew was coming her way. She also knew there was a third choice, one she knew she wouldn't take...she could make her way back home. She glanced at her companions, at Sasha and Lexi. She knew she couldn't leave them. She couldn't let the men of The Assemblage win. So long as one of them were alive, they would take advantage of those they felt were lesser than them. They would go after women they thought were helpless. They'd learned, much to their dismay, that people like Sasha weren't going to lie down and take it. There were only two of them left in charge and she already knew their greedy little souls were divvying up the remainder of their enormous wealth...what little she had left them. She calculated the time they had been in the dungeon and was willing to bet the wealth they thought they had was considerably less now, they just hadn't discovered it yet. They wouldn't know that their so-called computer expert was dead. She was sorry for the death of Evgeni Konstantinov; she had been an attractive woman. Unfortunately, her association with her uncle was her undoing and she had to die like the others.

Alice looked around once more. She decided she'd have to do both the remaining choices, but first things first. "Let's get under cover," she ordered the two women who looked to her for leadership.

They headed across the vast field towards the tree line. Alice was sure they were already being watched. You didn't let three enormously valuable prisoners run free, even if it was for something as stupid as hunting them. Alice was under no delusions; they were going to hunt them to kill them. She'd seen the looks in the faces of the men who guarded them. They'd rape the women too, if they had the chance. Once they got under cover of the trees, Alice stopped them.

"Shouldn't we keep going, find someplace to hide?" Lexi asked.

Alice looked up from where she had stopped to go through her bag. She was laying out the nail gun, the knives, the piano wire, and other supplies she had brought. The electronic tags she had stolen off those men were gone. She was wondering how much juice was in the battery of the nail gun, and then she found the second battery pack and the charger. They really had given them back the things they had packed.

"We need to assess what we have and what they've given us. We also need to look for bugs."

"Bugs?" Lexi pulled back distastefully from the bag she was carrying, misunderstanding.

"Electronic devices," Sasha clarified, seeing her girl girlfriend, unused to these harsh conditions, react to the word 'bugs.'

"I know that, but what am I looking for?" Lexi asked as she reached for her bag again and unzipped it.

Alice went through everything, twice, which took a while. She also went through the clothes they were wearing, which wasn't much. The other two looked awkward in army issue fatigues and if theirs were as rough as hers, they were going to be chafing as well. She found what she was looking for. The clothes, the bags, even the batteries all had nifty little bugs attached. She carefully pulled a plastic baggie from her bag and put the bugs inside.

"Why don't you throw those away?" Lexi asked, watching her. She'd been alarmed when Alice, with Sasha's permission, had frisked her and her clothing.

"We may need them as decoys," Alice told her, wishing they had something better than a plastic bag to hold the cache of bugs. She hoped she had found all of them and intended to look again when they had more time.

"Decoys?" Lexi asked. She was questioning everything Alice did, not having the trust in her that Sasha did.

"Come on, let's go," Alice answered instead as she zipped up her bag and hoisted it. Its handle was long enough that she could sling it across her back. She saw the other two lifting their heavier bags and hoisting them on their own backs.

"She may attach the bugs to something to throw them off," Sasha murmured to Lexi. She worried about her partner in this wilderness. She would follow Alice's lead. She didn't feel comfortable out here, but she'd seen Alice under many conditions and trusted her implicitly.

Alice quickly found some sort of animal trail as they began to hike through the woods. She circled around and set a couple of traps. They waited hours, but eventually she had an assortment of rabbits and a squirrel. Then using the meat from one of the rabbits that she killed, she put the bugs on some of the live rabbits and the squirrel. She also fed the meat to some other animals including an inquisitive crow who flew away with his prize. "There, that should confuse them," she said

with immense satisfaction. "I hope I got them all," she confided to her companions.

"Wait, we just wasted hours of our time to put them off our trail using animals?" Lexi asked, incredulously. She'd watched as Alice killed that poor rabbit without a moment's hesitation.

"Yes, baby. It vas necessary," Sasha assured her. She'd helped Alice once she understood what the woman wanted. She'd also watched Alice pick up the small snare traps and take them with her after she caught what she needed, something she was sure Lexi had missed. She hadn't left them set to catch other animals needlessly.

"We are going to need every advantage," Alice assured her as she picked a trail and headed farther into the trees.

"Where are we going to spend the night?" Lexi asked, looking around as the trees got more and more dense and the air became cooler. The trees stopped the sunlight from penetrating this far into the forest and the shade was cold.

"I'll find something," Alice tried to reassure her. She was thinking to herself that they would need more supplies. She wished she could find someplace to leave the other two so she could go out on her own and hunt. She knew she couldn't though. They were babes in the woods in more ways than one. She glanced back when Lexi tripped on a branch and Sasha, gallant and thrilled to have her partner back, helped her up. They were going to slow her down and that really was the point, wasn't it? Alice was sure that Konstantinov and his cohorts had figured out Alice was doing more than they expected.

That night Alice made a makeshift shelter, cutting branches and leaning them against the rock face.

"Don't make that too high," she cautioned the other two as they made a fire. She made sure it reflected against the rock, bouncing its heat back in the small space so they would all stay warm. They'd need it, they had no blankets against the cool of the night. They all slept that night as Alice didn't think they needed a guard this soon. They awoke all stiff and feeling gross since the 'facilities' left a lot to be desired.

"I wouldn't use that," Alice cautioned when she saw out of the corner of her eye that Lexi had grabbed leaves to wipe herself.

"Why not?" she complained in a hostile tone, annoyed that the woman was watching her squat.

Sasha looked at them both, angry that Alice was reprimanding her girlfriend and worried that Lexi would piss off Alice.

Alice was amused though and looked away as she answered, "If I'm not mistaken, those are leaves of three."

"Yeah? So?" the hostile tone hadn't changed as she wanted to clean herself off and get out of the crouch she was in.

"Weren't you ever a girl scout?" Alice asked in the same amused tone.

"Yes, I was..." she began to defend herself, seriously pissed at Alice's amusement at what she was sure was her expense. Then it occurred to her what Alice had just said and she was reminded of a saying from her girl scout days... *"Leaves of three, leave them be,"* was the phrase that indicated poison ivy, oak, and sumac. "Oh shit," she said aloud, as she'd already used some of the leaves.

"Yeah, that might," she cleared her throat before adding, "itch later," Alice continued, looking up into the canopy above them and trying not to laugh.

"Vhat? Vhat am I missing?" Sasha asked, seeing the expression on her girlfriend's face.

"You might want to take the water bottle and wash that," Alice offered as she started poking into the fire and pulling out some cans of food. The other two were a long time in returning to the fire and Lexi was walking oddly, almost as though she were trying not to let her split halves rub together. Alice tried not to laugh, at least not aloud.

After eating out of the cans of food, Alice felt queasy, which made her think the food might be tainted. She really hoped not. They had a lot to do today. When the others began to feel just as ill, she took the remaining food and buried it, cans and all.

"Wait! We're going to need that!" Lexi protested.

"Look, they either poisoned the food slightly or made it so we would be sick from it. Who knows, maybe there is something else in there as well. We'll do better living off the land," Alice pointed out.

"You're being paranoid."

"These people are hunting us to kill us," Alice said angrily.

Sasha played the peace-maker. She could tell Lexi was out of sorts with having to rough it.

"Ve also don't vant them to find our debris," she pointed out after calming her girlfriend and helping Alice bury the cans.

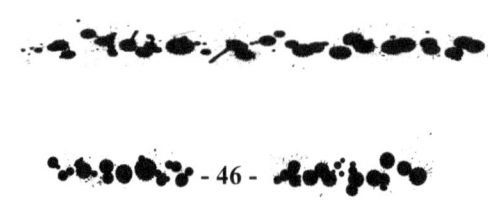

They found their first hunters the next day. They hadn't given them two days as they had promised, but then Alice hadn't expected them to. She'd finally gotten Sasha and Lexi to stop chatting as they walked along. They were hiking deeper into the wilderness and the chatting was scaring away any game Alice might be able to find to supplement their food. Their chatter had also kept her from hearing things, such as an enemy that might come upon them at any moment. They had believed, or at least Lexi had, that the hunters would give them the full two days they had been promised.

"That's not fair," Lexi protested as Alice pointed out the camp that was even now being set up where they had first entered the woods. She was pulling at the seat of her pants, shaking them out where they clung to her.

Sasha shushed her. "Your voice vill carry," she explained, seeing the look of anger in Alice's eyes. She knew Alice would do better alone. Heck, she and Alice would do better without Lexi, but there was no way she was leaving her behind after she had found her again. Little bits and pieces of their time apart were coming out and Lexi was appropriately horrified.

"What are we doing?" Lexi whispered, realizing they had come in a great circle back to the original spot where they had entered the woods.

"We need to see what they have in mind," Alice answered her, looking down at the camp. She wished she had binoculars. "Do you two think you could stay here out of sight while I go…."

"Ve should stay together," Sasha cautioned, seeing Lexi willing to argue with the bald woman.

"Yes, but I'll move faster and get more without…" Alice began and then saw that Lexi was frightened. She hadn't dealt with this for the past year and she hadn't killed. Sasha had just let on about her own active role in taking out The Assemblage players.

"Vy don't I get closer and listen," Sasha offered.

"I can…" Alice began, but Sasha, knowing that Alice was the better of the three, waved her off.

"My Russian is so much better," she pointed out logically. "I can listen and find out some of their plans."

"You are going to have to crawl," Alice told her.

Sasha nodded and realized, before this all began she would never have considered it. Her Armani suits and nice clothes were far behind

her. Lexi had already commented on the difference in her and she wondered if the new Sasha would still appeal to Lexi. They'd tried to consummate their love for each other, but had chosen an awkward spot and were forced to halt their lovemaking.

Lexi and Alice watched as Sasha started crawling away, at first on her hands and knees, and then as they watched, she ended up on her belly to get close enough to listen. Alice wasn't pleased with the idea. She knew she was the best of the three of them, but they needed to know their plans. She wanted to go in after dark to get some supplies including blankets and food.

"Why'd you lie to me about Sasha's involvement?" Lexi asked, nudging Alice's shoulder with her own.

"I didn't want you pulling away from her for what I made her do." Alice had been expecting this question and was ready for it.

"You *made* her do?" Lexi's elegant eyebrows raised in disbelief.

Alice smiled. She knew Alexis was too smart not to figure it out. "She loves you. When she saw a video of you getting beaten, she wasn't hard to convince."

"She's very loyal to those she loves."

"She's been betrayed by a lot of people."

"Yes, yes she has. Never me though, *never me*." Lexi stopped a moment to look over at Alice again. "I don't think you'd ever betray her either. You've been a good friend."

"Some friend. I helped her commit murder."

"You helped her retrieve what was hers. You saved her. And for that you have my undying gratitude. If there is anything I can do to help you, please let me know."

"You are going to have to go with us now. It's the only way I can keep you safe. You are going to have to look the other way too." Alice wasn't so sure Lexi could. Alice was, after all, killing people.

"Maybe I want a little revenge myself," Lexi admitted with a glint in her eye as she looked at the military camp below.

Alice looked at her in surprise. Revenge was a powerful emotion. So was hate and so was love. So many people wanted to have revenge on someone who had wronged them, but they didn't necessarily want to carry it through to the extent that Alice had.

Lexi had never hated these people. Instead, she felt pity for them and their greedy ways. She'd seen the results of Alice and Sasha bankrupting their families. Until now, she had thought the deaths an

unfortunate happenstance of what these people had done in their lives. Maybe karma was dealing them a blow? But she didn't realize that karma was acting through someone named Alice Weaver. She did feel sorry for their families to a degree, but she didn't feel sorry for the dead. They had deserved what they got. It was the result of what they had done to Sasha, *her* Sasha, and Alice. She had a sudden thought, "Does Kathy know where you are?"

"Kathy thinks I'm dead," Alice said quietly. She closed her eyes to conjure up the image of her wife. She hadn't allowed herself a picture, even one on her phone, in case she had been caught. She didn't want those people to know how much she loved her wife. For all they knew, they had split up and were about to divorce. Let them continue to think that. It might keep Kathy safe, and that provided Alice with the peace of mind to take care of what she must.

They turned their attention back to where Sasha had just disappeared in the long grasses. Alice was twitchy. She knew Sasha was right, but she had still wanted to go herself. Wisely, she knew she couldn't do it all, but she heard dogs in the camp and that worried her. The dogs would be a bigger enemy than the men who were making far too much noise. It did give her an idea though.

"Do you think you can stay here out of sight while I go get..." she began, but Lexi interrupted her.

"Sasha is in danger getting information," she pointed down to where she had disappeared. She was watching that general area, looking for a sign of her girlfriend. She was amazed that the elegant woman would do this, but she had changed a lot since she had known her. Some of it was horrifying and Sasha wouldn't complete sentences, leaving things up to Lexi's imagination.

"No, I was going to go back and get the food we buried," Alice surprised her.

"You're hungry?" she asked, confused.

Alice laughed slightly. "No, but I bet those dogs are," she pointed down into the camp where even now a dog was lunging at the end of its lead. She only hoped it hadn't scented Sasha. If it did, it might alert the men to her presence. She wondered where the Russian woman had disappeared to.

"But you said that food was tainted...?" only then did she begin to realize what Alice was implying. "So, feeding it to those dogs will make them sick?"

Alice shrugged. "Or kill them if that was the plan for us."

Lexi was horrified at first and then realized, once loose, those dogs could be used to track them. She nodded. "What should I do when Sasha gets back?"

"See that clump of trees up there?" Alice pointed to a denser part of the woods. "Meet me in there and make sure you aren't followed. If they find her and you have to run, just head uphill and I'll find you."

"Shouldn't I go help her if..." began Lexi, but stopped when Alice shook her head.

"If they find her, you can't help her."

Lexi was shocked, but realized at that moment how real this was. Those soldiers down there, even those who weren't real soldiers, were in it for the kill. This was real. She gulped and then nodded. She couldn't bear to see Sasha cut down. She'd want to help her, but if she went down there, she would be killed as well. If Sasha was killed, she had no reason to live, but seeing it...she could only hope and pray that Sasha got back, and soon. She watched as Alice watched her for a moment, saw her glance down into the field where Sasha had disappeared, and then head deeper into the woods.

Alice took a while to find their previous camp. She'd led them in a wide circle because she knew someone would be tracking them. She also knew they wouldn't expect them to be watched. As she went along, she couldn't help but think that very soon they would have to exchange their things for what she could steal. Somewhere, in something they wore or were carrying, there had to be a bug. There was no way those bastards would have let them go without some sort of advantage. If she couldn't find any more bugs, the safest bet was to change and start over. She only wanted to keep a few things. She found the camp with great difficulty because she had sprinkled leaves over their previous campsite. The only thing that gave it away were the fresh cuts of the branches she had used to make their shelter. She'd remember that in the future. She knew better, but it was getting too damn dark to correct it. She looked around as she dug up the cans of food and put them in her bag and realized the fresh cuts on the trees were glaringly obvious, any novice would have made the same mistake. With that in mind, her enemies would *think* they were novices. She sharpened a few sticks and left them to be found by the unwary or unsuspecting who would see the same fresh cuts and hurry in. She left the area, sprinkling some more leaves as she hid her own tracks.

It took longer to find the camp than it did to head back down the hill and find the two women. She was pleased to find Sasha back and whispering heatedly with Lexi.

"Psst," she called and gestured with a 'come hither' motion of her hand when she got the two of them to look up. She led them farther away from the camp and into the woods. "What'd you hear?" she asked Sasha.

"There are only ten of them and zat includes Konstantinov anzthat guy ve suspect is in The Assemblage."

"Have you heard his name or figured it out yet?"

Sasha shook her head. It was bothering her, but he stayed quiet and no one addressed him by name. "They vere laughing and enjoying beers," she added meaningfully.

"What about the dogs?"

"There vere three that I could see, maybe four total."

"Good, we'll feed them this," she indicated the cans in her bag.

"Yeah, Lexi told me. Do you think you can get close enough that they von't sound the alarm?"

"They are still jittery, and unless they were taught not to eat from a stranger's hand, we should be able to plant these and feed them."

"Ve?" Sasha asked, alarmed. She had seen the teeth on a couple of those dogs and that idea didn't appeal. In addition to a German Shepherd, she had seen a Belgian Malinois and those dogs scared the hell out of her with their intensity.

Alice sighed. Used to doing things her way and on her own, she smiled, "Then I'll go feed them and see what I can find for us to scavenge."

"She'll need help carrying away anything she finds," Lexi pointed out.

"I don't vant to crawl all that way into camp again. My nerves are shot."

"Then don't. I'm not asking you to," Alice told her, becoming impatient. "I'm going to wait until dusk to start and hopefully the dogs aren't fed until dark so I can throw some of this their way." She indicated the cans of stew and soups as well as meat and vegetables.

"You'll need help getting those open and to the dogs," Lexi stated. "I'll go with you."

"Fine, I'll go too," Sasha sighed.

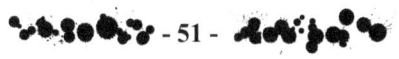

"I don't want to keep you from your busy social calendar," Alice teased.

Sasha laughed, but it wasn't heartfelt.

"What do you want to get from the camp?" Lexi asked Alice.

"I want to see what they brought and if any of it is of use to us. Mainly we need warmer jackets, blankets, and food they might eat, but who knows what else." Alice looked up the hill and gestured at the mountains beyond, "It's going to get cold."

"Are we going to the mountains?" she asked, sounding alarmed. It was quite a way to walk.

"Who knows where this will lead us, but I'd like to hit them tonight when they aren't expecting it, and hit hard. You know, discourage them," Alice smiled, but Sasha saw the glint in her eyes.

"You vant to get Konstantinov and his partner and perhaps end dis now?" she asked, her accent suddenly sounding thicker.

"That would be a bonus, but I think those good 'ole boys might continue the hunt out of sheer enjoyment." She hadn't missed the look in their eyes when they discussed it. There was more than a hunt on some of those men's minds.

At dusk, the three of them were crawling towards the camp. They'd emptied out the other bags and filled them with the food Alice had dug up. They put the guns, ammo, and other supplies in Alice's bag and left that, intending to retrieve it later.

"Remember, if you get caught, fight like hell because they aren't going to give you any chances," Alice had advised, mostly to Lexi who hadn't been in this fight. Sasha, she was sure, would be distracted by Lexi.

They crawled towards the camp, to a different spot than Sasha had crawled to since the dogs were on chains near a couple of the makeshift tents the men had erected. Lexi and Sasha opened the cans and Alice threw them, one by one, near enough that the dogs could access them. She was pleased they were hungry enough that they didn't raise the alarm over the incoming cans. There were enough cans that it took a while, and all three had to duck down several times as men walked to and from the tents. As they were finishing up and Alice was planning her next move, she saw a woman walk from what proved to be Konstantinov's tent, get in a vehicle, and leave the camp. Something told Alice this woman was important. She also looked vaguely familiar, but Alice didn't know why.

"Let's go," Sasha breathed as Alice finished throwing the cans of food.

"Supplies," Alice breathed back and began crawling to the nearest tent. She listened for a moment to determine if anyone was inside and then carefully used her knife to cut at the seam of the tent in a corner, the best way to avoid detection. She was disappointed that something heavy was blocking her way as she opened the seam to go in. Carefully, she climbed over it, realizing it was some sort of trunk. She cautiously opened it and found it held supplies, some she could use. Quickly, she filled a bag and passed it through the slit. Using a penlight, she looked around, saw a backpack, and grabbed that too. She found two blankets and shoved them and the backpack through the cut before taking one last look around for anything she could use. Finally, she exited through the seam.

"Any more?" Sasha breathed in her ear once she tucked up the tent in a way that wouldn't give them away too soon.

"Yes," Alice breathed back and then flattened herself to the ground as someone came around the side and unzipped his fly. The stench of fresh urine was clear in the air. The three of them held their breath until he zipped up and walked back where he had come from.

They decided to crawl away from the urine and headed for the next tent. Unfortunately, someone was inside. They could hear him laughing as he drank loudly so they moved on.

"Maybe ve should take vut we have and go," Sasha worried, seeing Lexi wince as she scraped her hands on sharp stones. Also, it was getting too dark to see very well.

"You go on and I'll catch up," Alice suggested, knowing the two of them were more likely to get caught. It would provide a distraction, but she didn't want them to be killed.

"No, we stay together," Lexi insisted and then shushed as someone in the last tent said something and the men there got very quiet, listening. Lexi pulled at her pants. They seemed to be binding her although she had been very careful not to itch.

The three women tried to control their breathing. Finally, one of the men said "Sobaki?", which meant dogs, and they started talking again.

Alice peered through the oncoming darkness and could see the dogs were still snuffling about the cans. One of them was already pawing at his mouth where a can was lodged around his muzzle. She moved on. At the next tent she listened, but didn't cut into it right away. It wasn't until Sasha and Lexi were right up next to her that she carefully slit it open as she had the first one. Again, with her penlight pointed towards the rear of the tent, she searched for things. She found clothes, which were a bit big, and shoved them through to the two women along with a couple of sweaters. For herself, she found a cap and put it on with relish. Her bald head had really been cold. She also thought it might have been like a beacon in the dark. The men, not expecting them to attack or steal from them, wouldn't have thought to look for them...not yet. She found a bunch of energy bars and teas, and stole his small teapot as well. Lastly, she pushed his two blankets and sleeping bag through the slit. She followed it and whispered, "Let's go." With this loot, they decided to head out. They didn't have enough, but at least they had more than they started with.

Slowly, they made their way across the field in the dark...at least they could crawl instead of slithering. They couldn't stand and run, not yet, or they would be seen. Alice had explained about three black shadows against the field and how they would stand out. Before they got away, Alice wondered if the dogs had been poisoned, but she couldn't see in the dark so simply followed the other two.

"Okay, you can stand up," Alice hissed when they got to the tree line.

The three of them had trouble finding where Alice had left her bag.

"Now what?" Lexi asked, trying to balance all the stuff they had stolen.

"Do either of you snore?" Alice asked.

"No, I don't. And I know Sasha doesn't," Lexi stated, puzzled.

"Then I think we should sleep right here, unless you want a fire."

"Vhat, so close?" Sasha turned to look down the hill where the campfires of their enemy were located.

"Yes, they wouldn't expect we'd be this close and maybe we can do something in the morning to upset them."

"Are you sure?" Lexi considered.

"We can't get far tonight, even to escape. We have some food," she pulled an energy bar from the bag for each of them and handed them to the women. "We need more supplies and they have them."

"Won't it make it easier for them to track us in the morning?"

"Vhat do you vant to do?" Sasha asked at the same time.

"I think they were planning on using the dogs. I don't know if that food was tainted or not, but it gave me the trots. How about you two?"

The other two were embarrassed, but admitted it had. Lexi had been particularly careful, but so far, no rash. They thought perhaps the water had kept her from developing the rash they all expected.

"Then I hope the dogs are out of commission. Maybe if you eat enough of the crap they let us have, it makes you sick by degrees or kills you. I don't know. Anyway, I thought I'd be really bold and sneak back in the morning and see how many I could take out of commission."

"Dogs?" Lexi asked, alarmed.

"Men," Sasha answered for Alice with a decisive note in her voice. She agreed with Alice. They needed to attack, and soon, when they wouldn't be expecting it. Once they realized the the women had been there, they would be on alert and they wouldn't be able to steal any more supplies. "I could help..." she began, but Alice was shaking her head as she pulled out one of the sweaters to put on. She liked that it was rather large and covered her quite nicely with room to spare.

"I need you two to create another diversion if I should get trapped down there," she began to outline what she had in mind, speaking sotto voce so their plans wouldn't be overheard. "I hope I don't have to tell you two what will happen if you get caught by these men."

"Are you a man-hater?" Lexi asked, the tone in her voice irritating Alice on principle.

Alice gazed at her in the darkness, wondering at the naiveté. "These men are exceptions. Most men are decent human beings, but men like this hire more men like them because they need that mentality around them to get them to conform...to have them obey commands without thinking twice. If they catch you, and they may, they will rape you and use you for vile things that I'm not going to enlighten you on. It's us or them."

"Surely someone will..." she began, but was interrupted by her girlfriend.

"No, no one vill," Sasha told her. "Ve could have gone to the authorities in Russia, but they are owned by men like this. To them, this is sport. They have their testosterone high and the idea of hunting another human being has them at their peak. Ve must kill them or they vill kill us…eventually. Only after they have their vay vith us." The sad note in her voice finally got through to the woman.

Alice continued to outline what she wanted the other two to do. They didn't have much in their arsenal, but what they had would have to do.

"That sounds good," Lexi noted as she explained. Using the penlight, standing between it and the camp down in the glen, they repacked their bags and the new backpack Alice had acquired. They each had a blanket and the sleeping bag could be a cushion between them and the forest floor. Sleeping next to each other for warmth, they went to sleep.

The gun was pointed straight at Alice's forehead. She used her hands and pushed it up and away from her, at the same time ducking her head out of its line of fire. The gun went off and Sasha flinched, knowing Alice had to be dead. In the time it took her to open her eyes again, she saw Alice was still alive and fighting. Alice brought the hands down, bending the gun towards the man's stomach, and then wrenching it away from him. She didn't hesitate. She immediately turned it on him and fired three times to make sure she hit vital spots. She kicked him in the privates as an added insult to his injuries. Staring at her incredulously, he grabbed his stomach and bent over, looking up at her as he slowly succumbed to his wounds. He fell over, almost in slow motion, and he was dead as he hit the ground.

"I thought you didn't like guns?" Sasha asked in relief, seeing Alice surviving this.

"Yeah, well, you use what you have," Alice answered as she began to frisk the body for anything she could use.

"Vat was zhat technique you used?"

"Krav Maga," she said shortly, finding a couple things on his person and pocketing them before someone came to check out the gunshots. They might not check immediately, assuming Alice had been shot first.

"Vhat is zhat?"

"It's an Israeli technique that is taught to all their soldiers," she confessed, standing up.

"You vere in Israel?" Sasha asked, sounding astounded. Perhaps this explained how Alice knew so much about killing people.

"No," Alice said as she began to walk by, putting the gun in the waistband of her pants after slipping on the safety. "What made you think that?"

Sasha stared at her back momentarily, shrugged as the answer, and followed her towards a waiting Lexi.

Lexi drove the vehicle off as soon as they all got in and they headed deeper into the hills towards the mountains. "Do we have enough supplies?" she worried.

"No idea, but we still need to be alert. I didn't get everyone," Alice answered from the back seat.

"I can't believe what I saw..." Lexi began and Sasha interrupted.

"That was incredible!" she enthused.

Alice shrugged, wishing to put it behind her. She felt absolutely no guilt over their morning shenanigans and the deaths that had resulted. Instead, she was relieved to get away...for now. Unfortunately, neither Konstantinov nor his partner were in the camp when Alice had conducted her raid. They must have left sometime during the night while Alice and the other two were sleeping. And who the hell was that woman they had seen leaving the previous day? Alice had a few questions she wanted answers to. She knew she wouldn't get them for now, but she was patient, although she was ready to get this over with and go home to the United States. She was ready to see if there was the possibility of a reconciliation with Kathy. She missed her desperately. Hearing Sasha and Lexi as they reconnected gave her not only indigestion at how syrupy sweet they were to each other, but a longing for her own woman. She really wanted Kathy back, but if Kathy wasn't willing, she would have to deal with it and move on. That was the part that bothered her the most.

They drove a ways before the road became too rocky to continue. Lexi, used to a four-wheel drive and having driven on dirt roads many times in her life, had volunteered to take the jeep-like Russian vehicle while Sasha had thrown the grenades that provided the 'distraction' that Alice needed once she started her kills. She'd gotten four of the men in their tents by crawling up and slicing into the tents from the back and then killing the men in their sleep. One wasn't asleep though. He'd been jacking off to a picture right out of Playboy, only Alice was horrified to find it was a picture of Lexi pinned up in the magazine and not the playmate of the month. She'd taken great satisfaction in slicing across his neck. His scream was quickly cut off and only a gurgle issued forth, but it had been enough to alert the other six men in camp and the chaos that ensued from the grenades Sasha threw had allowed Alice to get two more men: one in the kidney and one by disemboweling him. He'd stared in horror as his hands tried to hold in his innards before he fell to his knees. Alice hadn't seen the gunman until it was nearly too late.

Sasha and Lexi had crawled to the far end of the camp. If, and when they heard anything, one of them was supposed to throw the grenades Alice had confiscated the previous day. They had planned on looting the entire camp, but a few vehicles coming up the road, their dust billowing up and alerting the women, had changed that idea. They grabbed what they could, stole the jeep, and now they were trying to get as far away as possible.

The final bump made the vehicle scrape along the rocks horribly. They were no longer going to be able to use it to get away. Alice took out a pair of binoculars she had stolen and looked back. Yep, they were still being followed. The reinforcements were probably Konstantinov and more of his company. She was very angry that things hadn't gone as she had hoped. Perhaps it was the surprise of finding the guy jacking off? She might have hesitated a second and that allowed him to scream. Or maybe it was seeing a picture of Lexi superimposed on a naked body that allowed him to get out the warning, but she had planned to kill all of those in camp and take their supplies. She shrugged it off. The best laid plans often went awry.

They divvied up the supplies they found in the back, creating heavy packs for all of them as they left the vehicle and headed up into the rocky hills, disappearing among the pines. Alice had booby-trapped the vehicle before they left.

"What do you mean their tracks peter out?" Konstantinov raged as his man made a report.

"They obviously made their way up there," he indicated the rocky hillside. It was difficult to track anyone on rocks, but two of the three didn't hide their tracks as well as the third. If it wasn't for the fact that they knew there were three women, they wouldn't have known they were hunting a third woman; she was that careful.

"That is obvious, you idiot!" he backhanded the man. "Tell me something I don't know?"

"They may have circled back," he breathed, a trickle of blood running from his lip. He wiped it away with the back of his hand and stared at it angrily, careful not to show that anger to his employer.

"What makes you think that?"

"It's what they did with the first camp."

Konstantinov thought that over carefully. He had a small crew of men going over that first camp, burying the bodies, and backtracking the women. He'd lost one man when they found the women's first camp—sharp spikes had impaled him front and back, ripping into the man's kidneys and gut. It had been horrific and several men lost their breakfasts over that.

He looked up at the mountains the women were heading into. It wouldn't do them any good. There was snow up there that would prevent them from going over the mountains. Kazakhstan was a nation of over 2.7 million kilometers with over 17 million people. It was the ninth largest country in the world. This area was sparsely populated, which was why he had chosen to locate his hunting cabin here. It had grown over the years and he had only recently turned it into the palace it was today. He was very proud of his heritage. He was a direct descendant of Konstantin and he felt he should have a home that reflected that. Not in Russia where he was from, but here where land was cheap and the economy was growing at such a rate that people with his foresight would be able to capitalize on the emerging markets. Kazakhstan was where Europe and Asia came together. It had 130 nationalities within its borders and there was a unique opportunity for those willing to take advantage and having the know-how. As a member of The Assemblage, Konstantinov had known vast wealth. Watching The Assemblage brought down, member by member, he had known it was time to retreat to his country estate and regroup. He hadn't realized that anyone knew about the palace. Finding Sasha Brenhov and that companion of hers walking boldly up the dirt road to his home had vastly surprised him. Capturing them had been easy, almost too easy, and he wondered at that as he saw his men fall. He'd already lost a dozen of them.

One of the men following the women into the rocks was blown away as he tripped over the carefully placed piano wire that triggered a grenade. One of the men, a bit more zealous, followed the tracks into the forest. He outdistanced his comrades far too soon."Why?" he whined, losing control of his bladder as she held the knife to his throat.

"Your *employers*," she said disparagingly, "gave me no choice."

"But I didn't do anything to you."

"No? Haven't you, like your *comrades*," she spat the word, "been hunting us like animals?"

"It was my duty," he protested as he felt the sharp edge of the blade.

"To hunt women?"

He gulped, his Adam's apple scraping up against the knife.

"Perhaps you should have chosen different employers? Perhaps when you saw what they were planning, you could have quit your job?" she hissed into his ear as she sliced open his neck and the blood spurted out. She didn't wait for him to die before wiping the knife on his clothes and returning it to its sheath. He breathed a last gurgling sigh as she began to frisk him for things she might have a use for.

Alice glanced around to see if there were any more of them, but she had been careful when she attacked, singling out this one because he was alone. She continued her own hunt looking for these soldier boys as she gave Sasha and Lexi time to make it up the slope; it was steep climbing. Just then, she saw another soldier boy. This one was being a little more careful about looking around.

"I don't take prisoners," she told him conversationally as she ran directly at him and plunged her hunting knife into his chest. He tried to heave her over his shoulders, but the blade was so sharp it had cut in like a hot knife through butter. His move did throw her over him, but her grip on the knife pulled it from his chest. He looked down in horror as blood began to pump out in time with his accelerated heartbeat. He tried to staunch the flow with his hands, looking up at Alice in horror as she turned quickly and stared at him. She didn't wait for him to die fully before she began to rifle through his pockets for things she could use. His feeble attempts to stop her with his hands were brushed aside as she searched. She found a Zippo lighter, which must have meant something to him as he unintentionally lunged for it as she took it. She stared dispassionately at him as she watched the life fade from his eyes. His last look in her eyes showed yellow, nearly orange eyes. He thought that had to be a trick of the light as he could have sworn they changed into something he would have seen on a cat. He finally sighed out his last breath and Alice left him where he lay.

Alice continued up the slope, using rocks to her advantage to hide her passage as she went. She'd mentioned that to Sasha and Lexi, but they were either too tired already or just unknowing, as she was still able to track them. Alice stopped from time to time to listen around her. The birds told her more as they were either tweeting or silent, telling her if anyone was around. After a while, she stopped again to listen and heard herself panting from running too much. *"I better get back in shape,"* she thought. She slowed marginally to keep from sweating in the cold weather, not wanting to tire herself out or catch something.

It was late in the afternoon when Alice, swinging wide to let Lexi and Sasha come up on her, found a cabin. It was very primitive, very well hidden, and was obviously some hunter's cabin. In fact, she wouldn't have seen it, much less found it, if she hadn't nearly slipped off the rocks she was climbing. The cabin was made of native stone and only the symmetrical square of a window gave it away. She carefully approached and found the front door hidden in a curve of the mountainside, camouflaging the whole building. She carefully opened the door, armed with her knife, which was a silent killer, versus the gun in her waistband that would alert her enemies to her position. As she went inside, she found it had four bunks. Judging by the amount of dust that had accumulated, it obviously had not been used for many years. The four bunks had nothing on them but slats to hold a mattress. There was no sign of any mattresses. In a large box next to a fireplace in the stone wall, she found a supply of candles. She carefully assessed the cabin and backed out, making sure she stepped only on rocks and looking back frequently to mark its location as she went in search of Sasha and Lexi.

She found them in the trees about a mile from the cabin. She could hear them whispering, but only because the birds had silenced at her approach. They didn't even notice the lack of birdsong as they discussed their options.

"We should go back and give ourselves up," Lexi was arguing.

"If ve do that they vill take vhatever information ve give them and then kill us," Sasha responded heatedly.

"Surely they can't be that bad."

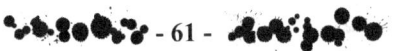

"They are…and vorse." She had already explained about the sex slave trade they'd been involved with…and who knew how much more they would uncover. She'd tried to fill Lexi in on everything now that she knew Sasha had, by necessity, done killing of her own accord and not because Alice made her.

They continued discussing things, wondering if Alice had been caught, but Sasha was certain she hadn't. They'd heard the repercussions of the grenades that Alice had told them about in the rocks. That piano wire was coming in handy now. She wondered how Alice had known they would need it?

"What if they have gotten her? We should turn back to civilization," Lexi persisted.

"No, Alice said to continue heading up here. I trust her," Sasha contributed.

"You have a thing for her, don't you? You are attracted to her?" Lexi sounded whiny and tired.

"No, I respect her. She kept us alive time and time again. If she said head up here, she vill find us."

"And so I have," Alice said as she made herself known. Both women made moves for the guns they were holding, but that would have been useless since Alice had the drop on them both. "I found a place we can hide for a while," she continued, not letting on that she had listened to their conversation for the last five minutes or so. She gestured and turned, expecting them to follow. Sasha did immediately, but Lexi balked.

"Wait a minute. Tell us what happened down there," she gestured down the hill. It had been hours since they had seen the bald woman.

"I killed some of them. Is that what you wanted to hear?" she asked as she turned back to see Sasha walking towards her and Lexi halted in her tracks.

"No, I just think…" she began, but Sasha whirled around on her.

"You think we can reason with these people? That they vill let us go if ve tell them vhat they vant to know? They are in dis for the kill!" she said passionately, her Russian accent becoming thicker. "I love you, Alexis, but if you can't see that they vill kill us—they vill kill you, they vill kill me—then you are foolish, and I've never thought that about you!"

"I'm sure some of them are innocent of…"

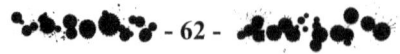

"They chose to follow Konstantinov," Alice said quietly. The birds were still quiet and that didn't bode well. "We have to fight back." She didn't add that she had to kill them all or they would keep on coming, they wouldn't give up. "Look," she tried to reason, "You're tired, you're overwrought. I found a place where we can hide and you can relax. Come on," she gestured with a come-hither wave of her hand while her eyes were darting about the spot, looking to see if there was anyone else here. The birds continued quiet was bothering her.

Lexi knew she was being childish and obstinate. Sasha trusted Alice so she should. Alice had saved them from what she knew would have been a bad situation, but they had been caught in the first place and that bothered her. As she caught up with the other two she asked, "How can I trust you? You think you know what you are doing and yet you were caught at the palace."

Alice turned slightly, first to look around at their backtrail, and second to give Lexi her attention. "That was *deliberate*." She smiled at the stunned look on the woman's face. Sasha looked like some of the things she had wondered about were finally making sense. "If Konstantinov hadn't captured us, how could I have gotten the faces of the two members that Sasha and I didn't know. And I wouldn't have the opportunity to take out two more of The Assemblage," she explained passionately.

"But they could have killed either of you at any time," Lexi argued. She gestured at Alice's face where the telltale signs of the beatings she had taken were still visible and healing. "That can't have been worth it?"

"This? This is nothing," Alice shrugged it off, gesturing at her own face. "We got two more of The Assemblage. The original twelve are now down to two. We now know who the last two are and we only knew of Konstantinov before," her voice had lowered to a near whisper. She was looking around them, making sure no birds flew off as she led them back to the rocks away from the forest. It would take twice as long to return to the cabin as it had for her to find them due to her caution. She led them across the rocks carefully, not bothering to talk. The birds had started tweeting again and that, more than anything, relieved her.

She had a moment or two where she almost couldn't find the well-concealed cabin, but she finally remembered enough of the rocks to recognize where she was. The other two were astonished when she opened the door that wasn't visible until you went around a curve in the rock and walked into the cabin.

"If you don't light a fire or go in and out too much, this will be a safe place to hole up for a while," she promised.

"Won't we need a fire for warmth?" Lexi asked, looking around at the dust distastefully, her own flashlight peering into corners and along walls.

"Unless it snows, these outfits should be warm enough," she indicated the mismatched outfits they had stolen and changed into. They left their original garments behind as Alice hadn't been sure that those weren't being tracked somehow. She'd had Sasha, who hadn't minded, look carefully at Lexi's skin for the telltale red mark from being shot with a tracking device. She didn't know where the bugs might be hidden and that was the part that bothered her the most. "We have blankets and sleeping bags now," she indicated the gear they had brought in. "Let's make this place livable."

Much to Lexi's surprise, Alice dug in and helped clean the place. It was small enough and between the three of them they quickly had the dust gone, aired the place out, and organized their supplies. Lexi looked astonished at the nail gun as Alice willingly gave them the gun she had stolen.

"Won't you need that?" she asked the bald woman who no longer removed her cap except to wipe sweat from her head.

Alice shrugged. "I don't like guns," she repeated her earlier statement. "I prefer something quieter," she indicated her knife, but made sure the nail gun was on safety as she inspected it to make sure no dirt had gotten in.

A while later, as they ate from the cans they had stolen, a candle lighting the room adequately, Lexi asked, "Now what?"

"Does it seem to you two that there is something else going on here?" Alice asked as she licked the spoon she was using to finish the peaches from her can.

"Vhat else?" Sasha asked, looking up from the canned pears she had chosen.

"There has to be a reason that Konstantinov built out here in the middle of nowhere," she gestured with her hands, the spoon in one hand, the can in the other, spreading her arms wide.

"Didn't he say something about it being his hunting lodge originally?" Lexi put in, watching to see if Alice's spoon dripped the

syrup from the peaches and shuddering at the sticky sweetness that would make a mess.

Alice nodded as they sat at the little table in the cabin. The walls, now cleaned of dust, showed the wood someone had brought up here to line them. Beyond that were the stones, making the cabin tight against the weather. "Yeah, but why here? Why in the middle of bumf–" she stopped what she was about to say to listen…there was a noise. She got up to investigate, leaving her spoon and can on the table. She opened the front door slowly and carefully. The angle made it impossible to be seen in the rocks, but she was also unable to see beyond the cabin without exposing herself, so she peered cautiously around it. She knew the only way in was also the only way out. They'd be trapped if anyone came up here and found them. She personally didn't want to stay in this snug little cabin. She put a few rocks on the window sill to hide its symmetry, the first thing she had spotted when she found the place. Relieved, she closed the door and turned around to see the fear on her companions' faces. "It's all right. It's raining." She hesitated a moment before pointing out, "If they still have dogs, the rain will hide our scent and it will also wipe out any footprints we left. If you just stay put, they won't find you."

"Vhat about you?" Sasha asked, picking up on the 'you' and not 'us.'

Alice smiled. Sasha had become very quick to pick up on these things in the last year or so. "I'm going out to create some mischief and whittle down the numbers."

"Vhy can't ve help?"

"Do you really think Lexi is up to this?" she asked, pointedly. "No offense to you," she turned to Lexi, "but do you really want to be responsible for the deaths of any of these people?"

Lexi immediately shook her head, but somehow it seemed unfair. "So, you take the risks for us all?"

Alice shook her head. "If I don't have to worry about the two of you, it will be better. Also, these few supplies will last longer. You should be fine so long as that," she pointed over her shoulder at the outdoors beyond the door, "doesn't turn into snow."

"It vas snowing in Russia," Sasha pointed out.

"It's snowing at higher elevations," Alice acknowledged in agreement. "It's only a matter of time before it moves down to this level."

Sasha nodded. That only made sense, and she had seen the snow on the mountains. She trusted that Alice wouldn't abandon them. "Vhat if they finally get you?"

"You won't know until you run out of supplies then, will you?" Alice said sadly. "But I tell you, I'm going to do my damnedest to end this. I want to go home. I want to see my wife and family."

Both women understood that. Since being back together, they hadn't had any real time alone. Both suddenly realized...with Alice gone from the cabin they would be alone, they could consummate their love for one another. They exchanged a look that told the other volumes.

"What if they do find us?" Lexi worried.

"Then use all of this," she indicated the ammunition and guns the two women had hauled up with them as well as the one she had just given them, "until it's all gone," she said warningly. She exchanged an understanding look with Sasha who hesitated and then nodded in agreement.

"They could out–" began Lexi again, but Alice interrupted her.

"They could," she agreed, "but I'm going to try to stop them. And if I can, I'll come back and restock you."

"What can one person do that three can't?" she nearly scoffed, not realizing who she was talking to.

"Trust me, baby, she can," Sasha shushed her. She knew how competent Alice really was. If Alice was willing to take the fight to them and her dear Lexi was out of it, she was content. She had done some things that she still had to tell Lexi. With Alice gone, she could have heart to heart conversations with her. She had to know if Lexi could get past the fact that Sasha had willingly killed people, had helped Alice to kill.

"Well, no time like the present," Alice said as she began to gather her gear.

"It's nearly dark. Won't you stay and start out in the morning?" Lexi offered generously.

"Yes, that would be a good idea, but there is no guarantee this rain will continue and I don't want to lead anyone back to you two." She didn't relish going out in the rain, but she had no choice...they hadn't stolen any raingear. "Just stay in here. That hole over there is the toilet. Just pour water down the hole and cover it back up when you're done," she indicated the corner she was certain neither of them had

noticed. "There is a barrel that catches the rain from the rocks," she pointed outside. "Try not to go farther out than onto the rocks," she added the warning. "The less you two move around or expose yourself, the less scent or tracks there are to find, and the less likely you will be *seen*. They can't find you if you don't move around or make yourselves known."

"You think they vill send dogs after us?" Sasha asked, musingly. She knew she should go with Alice. It was her fight, but she glanced at Lexi, her Alexis, and knew she couldn't have her killing people. Lexi hadn't seen Sasha kill anyone. Telling her about it was bad enough, seeing it would be so much worse.

"They'll send whatever they can use after us," she answered sardonically. Alice didn't want to spend a long time on goodbyes so she gathered her gear and left shortly thereafter as she began her hunt...alone.

~The End~

❧ MANIACAL MALICE ❧

BOOK 22

Alice is just finishing up a few minor details that have kept her from returning to her family—killing a few people that kept her away, blowing up a few things, taking revenge on the heartless...Can Alice FINALLY go home?

"Why didn't you just come *home*? Leave there and come home?" Kathy pleaded as Alice continued with her story.

"I had to finish what I'd started. If I had just left Sasha and Lexi there, they would have died. If I hadn't finished everything, those bastards would have come after you and the kids." Alice was angry as Kathy interrupted her thoughts, reliving in her mind what had happened to keep her away from her family.

"I don't know if I want to hear any more," Kathy admitted honestly, her hands going to her ears dramatically after all she had heard from her wife.

"I need you to understand. You are the only person I can tell this to…" Alice pleaded.

"You mean you need to confess. You need to get it off your chest to justify all the killings!"

"No, nothing like that," Alice shook her head, shocked at what felt like a verbal attack. Seeing the expression on Kathy's face broke her heart and reminded her why they had separated in the first place. "If you don't want me to continue…" she offered helplessly.

Kathy considered. Not knowing the story, the whole story, would bug the hell out of her. If she was honest with herself, she *needed* to know. But there was so much…there had been too much. "You had to kill more, didn't you?"

Alice didn't say a word. She just nodded her head, waiting for Kathy to ask.

Sighing loudly, Kathy closed her eyes wearily and rubbed her forehead thinking of all the deaths that could be attributed to this woman: this woman who had always been loving and faithful and giving to her and their children; this woman she had thought about constantly for two years; this woman she had been married to for even more years; this woman, the first and only woman she had ever truly loved! Kathy looked up at Alice. She could see the worry and concern on the face of the woman she still loved. She looked so haggard, so thin, and she had never been this thin. She looked gaunt. She looked…old. Kathy's heart melted, wanting to fatten Alice up, give her comfort, and make her happy. As she realized she still loved Alice, that she wanted Alice here, and wanted to make her happy, she realized she did need to know everything. "You better finish. Tell me *all* of it."

"Are you sure? I can gloss over…" she began considerately.

"No, I have to know it all. I need to hear it this once. I may never mention it again, but if I have questions…" she warned.

"I'll answer anything you may ask," Alice promised and then she took a deep breath to continue the story of where she had been for so long.

As Alice walked away from the rock cabin she wished she could have slept inside its safe walls. The weather was not going to cooperate and she looked up as the rain began to fall harder and harder as she carefully made her way across the rocks. At least no one would be able to track her back, no matter how good they were. Once she got out of the rocks she began a jog, one that would eat up the landscape and allow her to take longer strides to further hide any sign of her passing as the rain washed away her footsteps. She slipped once and nearly fell in the mud, and only then did she slow down. She needed to find a place to hide for a few hours, somewhere safe and dry so she could sleep.

It was getting too dark to see. She nearly fell into a gully and decided to go no further. Between the darkness, her fatigue, and the unfamiliar landscape, she could do more harm than good. She managed the best she could, crouching under a couple of fallen trees and wrapping herself in her jacket, hunkering down and pulling grass and bark around her to retain her body heat. She spent a very uncomfortable night in the rain that seeped through everything and woke a bit grouchy. It was then she realized she hadn't brought any food with her. It had been deliberate at the time, but she knew in her present condition—feeling cold, tired, and cranky—she wasn't at her best. She needed nutrition, vitamins, and protein, and with that in mind she began to look for the people hunting them.

She found only one guy. They too had hunkered down in the bad weather, looking for movement. She only spotted him when she climbed a tree to try and see further in the dense woods. He didn't look up as he crept up the side of the hill, using his binoculars to sweep the hills. Had he gone straight ahead about a mile or so up the rocky hill before him, he would have found their camp, but he didn't know that. He would never know that as Alice used the sound of the rain to mask her climb down from the tree. She could feel the fatigue in her battle-weary and injured body. It had been too long since she'd given it good food on a regular basis. It had been too long since she had allowed it to heal for any length of time. It was wearing on her and her strength was ebbing. Still, she timed her fall to land on him, using his back to break her fall. She knew she had to move quick and she barely made it. He was bigger, stronger, and used to regular meals. Only the element of surprise was in her favor…and the fact that she knocked the breath out of him.

Alice turned and snapped his neck, not taking a chance that he could fight back. She couldn't afford to take any chances, not now. She quickly frisked his body for anything she could use, adding items to her own pack including compressed cakes that could be made into soup, nutrient bars, and even some vodka that she took a slug of to warm her cold body. The blanket, the sleeping bag, and the knife, she added to her kit. She hid the body in a depression under some brush so his now naked body wouldn't be seen too easily.

She ate two of the nutrient bars, which rapidly filled her shrunken stomach, falsely signaling her body that her stomach was filled and she'd had a full and complete meal. She felt the fullness and any benefit she got from the bars wore off a couple of hours later. Since it was still raining, she had no problem filling her water bottle. She was grateful for the filter built into the cap since she didn't need a case of diarrhea at this point. She took care of her necessities, hoping no one would see her rather white buttocks, and used the guy's handkerchief to clean herself, burying it along with her poop. She needed to hide any signs of her passing and the rain would only last so long.

As she came out on the road they had used before, she watched warily as some trucks drove along. They were obviously familiar with the route, not slowing for the twists and turns or the rain. Her eyes narrowed as she contemplated this and before the thought was fully formed, she was moving and waiting for a turn in the road that wouldn't allow them to use their side mirrors, then vaulting up, over, and inside the last truck of the small convoy. She looked about wonderingly. The truck was carrying explosives and other gear. She began to use the turns in the road as an opportunity to throw gear from the back, counting on the curves to identify where she was throwing supplies and to hide her activity from anyone watching out the mirrors.

She found six boxes of MREs (Meals, Ready to Eat) that the military supplies for its service members. These went into a couple of the curves first thing. It was as she was throwing out the fifth and sixth boxes that she realized these were American supplies, not Russian! The rest of the supplies she stole before she herself dropped out of the truck were all Russian and most, if not all, were weapons and ammunition.

It took her most of the day to find the six boxes of MREs and haul them to the bottom of the hill below where Alexis and Sasha were camped out. She had to wait until dark to deliver them and she had to move carefully on the path she had memorized that would take her up that rocky hill in the dark and rain. She only hoped they wouldn't hear her and shoot her. The rest of the supplies—the medical kit and the weapons she had taken—she kept in her pack. She took a few sleeping bags and blankets up with the MREs and left it all on their doorstep, waiting until a crash of thunder coincided with her footfalls so she could drop the boxes two by two on the ground outside the door. Knowing these two women were well-supplied, she felt the many trips up the hill were worthwhile. She didn't even bother to knock or let them know she was there. She hurried back down the hill, skidding slightly on the slippery rocks. She knew she had to be more careful as she was tired and the nutrient bars were no longer doing what she needed.

In a curve of the hill, the same one that hid the cabin, she found two slabs of rock where she managed a small fire on a small butane-type stove. It was the size of her hand and perfect to heat up whatever she wanted from her supply. It was easy to squeeze water through her filtered water bottle into the small pot on top of the stove, adding a packet of something dried she found. She soon had a sort of beef and onion soup simmering. Because the portion size was made for a larger pot, the contents were rather compacted…and nutritious. For the first time in days Alice felt warm from the soup, dry from the rain jacket she had propped over herself and the fire, and safe…relatively speaking since she knew she wasn't too far from one of their camps.

After making her soup, she quickly extinguished the little stove, packed it up immediately in case she needed to leave quickly, and curled up in her sleeping bag, removing only her boots as she climbed in and wrapped the wool blanket like a turban around her head and neck. With all the rain, she had felt the pangs of a cold that day and knew she couldn't afford to get even a little ill. The protein bars had given her the dreaded diarrhea and she'd had to use military issue toilet paper, not much different than using rough bark from a tree. Water and exercise had allowed the first pangs of cramping and body excrement to pass. Ignoring the acidic and painful moisture, she had to stop, pull down her pants, and spray her water bottle in a bidet-like fashion. It was only later, as her stomach stopped telling her she was eating badly and rejecting all signs of it, that she finally breathed a sigh of relief. The hot soup and endless water were doing their job admirably as her fairly healthy body returned to normal.

Alice didn't sleep deeply. Any sound out of the ordinary—from water building up on the hill, to nature releasing it in a rush—had her opening her eyes again, sure she had been spotted and perhaps captured. She had no illusions of what they would do to her if they found her. She knew what they would do to the other two women as well. It wouldn't be pretty. Pain and humiliation would be inflicted upon them all at this point, before they were eventually killed.

The next day found Alice across the valley, far from where she had left the other two. It was still raining and the cold suggested at any moment it could turn to snow. She couldn't see up into the mountains due to the low cloud cover, but she was certain she would see white up there when she got a glimpse through the clouds. She hoped for a break in the weather for a few days so she could lead those searching for them on a merry chase, far from their intended victims. She had been right. Their camp had been within a very short distance of the cabin and if not for the rain they might have found it. She hoped the food and supplies she had left for Sasha and Lexi had been found by now.

She used the binoculars she had acquired to scope out the little she could see. She saw there was another set of roads leading out of the valley where the castle sat; those power lines she had noted led her to them. It was then she realized these were major power lines and major roads. Despite the weather there was a convoy of trucks traveling down them...all military vehicles. Slowly, she realized the comrades she had been whittling down for all their other nefarious schemes and activities must also be dealing in arms. The small convoy she had been a part of for that brief time had American rations and Russian arms. She wondered what the others might have, but it didn't matter as she didn't have a plan of how to take them out yet.

She started with some small guerrilla tactics to annoy them. One by one she ambushed, humiliating them by stripping them of their supplies and clothes, and leaving them alive to fight another day. When this didn't discourage any of these battle-trained men and a few women, she sighed. She would have to start killing them since she had learned from conversations she had overheard with her imperfect Russian that she and the other two women were to be killed on sight. It was then she started using the military supplies and armaments she had taken.

She timed a caravan of supplies—four large military trucks with who knew what on them—as they traveled down the mountainous roads. Behind them on motorcycle were some of their escort. Because of the grade and the slippery, rainy roads there was an adequate delay to allow her to get the last of the piano wire tied to a tree, run across the road behind the last truck while slipping in the mud, and bind the other end to another tree before continuing to hide some ways away. She left herself an out for when they realized they had been sabotaged and how. It took only moments, but the beheadings were instant. The speed of the motorcyclists while trying to close in on their caravan and doing their duty as guards had them completely unready for the nearly invisible, but very strong piano wire. Even Alice had to swallow twice as she saw the many dead from her trap. Untying the useful and reusable wire, she was nearly seen as one of the motorcyclists had gone down on his bike instead of hitting the wire. She used the butt of a gun on his helmet until it cracked under the pressure and then struck into the space between the helmet and his head. He wouldn't be reporting anything. Alice slipped back up the mountain loaded with additional contraband from the men she had frisked and disappeared, pleased with that day's work.

Most days were spent observing. She was bored and tired of it. She wanted to get something done and knew it had to happen at or in the castle. She watched the castle too, knowing they were expecting…something. While looking at the wires beyond the castle she got an idea. Using up the last of her grenades, she caused one of the huge towers to fall into a ravine, the power lines snapping and sparking impressively as it fell.

When someone came from the castle to check why their power was out and radio in their report, Alice took him out and threw his body into the same ravine. As the power was still live in the wires, his body snapped, crackled, and popped when it hit them. She winced thinking of the sensation he would have felt if he was still alive. The smell of burnt flesh wafted up the ravine, but the rain soon washed it away.

His radio broadcast brought out several more people including a team that began to turn off the power to the lines. A few days later, another team began rebuilding the huge tower, trucking in huge steel girders for their project. Alice's eyes narrowed as she recognized two of the people she had been hunting, one of whom had ordered her death as a member of The Assemblage, back in Russia. With her trusty nail gun, she took out his larynx. She was disappointed as she had aimed for either his mouth or between his eyes, but with the rain, the cold, and the distance, she had to be satisfied he was dead. Now, she only had one other to contend with…right?

The men scattered as they realized their comrade and boss, had been killed right before them. Some of the guards had machine guns and they began to fire into the surrounding woods and hills, having no idea where the nail gun had fired from. They didn't even know it was a nail gun. All they knew was he was down and dead, very dead, with blood splattered everywhere. The rain was already diluting and dissipating the blood on the ground. He stared blankly into the sky, not even realizing he was dead, but Alice felt little satisfaction over his killing. It had taken too long to get him and she was now hiding from the bullets winging around her. One ricochet caught her and she was grateful for the first aid kit as she sewed herself up by her little fire that evening, feeling her way around the wound, cold from the rainy weather and shock. She was grateful there was no bullet inside her, merely a deep and bloody wound.

"She's hit," the tracker they had brought in stated, finding where Alice had first been hit and seeing the blood and water under the beam of his flashlight. "We will stop here tonight. You go back down the hill," he ordered his comrades, not wishing for them to ruin any signs he might find of his quarry. She had proved elusive, very elusive, and he was admiring of her skills. He was also angry because he knew the other two had to be hidden. He guessed they were close, but had gone to ground. If they didn't move, they left no tracks, no signs, and he could not find them. He would not get paid, he could not go home unless he found them. This one was good, but not as good as he. He would find her. He smiled, his diamond encrusted front tooth showing for a moment as he hunkered down for a cold and long night.

The next day, the continuing rain hadn't diminished, but there were signs that an expert tracker could find. A bent plant, a broken branch, and if they were lucky, a boot print. He was very thorough and very excited. She had gone to the rocks to hide herself and he had his men surrounding the hill he thought she was on.

Alice watched, shading the binoculars from the sun that was finally peeking through after so much rain. She saw her tracker, recognizing his skills and even admiring them as she cursed whoever had found this man. That he was on her trail, she didn't doubt as she watched him skillfully navigate the rocks she had used to hide her tracks.

What Alice didn't know was he had been brought in from the wilds of Siberia where such skills as he possessed were still fairly common, where technology hadn't ruined nature, and where the people still hunted and foraged for their food. Things that were common there were uncommon in more 'civilized' places and non-existent in cities.

Alice cringed as she quickly looked through her bag for an ibuprofen, something to alleviate the pain she was in from menstrual cramps and various aches and pains. Finding some, she quickly swallowed two as she continued leading the men away from her previous camp to some traps she had set the first night they had begun to hunt her and her friends. The amount of time that had gone by since she set the traps had erased any signs of them and she nearly fell into one herself, barely missing the hole where her leg would have been impaled on the now rotting, short spears she had cut. She smiled as she avoided the trap, remembering now where others were and leading her followers.

The half dozen men, eager to finish trailing the woman and sure they were near their goal, became overeager and didn't realize why the tracker held back when seeing his quarry's hesitation in certain areas. He understood her hesitation when the first man went down, his leg pierced, ruined by the rotting and sharpened stakes. The men pulling him out of the hole only made the wound worse. Two others, eager to go on and catch the woman and certain she was only a short way away, were bayonetted, one on top of the other and then together as the spears came at them, making them human shish kebabs. The two men who had stayed to help their other comrade out of the hole heard their unearthly screams. The tracker moved up, saw where the spears had pierced their bodies and how badly off they were, and put them out of their misery by slicing their throats. He moved up the trail, unaware of the horrified looks of the two unhurt men behind him.

He stepped off the trail the woman had taken, keeping his nose to the breeze much like a hound dog on a trail. Unbeknownst to the woman, not only did she need a shower, but her blood flow also gave off a peculiar metallic smell. Unable to use modern products, Alice had been using rags that she washed out. She'd left a trail despite taking them with her or burying them deep. Modern products not only masked the smell, but absorbed the blood. The rags only absorbed so much and then left behind the odor he was using to identify her. The wind was blowing down the hill directly into his path. He knew almost exactly where the woman was, as any human bloodhound would. No chemicals had ever ruined his sense of smell and there were no modern conveniences to interfere with a totally natural and refined ability to track anything...man or animal. He smiled, showing uneven but very white teeth; his quarry wasn't far away.

Alice was tired and the cramps and blood flow of her period had made her ornery. She'd been on the run for far too long. She needed a couple days of sleep and peace as she was starting to feel cornered. Whoever this man was, he was good, very good, and she was sorry to have to kill him. Hearing the men's screams, she was certain none of them were from her tracker. He wouldn't scream. When his time came, he would quietly die. Alice moved off her path, knowing they would follow. She couldn't hide her tracks as the sun slowly dried the water-drenched earth. She remembered where she was and began to circle back, rewarded when she heard a thwap sound and could see the movement as a tree sapling pulled itself upright once again, hanging someone by an ankle. He did not cry out and she was incredulous to realize she had somehow trapped her tracker. She warily approached as she watched him.

The well-camouflaged rope, set up sideways and not upright as he had seen her other traps, had been a surprise. As he felt his leg go out from under him, he relaxed himself, knowing that fighting it would pull the rope tighter around his ankle. The tree was higher than he expected and he was sorry to see his favorite knife shaken out of its sheath at his ankle and well out of reach as it fell to the forest floor. He tried to bend at the waist to work on the knot, but it was reinforced with metal, something he had also not expected. His quarry was very clever. He was amused at first to have been trapped by her. This had never happened in his life and he waited to see what would happen.

Alice approached from behind her victim. She didn't doubt he was armed and ready to fight her. She wasn't sure where the others were. One was down in the hole and his leg probably useless, another one or two were impaled by the spears, but as she couldn't be sure of the count, she wasn't discounting that they might be nearby. She hurried to slit this one's throat, looking in his old and knowing eyes as the knife cut his skin. The momentary hesitation as he saw her unnatural eyes was his undoing. His stronger hands immediately came up to stop hers, but it was too late. Her blow had cut the carotid artery and the spray arced on the pine needles. His eyes opened wider, the blood flow from hanging upside down ensuring there was plenty of blood near his head, his heart, and flowing along the artery. His hands which had tried to stop her now tried to staunch the flow, but it was pointless. Alice watched only a moment, staying well out of the way of the spray and his hands. She leaned down and her adversary, so good at tracking her, watched her scoop up his knife, which had been the death of so many animals. He had hoped to kill her with that knife. The valuable things from the outside world that his wife and family had coveted and been promised would never be now. His vision was dimming, but he wanted to protest the loss of the knife. It should have gone to his son, but instead a woman, a devil woman judging by the eyes that had looked in his, would be taking the prized possession.

Alice quickly got away from the scene hoping to find a couple more of her adversaries, but they had counted on that and began firing as they saw her. The knife she had just acquired, perfectly balanced and as big as a Bowie knife, flew through the air as accurately as any bullet and hit the first man firing at her. The weight of the knife and the force of the throw ensured it went in up to the hilt. Even if it had managed to hit a rib and bounce off, the bruise might have killed him, but the knife had gone in, had damaged valuable organs, and he was dead even as his hand spasmodically pulled the trigger, nicking Alice's arm.

Alice jerked as the bullet hit her arm, saving her life as the other soldier pulled his trigger. Her nail gun swung around and she ignored the pain in her arm to pull her own trigger again and again until it jammed. The man looked like a porcupine with the quills reversed as the nails impaled his chest. Alice fell to the forest floor, crawling forward until the nail-impaled man fell. He died watching her as she removed the knife from his comrade, wiped the blade on his clothes, and searched him for anything of value.

Alice was breathing hard: first, to control the pain in her arm as she could feel the blood dripping down it and second, because this exertion had exhausted her. She was now running on pure adrenalin. Neither of the soldiers was well-equipped and she wasn't about to carry useless items. The knife was the only thing of value and she took that, trying to remember how many had been after her and how many she and her traps had killed. She worked out that there was one left and as she approached her victims in the traps, in the distance she saw someone running for their life. Taking one of the rifles her victims were carrying, she aimed carefully. Although she hated to shoot someone in the back, this time she did so. It was her or them, and right now she wasn't doing very well. She watched him go down as though he had just run too fast on the hill and tripped, then watched a moment to see if he would rise again.

She quickly frisked the three victims of her traps, finding nothing she didn't already have. She then made her way cautiously down the hill and through the trees to the grassy area where her final victim lay. She wasn't certain the gunshot wouldn't bring others, so she hurried as much as she was able, not willing to become a victim herself. She was surprised to find him alive and breathing heavily, but as she rolled him over she saw why. The shot, a long one at that, had split his spine. The man was paralyzed and she looked down on him with pity. She rolled him back over to look in his eyes. A little spittle came out of his mouth and rolled along his cheek. He reached for and failed to get his sidearm. Alice's boot stopped his hand and he was too weak to try harder. She reached down and pulled the weapon out. His weak hands tried to stop her, but her frisk showed he too had nothing she wished to keep, so she threw his gun away as well as the rifle she had used to shoot him.

"Otpusti menya iz moyego stradaniya," he gasped pleadingly. Alice just looked at him. He asked again in a voice that begged. He added, belatedly, "Pozhaluysta." Alice never even pretended she understood him as she looked in his eyes. He would have shivered at the orange glow coming from the woman's eyes, but he couldn't move. He had asked to be put out of his misery. He had even added 'please' to his plea, but she just looked at him with those strange eyes and then turned and walked away. It was only when he could no longer hear her footsteps that he realized she had deliberately left him to die here next to the forest, unable to help himself and with no supplies, no radio, and likely no help for many days. He swallowed, wondering if he would die of his injury, thirst, or in the jaws of some animal. None of the choices appealed to him.

Alice made her way slowly. Her arm was throbbing and she stopped to rip a strip of shirt, add gauze from her kit—something she had saved rather than use for her period—and stopped the flow from the deep gouge caused by the bullet. She took a roundabout way to the rocks she had hoped, apparently unsuccessfully, would hide her passage from the human tracker she had just killed. He had been too good, too able to follow her when she thought her tracks well-hidden. Even going to water hadn't worked as he had sent his men up and down the small stream that was now a rushing torrent of cold water from the rain and some snowmelt further up. She had nearly fallen in the stream and was grateful to make it across and come out on stones that quickly dried in the sun. She'd used things she had learned over the years: some she had read about, some she had practiced, and some she had even seen in movies, but nothing had shaken the man and she hadn't known why. That she had thwarted him had been an accident of fate. Her having used the combination of piano wire and rope had kept him in place long enough for her to slit his throat. Had she been a few minutes later he may have gotten out of her noose and learned from the experience. He would have been harder to get, warier, but fate had been in her favor and now he wasn't an issue.

Alice heard the helicopter long before she saw it. She had just been about to take the rocky path that would take her to the cabin. After the time away, she needed to be sure that Alexis and Sasha were okay. She also needed them to care for her. She changed her mind as she heard the rapid chop, chop, chop noise of the blades. She quickly took to the trees to watch the modern helicopter fly over. She peered at it with her naked eye, not daring to take out the binoculars for a good look as it swept by. She thought she saw a woman inside along with a pilot and two men manning the guns from the rear doors. She backed a little more into the overhanging trees, hoping the movement would remain unseen. They were too far up to see any features, but she wondered if they were looking for their tracker and his men. She gazed after it long after it was gone. Looking up the rocky hill where the two women were in the cabin, she rethought the planned visit; she couldn't afford to lead anyone to it on this sunny day. She hunkered down in the trees and unwrapped her bloody wound.

It needed tending, that was obvious. It had a nasty, jagged edge and she wondered if the bullet had been something like a hollow point that normally exploded on impact, causing more damage. She put her back to a tree and looked carefully around, unpacking her emergency kit and taking out a needle and thread. She poured an excessive amount of rubbing alcohol on the wound, wincing as the liquid seeped into every crevice. The wound bled pure red blood. Poking herself with a needle, Alice began to sew using neat and fairly even stitches despite the angle. It hurt like hell, but she gritted her teeth and concentrated. Sweat broke out on her brow as she continued, hearing the helicopter returning and worrying about being seen. She finished sewing quickly and gathered up the gauze, the needle, the scissors, and anything else that was bright and shiny and could be seen from afar. She quickly buried the bloody gauze, sifting pine needles down on the hole just as the helicopter flew over again. She looked down, knowing a white face could be visible from above and wondering briefly again if they had heat sensors.

Not a religious woman, none-the-less Alice prayed they didn't have modern technology like heat sensors or something that could detect movement. Her body, in response to the shock of her injuries and the cold, shuddered at the thought. It hadn't occurred to her with the first pass, but now she was worrying. The blood loss and the sweat now cooling on her brow were making her begin to shake. They went by too fast to really see into the trees where Alice was lying, looking down again so her white skin wasn't visible. It was then she wondered if they had found the paralyzed Russian and were taking him for medical attention. If he survived, he would probably be a paraplegic...that was *if* they found him at all.

Alice moved deeper into the forest away from her friends and their warm and safe rock cabin. She had almost given in, had almost given them away. She could not, would not approach the cabin while it was daylight. She also could not approach it unless it was raining. The smell could easily be tracked by dogs, she was certain of that...at least her increasingly feverish mind was telling her that.

Alice spent an uncomfortable night in the forest wrapped in her sleeping bag and blanket. First she was too hot and then she was too cold. She knew she had a fever and desperately wanted to throw a bare leg out to somehow equalize the temperature. She knew she was becoming increasingly ill. Her body wasn't throwing it off like it used to. She was too run-down and that could become dangerous.

The next day she realized how dangerous it could become as she saw a skirmish line starting from the field where they had originally camped and attacked the soldiers and going up through the woods where they obviously had found the bodies. By now she was certain they had found the man she left alive, but she didn't know if he had died or been found in time. All she knew was that men and women in army fatigues were walking in a line ten feet apart for a long way and coming toward her. She took off the other way, feverishly making her way and trying to stay away from the many people looking for her and her friends. She knew they wouldn't go up that hill from the angle they were heading, but they were going to chase her up some hills she had avoided, which led into the snow-covered mountains. She found she had no choice but to go.

All day long she trotted along, resting as long as she dared, trying to remain unobserved and out of sight. The helicopter had passed over several times and this time she clearly saw only three people inside: the pilot and two gunners. Her fever made her less alert than usual and she nearly trotted into a camp further up in the hills. It was a camp of soldiers getting ready to start their own skirmish line. She watched as they spread out and began to walk the hill. That was good. That meant they didn't know where she or the others were hidden and they didn't know she was observing them. She watched their camp, realizing that they had left only a couple of soldiers to guard the camp. Alice snuck into their camp when it was obvious the soldiers were going to stay out in the field.

She came across the first guard in a medical tent where she had been stealing supplies. Hearing him or her approach, she flipped a switch on a machine inside the tent. As the person entered, Alice was ready and used the paddles to give them a heart attack. They dropped like a stone and Alice made sure they fell into the tent instead of out. She rolled them over and found they were still breathing, but barely. She knew if they were oxygen-deprived for at least four minutes their brain would never recover, so she jolted them once again when the machine powered back up. This time she didn't hear the telltale signs that the machine would power up again and realized she had drained its battery and its backup, but she didn't care as she dragged the body to the side and finished loading up her kit bag with things she would need from the well-stocked tent. She slipped out the back, the same way she had slipped in, and crept up on the next soldier she found.

She watched in the dusk as the soldier gave himself a shot. Unconcernedly, he threw aside the vial and pocketed the needle in a case. She crawled to the discarded vial and tried to read the side of it, but it was too dark and the writing was in Russian. She had never learned to read those exotic symbols well. She knew common words, but would never be able to decipher the medical words. It was as she turned it over in the dark that she realized it had an English translation on the other side. She squinted and made out the letters...H-E-P-A-R-I-N. Heparin! Thinking rapidly despite her fever, she realized it was for a blood disorder. She tried to remember how it affected the human body, blinking quickly against her fatigued mind. She remembered just as the soldier returned from retrieving something and rose in time to knock him on the back of the head with a rock she grabbed. As he went down to his knees, she hit him again, momentarily knocking him unconscious. She searched his pockets, found the needle and another vial, and injected it into him. She found another vial and injected that too. Quickly she left the scene, knowing she had left behind a hemophiliac and the blood flowing from the blow to the back of his head would kill him...he would bleed out shortly, after the heparin thinned his blood.

Alice looked about, wondering how much other mischief she could get up to, but it wouldn't pay to draw too much attention to any one place. She wasn't up for a chase and she didn't really want to give away her position. She could not take on hundreds of soldiers and it looked like they were using her as an exercise of some sort.

In one tent, she found a good supply of tins. While it made for a heavy pack that she was already carrying, she loaded up with as many as she could reasonably carry and slowly made her way from the camp. She had only killed a couple of soldiers, but it would make the others warier...or so she hoped. Before she left she found a flamethrower and having discarded her jammed nail gun, she scooped it up. It might prove to be an interesting weapon. Loaded down, she made her way away from their camp and followed where she had last seen the skirmish line head out. They probably wouldn't think to search the same area twice, at least she hoped not.

Alice slept that night next to a moss-covered log. Another log had fallen next to it and there was a slight depression under it. Not a big depression—she hated to think if a wild animal found her or had made the area its own den. She made herself some stew, heating up a can over her small fire and blocking the view of the flames with pieces of bark, the heat bouncing back to her. She needed that heat and thought about a way to perhaps get rid of her fever later when she found just the right place. After a full meal of stew, she cleaned the can out, buried it and then turned off her small butane fire. She next wriggled into her sleeping bag and then under the two logs, being careful not to move about too much as she could no longer see if she was leaving signs. As she began to fall asleep, her brow sweating in the sleeping bag, she worried she would snore and give her position away. As a result, she slept restlessly, waking up often in case someone could hear her. It was not conducive to a good night's rest.

Alice was wrong, not something she liked to admit. They had decided to retrace their steps and many of the soldiers had followed the exact same path they had taken the previous day. Alice was trapped. Her only consolation was they took the path of least resistance and didn't look under the logs. She had one moment of panic when one and then another soldier decided to walk on the logs. Fear of the logs rolling and exposing her in her sleeping bag had her heart thumping loudly in her chest. Inappropriate laughter bubbled up as she imagined their looks had they seen her face below them.

She heard shouts a while later as she lay there and realized it was time to go. She rolled out from under the log, rolled up her sleeping bag and blanket, and packed her bag. The heavy cans were slowing her down, but she wasn't going to abandon them. The sustenance in them might mean the difference between life and death. She was sure the shouts she was hearing were about the bodies that were found in their camp. She made sure to use the paths and footprints of the soldiers whenever possible as she retraced their skirmish line as rapidly as she was able. She finished her bottle of water and was grateful when she came to a stream to fill it again. She drank all she could through the filter and refilled it. She continued across the stream and higher into the hills, unsure when the mountains started, but knowing she had come miles.

That afternoon, Alice began to scout for a place where she could hole up for a few days. Twice now she had to freeze under the canopy of trees and she knew the helicopter was looking for her. She couldn't afford to be caught at this point. She'd caused murder and mayhem down below, but it wasn't enough; she hadn't stopped the search. She thought only one or two players remained of the original members of The Assemblage, the ones that could afford to pay for this army, but she had to be sure. She had to get back to that castle and finish this once and for all.

It was near dusk when she thought she saw what she was looking for in a wall. She began to climb the rock face, hoping no one could see her. She was very vulnerable as she climbed, but she made it up to the hole in the rock she had seen. As she came to the darker spot, she saw a small, very narrow path leading further up the rock wall. She peered into the cave she had searched for. She heard nothing, but that didn't mean there wasn't something living inside. She slowly lowered her weighty bag. It was too heavy for her, had slowed her down immeasurably, and she was in no shape to be carrying such a substantial bag, so she was relieved to take it off. There had been several times she thought of discarding some of the contents. It had thrown her off balance on the climb up here to the cave, but she was grateful for it now. She took out the flamethrower and a flashlight, and looking out the cave once more, she scanned for any telltale lights. She could vaguely make out some man-made lights, but those were miles away. She only hoped no one would see what she was about to do.

Alice shone the flashlight around. The cave wasn't that deep—only about ten or twelve feet, narrow, and not that tall. In fact, she had to stoop to look around. It looked like some sort of nesting material at the back, but that could be years of debris being blown in through the cave mouth. She glanced out again to see if anyone could see her light. She wondered if she should use the flame thrower and scorch the rock just in case, but that would certainly give away her position if anyone was looking. She had to be satisfied with the cursory look with her flashlight until daylight. It had looked like it might rain again, which she welcomed as she had thought she heard dogs earlier. Dogs were way smarter than any human tracker, although that last one had come close. As she buried her last rag, she realized it was possible he had been able to smell the blood. She knew, as she wrinkled her nose in distaste, that the smell was strong. Still, she had no choice and while she was now able to use the gauze she had stolen more of, she was still woefully under-stocked for things such as menstrual bleeding. She thought it a bit ironic that men and the derivative menstrual cycle were the cause of her present problems as she unpacked her blanket and sleeping bag.

Using the blanket as a pillow, she lit her small stove and realized she might need to refill it soon as she heated up another can of stew. The one she'd had the previous night hadn't been sufficient to last her through the day and she was grateful she had the protein bars to keep her going. Still, nothing beat a good, hot meal and she indulged herself with boiling some water and inhaling the steam. In through her mouth and out through her nose, changing off to reverse that and breathe in through her nose so she could get the steam into her lungs. It felt good and she hung a shirt around her head and over the can of boiling water.

Her full stomach, the warmth of the cave, and her own fatigue soon had her yawning. Putting out her stove, she pulled off her boots, crawled into her sleeping bag, and was sound asleep within five minutes.

Alice awoke feeling stiff and a bit cold. Using the little stove, she heated up another can of stew, opened another can that contained peaches, and a third can that contained condensed milk. She didn't like the milk much, but she needed sustenance. She didn't plan on going anywhere that day, that was why she had looked for the cave. She needed to hide and she figured hiding in plain sight was best. She slowly ate as she contemplated her predicament.

If she were found in the cave, she would be well and truly caught; she'd be trapped. She thought perhaps they didn't think she was this high or this far, not yet. Using the empty cans to pee and then later to poop in, she left them near the entrance to discard as soon as she could. Now that it was daylight, she had been right about the rain, but she was high enough that the valley floor was being soaked and little fell up here. Still, enough of a trickle came down the narrow path she had observed that she knew she wouldn't be exploring today. It looked slippery and unsafe. The water gave her an idea though.

She filled the third can with water as well as her water bottle and another she had in her bag. Carefully, she began taking her clothes off on the sleeping bag. She took a shuddering cold shower with her water bottles and used the warm water, heated up on her little stove, to help clean her battered and disgustingly dirty body. She did this twice and felt much better as she changed into clean clothes, the first time in weeks since the hunt had begun. She looked at the battered and filthy clothes she had been wearing. The pants had blood stains, not just from injuries, but also where she had leaked out and bled down her own legs. She wrinkled her nose in disgust. She was too old to continue bleeding and she'd never have a baby from her body. Someday she would take care of that so she no longer bled since it would be years before menopause would take care of it for her. In the years since she'd been imprisoned her period had come and gone, not as frequent as it might be, but this cycle had been especially painful to her emaciated body.

She didn't know if she could wash out the blood stains or other gunk on the damaged clothing. The blood stain on the arm of the shirt was from her now healing cut. She examined the stitches and they looked okay. She rubbed on some ointment she had stolen and hoped it would soothe the wound and help with scarring. She looked down at her body. She had gotten a lot of scars over the years. She could see the bruises on it in various stages of healing, from yellows and browns to a really nasty almost black one. She smiled wryly. She had lived a very full life.

Still, it felt wonderful to be clean and dry. She reached up and felt the hair that was growing in. They hadn't needed to shave her hair off again. She knew they had done it to humiliate her, dehumanize her, and take her femininity away, but all they had accomplished was to make her more determined to exact revenge. And she would too. She just needed to rest a bit before she returned to the fray.

It rained two days this time and Alice was thoroughly disgusted with the odor of her own urine and feces from the cans in the cave. She had been tempted to go out in the rain and dispose of them, but the slippery slope and rocks had her well and truly trapped for the moment, so she used the time to rest, get over her fever, and eat. But eating more meant pooping and peeing more. It was a vicious and disgusting cycle. Still, it was necessary and she poured the urine out of the cans and down the face of the cliff and hoped the rain would wash it away before the dogs could scent it. Some noise sent her to the edge of her cave to cautiously check it out.

She had also stood up too quickly, forgotten the height of the cave, and hit her head hard on the ceiling. The result was she fell to her knees, swearing loudly to any who cared to hear her, and with her eyes smarting from the blow, she blinked rapidly to rid herself of the tears that coursed down her face. Gingerly she felt her raw scalp, wondering if having hair there would have cushioned the blow any. Instead she felt the blood in the short hair and cursed some more from the pain of touching the site. Sighing, she vowed to pay closer attention. She couldn't afford a concussion with all her other worries and injuries. Still, it gave her a tremendous headache that she had to deal with.

She saw nothing that would have caused the noise as she carefully looked out of the cave, blinking away her pain and tears. She looked up and around, hoping not to see the face of man or beast, and seeing nothing she could only hope she had heard rain causing rocks to give way somewhere.

On the third day, she felt caught up on her sleep. Not having to worry if she snored or would be discovered was a big consideration. She felt a lot better and her fever seemed to have abated. She was relieved. She carefully put the cans containing fecal matter into a bag she planned on disposing with them. The bag was actually the shirt she had been wearing when she got shot, which had other tears and rips she hadn't been aware of. She carefully made her way up the narrow path, looking down as she placed each foot so as not to slip. She had only looked up once to examine the path before her and did not see the eyes watching her. As she came above the level of the cave and up on top of the rock outcropping she saw it, but not before it saw her and roared.

Alice vaguely remembered having read that tigers lived in these mountains at one time. She also had read they had become 'extinct' due to too much hunting, trapping, and even poisoning. The Soviet Union had paid large bounties on the cats, one of the biggest reasons they had become extinct. Now, she knew the article lied. If she remembered correctly it had said that Caspian tigers, some of the largest cats that ever lived, had become extinct in the mid-1960s. They had ranged from Turkey to Central Asia, were about ten feet long, and weighed about three hundred pounds! She knew the cat roaring at her was not extinct, and fortunately, nor was it that large. Still, it was large enough. She froze where she had just come over the ridge from the cave, her bag in her hand.

Alice felt ridiculous. She had her knives of course, but the only thing in her hand at the moment was a makeshift bag of shit she had been looking to bury. It wasn't much in the way of protection against a huge cat!

The rest of the article began to come back to her and she remembered they had talked about restoring the cats or a relative cat to promising sites in Kazakhstan. Apparently *this* was a promising site? She knew it was remote, which was why the castle was located where it was. The roads leading into and out of it were ideal for hiding the weapons they must be dealing in. What would they care about a formerly extinct tiger or any near relatives introduced into the wilds of Kazakhstan? She wondered what tigers they had used. Her mind was a lot more agile after a couple days of rest and the name Amur tigers came to her. It must be from that article that had interested her. She wondered how long ago she had read it. Still, the name of the tiger wasn't important as it watched her suspiciously, and she still didn't move.

Suddenly, the thought of fighting off a tiger this large with a bag of shit struck her as funny. She couldn't help herself and began to laugh. The tiger didn't like the sound of that and snarled warningly. She should have stopped, but she could imagine throwing the canned poop and watching it exploding over the face of an enraged tiger and that set her off again. The cat, unnerved by her presence, unsure if it should attack, and disliking the sound of her laughter, began to retreat. But first it gave a few snarls, almost as a warning of what she could expect in the future or if she dared attack.

Alice waited until it faded away into the underbrush then knelt in the first dirt she could find and buried the shirt bag filled with the cans using the knife she had stolen from her enemy. She sprinkled dried grass and dirt over the mound to hide the freshly dug earth. Looking around frequently for any sign of the cat, she realized the cave she had been using could easily have been a cat's lair and wondered if that was why it had been there. She was unnerved by the big cat's presence having never seen anything like that up close outside of a zoo. She thought warmly of the times she had gone to both the L.A. Zoo and the San Diego Zoo with the children. She firmly put the thoughts of her children and wife out of her mind. She decided to take a third day of rest and returned to the cave.

Alice had to admit that third day was unnecessary. Her body was healing and she was feeling restless and determined…and bored. She used the day to spy on her pursuers. From what she could see with the binoculars they were looking in all the wrong places. She was careful, especially in the afternoon sun, to not the let the sun's glare shine against the glass. A quick flash could give away her position in an instant. Still, the view from up here was fantastic and gave her a good idea of places she could use that not only led into the valley where the castle was located, but might prove forbidding to her pursuers.

She was up and ready to go on the fourth day; no more lying about. Her body, while still battered and healing, was feeling well enough that she knew she had to take the fight back to them. As she climbed down in the early morning light, she realized it had started to snow. This could be very bad for her as it would leave visible tracks. She looked up at the mountains and saw a white blanket coating them, hiding the rocks and escarpments as well as the pitfalls and dangers. She also realized, if it got deep enough it could mean avalanches. She had no idea how deep the snow got around here and knew nothing of the weather in Kazakhstan. She sighed. It was time to finish this and she headed out with new determination towards her pursuers.

"We've lost her," he reported reluctantly.

"How the hell could you have lost any of them?" she asked, angrily. She looked at him, noticing that he avoided all eye contact. Sometimes she used that behavior to her advantage and sometimes it irked the hell out of her. It wasn't her fault that she had been born with nystagmus, a condition that caused involuntary eye movements, usually in rapid motions. It was hard to look anyone in the eye when they were busy looking all over, but especially someone in her position of authority.

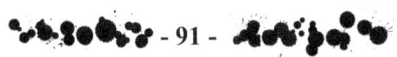

"With the rain, ma'am–" he began his explanation, but she waved her hand aside, dismissing anything he had been about to say.

"Of course, the rain," she returned heatedly. "What happened with that tracker you people insisted I fly in from Siberia?"

"We found his body..." he began again, reluctant to give her any more bad news.

"Of course, you found a body," she sneered. They had underestimated Sasha and this Alice person. It hadn't been that American they were after in the first place. It was unfortunate she had become involved. Whoever she was, she was certain the American was the key to killing Sasha Brenhov and now her girlfriend, Alexis Valour. How they had thwarted the great Assemblage was unfathomable, but now it was a matter of pride to kill these three women and they had men in the field trying to do that very thing. Who the hell were they that these men were ending up dead, one by one, in such gory ways? She was certain it was not Sasha or the dainty Alexis. She herself had investigated this Alice person, but she wasn't very well known and not a lot could be found about her. She was a businesswoman and an investor. She had a bit of money, but nothing like The Assemblage had at their disposal...or used to have. She inwardly sneered at all they had lost. This Alice person would pay, and pay dearly when they got hold of her...then she mentally and realistically added, if.

"Get the dogs out there and any man who catches her gets a hundred-thousand bonus," she promised, knowing on a soldier's pay this would be a great incentive.

"At once," he promised and left her presence, relieved she hadn't taken her disappointment out on him.

Alice heard the dogs long before she saw them. They were using hounds. She couldn't determine what kind, but she heard their baying clearly as she entered the valley once again. There was another dog or two, but their barking was rarely heard. She wondered what other kind of dogs they were, but later she would wish she was still wondering as she saw the two most enormous dogs she had ever seen in her life. She realized these beasts must be Tibetan Mastiffs. They were huge, shaggy, and looked intimidating. They had been used as guard dogs for

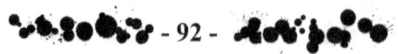

herding animals, but she had also heard they had been trained to guard other things. Their presence worried her since they were more than twice her size, enormous, and looked ferocious. She didn't like the idea of having to kill an animal, but she might have no choice.

Alice scoped out the lines leading into the castle again. They had a temporary tower to hold the many lines up and out of the way, but she could tell by the lack of lights that the power was still off except in a couple of spots where generators must be working. The wooden structure would be easy to take out and she could see where metal girders were being constructed to make the more permanent tower. She also realized that the top of that tower would afford her an incredible view if she made her way up there. She decided it was worth the climb.

First, Alice rigged the new tower and decided to climb another one, the tower nearest the castle. She also rigged this one with explosives she had stolen from the convoy. The two riggings had timers that she could remotely activate, but it took her a while to figure out the different settings since it was all in Russian. She took days to figure out not only the electronics, but the feasibility of blowing both towers, and the timing with men working so hard all day long, every day, on reconstructing the one tower.

Alice had come down out of her cave and hit a stream that led to a river. She kept her boots in the water to hide her trail from the dogs and anyone else they brought in. They had found one expert to track her, they could and probably would find another. Because there was no fresh scent, the dogs were left looking for Alice in the wrong areas, for now. She had bought herself some time to reconnoiter.

Climbing down from the rocks had been a lot easier with her pack lighter after the food she had consumed. The cans had been heavy and she was surprised at how much she had eaten. She briefly considered checking on Sasha and Alexis, but didn't want to leave a trail to them. Instead, she headed for the castle, sticking to the water as long as she could and then to the trees to keep herself obscured from any observers. With the aid of her binoculars she had seen that men were stationed in trees, but they were on the wrong side of the valley where she had killed their comrades. She was sticking to this side to obscure her scent.

Alice chose to climb the last tower after dusk when the men building the other tower had left for the day, returning to their camp since the area was so remote. She'd observed this camp a couple of times and determined they were in no way involved in the hunt for her. She gave it a wide berth as she hunted her pursuers. The tower was hundreds of feet tall to allow the lines to pass over the tallest trees and even a few hills. It commanded an incredible view.

As she gazed far into the distance and the sun set over the mountains to the west, for just a moment she wished for some peace. She had been at this far too long. It was cold, she was tired, and her body needed to heal...both physically and mentally. She missed Kathy and the kids, and her life back in California. Here she sat, hundreds of feet in the air on a tower in the middle of Kazakhstan. Where the hell had her life gone? There was no way she could have predicted the turns it would have taken, the people she had killed over the years, or where she would end up. As she gazed at the beauty around her she thought she heard a sound, a whiff, and then she heard the report of a bullet. Time and distance were factors and only the fact that she was so high up kept her attacker from being more accurate. She looked down and around at the sound and saw a lone gunman taking aim again. She quickly moved, but there was nowhere for her to go! She was stuck out in the open at the top of the tower and had assumed no one would be out and about and see her. How foolish she had been! She was exposed and she was certain that other soldiers would join their comrade at the sound of the gunfire.

She heard the report of another near miss. She was a blob at the top of a spindly tower, but it was only a matter of time before he either got lucky or more guns would start firing. She could faintly make out flashlights bobbing in the distance, hurrying towards the lone gunman. She also heard the sounds of dogs, excited dogs, and she made a hurried decision. Climbing down was not an option as they would simply wait for her at the bottom or shoot her as she came down. Blowing the tower was also not feasible as she wasn't a martyr or suicidal. She reached into her pack, careful not to drop it or she was dead, then searched for and found a set of lanyards. They were made of one inch nylon webbing with an adjustable opening and auto-lock snap hooks on each end. She heard the ping of missed shots on the metal of the tower and the whap as one lucky shot hit her bag. She was grateful she was so high up until she looked down and the enormity of what she was about to try hit her.

Alice knew the power was still not in the lines since they were attempting to rebuild the tower she had taken out. She was grateful for this one small consideration, but not happy as she attached the lanyard clips to her belt and waist after throwing one end over the line above her. It was thick, a cable wound with more cables, and she could imagine the thousands of volts that would have electrocuted her had it been working. She faintly heard shouts as others joined the lone shooter. She also heard the dogs clearer and louder in their excitement. She pulled the detonator from her pocket, careful not to let it go, and flipped one of the switches. For a heart-stopping moment she heard the sound of another rifle coming into play and at the same time worried the lanyard wouldn't carry her weight and she would fall. Then in that instant, she worried that the switch would not work as she flipped it and jumped from the tower at the same time.

The explosion on the wooden tower was enormous, also taking out the struts of the metal tower they were erecting. The 'diversion' momentarily distracted the armed men from Alice as she sailed down the wire, grateful it wasn't powered up and flying freely down its length towards the castle. Her weight caused a bow in the taut line as she went. "I wouldn't want to do this as a ride at an amusement park," she spoke aloud, feeling the adrenaline rush and realizing the exhilaration was not a stunt she wanted. She hadn't thought about slowing or stopping as she jumped and she realized she was about to slam into the castle, into a stone and mortar tower that was going to hurt her very badly on impact. She turned and used her legs to absorb most of the impact, bouncing back as though she were a spring. The jarring hurt. She was going so fast it numbed her legs and gravity pulled her straight to the ground or in this case, the bricks. She was momentarily stunned and looked for a way to get off the wire she was tied to, realizing she could pull herself up.

Weakly, Alice pulled her emaciated body up and unhooked one side of the lanyard, letting it fall, then pulled herself onto the roof of the castle. She heard other dogs down in the courtyard of the castle as she lay there catching her breath out of sight of her would-be shooters. She wondered if they had even seen her jump or realized where she went. If they had, she would need to get moving, and soon. She was so tired though. And if she had thought about the jump, she would never have done it. The adrenaline had her getting up much quicker than she would have liked and making her way across the roof. She found a trap door, pried it open, and looked through. Apparently, she wasn't expected and she carefully made her way inside, closing the hatch with a thump.

Alice found herself in a turret, a medieval one at that. Everything she had ever read about castles was holding true as she made her way down the circular staircase. It was incredible and the aesthetics were pleasing. Normally she would have enjoyed the architecture, but the reality was her poor legs were having to traverse the miles of stone steps. Alice moved along cautiously, never knowing if she was about to run into a guard. Ostensibly, they had never thought they might be invaded from above and no one was stationed in this tower. Alice held the Bowie-like knife at the ready just in case.

As the blonde explored the castle, her pursuers had lost sight of her with the explosion. Alice had underestimated her explosives; having no knowledge of their capacity, she over-used them. The dirt and debris had been blown sky-high. They cautiously made their way to the site of the tower as the workers came running, cursing at all the work they had done that was now blown up. Comparing notes, it was decided that somehow that American woman they had been hunting had done it. Over forty men, dogs of various breeds and nationalities, and workmen made their way cautiously towards the next tower with flashlights, looking for her and any signs of sabotage she may have done there. For all they knew, she had rigged each and every tower and they would be a nightmare to replace.

Alice looked out the window of the high tower as she made another one of many countless turns. She saw the flashlights and the direction they were heading. She waited, watching, and resting her poor legs before continuing down the stairwell. When she saw the flashlights pause for a length of time and then begin flashing about on the ground, she knew they were looking for what she might have done to the second tower, the one she had actually just flown from. She couldn't let them dismantle the bombs she had left there. She reached into her pocket for the detonator and flipped the second switch. Even as she saw the explosions and heard the reverberations against the glass of the window, she was throwing away the used detonator and making her way down the steps. The emergency lights, lit by what she assumed was a generator, flickered, and she wondered if she should pull out a flashlight.

At the bottom of the tower Alice could hear voices as the men discussed what they believed happened up on the hill behind the castle.

The first tower exploding was already a fact, but they weren't sure about the second one and what had happened there, not yet. Alice didn't fare well as they discussed what they would do when they got hold of her—not if, but when. She smiled. Many had tried, in fact they had her in custody several times, and still she eluded them. She waited in the dark, shamelessly listening to their mutterings, glad for the Russian language she had learned from Sasha and her hard studying. Even the different dialects, while sometimes difficult to understand, could gradually be figured out.

The men, realizing they had their duties, eventually left the area and continued their patrols. Alice followed one of the two, hoping to get more information. She saw him go into a room, leaving the door ajar. He must have sensed her presence as he turned just as she followed him in. Alice was prepared and used the Bowie-like knife effectively across his abdomen. He was instantly in shock as his guts began to spill out and he tried desperately to catch them. As he looked up in horror at what Alice had done, he realized how odd her eyes looked in the muted light, how the short hair on her nearly shaven head made her look scarier, and how he needed to sound the alarm. He went to open his mouth to shout and Alice punched him, breaking a tooth on her knuckle, causing her and him pain. He went down from the blow, but more likely because he was bleeding out at the gut. She kicked him backwards and he fell, whining slightly at the pain. She looked around the little office she found herself in, noticing the diagrams of the castle and the surrounding estate. She saw the two roads, both coming into the valley and leaving, and saw a manifest. Pulling it to her, she was shocked to see it was in English, showing inventory of what was to arrive in the following days. They were moving some very heavy equipment and supplies. The convoys she had seen were nothing to what was coming. She threw it down, making a noise and she heard the other guard call to this one.

"Vasili?" she heard in Russian. She slowly hid behind the door of the office, waiting.

"Is that you?" the voice echoed in the hall and she could tell it was coming closer.

"Vasili?" the voice asked once again as he came through the office door. He nearly stepped in the pool of blood before him as the man on the ground made a gurgling noise. "Vasili!" he shouted in concern, and before he could take in what had happened to his friend Alice hit him over the back of the head with the chair she had lifted. He went down, momentarily stunned. He was only vaguely aware as Alice hog-tied him to the chair she had just used to hit his head. As he became a little more aware, he realized she had stolen his keys and emptied his pockets. Suddenly, he became aware of the plastic bag she had found to put over his entire head.

She watched him as the bag over his head began to run out of oxygen, the plastic clinging to his face as he inhaled and the bubble forming as he exhaled. His eyes were bulging as he realized he wasn't inhaling oxygen anymore and was running out of time. Before he could pass out, she popped the bag around his mouth and he inhaled great heaving gasps of clean air.

"I could do this all day," the blonde told him conversationally as she looked at her dirty fingernails, but they both knew she didn't have all day. Then she looked at him closely, making sure to make eye contact. "I'm a *real* patient woman. I'm sure you have learned that. I'll tell you this though, I've run out of patience. You and your people have kept me from my family for far too long. Now, I'm getting pissed off..." she left off as she put another bag over his head, covering up the hole to watch him repeat the cycle—the bulging eyes and the realization that he was running out of air. His eyes bored into hers pleadingly through the plastic of both bags and he inwardly shuddered at how unemotional this woman truly was.

Alice considered letting this be the last time, but she had a few more bags. She let it go a little longer this time, the lack of oxygen causing the alarm in his eyes to register with hers. He wriggled at the bindings that held him to the chair. She found it fascinating to watch as they changed from alarm to an almost deadpan look as he struggled more in a vain attempt to save himself. She knew she couldn't play too much longer and popped the bag at his mouth again to allow him to breathe. Great shuddering rasps were heard as he drew in what oxygen he could through the small hole, the double bagging fluttering in and out of his mouth, his chest heaving as he gasped.

"I suggest you start talking, and soon." She looked at her nails again, pulling out a knife to use the point and flick dirt from under them then looked at him again when she heard the difference in his breathing and he wasn't gasping as loud. "Or do I put another bag over your head and leave?"

He shook his head and started in a breathy voice. It was obvious he needed more oxygen to really talk, but he didn't want to end his life too soon. He was certain she would kill him, but maybe if he cooperated, she'd keep him alive a little longer. Maybe someone would find them, maybe someone would keep her from ending his life, maybe someone could finally kill this bitch.

Alice pumped him on the guards in the castle, where she could find the roster and the times. She pumped him on what he knew about who was sent out in the field to hunt for her. She interrogated him for a long time until she was certain he knew no more. He knew the longer he talked, the longer he lived. She was almost sorry to have to kill this one. It was just as she was considering killing him that she heard someone out in the corridor coming their way. The man in the chair attempted to yell and she slugged the air out of his stomach, hurting her knuckles that had previously been cut on the teeth of the other man. The decision was made for her and she nonchalantly put another bag over his head. He realized the significance of this third bag immediately and knew she would not be popping the air hole this time. He watched in horror as she left the room, preparing for whoever was in the hall. He attempted to suck the plastic into his mouth and rip it with his teeth, but between the other two bags and the tightness of this one, he had no luck. Slowly, he smothered in the plastic.

Alice never gave the young guard a chance. She attacked, quickly and viciously. It was a good thing too as the young man would have easily overpowered the much older Alice, the much more exhausted woman whose emaciated body would have been no match for him normally. Instead, her surprise was absolute and she soon looked down on the body with regret, knowing she had had no choice since the order was to kill her on sight. She made her way down the passage, the map of the castle in her mind making it a little easier. Using the key card she had stolen so long ago, she explored the various rooms, even if only briefly. She found the room she had been looking for near the guard entrance and she loaded her pack down with explosives and detonators, taking the time to rig them all to the same two or three radio frequencies. She unplugged the camera system, knowing that some of it was already down due to the power and the generator couldn't handle all that and keep the lights on as well. As she made her way through the castle she stopped to leave little packages, using double-sided tape whenever possible and breaking the noticeable red blinking light from the devices. She didn't want her parcels discovered before she was ready.

Alice found the elevators she had ridden in before and made her way down a floor, keeping away from the guards that she knew occupied each floor. She used the darkness as her friend and the night goggles she had stolen from the ammunition room to her advantage. She positioned packages all along this prisoner ward, noting that no one was being held right now. She wondered if she, Sasha, and Lexi had been the last? Hearing a large gathering of a dozen or more guards in a room, she peeked in and saw they were watching a big screen TV. They were watching porn, cheering on the BDSM (Bondage and Discipline, Sadism and Masochism) that was showing on screen, and degrading the women on the screen. She shook her head. They always seemed to hire the same types of men. Not one woman had been in that room and she knew they hired both sexes, she had seen them. Slowly she withdrew the flamethrower from her pack, knowing she would only get one chance to use it. She lit the end with a slight click of the trigger.

Pulling the trigger wide as she stepped into the room, she shot flames across the room, holding it low to where the men were sitting, some on couches and some on chairs. Some were clapping at the scenes shown on the screen, some were masturbating, rubbing their crotches as they watched, and some held their peckers boldly in their hands, but none were prepared for the flames that began to consume them. The yells were intense as Alice burned them, turning to fan the flames around the room and miss none of them. The jet took in the big screen causing it and the scene on it to explode, showering those in the front with glass shards before their uniforms, hair, and then skin caught on fire. There were shouts, screams, and even crying as Alice panned the flames over and over across the room, repeatedly burning any who still moved when she returned. Slowly the liquid in the flamethrower was used up and by then barely any moved as they died in that room, burned to a crisp. Alice threw the flamethrower away when only a little flame burst out of its nozzle. She looked once more around the blackened and now darkened room, shining a flashlight over the carnage. She wrinkled her nose distastefully as she smelled the burnt flesh and hair. "Now that's a weenie roast," she commented wryly as she checked her victims. When she was satisfied that none of the room's occupants were alive, she attached a package to the wall and left the room. She was searching for more people in the castle, searching specifically for one or two.

Alice was running out of packages as she made her way back to the elevator and upstairs. She knew there was only one man and one woman left in the castle from The Assemblage, but there were others left who were second or third generation and she had killed their parent or parents. Their hearts weren't going to be into the same illegal activities of their parents. They had seen the price that had been paid to be a member and many had no stomach for it. These last two weren't original players, but the guard had thought perhaps the woman was, he wasn't sure.

Alice made her way to the library. She left her bag outside the door, under a chair so it wasn't as noticeable, then thinking again, she removed the switches she had wired as well as the extra packages and slipped them into an alcove out of sight. She glanced around repeatedly, wondering if there were more people about, more guards, and hoping there weren't. It was hard to see as the lighting was minimal and she knew their generators were only keeping certain things up and running. As she slipped inside, the dark wasn't as noticeable here as several Tiffany lamps were lit on the desk and a nearby couch. The library still reminded her of a smaller version of the Wren Library in Cambridge, England, the architecture of the room itself as seen above the bookshelves.

On the upper walls were scimitars, swords, and even a set of Japanese swords called daishō. The large sword was a katana and its companion, the smaller sword a wakizashi. Alice eyed the them, admiring them and coveting them, but this wasn't why she was here. She looked at the person behind the desk. The man had obviously been waiting for Alice. He didn't look surprised to see her standing there.

"Ah, you have come," he greeted her. "Please, have a seat," he offered generously, indicating the plush chairs across from him.

"You know why I am here," Alice answered him. He was the last one they hadn't been able to name. He had kept quiet and out of the view of most of The Assemblage activities, but still, he had benefited from them and what they had done to many people…what they had done to Sasha and then to Alice.

"I do, but you may not succeed," he pointed out, wondering how long the woman had been in the castle and where were their guards. There was more than a dozen of them in the castle alone, so where were they?

Alice was so fatigued and so tired of this game. She wasn't about to listen to this man and what he had to say or the delay tactics he might be using to waste time and allow the guards that still might be in the castle to come. She glanced beyond him and saw the telltale shadow in the bookcase as someone gazed at them. She moved suddenly aside and a gun went off, missing her and taking out the fine wood door behind her. They hadn't been fooling around, using some gun that left a huge hole in the door. Alice didn't stop moving as she glanced behind her and, using the chair in front of the desk, bounced up on the seat and on top and across the desk in order to put her knee in the face of the man sitting there and propel him and his chair to the floor.

"That had to hurt," she said softly in Russian as she heard the satisfying crunch of his nose beneath her knee cap. He tried to pull her off him, but her weight, slight as it was and unexpected as it was, had him at a disadvantage. Alice didn't waste time. She pulled the knife from her boot and sliced across his neck, satisfied as the blood spurted across her shirt. She sliced twice, just in case and then got up, heading for the bookcase and beginning to hurl books to the floor, regretting the first editions and beautifully bound books that she heaped in a pile. It was when she began hurling fake books that she knew she was getting close to what she was looking for and managed to pull aside just in time before a second blast came from the bookcase. It was obvious the bookshelf was either on a hinge or just a hole in some wall and she began to climb it. She tested her weight against it and feeling it begin to topple, got out of the way as it crashed against the desk, the remaining books falling all over the man gurgling on the floor, trying to stop the inevitable flow of blood from his neck. Alice didn't worry about him as she stepped on the leaning shelf to pull the gun barrel that was jutting slightly outside the hole in the wall she saw there. She pulled it until she had a good grip, the barrel hot from the two blasts, and then she shoved it hard into the hole, hearing a very unladylike swear word in Russian.

Alice began to look for a way into this concealed, secret room, suspecting she would finally find the person she was looking for hiding inside it. The adjoining bookshelf did not quite fit. That hadn't been noticeable when all the shelves were against the wall, but now that she had removed one she could see it was some sort of door. She ducked under the hole where the gun barrel still protruded, now at an angle that told her it had been dropped, and pulled on the next bookshelf. She'd pull them all down, one at a time if she had to. She was pleased as it began to pull out and then pivot. It must have to come out to avoid the bookshelf next to it.

She cautiously began to edge around this door, but was immediately set upon by a dirty-blonde woman who immediately attacked and went for her throat. Propelled backwards a few feet, Alice set herself and brought her hands up and out, knocking the woman's arms away and bringing the palm of her hand up and against the blonde's chin. The woman's head snapped back and she started to go down, grabbing at Alice to try and break her fall. Alice was slightly off balance and nearly fell, but instead, gasping from her exertions in the last few minutes, she leaned over the woman, looking at her incredulously.

"Who are you?" she asked in Russian. The woman looked...familiar and Alice knew she had never seen her before, at least not from the front. She glanced around the small room. With the electricity to the castle off, the computers and other electronics in this chamber were also off, but at least there was no one else present.

The woman had the breath knocked out of her from the fall. She glared up at Alice with hate-filled eyes. She started to reach in her waistband and pulled a gun, but Alice kicked the gun from her hand and it slithered across the room. In one smooth draw, she had the long ago confiscated Bowie-like knife in her hand and at the woman's throat. "Who are you?" she repeated, this time in English.

"Lidiya," she spat, almost as though it was a vicious word.

"Lidiya, what?" Alice asked, the blade flickering in the low light of the room.

The woman stared at the huge blade of the Bowie-type knife and then up at Alice's eyes that were narrowed. She could see they looked...yellow, or maybe...orange. It must be a trick of the light. "Brenhov," she whispered.

Alice looked at her in surprise, wondering at the accent she could hear in Russian, which wasn't quite like Sasha's. Something about the woman bothered her and it wasn't the eyes that couldn't seem to sit still in her lovely face. At her words, Alice put two and two together and she asked, "Sister or cousin?"

"Sasha has no cousins," the woman confirmed defiantly.

"I wasn't aware she had a sister either," some humor could be heard in Alice's voice as she watched her quarry carefully.

"She doesn't know," the woman hissed. She made a movement and Alice took her boot and set it down deliberately on the woman's arm, breaking it. "Khristos," the woman swore. She made a move as though to hold her broken arm with her other and Alice deliberately stepped on that arm too, bouncing a little in her stance and breaking this arm too, but a bit higher. "Yeblya suki," she swore as the pain made her arch her back, nearly unseating Alice in her awkward position.

"Yeah, but if I'm a fucking bitch what does that make you?" Alice asked in response.

"Your Russian is terrible," Lidiya tried to insult her through gritted teeth. The pain was insane and making it hard for her to talk.

Alice laughed, a genuine laugh, and shrugged, removing herself so she didn't fall on the woman and stab her with the Bowie-like knife. She watched as the woman attempted to hug herself from the pain, causing herself more pain with the gesture. "Are you the one that started all this?" Alice gestured at the castle and into the air. She saw the woman's wary look as she looked in her eyes.

"What if I was?" she asked, belligerently.

Alice smiled, but it was an evil smile. Accompanying her blazing yellow-orange cat-like eyes, it was truly frightening. "I take it you are illegitimate?"

Lidiya looked at her, alarmed. That Alice had jumped to that conclusion so accurately and so quickly was upsetting. Most assumed she was just a younger sister that had been hidden. It had opened doors that Sasha wasn't aware of. She didn't answer Alice. She thought she heard a noise outside the library door, probably due to the fact that the doors had holes in them now.

Alice leaned down and gently nudged the woman's shoulder. The pain was radiating upwards from the break and her nudge sent the woman arching in pain again. Her breaths were drawn in deeply through her nose and nearly whistled through her clenched teeth. "We can make this easy," Alice started conversationally, remembering the

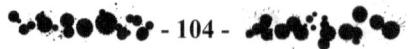

man with the plastic bag as she examined the room a little closer, but still keeping her attention on the woman before her. "Or I can make it hell for you," she informed her. She too heard a noise and backed up a little so she could look out into the better-lit library. Her eyes opened a little wider as she saw the doctor she had met down in the prison. Addressing him as he looked wide-eyed through the hole in the door, she called, "Quick, get a gurney, she's hurt," hoping her Russian was adequate.

The man nodded, not recognizing her voice and not able to see who was addressing him. He turned to someone behind him to command them then turned the handle on the door and came into the room. "Can I help?"

Alice backed out of sight and picked up the gun that Lidiya Brenhov had been about to use on her. She had it in her hand as the doctor came into sight around the corner of the now open bookshelf. Alice could see by his amazement he too had no idea about this hidden room. His eyes opened wider as he took in the woman on the floor moaning in pain and Alice, holding a pistol in her hand. "Come in, Doctor," she said imperfectly in Russian. She gestured with the gun towards Lidiya and said, "Do what you can for her."

"Why bother? You are only going to kill us all!" Lidiya spat through her pain.

Alice just smiled and the doctor went to work examining the blonde on the floor, ascertaining that both her arms were broken. Alice watched carefully, waiting for whoever was bringing the gurney. And when they arrived her eyes opened a little wider as she recognized one of her attackers from the last time she was in the castle…the one who had punched her in the crotch. Without a second's hesitation, she lifted the gun and shot him in the face. His look of surprise turned to horror at the sight of the gun and then was instantly obscured. Everyone jumped at the explosion of the handgun and looked from Alice to the man in horror. She had warned him she would get back at him, if not with words, with the look she had given him when he punched her.

"That wasn't necessary!" the doctor began in a strangled voice as he realized who Alice was.

The second man who had helped to wheel the gurney, held up his hands as Alice turned the gun to him.

"Slide your gun over here," she told him, recognizing one of the guards in the castle by his uniform and wondering how many she had missed. She was so tired of the killing. It was senseless, but she knew it was her or them and she wanted to get home to Kathy and her children. She simply wanted to get out of here alive.

He gently took the gun from the holster by two fingers. He had briefly thought to grab it, but seeing how she had so easily killed the other man, he thought better of it. He bent over and slid it across the floor where she stopped it with her boot. He glanced at the downed man where he had fallen with his gun exposed. Briefly he thought of being a hero, but she beat him to the thought.

"Now, his gun," she told him and he glanced up in surprise, almost as though she had read his mind.

When she had all three guns, she slid two of them into her own waistband behind her back and gesturing with the gun, she spoke to the doctor and the gurney bearer. "Pick her up and put her on the gurney."

The pain from her breaks was so intense as they lifted her, Lidiya screamed. The soldier nearly dropped her when she screamed, but the doctor held on bravely, putting her gently on the gurney.

"Now let's get her down to the infirmary," Alice ordered and walked forward to keep them both in her view. She moved up on the soldier whose back was to her and with the butt of the gun, hit him on the skull, knocking him out and pushing him aside. She pushed the gurney herself, one-handed, her other hand holding the gun on the shocked doctor. "Let's get going before someone else tries to be a hero," she told him. She glanced at the man she had knocked out as she passed him. She leaned down and scooped something she saw hanging from his belt loop. She didn't have to kill him and he hadn't participated in the hunt for her. He would be dead soon anyway. '*Maybe she was getting soft,*' she thought to herself as she pushed the rolling bed.

The gurney was a tight fit through the library door and Lidiya passed out when they accidentally bumped her shoulder into the door frame. Alice made a move to awaken the woman and the doctor said, "Leave her. It's better she is unconscious for now." Alice nodded and they continued.

Alice stopped where she had put her kit and was surprised to see it was gone. She swore under her breath and retrieved the packets and switches, stuffing those in the pockets of her pants. She silently thanked whoever had made these army issue pants that were full of pockets. She glanced around, wondering who had stolen her bag.

It was a tight fit in the elevator with the gurney. The doctor swallowed constantly, staring at his patient, Alice, and the gun. Alice watched him warily, wondering if she would have to kill him too and resigned to it. As the doors to the prison level opened, Alice watched the doctor to see if he reacted, if anyone was there, and was relieved she didn't have to shoot anyone. She hated guns; she hated the sound of them and she hated the smell of them. The shots in the hidden room upstairs had nearly made her gag.

They moved to the infirmary and the doctor took out a syringe.

"What are you giving her?" Alice asked.

He told her, but Alice didn't know the word in Russian. She shook her head and he put the syringe down on a tray, rolling it so the English word was visible.

"No, I don't want such a strong painkiller. I want her conscious as soon as possible," Alice instructed him.

His eyes widened as he realized she knew sedatives. He pulled another from the cabinet and put it on the tray. He rolled it so she could read what it was. Again, Alice shook her head. He tried again and again, choosing less strong palliatives until she was satisfied. "You realize this is basically aspirin?" he asked to be sure.

Alice smiled, an evil smile and nodded. "Do you have vercuronium?" she asked and his eyes widened at the English word that he understood. He shook his head. "How about rocuronium?" Again, he shook his head. "Pancuronium?" He shook his head a third time, but he was getting the gist of what she was looking for, and anticipating her next question he pulled a small bottle from the cabinet and held it up. It read succinylcholine and Alice nodded, indicating he could administer it.

He pulled out a needle and carefully measured out the succinylcholine, put a tie on her arm waiting for a vein to rise, and shot it into the unconscious Lidiya. He quickly measured the equivalent of the palliative and shot that in too before quickly removing the tie. He moved as though to straighten Lidiya's broken arm and administer to it, but Alice shook her head.

Gesturing with the gun, she indicated he should sit on the other side of the room where there was a bathroom. She spotted a safety rail, the kind used in facilities for the handicapped, and handed him the cuffs she had scooped off the belt of the downed soldier. "Put these on," she told him and he looked at her and glanced back at the unconscious

Lidiya. "Don't worry, I'll take care of her," she promised and he shuddered at the look in her eyes as he put the cuff on one his wrists and slung the chain around the bar. Alice moved up and holding the gun, she grabbed the other cuff and held it until he put his wrist through it, locking it and trying both cuffs to assure herself he was chained. "Now, be a good boy and stay here," she told him, generously, she thought, then closed the door so he couldn't see what she did with his patient.

Alice was feeling impatient as she waited for Lidiya to wake up. The resemblance to Sasha that she could see in Lidiya's face was uncanny now that she had time to examine it. She was willing to bet that Sasha had never suspected she had a sister, much less one in The Assemblage. It explained why they had never seen this last member. The original twelve had been a lot more and now she remembered some of the video footage that contained a female voice or the back of someone, but never the front, or they might have figured this out long ago.

Alice wondered how Sasha would feel if she knew she had a sister, one who had tried to have her killed for so long and one who had stolen her fortune, bit by bit. Alice and Sasha had gotten it back…and more, but how would she feel if she had known? There were questions that needed answering and Alice was impatient to begin. The woman was taking entirely too long to wake up. Was she as tough as her older sister? Alice was sure she wasn't. Sasha herself hadn't known how tough she was until Alice tested and taught her. This pansy looked like she had been well-fed for far too long.

Alice looked around, pondering if there was some drug she could administer to wake the woman up. She found her kit bag and looked at it in surprise. She would bet that one of those last two soldiers had brought it here, but why here? She went through it cautiously, looking for traps of some kind and checking to see if anything had been taken. Surprisingly, nothing was missing and she wondered if they hadn't had time. Still, she left it by the door for herself and began to look through the medical supplies. It was well-stocked. Were they expecting a siege?

It was time-consuming looking at the bottles, first in Russian, which she couldn't make out since the medical terms were beyond her limited vocabulary, and then looking for an English translation somewhere on the labels. She was looking for sodium thiopental, marketed as pentothal or any other psychoactive drugs. She wasn't going to worry about any drug interactions with what they had already pumped into Lidiya. She found something that sounded like what she was looking for and without a qualm pulled the syringe from the tray and emptied half the bottle, shooting it into the same vein they had used before. She didn't worry about cleaning the syringe site either. She waited, and waited some more.

When Lidiya first began to show signs of waking, only her eyes and mouth began to move. As she became aware, her facial expression at first looked puzzled, then annoyed, and then concerned as she tried to look around. She moved her eyes since her head wouldn't move, and then tried her hands, her arms, and nothing. She glanced as far as she could around the room, recognizing the infirmary and wondering how she had gotten there.

Alice noticed the eye movement and came into view. The blonde's eyes widened at the woman's visage. Alice hadn't cleaned her face of the blood that had spurted across her shirt and splattered onto it. She looked like a horror. "You are probably wondering why you can't move?" she asked in a carefully-controlled voice.

"What have you done to me?" Lidiya asked, gulping, trying to get the dryness out of her mouth.

"You've been given a shot and you can't move. In fact, I'd be surprised if you could even feel the pain of your broken arms."

"Why? Why don't you just kill me?" she demanded. She sounded angry.

"Maybe I will. Or maybe I will just keep causing you pain," she promised and watched as the woman looked...worried. "I have a few questions to ask you."

"I will tell you nothing. Nothing, you hear?" she arrogantly answered.

Alice smiled. "There is pain you haven't even thought of as the drugs wear off."

The woman stared at her, wondering if this woman was the one who had killed so many of The Assemblage. Looking in those cold, cat-like eyes, she realized it was possible. She had never really given credibility to the idea that her sister had hired her killing done. She wanted to shudder, but her body wouldn't let her. She wanted to sleep, but couldn't even though she felt drowsy and yet...dreamy.

Alice began to ask questions and compelled by the truth serum, Lidiya began to answer them.

The Assemblage had been her idea. Using her similarities to Sasha, she had conned a few of the early members into investing in her proposals. It had grown from there. When Sasha herself had been approached, they had been going after oil futures, the mines, and other properties they coveted in the vast Brenhov fortune their father had left the legitimate sister; the properties that Lidiya had coveted. She had never inherited anything from their shared father. She hadn't even known who he was until late in her life. She had grown up in an orphanage and hadn't known he knew about her until her college tuition was paid for her; a full scholarship, but nothing more. She was expected to make her way in the world after that on her own...no inheritance, no nepotism, no communication, no nothing. Using street smarts and a savvy way she had about her, she used whatever she could to get ahead and figure out who the Brenhovs were. By the time she had enough on them, he was dead and Sasha had inherited it all. The unfairness of it all had galled her.

As Sasha had slowly turned several illegitimate enterprises to legitimate ones, getting away from the mob mentality and influence, she made many enemies. Those enemies became Lidiya's friends and business associates. They had formed the basis of The Assemblage. As they all grew in influence and money, they extended an olive branch to Sasha Brenhov, who refused. Not needing their money, their business, or their influence, Sasha kept going alone. This arrogance alone had infuriated the members. That she didn't need them, enraged them, none so much as Lidiya who had hoped to have some sort of relationship with this sister of hers.

Lidiya had learned a lot about Sasha over the years and she had admired her. She wanted to be like her, even emulated her, enough so that people knew they were related, but no breath of this was put into the gossip mills. It wasn't until they had a good portion of the Brenhov holdings in play that Lidiya began using the surname. It was on her orders that her sister was kidnapped. Those idiots had bungled the job, capturing both Sasha and Alice, not realizing which was which. Things hadn't gone well since.

Alice smiled at this revelation. Of course, they hadn't gone so well for her either. She was separated far too long from her wife and family. So many people had died for this one woman's greed, and Alice had suffered physically as well. This woman needed to suffer for her actions. Alice contemplated what she would do to her as Lidiya filled in the story and Alice continued to ask questions.

Alice couldn't remember the last time she had eaten and she knew her metabolism was getting low. She checked on the good doctor, saw where he had rubbed his wrists raw from trying to get out of the cuffs, and then rechecked Lidiya. She could tell the woman, though paralyzed, was beginning to feel the pain again and that was good.

Alice went looking for food while her victims sat in the infirmary. She found the room she had used the flamethrower on. Each one of those men had been ordered to kill her on sight and she didn't doubt they would have, had they been given a chance. Alice hadn't given them an opportunity and she didn't regret their deaths. What she regretted was the many deaths she could lay at Lidiya's feet. The woman had calmly ordered people, troops, and others to do her dirty work and hadn't blinked an eye, all in the name of envy and greed.

Alice found some energy bars. While they didn't taste that great, she ate them anyway, washing them down with water from her bottle. It took a while, but she finally felt a little better. She wasn't full, but at least she'd eaten. She returned to the infirmary and continued questioning Lidiya.

The woman began to squirm, as much as she could while paralyzed on the gurney. Alice knew she could give her more painkillers, but refused to do so. When she sensed she had gotten all the story out of the woman, she asked her, "Are you happy with what you accomplished?"

"I was rich for the first time in my life and I was respected," she bragged, her slurring becoming a little clearer as the pentothal wore off too.

When Alice could see her hours of interrogation were also wearing off the succinylcholine, the spasmodic twitches of her victim giving her away, she administered the other half of the bottle. She watched for the telltale signs that Lidiya was once again paralyzed. "Do you know how many died to achieve your goals?" Had Lidiya known Alice better she would have seen, much less heard the genuine regret in Alice's voice and demeanor.

The woman went to shrug and found she couldn't. Lidiya briefly wondered if it would have hurt as the paralyzation took effect and she began to realize the other pains in her body, including the breaks.

"You didn't care how many died so long as you had your fortune, Sasha's fortune?"

"You don't know what it's like to watch your sister succeed, to watch her not even acknowledge you!" she spat, becoming clearer and realizing how much she had told this...this...American! She totally forgot to add that Sasha didn't even know of her existence.

Alice briefly remembered her own sister, as selfish and self-absorbed as they came, and knew they couldn't compare. Besides, her sister was long dead. "Maybe if you had gone to Sasha and explained who you were–" she began, but Lidiya cut her off.

"She was rich! She was rich beyond anyone's dreams. She had everything!" she sounded bitter and angry.

"So, it didn't matter how many people died so long as you took all Sasha's things, all her money, and got your way?" The anger and her own bitterness crept into Alice's questions.

"Exactly. She got what she deserved!"

That did it for Alice. Lidiya showed no remorse. She showed she was vicious, calculating, and immoral. She'd gathered together all the people who were as greedy and ambitious as she was and had stolen, connived, and killed for the billions they felt they deserved. Screw the little guy. Since Sasha hadn't been the little guy, taking her down had taken longer, but at what cost? How many people had to die so they could get another million or even a billion to achieve their goals. "But you lost," Alice pointed out and looked around the infirmary again. She found a silver set, complete with forks, knives, spoons and even a sharpener for knives. The knives looked dull and she considered them carefully before she reached for the spoon and sharpened the narrow point a little.

"Why don't you just kill me?" Lidiya goaded the American.

Alice smiled as she showed the spoon in her hand. "Because then you won't get to see what happens to you."

Using her Bowie-like knife, Alice ripped open her victim's blouse, exposing her chest. Lidiya watched her in wonderment. Seeing the knife, she had thought Alice was going to cut her, but was shocked to see her begin to use the spoon against the skin of her chest. She was horrified to realize it was cutting into the flesh.

"Wha...what are you doing?" she sputtered, trying to move and unable to as she looked down in horror at her own chest.

Alice smiled and went to get something else she had found—an arm that was used to hold lights. She attached it to the gurney, adjusted it above Lidiya, and then attached a mirror using duct tape. She got behind Lidiya on the gurney, adjusting the arm several times and then the mirror. "There, now you can watch what I'm doing," she finally answered.

Lidiya was shocked. She had a perfect view of what Alice was doing. She watched as the blonde pulled back the skin she had cut with the spoon and exposed the breast bone. The bone looked white and glossy from the blood and fat. Alice used the Bowie-like knife to help cut the breast bone and detach the ribs, using brute strength, clearing a way. "Oh, my God, what are you doing?" she tried to scream, but it came out as a disturbed whisper.

"Well, you don't need this, so I'm going to remove it," Alice told her matter-of-factly as she probed inside about five inches or more with the spoon and began to sever things that Lidiya didn't know the names of. The gruesome exposure silenced Lidiya as she stared in fascinated revulsion.

Slowly, Alice exposed the heart, the beating and pulsating heart that was Lidiya's. Using her bare hands, she reached in and gently pulled it to the surface. The mirror showed the dirty-blonde exactly what her heart looked like, the darker vessels coming from it in a rich red, almost black appearance. There was white fatty tissue as well as plenty of pink pulsating flesh. Alice held it up beyond the mirror so that Lidiya could clearly see with her horrified eyes as her own heart was pulled from her chest. "If you could have felt this, you would know it hurts more because I used a spoon," Alice explained conversationally.

Lidiya's eyes widened as the realization sunk in, but Alice continued, "You showed no heart for the people you had killed, that you arranged to kill, or for the monies you had stolen. Since you do not need this, I'm taking it out," and with that Alice yanked the rest of the way, detaching the life-giving vessels from the pulsating organ and holding it up for her victim's viewing pleasure. Alice watched as Lidiya realized in that moment what she had done to her. The words about the spoon hadn't gone unnoticed and the admonition about her having no heart either. As her heart stopped beating, Alice watched in bemused fascination as the realization sunk in. The blonde's eyes told that she was dead and had watched herself become a victim. She would have screamed, she should have, but now it was too late. She died on that gurney in the infirmary of that castle in the middle of nowhere...for what? Alice left her on the gurney, her eyes staring up at the ceiling.

"What is going on out there?" the doctor called for the umpteenth time, the rattles of his handcuffs against the bar distracting. Alice had heard him for a while, but ignored it all. Now, she suddenly realized how loud he really was. Putting her hand behind her, she reached for the door handle with her other bloody hand and opened it wide.

"Can't you be quiet?" she asked.

"What is going on? Will you release me?"

Alice looked at him. "Did you willingly work for these people?" she asked conversationally. She tilted her head to indicate the people in the floors above, the ones that weren't there anymore. She'd found people revealed more if she showed no hostility towards them.

"Why, of course I did," he confirmed, confused at the question. "They needed medical expertise now and then."

"So, you knew The Assemblage and what they were doing?"

"Theirs is a noble cause..." he began and then stopped as Alice brought her hand around from in back of her and showed him the bloody heart. He stared in fascinated horror, realizing immediately what it was.

"People like that," Alice indicated with her bloody hand, pointing back at the woman on the gurney now that she pushed the door wide and he could see out, "tend to get what is coming to them. Their cause was not noble," she argued. "Their cause was greedy and obscene." With that she threw Lidiya's heart in his lap. To give him his due, he did cringe away from it. The heart fell to the floor and his eyes bugged out of his face as he realized what Alice had done. He glanced at the blood on her and back to the heart on the floor, swallowing convulsively to keep from vomiting.

With that Alice turned, grabbed a towel, and began to wash her hands and arms. It was as she had been adjusting the mirror for Lidiya that she realized she had blood on her face too, probably from the man back up in the library. She desperately wanted a shower, a hot shower, or maybe a bath. She glanced around at the time. She'd wasted a lot of time here in the castle, hours and hours. She wondered why none of the soldiers in the field had come to check on the occupants of the castle. Remembering how many might have been by that second tower when she blew it, she wondered if maybe she'd taken out more than she realized.

Alice picked up her kit bag and left the infirmary. Going to the elevator, she used the card she had stolen so long ago to return to the level the library was on. Listening carefully, she slowly walked to the library and looked around once more. She viewed the scimitars, swords, and the set of Japanese daishō. She put down her bag and climbed up to begin throwing down the ones she wanted. The katana and its companion sword, and the smaller wakizashi came down, as well as few of the scimitars. "To the victor goes the spoils," she muttered as she gathered her treasures and rolled them in a small, expensive rug. It was then she realized that the soldier she had knocked out instead of killing was missing. She knew she shouldn't have left something like that undone.

Alice rifled through the desk, looking for something, anything, and not knowing what she might find. Then she looked for and found the safe behind another bookshelf...these people had been obsessed with their bookshelves. She was annoyed that it took her three tries with her agile fingers to hear the clicks on the safe and manage to crack it. She consoled herself with the thought that she was listening for other signs of life in the castle, listening for someone that might come and try to stop her. Where was that soldier?

Once Alice had the contents of the safe and her swords, she left the library. Looking out at the night, she contemplated her next move. Shrugging, she headed up the luxurious stairs in the foyer and looked for and found the master bedroom. She locked the bedroom door behind her. It was set up in harem style and she laughed at it. There were no women here, but she did find a luxurious bathroom. Setting her kit and the rug filled with stolen swords down, she placed one of the guns on the edge of the tub and began to fill the tub with water. Carefully she undressed, noting in a full-length mirror the many scars, scabs, and bruises she had in various stages of healing and realizing it took her a longer time to heal these days. She must be getting old. Looking at her nearly bald pate, she was pleased to see the hair growing back and grimaced at her face. She hadn't done a very good job of washing up downstairs. Her body was very thin, ribs showing, her bust gone. Locking the bathroom door, she slid into the bathtub with a sigh of relief, scrubbing away the flecks of blood, dirt, and sweat from her emaciated body.

Alice luxuriated in that bathroom for far too long. She knew it, but she couldn't help herself. If she was going to die in the next day or the next week, she would at least be clean, for now. She was so pleased not to smell the sweat anymore. Not having access to antiperspirant, the acrid smell of her own pits had nearly asphyxiated her time and again. She used the soap repeatedly, deep cleaning her pores, and rinsing away the suds she created with the hand shower on the side of the tub. Feeling clean for the first time in ages, she used the fluffy towels and rubbed herself dry as she watched the large oval tub drain, the water brown from the blood and dirt. She looked down at her now clean and pruney body, she examined the various cuts and sewn wounds, now white and puckered around the edges and wondered how long it would take for these to heal.

Looking at her clothes, she hesitated to put on the dirty fatigues she had been wearing. Her body was clean and she wanted to keep that feeling for as long as she could. Remembering an extra set of clothes she had stolen and placed in her kit, she pulled them out and grimaced at their ugly visage. Still, they were clean and she might thank herself for them as she tried to get away from the castle. She was planning on leaving shortly and nearly left her dirty clothes on the bathroom floor as she caught up her kit and rug full of swords. At the last minute, she remembered to go through the pockets. With all the extra packets, she had almost left one important item here in the bathroom. She put the switches in one of her pants' pockets. She had left one of her last packets in the library and wondered if she had enough to complete the job. Having no idea of their explosive power, no knowledge of explosives, all she could do was hope she had distributed enough.

Feeling wonderful despite her fatigue, she debated sleeping in the luxurious bedroom, shrugged, and crawled into the bed, leaving her boots on the floor. The huge bed was bigger than a king-sized bed, even a California king. She didn't care, she only hoped when that soldier sent others to investigate that they didn't come up here too soon. She needed her sleep; she was exhausted. The bath had relaxed her so much that she fell asleep almost immediately.

Alice didn't sleep deeply. She was too concerned with being caught out, but the thought of sleeping on the cold hard ground versus this luxurious and soft bed was too much. She did sleep well despite waking occasionally to listen carefully at some imagined sound. Still, she rose before dawn and gathered her things. Using a flashlight to check the other rooms, she felt the castle had been abandoned and wondered why no other soldiers had come to check. She knew she hadn't seen it all, so using her pass card time and again, she went into areas whose function made no sense to her. She left packets in each of them, double and triple checking to be sure the radio frequency matched her switches. When she ran out of packets, she returned to the guard's munitions room. It took a while to find it in this large facility and to restock, taking the last of their explosives and setting their frequencies as she continued to explore.

Alice found a plastic rifle carrier with sponges to hold the weapon in place. Into this she carefully placed the swords, using cloth to wrap each one individually so they didn't scratch against each other. She knew the odds of taking these all the way home and keeping them for herself were not great, but she was going to try. Meanwhile, the case was more comfortable to carry than the rolled-up carpet. Looking at the carpet, she realized it was Persian and folded it into the case as well. "Spoils of the victor," she mumbled again.

She knew she didn't find everything in the castle, but the map she had memorized helped somewhat. She was frequently lost in the huge building, but she knew she had to get out, and soon. She was making her way to one of the exits when she finally heard something that caused her alarm. The sounds were coming from the exit she was making her way towards and it sounded like a lot of people were entering. She turned right around and headed in the opposite direction of the noise. She glanced back in time to see the soldiers she had long been expecting. They were armed to the teeth and cautiously making their way inside, inspecting each and every room.

Alice made her way down one hallway and then another. She kept trying doors that seemed to be locked or didn't take the pass key. Her heart began to feel like it was climbing into her throat. After all this time, they were going to catch her. But after feeling so good the past few hours, clean and away from all that, she wasn't going to go easily.

She heard them spread out…they kept coming in and there were so many! She made her way to an area that seemed familiar, realizing it was where she had come into the castle in the first place. She quickly exited by an exterior door and confiscated one of the ATVs. Rapidly, she sped away from the castle from the opposite side that the soldiers had entered and then circled around so she could observe. She had good cause for panic and alarm. Whoever had raised the alarm had brought a lot of friends. They had poured into the castle and were probably going up floor by floor. She wondered if they had discovered the burnt-out room or the infirmary yet, but she didn't care as she reached for the pocket that contained her switches. She'd used up the last of her second set of packages in the many passages she had explored or been lost in. As she readied the switch plate, she knew the radio-controlled devices would go off depending on which signal they were wired to. She hadn't been too particular so long as they were switched to the five frequencies on this plate. She contemplated flipping the switches one at a time, but that might mean some went off here or there and she would rather they all went off at the same time so no one would get out or be warned. She used the flat of her hand and flipped them all at once. She was disappointed that nothing happened. It was a hell of a letdown after she had placed so many explosive packages all over. She was suddenly angry: at herself, at her position, at the apparatus. What a waste of time.

Alice was getting up from her position, intent on getting on the ATV and getting the hell away from this area when she noticed a switch on the side of the small panel. Turning the switches back to the off position, she flipped the little black switch and tried with the flat of her hand to turn them all on at the same time again. It took a few seconds, but the explosion was horrendous when it came. Alice looked up from the switch plate in time to watch walls bursting out and turrets moving backwards like missiles, collapsing into the buildings. As the concussion began to echo around the valley, Alice felt it. It was like a burst of air that knocked her on her ass, the switch plate flying out of her hand as she landed. She blinked a moment and got up as soon as she could. "I guess I used a few too many," she murmured as she looked at the devastation of the castle and the surrounding landscape. Trees had been knocked down and were laid flat. Plants that had beautified the grounds were no more. No life moved, not a bird tweeted. The horrible destruction seemed to have silenced everything for miles around.

Alice could feel an odd ringing in her ears. She moved her jaw to try and get her ears to pop. She tried yawning and shaking her head. That was a mistake. She had a headache and hadn't even realized it. She looked down on the devastation she had caused for a while. Then she made her way to the ATV, made sure her kit was slung on her back and the rifle case below that was across her buttocks, and started the engine up. If it didn't have gauges that told her the machine had started, she wouldn't have known. Apparently, she was deaf. This worried her as she needed to hear if anyone was coming her way. Still, she had to get out of here. She didn't know how many soldiers had been in that castle and she didn't care, but someone might. They might investigate. They might decide on revenge for the deaths of their comrades.

She carefully made her way down the trails she found, towards the road behind the castle. If she hadn't already blown the two towers, the castle might have taken out at least one when it blew up. The trees were laying as though someone had cut them precisely, like matchsticks, and this was an unsettling sight.

Alice drove a while before she ran out of gas and had to start walking. She used the trees for cover once again, which was a good choice. She hadn't heard them, but several vehicles that looked like modified Hummers on steroids came hurrying down the road she had been on. Fate had been kind to her. If she hadn't run out of gas, she wouldn't be walking and she would have run right into them. The machine guns bristling from the vehicle itself much less the soldiers in them told her she would have been mowed down. As she watched them pass from the shadows of the forest, she wondered if anyone had time to have called in reinforcements or if anyone had survived that blast. Having seen the devastation first hand, she didn't think anyone could have survived. She didn't know much about explosives, but the amount she had used combined with whatever else was stored in that place probably had caused a much bigger explosion than anything she could have anticipated.

It was about an hour later that Alice realized she could hear a little. It made her feel better to realize the deafness wasn't a permanent thing and that was a good thing as she was approaching the rocky hill where she had left Lexi and Sasha so long ago. She hoped they were still there as she carefully made her way, walking slowly since she had to look around a lot, using her other senses which she felt were a bit dull without her hearing and from a lack of nutrition. The sun was going down beyond those western mountains and she planned to spend the night. She had looked around carefully before taking the path that only she could see in her mind. She didn't want to be observed and had carefully used the binoculars to detect movement of any kind, but saw nothing other than birds that were stirring. As she approached the hill she even could hear a little birdsong. It was still muffled, but at least she *could* hear.

Alice nearly missed it, the camouflage of the rock wall was so absolute. The window was no longer square and she was coming at it from the wrong angle. Still, she had to look several times before she was close enough to recognize it and call out...after all, she didn't want to be shot.

"Sasha? Lexi? It's Alice. Are you there?" she called with a look along her back trail to see if anyone had followed or if she had missed any movement. She thought she called normally, but with her deafness she was actually pretty loud.

"Alice?" a familiar voice came to her as Sasha opened the door in alarm. To Alice, the voice sounded like it was muffled, but she put that down to her ear problems.

Alice smiled. She was relieved to see her longtime friend as she walked the last few feet across the rocks to the cabin. "Are you two okay?"

"Why are you so loud?" Lexi asked, worried.

"Sorry, I seem to be partially deaf, but it's slowly coming back," she nearly whispered as they welcomed her in and left the door ajar for air flow. Still, the cold air was welcome and refreshing. She hadn't forgotten that just a few days previous it had started snowing, but fortunately that had all melted away. Alice had forgotten about her rifle case and nearly fell on her backside as it effectively stopped her at the door. She turned it sideways and entered.

"Partially deaf? From what?" Lexi asked looking at the fairly healthy-looking Alice with her cheeks flushed from exertion and wondering what she had been up to. After Sasha had told Lexi the full story of what they had been up to, she wasn't sure she shouldn't be afraid of this woman.

She didn't hear Lexi's question. "I need to sit down," Alice said as she made her way to what was obviously an unused cot and took her kit off her back to sit down. She carefully placed the rifle case next to it as she removed that too.

"Are you hungry?" Sasha offered. "All we have are those rations."

Alice shook her head. She had eaten what she found in the kitchens at the castle. She took out some of the treats she had packed and handed them to Sasha and Lexi. After so long without such sugary

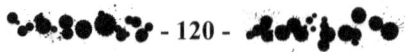

treats she cautioned them about scarfing them down. "You'll regret it," she warned.

"Vere did you get dese?" Sasha said through a mouthful of Twinkie.

"At the castle. I blew it up today," she said as though informing them of nothing in particular.

"You blew it up?" Sasha smiled delightedly. "Is it over?"

Alice shook her head. "Not quite," she said as though they were deaf, the sound of her words was loud in the small, enclosed space. "I saw more troops arriving just before I got here. I think it's time we started heading back to town and somehow make our way out of here."

"How?" Sasha asked with a glance at the more delicate-looking Lexi. Alice looked very fit and clean to her eyes. She herself felt gross and despite the cold, had welcomed any rain to wash herself with.

"I think," she said loudly, enunciating the words as though that would help restore her hearing, "that we should," she said slowly, "go out the way we came in."

"Can we do that?" Lexi put in, watching Alice and wondering if somehow Sasha had pulled her leg at all she had done. This petite woman surely wasn't capable of all that. Blown up the castle? Indeed!

"Well, we will skirt around the castle site," she was still fairly yelling, "but I think it's better to go with what is familiar. Right now, I suggest we get a good night's sleep before heading out in the morning."

"I'll make dinner," Lexi offered, pulling out some of the bars they had been eating and a few MREs.

"Here," Alice forestalled her, pulling out cans of beef stew and some crackers.

"Oh, heaven," she said, pulling the cans to her, hugging them as she read the labels. "How am I going to open these?" she asked Sasha, turning away from Alice.

"WHAT?" Alice said loudly.

"How are ve to open dese?" Sasha said carefully, mouthing the English words to Alice.

"Oh, HERE!" Alice said as she pulled the big Bowie-like knife out and began to open the cans, stabbing into them with apparent relish as she then worked the metal piece on the back edge of the blade to open the tins. Lexi stared wide-eyed at the huge blade on the knife.

For the first time in a long time, Lexi and Sasha ate a decent meal, even if it was canned. They finally felt full, if not stuffed. As they drank great sips of the water to wash down the salty stew and crackers,

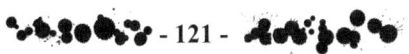

they felt like they were dining in a fine restaurant with wine. Alice filled them in on some of what she had been doing, but it was difficult as her hearing still hadn't returned and she was frequently overloud. They also had to repeat their questions quite often as she tried to read their lips and figure out what they were saying. It was a relief when all of them became sleepy from the rather large meal and sought their bunks.

Alice awoke refreshed, feeling safer than she had in a long time. It was still fairly dark, but she could tell dawn wasn't far off by the cabin's single window. She yawned and felt her ears pop. Her hearing hadn't quite returned fully, but she could tell she was hearing a lot more than she could the previous night. For instance, she could clearly hear the sounds of her cabinmates making love. She could also make out the odor that told her they were engaging in sex. She turned her head so that neither could see she was awake in the predawn light. Lying there, she thought about Kathy, wondering what she was doing at that exact moment. After a forced abstinence of so long, she wondered if her passionate wife had remained celibate or had moved on. Surely, she had moved on, she decided. The thought depressed her immeasurably. Kathy had been solely hers from the beginning. She had been Kathy's first and only for a long time...until...she let that thought go or she would become angry and depressed about that long-ago incident and the time lost to them. She had taken care of that and it had been a long time before her wife had come back to her, both physically and emotionally. Alice feigned sleep until the two lovers were done, stifling their cries into each other's mouths as they came. Alice was gritting her teeth at this point, wishing she had reached into her own pants to take care of her driving need. Their sounds had brought home her own situation and she pretended to sleep as each of them got up, washed, and then returned to their warm bed. She waited a good half an hour before pretending to just get up

"Oh, you're avake," Sasha greeted her from where she lay next to Lexi, the two cuddled in post-coital bliss with their clothes on.

"Yeah," Alice grunted, needing the hole in the corner of the cabin and grouchily heading for it. Knowing she was going to use the facility had both Lexi and Sasha discreetly turning away. The odor of urine was strong in the cabin as they heard her make her stream. Alice finished and closed the lid to the hole in the ground. She got up and opened the cabin door slightly, looking beyond it to make sure they were still without company. Seeing and being able to hear the birds pecking among the rocks reassured her they were alone...and told her that her senses were returning.

"How is your hearing?" Lexi nearly whispered, but Alice heard her and smiled in her direction.

"Better, but still not perfect. There is a slight ringing, but I hope in time that will go away."

"At least you aren't shouting anymore," Sasha dared to tease.

Alice smiled and went to her pack where she pulled out a couple cans of peaches for their breakfast. "We should get going while it's still dark, in case we need to retreat here."

"You think we will?" Lexi asked as she got up from the warmth of the shared, but narrow cot where she sat with Sasha.

Sasha got up behind her. "Ve must be prepared for anything."

Alice wanted silence with her breakfast, but now that she could hear they asked even more questions, clarifying things she had been doing.

"So, there isn't any way to communicate with the outside world?" Lexi confirmed.

Alice shook her head. "The two towers are down and the satellite dish was on top of the castle."

After their breakfast, the other two prepared two packs containing sleeping bags, blankets, and food.

"Don't make it too heavy. You have to carry that for miles and believe me, it wears on your body," Alice recommended.

Still, they were ready to go soon enough and Alice stomped into her boots and tied the laces, seeing the other two do the same in preparation. Alice cautiously opened the door of the cabin, looking to see if the birds had changed any of their behaviors. They were still pecking around happily and only shied away when she took a step onto the rock path from the cabin. Lexi stepped out behind her and then Sasha, who closed the door behind them. They carefully set off, the sun slowly rising to their right as Alice took them rapidly down off the rocky hill and into the trees.

"Don't talk unless you have to and then only in whispers," Alice recommended. They still didn't know if they were being hunted or if anyone was out there. It may be that they saw someone too late.

They made their way back on the route Alice had traveled the previous day, passing the ATV which had been gone over and been used as target practice. Alice was surprised to see this as they hadn't heard any of the shots in the well-protected cabin. It took a lot longer to make up the miles between where she had abandoned the ATV and the castle. As they crept up over one of the last hills that separated the valley from their cabin refuge, Alice cautioned them.

Sasha and Lexi looked at the valley in awe, the destruction was incredible to view. Alice pulled out her binoculars to look at the men who looked like ants that were going over the rubble.

"When you said you blew it up, you weren't kidding," Lexi quipped quietly.

Alice smiled wryly. "We better get going while their attention is engaged elsewhere."

"What are we going to do?" Lexi asked, gazing at Alice speculatively. It was obvious she didn't like or really trust the stubble-headed blonde. Still, Sasha trusted her implicitly and that would have to be enough for her.

"Over there you've got the steppes," Alice waved to her right as she looked from the hill overlooking the remains of the palace. "You have some huge mountain ranges to the south," again she waved her hand, "then, we could go to the Caspian Sea," she offered, pointing in another direction. "I suggest we find our way back to Astana and get the hell out of this beautiful country and back to Europe. From there, you two go your way and I'll go mine."

"Switzerland sounds pretty good to me right now," Sasha told her.

"Me too," Lexi answered, remembering other, more pleasant times there with Sasha.

"Well, it's not going to get us there any faster if we don't get moving," Alice said as she pulled herself from their lookout and back from the edge of the hill so they wouldn't be seen. After one long look at their safety and prison, the other two followed Alice down the rock-strewn hill.

The trip back to Astana was to prove longer than the trip out. Each time they heard vehicles, they scattered back into the trees and later into brush or grassland. Alice had emphasized that no one was their friend.

As Alice had predicted, someone might be watching. The third time they went to hide, they were pursued. She started to run, hoping to lead their attacker away from the other two women, only to find they had followed along. They were all too soon breathing heavily as she looked for and came across a trail that she blindly followed. Maintaining a run didn't make sense as they were all too physically tired, but they had to get away from their pursuers who were still shouting in Russian or a dialect close enough that Alice understood. They were shouting that the women should stop, but Alice had no intention of stopping. She trusted only these two women, and one of them only because the other happened to love her. Lexi's fear of her and animosity toward her hadn't gone unnoticed. Alice understood that. She also knew that Sasha had probably confided a bit too much about their adventures since being in prison. Only those things would make Lexi fear and distrust Alice.

The trail began to peter out and Alice worried since she had no idea where they were. She nearly ran off a cliff as her lungs began to give out. It was a near thing and she threw herself backwards from the edge, landing on the rifle case on her butt. "What the hell?" she swore as she looked at the deep chasm they had encountered, knowing they were now trapped and too out of breath to do anything about it.

"There," Sasha panted, her own breath coming in gasps as she pointed.

"No, surely not!" Lexi pleaded as she almost sobbed out her objection.

They all saw the suspension bridge. It was merely a series of thick ropes in an inverted triangle where you walked on one of the points and held onto the other two corners of the triangle. It spanned the width of the gap, bowing in the middle from the length.

Alice headed for it immediately, knowing their pursuers probably thought they had the three of them trapped against the gorge and realizing they knew the lay of the land much better than the three of them. She could hear them gaining on the trio and hurried to the bridge.

"No, I can't!" Lexi stated, looking down at the deep walls and what looked like a stream at the bottom, far away and down.

"Would you rather be raped or killed?" Alice turned on her to scare her, not only with her words but with her expression; her eyes were narrowed and orange.

Lexi unconsciously took a step back and looked away only to see how quickly the soldiers were gaining on them, unslinging their rifles as they ran. Her only other choice was to be shot and she desperately wanted to survive this. She glanced at Sasha and nodded, indicating they should go first.

Seeing the nod, Alice hesitated only a second before walking out on the bridge, her hands clutching at the ropes, desperately hoping they would make it across before the ropes were cut. Her rifle case grazed both sides of the handholds. She took another step, looking out instead of down. She felt the fear enter her legs, making them feel leaden, and kept looking out, not down, to keep from freezing up. She took one step and then another, not daring to look behind her to see if the others were following. She just kept going a little faster as she felt the suspension bridge begin to sway. It wasn't swaying from her, so she could only assume the others were behind her.

Sasha took one look at Lexi, her eyes pleading and hopeful, and at Lexi's nod she followed Alice onto the rope, grasping at the handholds tightly as she copied the woman.

Lexi wished the other two would hurry as she could hear the soldiers behind them and then she stepped out onto the rope. This reminded her of something she and her friends had done as children. She hadn't been good at the balancing act then, and now, as an adult, this was worse. She could feel the adrenaline pumping through her veins as she looked down at the spot to place her next foot. She couldn't help but see the distance to the bottom. Her legs froze and her heart accelerated. She quickly looked up and out, a trick to avoid worrying about what was behind her and below her, and then followed the other two women, going as fast as her legs would let her.

Alice found it was a little easier than she had anticipated. The bouncing caused by the extra weight was throwing her a bit and the rifle case scraping was slowing her slightly, but overall, she thought she could do this as she worked on her balance. What choice did she really have? She didn't dare look behind her.

They were about a third of the way when they heard the soldiers behind them, shouting at them to come back. Were they serious? Who would obey that command? Additional vibrations on the rope told the women that the soldiers were either cutting the rope or following. No one looked around to find out.

The bridge began to bow as the weight of the three women reached the middle. Alice heard Sasha swearing behind her in Russian and a few other languages. It was kind of funny, but she kept going. She had no choice…to stop would be a death sentence, and if the additional swaying of the bridge meant anything, it meant they were being followed.

"Christ," Lexi spat out as she slipped. Sasha's heart leapt into her throat as she turned to see her girlfriend with the rope under her armpit and grasping out at the other rope handhold. One of Lexi's legs was swinging out into space and the other was trying to get a footing. She reached out to grab the free hand and help balance Lexi. Taking her time and looking behind her girlfriend, she was shocked to see how close the soldiers were and just in time to see one slip as Lexi had. He wasn't as fortunate as Lexi and she watched in horror as he fell and fell and fell, before hitting the rocks along the stream below. His body splattered from the impact. She swallowed and didn't let on to about what she saw as Lexi indicated she was balanced enough to go on. Sasha turned around, pleased to see Alice had kept going and they could now move a little faster. She held on tightly to her own ropes as she sped up marginally, Lexi keeping pace with her.

Alice was about ten feet from the other side of the bridge when she also slipped off the rope that was their footing. She swung back and nearly over as both her legs hooked on the rope at the knee. "Keep moving!" she shouted at the other two women who stopped to help her. "It's when you stop that the weight begins to pull you down." She began to pull herself up as Sasha obeyed her command and stepped over her, followed by Lexi a moment later.

"Are you sure? Can't I…?" Lexi offered to help Alice.

"Gravity sucks, you know!" Alice quipped as she pulled, using the last of her strength to get up and back on the rope, angry at the unbalanced load on her back. She briefly thought about letting it all go, but they were so close that she decided not to. As they made it to firm ground, she looked back at the soldiers following, dropped to the ground, swung the rifle case from her back, and opened it. She unwrapped one of the swords and handed it to a shocked Sasha. She unwrapped another and began to hack at the ropes. Alice attacked the rope the soldiers were walking on and Sasha began to hack at one of the handholds.

"Let me help?" Lexi asked and unwrapped a breathtakingly beautiful sword and began to swing it at the ropes.

The soldiers, seeing what their quarry was doing, began to unsling their rifles and bring them up, but the threads giving way under Alice's extremely sharp blade unbalanced them. They had no good shot and the bridge began to sway more and more as it became unstable. The blades, having never cut anything, had been kept oiled and razor sharp, so they cut quickly and accurately. Alice was the first to cut through and the threads unraveled back along the bridge. Sasha's was next and this had the bridge leaning precariously to one side, the soldiers now hanging on to the last taut line, their legs wrapped around the line and pleading in their various languages and dialects. Two of the five soldiers who had followed them raced back toward the other side. The soldiers who had remained on the other side began to fire at the woman, but it was too far and their accuracy was in question. Lexi finally finished cutting through and the whole bridge fell toward the other side. The soldiers on the bridge peeled off one at a time as they fell. The last two, gripping hard, were bounced against the wall and fell to their deaths.

"That had to hurt," Alice quipped dryly as she began to wrap the sword she had used.

"I thought you had a rifle in there," Lexi panted as she looked at the sword she had cut the rope with.

"Nope, just a couple of souvenirs," Alice answered, gently and reverently taking the sword from Lexi as she handed it to her handle first. She quickly wrapped it carefully away. "Besides, I don't like guns."

"Dis vas much better than a rifle," Sasha grinned as she handed Alice the third one and watched her wrap it almost reverently.

"Damn right," Alice said as she carefully closed the case and then slung it around her again, looking across the deep chasm and wondering how the hell they were going to get back to Astana.

It took four days. They first had to walk far enough out on the plains they found themselves on to hide from other dedicated soldiers, and then they headed west towards Astana. They eventually found the ground tapered off towards a stream, which became a river, and then they found an absolutely prehistoric bridge to cross over it. They arrived in the town dusty and starving...Alice's pack had been emptied of all food with the three of them eating it, the last of the MREs and energy bars sustaining them that last day.

"How are ve going to get out of here?" Sasha wondered as they found a hotel and cleaned up. Alice

needed to buy them something besides fatigues, but as the town had many soldiers in it they weren't questioned...at least not yet.

"Let's worry about clothes first, food second, and passports third," Alice ticked off on her fingers. Sasha nodded and using her Russian, negotiated for some local clothes in the open-air market they came to. They pretended to be soldiers who were enamored with the clothes and let Sasha negotiate the prices. Alice slipped her some of the money she had stolen from the library when she had emptied things into her pack.

They were able to share a room, using the community tub one at a time to clean themselves and change. Sasha insisted Alice go first since she had used up their supplies for all of them. She hadn't known how they would get out of that valley and was astonished to find herself still alive. She was eternally grateful to Alice. She watched as Alice took her share of the clothes, dropped her pack and rifle case at the end of one of the beds, and headed off to the bath.

"How are we going to get out of here?" Lexi asked, still unsure of Alice and her 'skills' despite Sasha's reassurances that the woman was phenomenal. Her hands spread wide as she took in the town they were in as well as the country.

"Trust her, baby," Sasha took Lexi into her arms to kiss her. The last four days of walking had made the midwestern woman very cranky, but maybe it was also the presence of Alice. They had enjoyed their time alone in the stone cabin, but worried constantly that Alice would never return. Worse was the thought of what Alice had to do to effect their escape. They tried not to think, much less discuss the blood of the dead that were on Alice's hands.

"No more killing?" Lexi asked hopefully as she leaned in for the kiss, relieved that Sasha was in her arms.

"I won't promise that," she said seriously, looking at how dirty her girlfriend was.

"Could you make her promise?"

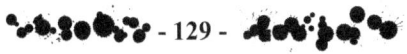

Sasha shook her head and looked in those lovely eyes. "I vouldn't ask her to. You don't tink she *likes* doing vhat she has to do?"

"How many people were in that castle when she blew it up?"

"I don't know. I don't care either. She got us out of dere and The Assemblage is no more."

"You don't care how many were killed?" Lexi was shocked and dismayed. She wondered how much Sasha hadn't told her about their adventures. She wondered how hard her girlfriend had become compared to the sophisticated businesswoman she had known and loved.

"No, I don't. You see, dey came after me, after you, and dey *accidentally* got Alice. Ve did vhat ve had to. She did vhat she had to. I was shocked too when this began. I learned that dese people didn't care what dey had to do. Destroying dem was the least ov it," she tried to explain. She had tried before, but Lexi didn't quite get it.

"It doesn't seem to bother her to kill. She does it as though she's done it many times."

"She probably has." Sasha had often thought that over the many, many months they had been together. Alice knew too much and thought differently than she or anyone she had ever known. She was too good at this.

Alice had never told Sasha about her own sister's involvement or that she even existed. That little bit of information was better off left unknown.

While the other two took turns bathing, Alice went down to the bar. She knew enough Russian that she could order a drink and she had enough money to pay for some information. There was always someone willing to talk...someone willing to make a buck, or a Euro, or a ruble. She soon had the information she needed. She had someone go upstairs and slip a note under their room door while she sought the people she would need to leave the country.

Alice was gone for hours, many hours, and Sasha and Lexi had gone down to find something to eat. The note had read, *'Found a lead to get us out of here. If I'm not back right away, do not worry. Alice.'* Still, by that time it was quite late and they were very worried. Finally, they heard a knock on their door and Sasha held Alice's Bowie-like knife while Lexi answered the door. They were both relieved to find Alice standing outside the door.

"Sorry, I didn't take a key," she began.

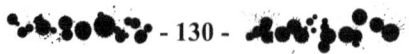

"What was so important that you had to leave?" Lexi felt bold enough to ask.

"Well, I found a flight out of here, but it doesn't leave until tomorrow afternoon so we have to stay here. We must remain low-key until it is time to go," she found herself explaining, surprised, as she hadn't liked Lexi's tone.

"How can ve leave witout passports?" Sasha asked.

"You mean these?" Alice said as she dug into her pack for the packet of papers, money, and other things she had stolen, surprised they hadn't gone through her things while she had been gone so long. She knew she probably wouldn't have been able to resist.

"Vere did you find dese?" Sasha was incredulous as she looked at the fake passport Alice had made for her so long ago.

"They, along with this," she showed Lexi her real passport, "were in the library and I thought we might need them."

They shared smiles and the relief was obvious. "Who vill fly us out?" Sasha asked next.

"Someone that needed money more than ethics. He will fly us out, then we can pick up a commercial airliner and use those," she indicated the passports both real and fake, "and get a flight to Europe."

"And then?" Lexi challenged her. She didn't care for how high-handed Alice was being. She didn't care if it would get her killed, she wasn't going to be frightened by this woman.

Alice looked up at her. Only the fact that Sasha loved this woman had kept her from abandoning her on their trek back. She'd been game, but she hadn't been exactly...pleasant. "Then you hide in a house in Switzerland as you recover. You can contact your children and let them know you are alive, but delayed due to some 'business.'" She made air quotation marks to emphasize what she was saying. "Then in a few months you can go about the business of having Sasha declared undead."

Sasha frowned and started to ask a question, but Lexi was too quick for her. "Why a few months? Why not start it right away?"

Alice had been prepared for that question. "Because we need to let this," she gestured to the east of them, clearly indicating the castle and what had occurred there, "blow over." She smiled at the pun and Sasha grinned behind Lexi, appreciating the humor. "Also, I too have to go home and be declared alive. I need to see what happened while I was gone and assess the situation. That will take time."

"Why do you get to go home and I can't?"

"You don't think we got all The Assemblage's minions, do you?" she asked, sick of the challenge to her knowledge and authority. Sasha recognized the signs of anger in her friend's expression even if her girlfriend did not. "They can and will try to kill Sasha if we appear too suddenly. We all need to heal and you need to lie low so it isn't an issue. I assure you, you will be in the lap of luxury."

"I don't care about that," she waved away Alice's words and assurances. "I care that my children will have thought that I'm dead..." she began to argue.

"I already said you can call them and tell them you were delayed. Don't tell them Sasha and I are alive. Not yet, not this soon."

Alexis went to argue some more, but Sasha pulled her away and murmured in her ear. She continued to argue with Sasha while Alice spilled out the contents of her kit. She still had her sleeping bag, a blanket, and other survival items, but it was the paperwork she wanted to go through a bit more thoroughly now that they had time.

The small, single engine plane sputtered and barely made it over the mountains as it took them away from Astana and away from the main airport and the many soldiers watching in the city. Alice felt like she was on a bad carnival ride as she sat in the front seat next to the pilot with Sasha and Lexi in the back. She had given each their passports to hold in case they got separated or something happened. They had left their fatigues back in the hotel and were wearing colorful local garb that allowed them to blend in, except for their distinctive European features.

"You will need to go over to that terminal," he pointed as he taxied to a stop in an area of small planes. They could see the larger planes parked on the far side of where he pointed. They nodded and Alice handed him an envelope, which he took gratefully. He watched as they walked towards a door that led into the terminals then turned to find someone to gas up his plane for his return journey.

They made their way inside and Alice had Sasha buy them three tickets to Switzerland, only the first stop in their long journey where they would have to change planes. Their passports passed a cursory glance at the ticket counter where the man selling them the tickets looked at the amount of cash suspiciously. After that, Alice had Sasha exchange their money for Euros before they went through security. Alice had checked her baggage containing the swords and prayed it would make it to Switzerland without being 'diverted.'

They sat down and waited for their plane to be called and only breathed a sigh of relief when they were on board and it took off. The hours on the plane were long and boring and only Sasha and Lexi spoke. Alice was left to her thoughts and that was probably a good thing. She was tired, physically as well as mentally, and the thought of what had gone on at home while she had been away plagued her. Still, they were heading in the right direction as they flew north to Switzerland

Only when they landed and were able to pick up their luggage did Alice breathe a sigh of relief. She could finally speak for herself and didn't need Sasha to translate anymore. She explained she was a collector as customs went through her case. She cautioned at the sharpness of the blades and showed a document written in Russian that she claimed was a bill of sale. Unable to read the beautiful Russian letters and script, the French-speaking customs' official that had gone through Alice's case believed her.

Alice spent one night in the 'safe' house. She and Sasha went through the programs she had set up on the computer and examined some of the data. "This vill take months," Sasha commented as she saw all it had recorded.

"I'll make a copy for you to go over. We should video conference once you've read over your copy," Alice advised, ignoring the dirty looks that Lexi was giving her. She sensed the woman would be relieved once she was long gone.

The next day, another passport with another bogus name had Alice heading back to the United States. From Switzerland, she landed in Los Angeles, but not before she recognized someone traveling in coach when she used the first-class bathroom. Sitting in her first-class seat, it took a while to remember who the woman was and why she looked so familiar....

~The End~

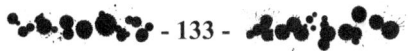

❧ MONITORING MALICE ☙

BOOK 23

Alice is home and must explain to Kathy why she watched her family go on with their lives and didn't show herself.

While she watches her wife being set up by thugs in positions of authority and is forced to witness Kathy's first foray into dating since being widowed, Alice struggles to control her murderous temper! She must learn to be patient...very patient.

Come along for the ride as we see things from Alice's distinct point of view.

After departing from Switzerland, Alice landed in Los Angeles but not before she recognized a passenger traveling in coach, who had snuck up to use the first-class restroom. As she sat in her first-class seat thinking, it took a while to remember who the woman was and why she looked so familiar....

The flight was long and boring, and Alice couldn't avoid using the restroom. The meals in first class were, well, first-class. But the meals seemed to travel through a person faster than the plane traveled through the air. It was as she glanced down the aisle towards the curtain separating first class from the economy section that she thought she recognized someone. The second time she queued up for the restroom, the wait was longer, and that's when she realized she recognized that person from...somewhere. She sighed, wondering if it was one of the Russians she had been pursuing for so long. She was tired of them. She thought she had cleaned everything up so tidily back in Kazakhstan.

When she returned to her first-class seat, she really worked on trying to remember where she knew the person in economy from. A man sitting on the outside of the aisle tried to strike up a conversation with her, but she pretended not to speak French, so she could concentrate on her thoughts. She finally had to give up on remembering for a while. After having had so much going on for so long and being without regular meals, her mind simply couldn't identify the person.

When the plane's staff dimmed the lights to simulate nighttime, she lay there trying to catch some sleep. An uneasy feeling began to build in her, and she had learned to trust that feeling long ago; that feeling had kept her alive too many times to disobey it. She began searching her memory again for that person in economy. Who was she? Why did she know her? Where did she know her from? As Alice's mind began flipping through the list of names in her mental Rolodex, it came to her. Bev Hanneman! The name finally clicked.

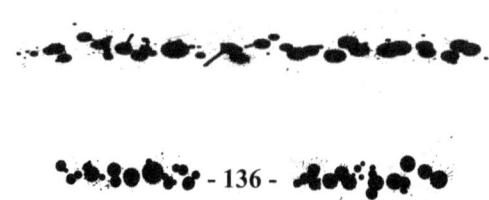

"So, you arrived in L.A. and didn't come to us immediately?" Kathy interrupted Alice's spoken musings, and Alice went silent.

Alice blinked for a moment, trying to remember where she had left off in the story she was telling Kathy. Covering, she answered, "Well, no. I had to scope out the situation and see where you were at. I couldn't just ring the doorbell, now could I?"

Kathy wished she had. She wished that so much it almost hurt her to realize how much she had missed Alice. During Alice's recitation of what she had done on her trip, which had taken days, Kathy realized how much she had truly missed this woman whom she couldn't forget. Still, Alice was a killer, and had Kathy been keeping count of all the bodies this woman was solely responsible for, she couldn't even imagine the total. And that was only the ones Alice had confessed to her. She was certain there were many that Alice had no intention of ever telling her about, so she could only guess at the full body count. "Yes, you could have. We needed you!" She sounded angry and confused.

"Well, it wasn't as if you were expecting me back," she pointed out with a wry, little smile.

Kathy chuckled. "No, I guess I wasn't. So much time, Alice. So much wasted time!"

"I know," Alice acknowledged. "But I'm here now, and we have to decide where we go from here."

"We'll have to inform Portia you are back and have her begin the process to declare you alive!" she began. She'd been dodging her good friend's phone calls for days as Alice told her the story that had kept her from her family.

"I'm already on that. I have my contacts too," she smiled, the thinness of her face making her smile look bigger.

Kathy longed to caress that face; she had been through so much without her. Years' worth of stories that had nothing to do with her or their marriage. "You could have made yourself known sooner," she pointed out.

Alice nodded musingly. "I could have, but I had to make sure the timing was right too. I had to find the lay of the land...and to be honest, you had moved on."

"Well, I thought I was a widow!" she answered defensively, feeling flushed about the reference to the failed romance she had started.

"Of course, you did," Alice agreed with her, hoping to defuse the anger she could hear building in her wife's voice.

"Now, what?" Kathy asked after they were both silent for a while, lost in their own thoughts.

"Now, I try to get my life back. What about you? Do you want me in your life, or do you want me to sleep elsewhere?" Alice asked her boldly.

Kathy considered. They would have to go about having Alice declared alive. She would also have to deal with the taxes that an increasingly frantic Portia was calling about. Did she want to resume her relationship with Alice? Did she want to live with a killer? She heard a noise and saw that Alice heard it too. They both got up from the couch they were sitting on, and Kathy went to the stairs to look for the cause of the noise. Alice seemed to melt into the spare bedroom, hiding effortlessly in the shadows as she had for months. Kathy didn't find anything and breathed a sigh of relief. She wasn't certain she wanted the children to know that Alice was alive, at least not yet. She was still trying to come to terms with it herself. She returned to the couch and looked up as Alice joined her again. "Where were we?"

"It wasn't one of the kids?" Alice, curious, asked her softly.

Kathy shrugged. "Just something settling in the house I guess."

Alice nodded as she went to sit down on the couch. "I need to know your decision. Do you want me here or do you want me to move out?" She waited for Kathy's answer.

"Have you really moved in? It's more like you've hidden here," she hedged, not really answering Alice's question.

Alice shrugged. She knew what Kathy was saying and sighed. "Okay, I guess I should get a place then?" She formed it in a question, but she was annoyed. This was her home too, and these were her children too. Either Kathy wanted her in her life or she didn't. She could sense her wife's confusion.

"Why don't you finish your story? We don't need to decide right now, do we?" Kathy felt relieved to be able to put off this decision. In the days while Alice had been telling her story, Kathy had been strangely excited to have her around, and yet….

Alice got up to take Kathy in her arms. "I still have a bit to tell you, but I want you to know, whatever you decide, I will love you forever."

When the plane landed in Los Angeles, Alice didn't have much in the way of luggage. She had some nice, new clothes from Dubai but nothing old and familiar. She hungered for the familiar but knew it would be a mistake to go straight home. Instead, she checked herself into a hotel that she knew wouldn't have cameras, where no one would recognize her and she could remain anonymous, at least temporarily. Los Angeles had a few thousand such hotels or motels. She had watched Bev Hanneman collect her own luggage and catch a taxi. Alice followed her and learned where she was staying, but she had no intention of following through on the threat she had made to the woman so long ago, not yet anyway. She just hoped Bev hadn't been looking for Alice Weaver, or she would live only long enough to regret that. Bev had been warned, and Alice was not willing to give her a second chance.

"What happened to you?" Kathy asked, looking at the short hair and emaciated body so reminiscent of Emily's body just a few months ago. With that thought, Kathy pulled back to look in Alice's amazing eyes. "It was you, wasn't it? You are the one that donated blood for Emily's treatment?"

Alice nodded. "Yes. I got back and found out what was going on, so I went to Doctor Wilkerson and we worked out a treatment for Emily."

"But that was months ago. Why didn't you tell me you were back? Why didn't you let me know you were alive?"

"Well, you weren't exactly waiting for me with open arms," she teased as she slowly extricated herself from her wife's arms. "You were involved with the cop, remember?" she reminded her wife of their earlier conversation. They sat back down on the couch to continue their conversation.

"So, you broke us up?" she asked, feeling a bit manipulated.

Alice shrugged. It was a familiar, endearing gesture and very much Alice Weaver, despite her appearance. "Yeah, well, she wasn't good

enough for you, and eventually, she would have asked too many questions."

"Yeah, I came to that conclusion myself," Kathy admitted.

"Why not sooner? Why come back now?"

"Because you *needed* me," she said simply.

"You've been in our rooms when we slept, haven't you?" she asked, remembering the times she felt she was being watched and the times she woke thinking she saw her wife.

Alice nodded again. "I've *missed* you." She began to tell her about the time she spent in LA, watching her wife closely.

"I'm sorry you got rid of all our cars," Alice began, a sardonic look in her eyes as her eyebrow raised, questioning Kathy.

"I really had to after…" she began defensively and then narrowed her eyes. "You know *why*, don't you?"

Alice nodded, a grin on her face. "It took some figuring out. The replacement of the safe," her hand gestured towards where it was hidden, "then the money you paid out. Reading the newspaper and finding that man was related to a cop…How scared were you?"

"You figured all that out by reading newspapers?" she asked, horrified that the clues were so easy to decipher. What if Linda…?

Alice shook her head. "No, it took me some time. I had a *lot* of time on my hands and figuring your situation out took up a lot of that time. I didn't know how to say, '*Honey, I'm home,*' without causing you a heart attack. I held back, I observed, and when that cop got a little too cozy and a little too nosy, I intervened."

Kathy flushed, realizing Alice had followed her and watched her for a long time.

Alice began to explain again. She had rented a car to look around, then she had checked on Bev Hanneman to make sure the woman wasn't looking for her, but she didn't tell that part to Kathy. There were parts of her past and certain stories Kathy didn't need to know…*ever*. Bev Hanneman had followed Alice to one of her favorite spots in the Caymans years ago. She had attempted, badly, to switch bags on the flight out to the Carolinas where Alice lost her for a while and was able to take another plane. When the woman made the

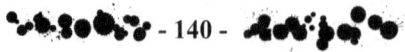

mistake of following Alice to her hotel and was spotted, Alice taught her a lesson that should have frightened her for life. Alice was relieved to discover Bev was in Los Angeles for an interview, and it didn't appear she was looking for Alice. For that, Alice was grateful and not terribly surprised. Bev had been warned in a rather unique way, and Alice would have been shocked if she had disregarded that warning. She was sick of killing but wouldn't hesitate to kill again if she had to.

Instead, as she told Kathy, she drove by the house but couldn't see much. She turned to the house in the valley, parking a block away in order to walk and look around. To her it was obvious someone had been there, and she ascertained it was Kathy when she looked long enough. She checked out of her comfortable hotel room in order to take up residence at the house and lay low for a while. She was still recovering, and that would take a long time. She couldn't clean up the house. If Kathy came back, the house had to look like it was abandoned, which also meant she couldn't work out. That annoyed her, but there were exercises she could do without equipment, and there were gyms she could go to if she really needed the physical exertion. Still, she didn't want anyone to see her, so she kept a low profile.

Spying on her own family was the worst as she tried to figure out what was going on in their lives. She waited until a day when she saw Mrs. Fernandez was off and Kathy and the children had left the house before she checked it out. This brought back overwhelming memories as she enthusiastically greeted Coco, who was happy to see her and followed her around as she looked through her own house. Following her from room to room, Alice smiled and petted the excited dog, reluctantly shutting the back door on her face as she left when she was finished. She would be back though, many times, as she hungered for her family. It was rough seeing how much the children had grown while she had been estranged from Kathy and gone from their lives. She wanted to walk in and say she was home, but she needed to know everything that was going on in their lives before she did that. Something was going on and she had to wonder what as she tapped into the computer system in the home, using a back door that she herself had created in the system in order to gain access.

It was going to be harder getting into the house with cops watching it. Alice figured out if she parked a mile away and hiked along the path that ran in back of the houses along this section of Palos Verdes, she could watch the house, but she could only get into the house if she knew no one was home. This required a lot of observation, which was hard to do without making it too obvious. She made herself a duplicate of the spare key for the back gate, so she had easy access in case anyone came along. Being seen jumping a fence was a sure-fire way to get the security companies and the police called. She still wondered why cops were watching the house.

She found where Kathy had replaced the safe. She searched and found Kathy hadn't written down the combination of the new safe. It took a few tries, but she finally hit on the combination by using the children's birthdates. She had cleaned up blood splotches she found on the floor that were visible with a black light and luminol. Something told her there was a reason why Kathy had replaced the safe but finding the blood had been a surprise. She could tell Kathy had tried to clean the blood up, and she finished cleaning it well enough that no one would ever be able to tell. Now, she wondered if the police were watching their house for that reason. It wasn't until she learned the locksmith who died was related to a cop that she thought of possible reasons for the presence of blood stains. Kathy had hired that locksmith, and maybe he had been hurt when he opened the safe. She remembered the traps she had put in the safe. Yes, that would explain it. She saw in the upstairs closet where Kathy had cleaned out her stored cash. Now, she would watch the cops watching her family and figure out the players in this scenario.

It was a curious time. She used a remote to her new computer to watch the house, but it provided no sound. She found it strange that Emily was home a lot, and it took her a while before she caught sight of the catheter in Emily's shoulder and became concerned. She hadn't put cameras in the bathrooms or places where she felt some privacy should be allowed. The child looked positively ill and was losing weight at an alarming rate. What was wrong with her? She followed Kathy one day, well behind the police vehicle that was following her wife, and found she was going to see Doctor Wilkerson. She knew she could just go to see him herself, but she didn't know if she wanted to reveal herself just yet. The bags of liquid that Emily was taking through her catheter seemed to be making her feel better, but why was she seeing the specialist instead of their regular pediatrician?

Alice saw Kathy being pulled over twice in the Porsche. What the heck was that about? She could have taken care of the men who were watching the house in the darkened car but was amused when the police stopped to ask the occupants of the car what they were doing. Eventually, they moved farther down the street, so it wasn't as obvious they were watching the house. Something was definitely going on. Was Kathy involved in the murder of that locksmith? The blood, the money, and now seeing her being watched by the cop's friends were puzzling Alice.

"What have you gotten yourself involved in, my love?" she murmured as she watched and waited. She knew it was simply a matter of time before they either saw her watching them or they took action. She could see they were impatient. Pulling Kathy over was an annoyance, and Alice had driven by in her unobtrusive rental, ensuring she wasn't noticed. Returning to the valley, she was getting tired of parking blocks away in order to slip back into the house to sleep. She carefully made up her bed on the thin hiking air mattress and sleeping bag she had purchased. She wanted better and thought longingly of a five-star hotel, but she didn't want to be seen just yet. She could have used another ID. This was Los Angeles, where she could hide in plain sight, but she also knew that fate was a tricky bitch, and the odds were, even in a large city such as LA, she might run into *somebody* she knew.

The final time Kathy was pulled over, she was driving the Porsche, and as Alice drove by slowly, she saw them arresting her wife. They didn't see Alice drive by a second and a third time. They were taking their sweet time hoisting the Porsche onto the flatbed tow truck, and she could see by the lights of passing cars that Kathy looked upset in the back seat of the police vehicle. She cringed at the sight of her Porsche on the flatbed, imagining them scraping the undercarriage in their attempt to transport the low-slung vehicle.

Alice considered contacting someone she knew to determine what Kathy was being charged with but nixed the idea. She didn't want people to know she was alive, *not yet*. She hadn't figured out what she would tell people, much less Kathy. Alice was annoyed as she tried to remain unobtrusive near the police station the next day and was relieved when she finally recognized Portia entering the station. The attorney looked smart, svelte, and professionally dressed. She was in there for over an hour before hurrying out and going to her car. She wasn't aware as Alice followed her to the clinic across town. Hmmm, this was getting interesting. She saw Portia return to the courthouse and stride determinedly inside. Alice got out of her rental. She had tossed a jacket she bought at the used clothing store on her shoulders and was wearing jeans and high-top sneakers. She detested the clothes but thought it best not to dress like she normally would have. Sitting in the back of the court as though she belonged there, she watched the different cases with interest. She watched Portia fidget as the docket wound through the various cases; LA courts were notoriously slow.

Alice perked up when they finally brought Kathy in for her case. She looked haggard, especially in the ugly clothes they had given her to wear. But Alice was more interested in the cop she could see looking on avidly, almost hungrily at her wife. He was far too interested in this case for it to be casual. The cop beside him kept up a running, whispered conversation until the judge called everyone to order.

"Your honor, my client is a member of the community in good standing. She is being harassed here. If you will look at the–" Portia began, but the district attorney jumped in.

"She was carrying enough narcotics to–" he began heatedly.

"Which we have the prescriptions for right here. They are signed by her doctor," Portia interjected.

Alice avidly watched the proceedings, keeping a close eye on Kathy and her reactions. She could see something was disturbing her wife. She also saw that something about the cop on the bench behind Kathy was bothering her.

Kathy let the hum of arguments flow over her. She heard them, but she didn't *hear* them. She let her peripheral vision take in Detective Leskowitz, who sat forward anxiously in his seat. She noticed that sitting next to him was one of the cops that had pulled her over once. She refocused her attention once again when she heard the judge offer bail, and she was staggered by the amount.

"Don't worry," Portia whispered, cautioning her. "It's in balance with the value of the narcotics you were found with."

"But I didn't–" Kathy began, but Portia shushed her.

"I'll have bail within the hour, and then, we will talk."

Alice let Portia leave the courtroom before rising to follow her. For a second, she saw Kathy look back, seemingly straight at her, but pretended she didn't see her as she turned and slouched away following Portia.

Kathy watched as Portia put a few cars between their cars to keep an eye on her for the route home. She hadn't said anything to Portia about Detective Leskowitz being in the courtroom today or about his visit to the jail. She also hadn't said anything about the flash of blonde she had

seen. It had belonged to a punk rocker chick in the back of the court who sat back insolently as she waited on her own case or whatever the dozens of other spectators were there for. For a second, Kathy had thought she recognized the woman, and then, just as quickly, she dismissed it as her imagination. Kathy was more concerned with her own freedom right now.

Portia watched Kathy drive confidently along, and she didn't see anyone watching the Porsche. She admired the car Alice had once owned. Her own Porsche wasn't nearly in the class of that one. She never noticed the ordinary sedan following her as she followed Kathy.

One night, Alice was just getting ready to leave the house after watching her family when she saw the cops getting out of their car and heading towards the gate. They climbed over the fence. She ducked in the hedges to watch them, knowing the dark hid her better than anything else. She snuggled into her warm jacket to fight the cold.

She could see Coco barking at the cops. Coco was wagging her tail as she approached them, then one officer pulled his firearm and shot her. The dog went down with what looked like convulsions. From what Alice could see, the officers were discussing the situation when lights began to come on in the house. One officer climbed over the gate as the other officer shot Coco again, this time in the head, before he too headed over the fence. Alice would have lunged after the two men, but she knew their drawn guns would be aimed at her in an instant. She saw lights come on in the house. She watched the officers climbing over the fence, and one of them was having a little more trouble than the other.

"What is going on here?" Kathy called before she was halfway down the driveway. It was then, she saw Coco. Alice could make out her wife's expression as she stared in horror at the sight of their dead pet.

"Are you the property owner?" the police called from beyond the gate.

"Yes, I'm Kathy Weaver, and this is my property. What happened here?" she asked as she got closer.

"That dog attacked one of our officers," he began lamely.

"A Golden Retriever attacked one of your officers?" she clarified in a disbelieving voice. She looked down at the obviously dead dog, which had two holes in its beautiful body.

"Yes, it came right after him and grabbed his leg. He was in fear for his life," he told her, watching her reactions. He could see she wasn't wearing much, and he appreciated the view. The shirt Kathy wore did nothing to hide her cold and erect nipples. He had, of course, been looking to see if she had any weapons. Alice wanted to slap the smirk off his face as he looked at her wife...*her* wife.

"What was the officer doing on my property?" she asked incredulously. Anyone who knew Golden Retrievers knew they were the most congenial of dogs.

Yeah, put him on the spot, thought Alice as she watched the scene before her.

"He wasn't on your property. She grabbed his leg through the gate," he said, gesturing to the gaps in the iron fence.

"You're lying," she answered angrily. "I saw him climb over the fence. Now, let's try this once again...What was the officer doing on my property without a search warrant?" she asked ominously.

He flushed as he realized she had caught him. "We were investigating a missing child," he told her.

"And you thought the child was on my property?" she asked, looking down at Coco again. Her coat began to blow in the breeze that had come up.

"We were investigating," he said lamely.

"I want your names and badge numbers," she answered.

"Ms. Weaver," she heard a voice behind her and saw Nan coming up with her cell phone in her hand.

"Nan, take pictures of this," she gestured to the dead dog and the officers.

"It was a mistake. The dog attacked an officer," he began to defend himself and the actions of his partner lamely.

"It surely was a mistake," she returned hotly. "This was a family dog and the friendliest dog you would ever want to meet. If you were on my property, she had the legal right to defend it. She lived here, you didn't." Her voice was rising in her ire.

Easy, Kathy. Keep your cool.

"We had probable cause–" he began again but she interrupted.

"You're a liar," she said disgustedly. She could hear the cell phone camera taking pictures behind her. She turned to Nan and asked, "Do you have the capability to film with that?"

Nan nodded, and at Kathy's nod, she pressed a few buttons to activate the video on her cell.

Alice shrank farther into the shadows just in case the camera might catch her.

Kathy turned back to the officer that was speaking and looked beyond him to the officer on the other side of the police car. She could see a couple neighbors coming down their driveways too. "I want your name and badge numbers NOW," she said ominously.

"Now, ma'am. I'm willing to give them to you, but you need to calm down," he answered patronizingly.

"Coco!" she heard the distress in the voices of her children. Alice had never wanted to go to her children and comfort them more than she did at that moment. She remained hidden, angrily watching the cops and her wife.

Kathy turned around to see her children hurrying down the driveway. "Go back to the house *now!*" she ordered. Both Emily and Sean halted at her tone, but she could see the anguish on their faces. They could see the dead dog at her feet. "NOW!" she ordered again. They both looked up at her with tears running down their young faces and reluctantly turned around. They looked back repeatedly as they headed back up the stairs to the front door where they had been watching, putting their arms around each other for comfort. Alice was seething. She wanted desperately to help her family.

Kathy was furious and turned on the cop again. "Badge numbers and names," she repeated for the third time, and the camera phone recorded the officer's response. The officer that was hiding didn't give his name or badge number, but the one in front of her that had identified himself as Officer Michaels gave them the name of Officer McGuiness. Just as he finished providing this information, their security company came driving up. Seeing the cop car parked there, they pulled up and stopped alongside it. Alice mentally repeated the names of the officers several times, so she wouldn't forget them. Her agile mind knew it wouldn't forget them or their faces despite the shadows.

"Can we help?" someone called from a window in the security vehicle.

"These officers just shot and killed my Golden Retriever," Kathy called loud enough for the neighbors to hear as well as the security officer in the car.

That's it, Kathy. Get the word out to as many people as will listen. Don't let them get away with this.

"Now, ma'am. It was an accident–" the officer began before Kathy turned on him again, interrupting.

"An accident is something that happens by *accident*. This was deliberate murder!" she countered. "How dare you come on my private property uninvited and shoot my dog when she is just doing her job!" she shouted. "You and your partner," she sneered, "have a lot to answer for!"

"A mistake has been made here, ma'am, and we will straighten it out," he tried to placate her as her voice got louder in her angst.

"Your partner deliberately killed my dog, and then, you tried to lie about it to me. I clearly saw your partner climb back over the closed gate. You are an idiot if you think you can whitewash this and call it an accident or mistake."

He swallowed audibly and looked decidedly uncomfortable.

She glanced at his shoulder patch. "What the hell are L.A. police officers doing here in Palos Verdes?" she asked. She watched as the security officers got out of their patrol car. They looked a little uneasy.

"I told you we were following up on a lead," he began lamely.

"Bullshit. You are out of your jurisdiction, and you know it!" she told him bluntly. She looked at the security officer and ordered him, "Call Palos Verdes Police and get them out here immediately." He nodded in response and reached into the patrol car.

Kathy looked at several of her neighbors, many who were standing a good ten feet away from the patrol cars, and she addressed them, "They killed Coco, and they were trespassing on my property," she explained. She immediately saw the compassionate looks on their faces. Many were pet owners too and everyone knew each other's *fur kids*, as well as the children from the various houses. She heard a murmuring begin among them.

"Now, ma'am, you are blowing this out of proportion," the officer tried to bluff her and intimidate her, but Kathy wasn't having any of it.

"I'll give you 'blowing it out of proportion.' You will be lucky if you get to keep your job," she told him succinctly. She rubbed her arms again against the cold ocean wind.

"There is no need for threats," he tried to warn her.

"Oh, no. This isn't a threat, this is a *promise*," she warned him with a little smile.

By the time the Palos Verdes police and the L.A. County Sheriff's office showed up, there were many more neighbors standing about and discussing the situation. Kathy was livid and had told her story repeatedly. She told how she had awoken to the sound of a gunshot and heard a second shot ring out as she went to investigate. She told how she saw the rotund officer heaving himself over her wrought iron fence, and she repeated the lie she had been told. When she mentioned they had visual evidence of everything on the cell phone, the police demanded the phone.

"Oh, no. I'm not stupid," she told them. "You can get copies of this video from my lawyer tomorrow," she added, refusing to give up the phone and gesturing Nan back from the now open gate.

"We need that cell phone for evidence," one of the officers countered and held out his hand.

"No, you need the evidence, so it disappears," she returned and blocked his attempt to take it from Nan, who backed away warily.

"You are interfering in an investigation," someone else tried to bluster her into turning over the phone.

Don't give in to their bullying, Kathy. Stand your ground.

"Yes, I'm sure I am, but I'm also sure that the officers trespassed and shot an innocent dog," she countered. She wasn't backing down.

Atta girl.

"We can arrest you for interfering," one of the sheriffs tried.

Kathy smiled. "Do you realize the negative publicity that would ensue?" she gestured toward the neighbors, many who had taken out their own cell phones and were filming the encounter.

The cops backed down but insisted that the *evidence* be in their hands by tomorrow. Kathy had a list of badges and names that Nan recorded before her battery died. By the time the officers all left, Alice was exhausted from trying to memorize all the names.

"Ma'am, can I help you with the body?" the security officer offered, holding up a wool blanket he had pulled from the trunk of his patrol car.

Kathy nodded once and thanked him, then watched as he wrapped the dog in the blanket, hiding it from view.

"Where do you want me to put this?" he asked kindly as he lifted the heavy and previously robust dog.

Kathy directed him towards a spot in the garden, and he left the swaddled body there. Alice looked up towards the house to see her

children's faces pressed against the glass, watching everything that had happened. She thought she could see the tears on their ravaged faces even from this far away. Alice watched as Kathy and Nan made their way back to the house, cursing under her breath when she heard the sprinklers come on and they inundated her. She made her way back to her car, which was parked quite some ways from the house, narrowly missing being seen by the increased patrols in the area. She was relieved to get back to the house in the valley but had to stop at the gym first and take a hot shower before going to the house to crawl into her sleeping bag. She fired up the computer and checked the security footage of the house. She saw the cops and was relieved there was no sign of herself on them, then signed off the computer and lay back down. This situation was getting out of hand, but she didn't yet know what she could do.

Alice watched the security footage in the house whenever she could see her family on it. She was thrilled to see Kit looking older, and of course, hale and hearty. She realized she must be at college now. She yearned to take her oldest daughter in her arms and give her a hug. She saw, but could not hear, Kathy arguing with the teen during her visit. She surmised by the gestures they were talking about Emily, who was looking worse than ever. She knew she would have to talk to the doctor and soon. Emily looked terrible. She was becoming thinner and thinner. She reminded Alice of concentration camp survivors she had seen on documentaries. Since the cameras only showed black and white, it made everything look quite sinister.

When she saw the television coverage of the killing, Alice was pleased that Kathy had given the reporters the tapes that showed the officers going over the fence. The lust to kill those men was burning inside her, but she had to be careful as she began to follow Officers Michaels and McGuiness and learn about their lives and routines. Right now, they were too well-known, too carefully watched, and she had almost been seen a couple times as she compiled a dossier on both the officers. She was even more interested when they met with other officers, particularly Detective Dewayne Leskowitz, the brother of the locksmith, the man that had been killed. She wondered at their friendship as she observed them.

Things got even more interesting when Internal Affairs became involved. Alice was annoyed when they assigned Special Agent Miller to the case. Something about the woman just bugged Alice. Maybe it was because she was usually dressed in a clean-cut suit. It looked tailored and fit the woman's physically fit body perfectly. She always seemed to stand at attention and Alice wondered if she worked out. She wasn't beautiful but obviously took pride in her appearance. She had short hair, almost as short as Alice's, which had begun growing back, but the officer's hair had blonde feathered tips, which gave her a masculine look. Something about her just irked the hell out of Alice.

She didn't like that she wasn't *in* on the information, so she tried to break into the cop's computer but found the laptop she had purchased was inadequate. She longed for the computers she had at the house. Some of them were outdated, but they contained programs that enabled her to find out anything she wished to know. She consoled herself with tapping into Portia Spiros' computer and finding some of the information. Eventually, she learned that Kathy was exonerated and the three cops—Officer Ramirez, Officer Rogers, and Officer Green— were admonished by the judge. Still, they continued operating, and now, she had three more names to add to the portfolio she was creating.

Gathering information took a lot of painstaking work, and Alice was worried about Emily since she could only get so much information from the security system. Hiding in the house was easier now with Coco gone, but the two employees working there still made it difficult. It wasn't often they were both off or the children were not at home. She didn't find out until the third day of her stay that Emily was in the hospital. Slipping into the hospital was fairly easy, but she was nearly caught by Kathy as she gazed longingly at her daughter. Backing into the shadows of the large handicap accessible bathroom, she watched over her wife. She was grateful when Kathy fell asleep in the room and she was able to make her escape.

From the data on Portia's laptop, she was able to find one Sara Penn, the woman who used her cell phone camera to tape when Kathy was pulled over and arrested. Alice anonymously mailed her one thousand dollars cash. She had clearly captured the damning video evidence against the police. It helped Kathy's case that Sara had gotten a clear recording when Officer Green muttered, "Got the rich bitch," to another officer. That was well after the female officer tried to give chase and a clear, "Hey, give me that!" was heard before the recording got bouncy and distorted from the bystander's escape. Sara had returned to the scene though, and she stood behind the crowd to get a second recording that destroyed the case against Kathy.

Alice watched as Sara went to her mail box and found the envelope, looking around almost guiltily as she opened the solid envelope and looked inside. She quickly went indoors, and Alice walked away. She would have to send more money but in smaller bills. She had thought one-hundred-dollar bills would be best, but after seeing how the woman lived, she realized she was barely subsisting on disability. Alice was pleased when she learned Kathy and Portia had given the woman a part-time job. Still, she was certain the cash money would be welcome and made the effort to send her more.

Alice also learned both Officers Michaels and McGuiness, who were sued by Kathy and Portia, settled out of court. Alice grinned when she saw Kathy had donated that money to the local animal shelters. She wondered if Kathy would adopt another dog for their grieving children.

Alice was idly watching security video of the house one night when she saw Kathy coming down the hall all dressed up. She lost her for a second but picked her up again when she came down the stairs. Kathy looked stunning, and Alice was pleased until she realized there was someone standing in their foyer. She zoomed in slightly on the footage. It was that detective! Dammit! Kathy was *dating*? Alice wasn't sure how she felt about that. She knew Kathy thought she was dead, but still, wasn't it...? Then, she began to count the months she had been gone and the months she had been back but not made herself known. Shit! No wonder Kathy was moving on. She watched on the outside camera as the woman followed Kathy out of the house, nearly stumbled, then quickly recovered and ran down the stairs to open Kathy's door. It was a typical cop car, and she zoomed in on it. A Grand Marquis. Figures! She watched as the woman opened the door and tucked Kathy in...as if Kathy couldn't do it for herself! She watched them drive down the driveway and down the street before they were out of sight of the cameras she could use.

Shit, shit, shit! Her wife was dating!

Alice was able to follow the couple on their second date, at least she thought it was the second date, but she might have missed others. It was easy to watch her family because Kathy had brought Sean and Emily on her date with the detective to the Santa Monica Pier.

'Detective Linda, what are you doing with my family?' she thought as she kept herself hidden but couldn't help watching them.

She could see Sean wasn't happy with Linda around, but Emily, who looked so pathetically frail, was having a good time. She could see Kathy would sit down and rest when Emily got tired, so it wasn't awkward for the teen. She also saw when Kathy pulled Sean aside and gave him a good talking to. He behaved after that. Alice had to be very careful in her surveillance. Linda was a cop, and from what Alice had observed, she was a good cop. There were several times Alice had to stop watching, turn away, or even move away quickly because Linda looked up a little too suddenly. Perhaps her cop senses were going off.

Alice was busy, so she couldn't be there for all Kathy's dates. She'd completed portfolios on each of the officers involved in setting Kathy up and the ones that had killed Coco. She was getting ready to make a move…or two…or five.

Officer Michaels was her first target. She had to make it look accidental, and learning his routine was easy, especially since he was fired from the police force. He spent a lot of time sulking about his situation and this made it easier to observe him. He was also careless, which surprised Alice at first. After all, he was a cop. Then, she realized it took all kinds, and really, he was a bad cop, so it all made a lot more sense. As she slipped through his unlocked patio door, her gloves ensuring she left no fingerprints, she listened to see if he had company. She could hear his snores coming from the couch. It had been a long time since she did any sort of breaking in, and she realized she was unpracticed. Even gathering the tools she needed had taken more thought and time than she had expected.

Carefully and slowly, remembering the house as she had seen it in daylight when she cased it, she walked around the dining area table and towards the couch. Slipping a vial from her pocket, she checked it in the light of the television to make sure she had the right one. The light from the TV was the only light in the room. She hadn't expected to be able to give him anything orally and didn't want to leave any traces of what he ingested. She had another vial in her pocket, just in case, and she was glad as she dripped one drop below his nose as he snored sonorously. He snorted slightly at the moisture on his upper lip, but the fumes from that one drop entered his nasal cavity and were soon permeating his system. It took no time at all for the snores to cut off as he fell into an even deeper kind of sleep. Alice waited to make sure he was unconscious before she walked around the couch and closed the blinds. She turned and was disgusted to see he was exposed, his male parts hanging out of his shorts.

She had planned this carefully but was prepared to change her plans if she had to. Seeing him laying there, helpless, she considered all sorts of things she could do in revenge for him killing Coco. A Golden Retriever was one of the happiest dogs on Earth. Why he would even try to tell a story of the dog attempting to bite him and then, deny the actual film footage, she didn't know. She would make him pay, and seeing him exposed, she considered exactly what she would do.

Michaels woke up slowly. It was early morning, so he must have fallen asleep in front of the television. Suddenly, he realized he was tied up. What the hell? He was also naked and spread-eagled on his bed. He realized something was in his mouth and was horrified to realize it was his own underwear. By the smell of it, it was dirty. Not the most fastidious of men, he realized he hadn't done his laundry in a while. Looking around the room, he was shocked to see someone dressed all in black sitting in the corner watching him. It was a blonde with very short hair. She was overly skinny, no meat on her bones, and he liked women who were curvy. The black of her clothing looked shocking against the white of her skin.

"Mmmm," he tried to speak and saw an almost feral smile appear on the blonde woman's face, but it was her eyes that truly unnerved him. They appeared to be cat-like, and they were a strange color. Yellow? Orange? He must be imagining things. "Mmmm mmmm," he tried again, pulling against the bonds on his wrists and ankles. It was then, he realized she had used clothing to tie him up. Why not ropes? He raised up enough to see his feet tied with jeans and was beyond horrified to see a tie clip on the foreskin of his penis, which looked like it was attached to a lamp cord. His eyes opened wide at the sight, and he looked beseechingly to the woman, who was watching him examine himself.

Alice rose from her position. She had been waiting for the moron to wake up. She was becoming impatient, and there was nothing interesting on the man's television. He had only basic cable, and from everything she had learned about him from rifling his home, he was cheap. As she tied him up using his dirty clothes, she made sure he couldn't escape. She could tell the man needed a shower. He had a perfectly nice bathroom, which she used, making sure to wash it down afterward so she didn't leave any traces of DNA.

"Hello, Officer Michaels," she said conversationally. He kept glancing at the gag in his mouth and the ties on his wrists. Occasionally, his eyes flicked down towards his penis. She watched him struggle against the bonds. "You won't get out of those bonds. I was taught by experts. They also taught me about interrogation and torture," she told him, watching when his eyes widened as he realized the significance of the tie clip and the lamp cord. "You see, I have some questions for you, and if you answer them honestly, you will make things much better for yourself. If not, well," she gestured at his prone and very exposed body, "it won't go well for you." Alice had learned a long time ago that people's imaginations could be used against them. They could always be relied on to make things worse in the right situation, and this was one of those times. "Now, I know you were a police officer, but what I want to know is how you know Detective Dewayne Leskowitz and why you were doing his bidding?" She watched his facial expressions closely, his eyes especially. She could see the fear in them, not of her so much but of the information she had just given him. She also read when a crafty look came into his eyes, so she continued, "Yes, you could yell or scream bloody murder when I take the gag off, but I suggest you answer truthfully and fully."

She lifted the cord to the lamp. It was one that had a dimmer switch on it. He recognized it as the one from his bedroom. "You see, if I turn it on, it begins to send electricity into the cord, and you know where that goes, right?"

He glanced at his penis. It was limp and beyond shriveled. If it had a mind of its own, it would invert and disappear right now. He could feel the need to pee beginning, and at that thought, his penis enlarged slightly.

"Arouses you a little?" she asked, laughing at him and the morning wood he was experiencing. She might not be into men, but she knew enough to know their physical peculiarities. "Think of the electricity coursing through your penis as I increase or decrease it with this little dial." They both watched as he shriveled immediately.

Michaels knew if she turned on the electricity, he would pee himself. The need to pee was growing, and that would cause him to become erect if he didn't keep thinking about the pain she was threatening. If he told her about Leskowitz though, he just might be killed. The man had paid him to do a job and had warned him about squealing to internal affairs. He wondered who this woman was and how she knew so much.

"I bet you are wondering how to get out of the predicament you find yourself in without telling me what I want to know, aren't you?"

He shook his head, denying her statement and question. She'd watched his face and eyes closely and knew he was worrying. Sweat was starting to bead on his forehead.

"So, if I show you how much this is going to hurt," she indicated the lamp cord and dimmer switch, "will you be more cooperative? Or should I trust that I don't need to demonstrate?"

He shook his head. "Mmmmm, Mmmmmf," he tried to speak through the dirty underwear. He was trying not to think about what was on them. They were wet from the saliva in his mouth, and he was worried he might choke on it.

"So, do you want option A," she held up the dimmer switch and paused, "or do you want option B?" she pointed at the gag in his mouth.

He shook his head at option A and nodded emphatically at option B.

Alice smiled, and he almost instinctively shuddered. There was something about her that told him she was dangerous...those eyes! Alice leaned over him and warned, "Remember, honest answers only."

It took a moment after the underwear had been removed from his mouth for him to get the saliva in his mouth working properly. She'd merely pulled the underwear to his neck and he could still smell the dirty garment. He swallowed and began, "I just work with the detective. He promised me some money to do some things for him."

"What things?"

"I…" he began, hesitating, and Alice knew there was more than her wife involved in this relationship. He told her things that she filed away for future uses…maybe. Still, he didn't get around to why he was following Kathy or why he had killed Coco. He'd been talking for a few minutes when Alice saw he thought he'd lulled her into a false sense of security, and as he took a deep breath to scream, she used her thumb to roll the dimmer switch to the on position. As he began to scream, it was cut off midway when Alice shoved the dirty underwear back in his mouth. She was glad she was wearing gloves and didn't have to handle it.

She saw the tears welling in his eyes and turned off the dimmer switch. He had stiffened as the electricity coursed through the cord into the metal of the tie clip and through the sensitive foreskin of his penis. She smiled evilly. "I did warn you," she said conversationally. In fact, her voice had never changed tone. He couldn't tell if she were angry or excited or what. Instead, those strange yellow-gold eyes squinted slightly at him, making them look more feline. Was that his imagination?

He blinked away the tears as the pain left his body, but there was an odd tingling in his groin area.

"Let me tell you something, Michaels. If you cause me to turn this dial again, I'm going to leave it on and walk away until you die from electrocution to your cock." At the widening of his eyes, she continued, "I've run out of patience with you, and you haven't even begun to get to the good stuff." He frowned slightly to show he didn't know what she meant. He thought he'd told her a lot. "Tell me why he had you follow Kathy Weaver and harass her?" His eyes widened at the specifics she was asking. "Are you ready to talk now?" At his emphatic nod, she reached for the underwear. He tried to lunge against her, but his arms were too taut, and he merely knocked against her.

She immediately turned the dial back on and watched as the man realized his fate. She untied him after he was dead, rubbing any telltale marks from his wrists and ankles. She threw the dirty clothes back onto the heap she had found on the dirty floor. She left him naked on the bed and turned the electricity on again. She turned it up higher and saw the lights flicker in the early morning. She figured when they found him, they might think he was into this kind of homemade kink, so she left his hands near his penis as though he had been enjoying himself.

She slipped out of his place before the sun was fully up and tried to look like a jogger in the neighborhood as she made her way back to her car, having exchanged the rental for a good, used, unmarked car. She now had more information on Leskowitz and was wondering how she could use that to interview McGuiness, who she had also been stalking. He was next on her *interview* list since he was the other officer who had helped to kill Coco.

Alice researched new cameras. She wanted to put a few in the house that she could control and weren't so obvious. She was enjoying herself in the stores, feeling as though she were a spy as she played with the gadgets. Some of them had audio as well as video and were much smaller than the system she had installed around their house when they originally bought it. She was almost relieved when Kathy left the house with Emily for a doctor appointment. Now, she only had to worry about the employees. Watching her family leave through binoculars as she pretended to bird watch, she quickly made her way through the back gate and into the house to set the cameras up in the most inconspicuous places, spots that were currently blind. She removed the cameras' red lights, so her family wouldn't know they were there. As she looked at their locations later, switching them on remotely, she made mental notes to move a few at the next opportunity.

Alice got stuck in the house once. Mrs. Fernandez came back much sooner than she had anticipated and effectively trapped her. When Nan joined her, she was sure she heard something in the house. She looked for the source of the noise Alice had made, then shrugged it off when she couldn't find anything. Nan would never know how close she came to be strangled. Alice couldn't afford to be found...not yet. She wasn't ready; there were still many things to figure out here. Kathy had complicated things by dating a cop. As she watched her family go about their daily lives during the night she was trapped there, she snuck into their rooms. Sean nearly caught her as he turned over in his sleep. Emily looked horrible, and Alice knew she would have to go see the doctor. That meant revealing herself to the man, but they needed him, and he needed to save her daughter. As she gazed at Kathy, she heard her breathing change and ducked down before she caught Alice watching her sleep, the moonlight shining across her. Something must have told her she was being watched though, and she looked around her room carefully before falling back to sleep. Alice watched her through her night-vision goggles, having come across some of her old toys. Alice was cramped up in a crouch before she allowed herself to move, watching Kathy carefully before she slipped out of the bedroom and then the house, reactivating the alarm with a delay, so she could get away.

"You were watching us. Why didn't you let me know you were alive?" Kathy asked, indignant at the story and getting angrier.

"Because you were dating a cop, who, for all I knew, was as dirty as the others. I had to find out and it took a while," she pointed out.

Kathy didn't like it but had to know the whole story. While she knew logically that Alice wasn't telling her some of the details, she also knew she should shut up, so her wife could finish the tale, which she suspected was coming to its end.

Alice watched on the computer as her wife watched television with Linda the cop. She sneered as they made out occasionally and nearly cheered as Kathy stopped it from going too far. She could see that the cop wanted to go further, but she had made the mistake of letting Kathy think she was setting the pace. Logically, she could see why Kathy was attracted to the cop. She could see that Linda was physically fit. *She* wouldn't have been attracted to Linda, but she could see why Kathy was.

With the information she got out of Michaels and using her own special talents, she found McGuiness was much more forthcoming about Leskowitz and his activities. She had very little trouble making him disappear. At least he had a wife and a life, unlike Michaels, who had been pathetic. She had to rush things a little at this point because she had seen from the computer video link that Kathy was planning to go out of town. She'd watched her pack a small bag and had packed one for herself.

As Alice followed Kathy one day, she wondered where she was heading. As Kathy got on the interstate heading north, Alice wondered if she had found out about one of Alice's many secrets? Interstate 5 was busy and that was probably why Kathy didn't notice the sedan following her. Alice was more worried about running out of gas or the old clunker falling apart. After all, Kathy was driving her Porsche, but as they got farther north Alice suspected where Kathy was going. That was fortunate, since she was finally forced to get off the interstate for gas long before the more fuel-efficient Porsche. Back on the interstate, Alice pushed the old car to the legal limit, following a speeder's tail but leaving several car lengths between her and the speeding car in case of an accident. She hoped that would encourage the police to go after them first for speeding since they were in front. Eventually, Alice caught up to Kathy.

The Motel 6 that Kathy pulled into in Sacramento was a pigsty, and Alice, who was much more fastidious, had no choice but to sleep in the sedan to keep an eye on Kathy since she took one of the last rooms.

Alice had gone for something to eat and was parked outside the rental storage facility when Kathy arrived in the Porsche. Alice sighed. Somehow Kathy had found out about the rental unit. Alice wondered what she would do, but if she continued to watch her, she would have exposed herself. Within an hour Kathy was backing out of the place. Enough time had gone by that Alice felt she must have found the sedan in the storage unit she kept there, which was not unlike the one she was driving now. She wondered if Kathy had perhaps also paid the bill? It was then, she realized she'd had the bills for the Portland storage facility sent here to the Sacramento facility. Her educated guess was right on target, and she followed Kathy as she turned north towards Portland instead of south, which would have led her home to Los Angeles. She sighed. Damn Kathy and her curiosity. She only hoped the cop her wife was dating didn't know where Kathy was or where she was going.

Alice wondered what Kathy was thinking about as she watched her sitting in a coffee shop after her visit to the storage facility. At the Portland facility, she was able to see Kathy cut the locks on not one but two storage units. One held the Jeep she had used years ago, and the other was a workshop. She watched Kathy rummage around in them after she got the Jeep going. She eventually got the Jeep to turn over after several tries and then left it running as she went through the units. She finally drove it back inside and left it, locking up both units and heading for the office. Alice could only surmise Kathy was paying the bill. She hoped she paid in cash, so there wouldn't be a trail to follow back to her. That was why she had had the bill for this place sent to the Sacramento storage facility. The bill for Sacramento, which was paid once a year, was sent to a post office box she kept. Kathy must have found it and traced everything back.

Alice wondered if Kathy remembered why she had been up here in Portland all those years ago? Kathy had been missing, and it had appeared she was dead, but Alice had found out differently. She remembered the incident and Alex 'The Flybird' Johansen's involvement in their lives very well. A lot of people had died for what they did to her wife. As she watched Kathy leave the facility, she worried about the memories that might be going through her wife's mind. Kathy had been quite fragile for a long time after that episode. Alice watched her looking thoughtful in the coffee shop, her own food on the car seat next to her, the garbage building up on the floor of the sedan. Fastidious by nature, Alice wished Kathy would just go home, so she could clean out this car. It was a piece of crap car, nonetheless she needed it to remain anonymous, so she could continue to follow her wife.

Alice was relieved when Kathy headed south once again on the 5 Interstate. The time spent waiting for her wife to leave had her thinking back to the hospital here in Portland and the fact that her wife had nearly been lost to her for good, mentally. Only going to the island Alice owned had finally allowed Kathy to slowly heal. That, and a bevy of mental health care professionals before it, plus the revenge they took on the last of the people who had not only tried to keep Kathy a prisoner as a sex slave but had started in on Emily. She didn't want to think of that awful time, but if those people hadn't gone after their daughter, Alice wouldn't have been on to them and discovered Kathy was alive. Fate was a bitch like that.

Alice was confused when Kathy headed not to Sacramento but towards San Francisco, but she understood when Kathy stopped at Stanford. Alice's heart nearly melted as she watched their daughter, Kit enveloping her mother in a hug. She'd grown up so much. She smiled as Kit began to show Kathy around the campus. Years had passed since any of the adults had gone there. Alice remembered the years her sister, Constance had attended this school and had introduced her not only to her future wife, Kathy, but also Portia Spiros, now a lawyer and Andie Wilson, an accountant. They were both working for Kathy now, untangling Alice's complicated financial life. She was waxing nostalgic about her dead sister, Connie when she became aware that Kathy might have seen her. Ducking around and trying to make it look natural, by the time Kathy moved to see her better, she had disappeared. The near disaster left her upset with herself as well as the students she bumped into trying to get away.

"I thought that was you!" Kathy exclaimed as Alice told her about the visit. "I couldn't see for sure, and then, you were gone."

"Yes, you almost caught me," she admitted with a grin as she remembered. She wondered if she had wanted to be caught. She continued her story. She had promised to tell her wife everything, and while some of the details had been left out, she was being as honest as she could with her wife. She only hoped the information would be used to help them repair their marriage and move forward together, not as ammunition against her.

Alice hadn't needed to follow Kathy back from Stanford once she set out on her return trip to Los Angeles. The long, eight-hour drive meant that Alice had to stop for gas more often, and once Kathy was out of sight and headed south, she let her go and followed at a leisurely pace. Alice checked to make sure her wife was home safely, then returned to her life, such as it was. She had become a watcher and didn't like it.

Alice was annoyed. Not only was Kathy going on regular dates with the cop, but it just might be getting serious. Watching them go to a pizza joint, she realized she couldn't blend in, so instead, she was forced to sit out in the rain, hunched down because there were cops everywhere. This must be one of those places where the cops all hung out. She guessed that 'Linda the cop,' that's how she thought of her, was introducing her personal life into her professional life. Cops were notoriously protective of their own. She wondered how Kathy would get along with the other police officers once they realized she had sued the dirty cops who killed Coco. Even dirty cops had loyal 'friends.' Watching her wife on a date with the woman and unable to see clearly through the torrential rain that had struck LA, Alice was miserable and unhappy. She only hoped that none of the cops spotted her watching them.

Alice perked up when the two women finally left in Alice's Porsche, but she was concerned as she watched Kathy driving a little too fast. From the silhouettes she saw in the windows occasionally, it looked like the women were arguing. That made her happy until she saw Kathy take the Porsche through one of those rain-filled dips in the road a little too fast. The roads were slick from the storm, and while Kathy was a careful driver, that didn't mean others were as careful. Alice watched in horror as another driver shot into the path of the Porsche. She saw Kathy pull hard on the wheel and then, the Porsche was spinning out of control. It struck the other vehicle and the two cars careened apart, ending up on opposite sides of the road. Alice got out of her car and ran frantically to the upside-down Porsche, sure she would find her wife dead. She could see both airbags had inflated. She kicked at the windshield until it shattered, then, quickly poked and prodded at Kathy to assess the damage. She tried to pull at her wife, but the steering wheel and airbag was in the way. Using her pocket knife, she popped the airbag and pulled at Kathy again, but the seat belt held her tight. Alice could smell gasoline and worried she wouldn't be in time as she cut the seat belt and gently lowered Kathy to the ceiling of the totaled Porsche before pulling her away from the crash. For a moment, she considered leaving Linda the cop in the wreckage but thought that would seem suspicious. Besides, what if Kathy loved this woman? She finally decided it was the decent thing to do and pulled the woman from the car, laying her next to her wife. She checked Kathy again, making sure she was breathing. For a second, she thought Kathy had opened her eyes, but then, she was unconscious again. Alice could hear sirens and quickly left the scene.

"That *was* you!" Kathy interrupted her. She had thought she was losing her mind when she saw Alice at the crash. Someone had pulled them both from the totaled Porsche, that much was evident from the cut seat belt and the fact they had been moved well away from the accident and were both laid out waiting for the emergency personnel. "I called for you," she remembered.

"I'm sorry, I couldn't be seen…not yet," she repeated the refrain. "I was just so relieved that you weren't hurt worse."

"Did you check on me at the hospital?"

"Of course. I had to know how you were."

Somehow, the knowledge that Alice had rescued her and her girlfriend, then checked up on her at the hospital made Kathy feel all warm and cozy.

"You didn't look too good," Alice teased.

"Look? Hell, I didn't *feel* too good," Kathy answered, remembering the concussion as well as the cuts and abrasions.

"You also ruined my Porsche," Alice pointed out.

"Yeah, well, there was that," she remembered.

Alice didn't bring it up at that moment but seeing Emily under the lights of the hospital when she visited Kathy had been horrible. It seemed even worse than what she usually saw on the computer screen from the videos. That poor child had been so ill. It was seeing her like that that made her realize how much Emily looked like her. While Alice hadn't been skeletal like this, the shape of the young woman's eyes reminded her of her own; the same feline look was there. After checking things out with her own eyes, Alice nearly revealed herself, but she knew the hospital was not the time or place with the cop there all the time.

Alice didn't mention that she had also gone over in furious anger to check on the other driver. Finding the idiot slightly drunk and awake, she had punched him right in the face, hurting her wrist in the process.

Alice had especially looked out for Kathy that first night in the hospital, which was a good thing since someone snuck into the room. She had sunk back in the shadows of the bathroom. He appeared drunk by the way he weaved as he came into Kathy's room. She heard him clearly whisper to Kathy, "I could cut off everything you need right now!" She knew her wife was too weak to fight him off, but Alice wasn't. He continued, "We both know what you did to my brother. It wouldn't take a moment for me to do the same to you!" Rather than

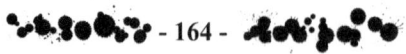

kill him there, Alice remained still, the rage inside her building. She was going to be especially inventive when his time came. She had been moving up her list. She was about to follow him out after giving him a few seconds head start, when someone else came into the room. Linda the cop settled into the chair. Alice had to wait until she dozed off in order to make her own escape and that took an unbearably long time.

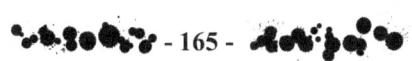

Dr. Wilkerson was pleasantly surprised to see Alice, not at his clinic as would have been normal, but instead, she appeared at his apartment. Not one to spend much time at home, dedicated to the fascinating research he adored and loved, he was staggered that anyone would be at his building, much less inside it when he got home one evening.

"Mrs. Weaver," he gasped, always respectful. "I thought you were dead?"

"Tales of my death are greatly exaggerated," she quipped, prepared to get up quickly if he acted inappropriately, like lunging for the gun she had found in the desk or going for the phone to call for help. "I understand my daughter is ill?" she underexaggerated.

He nodded, unsure what to say, but the question prodded him to explain about her blood. "I can't tell you how relieved I am that you are alive. We desperately need your blood in order to make an antidote to the infections that are attacking her blood."

"It's leukemia then?"

"No," he shook his head. "I think it's more a result of us combining the DNA of both you and your wife to make these children. I'll have to research it further, but I suspect that it only attacked the female child. Sean shows no signs of illness and is hale and hearty."

"Why couldn't you take his blood then?"

"They weren't a match," he explained, warming to his subject. He spent an hour outlining what he perceived to be the problem, what other things he could only guess at, and what he believed would happen if Alice would only come in and donate.

"So, you need a pint of my blood and then, she'll be better?"

"No, it's much more complicated than that. There are platelets, you understand that?" At her nod, he went on to explain how they would strip the blood down even further, add some medicines they had developed, and that combination might save Emily's life.

"So, you aren't certain it will even work?" she asked, wanting reassurance that her daughter was going to live. Seeing Emily in the hospital had really shaken Alice and compelled her to visit the doctor.

"No, there are no guarantees, and her weakened immune system is so far gone…" he said sadly.

Alice nearly kicked herself at the delay. She hadn't realized how dire Emily's situation was while watching her family these many months, and yet, she had seen the child was wasting away. It was all her fault! "Why isn't my wife a match?"

He explained that they had combined the DNA, but Mother Nature had determined who the child's genetic makeup would take after. "That's why I am not one hundred percent sure the treatment will work, but I'm betting you're closer a match," he said eagerly.

"You have to make sure no one sees me. In fact, I don't want anyone to know I'm alive yet—not my wife, not my children, no one," she emphasized, and he nodded.

He had wondered why she had come to his home instead of his lab. Too many people at the lab owed their livelihood to this benefactor and knew who Alice Weaver was. Her investment in their labs and research years ago had propelled them to the forefront of this technology. Her volunteering them for human experimentation, although her wife had been unaware of what she had volunteered them for, had given their lab an edge. Their company's theories had been born out and had produced Emily and Sean as well as other babies whose parents were willing to try the experimental procedures. Now, they had to counteract Mother Nature's attack on young Emily's system.

Alice donated blood the next day, late, after everyone else had left the lab. Dr. Wilkerson had shut down the cameras throughout the building for the hour the process took to complete. He called Kathy with the story that they had another treatment to give Emily, if she would please bring the child in.

Ready to give up, Kathy had almost refused, but the doctor was so persuasive, so eager, and so sure this would work, she couldn't say no. She brought the reluctant teen in for the first of many more treatments.

Alice was surprised at the car Kathy purchased to replace the Porsche. She had known she wouldn't get another Porsche, it wasn't her style, but the Lexus IS 350C in blue was a shock. It was classy, sophisticated, and when Alice thought about it, the car fit Kathy to a T. Watching her drive the four-seater convertible, she was envious and wanted to ride in it too. Alice wasn't happy to see the cop enjoying the ride with her wife. When it started to rain, Kathy put up the top and Alice admired its sleek lines. But she didn't like seeing the windows fog up when the cop sat in the car outside their garage talking to Kathy and the two women started making out. Alice wasn't certain, but she thought her wife was getting felt up and possibly more. She had to do something to make it stop. It was getting hard to see in the dark and the rain, which had become a light mist, and the two women making out was bugging Alice. She looked around for something she could do to distract them. She saw where the gardeners had missed cutting back some growth against the house and very deliberately pushed a tree branch through a window in the garage. She quickly moved away from the house, going deeper into the shadows and away from the yard light, but had anyone been looking, they would have seen her shape as she moved around.

She didn't know it at the time, but she had missed Sean by just moments as he looked out his bedroom window, peering through the darkness at the yard light to see if his mom was still out there. Alice listened to Linda and Kathy's conversation. They were making bad jokes about the broken glass.

"A pane or a pain?" Linda quipped with a grin.

"That's awful."

"Awful is as awful does," Linda answered and tried to take Kathy in her arms.

"Nuh uh, you have observers," Kathy said, avoiding her and pointing to where Sean was peering through the bedroom window again. Alice suddenly worried that her son had seen her duck into the shadows.

"Foiled again," the cop answered, sounding like some stupid TV show bad guy.

Kathy laughed, and they headed towards Linda's car. "I enjoyed our evening. Why were you so late to arrive?"

"You remember Officer McGuiness, the one who disappeared?"

Alice was suddenly alert, wondering if they had found him. It had been weeks. She saw Kathy nod before the cop continued. She had to be careful where she walked, staying to the shadows.

"They found him. It looks like suicide this time too," the cop told Kathy. Alice breathed a sigh of relief, wondering for just a moment if she had made it look authentic. The cops weren't stupid, and she couldn't allow a pattern to develop. It had been a while since she'd had to cover her tracks and vary her patterns. She'd left a lot of bodies back in Russia and Kazakhstan and hadn't had to cover those.

"What does that mean, 'this time too'?" Kathy asked her, and Alice wished Kathy would stop asking questions.

"You remember Officer Michaels, the other officer that committed suicide?" the cop asked her. Alice shook her head, *Don't make her think. Don't keep this conversation going.* And yet, she wanted to hear the information. She saw Kathy nod before the cop continued, "He committed suicide, but there are enough similarities to his suicide that they are re-opening his case. He may not have committed suicide after all. They both might have been set up."

"Why? How? They were dirty cops. Did someone–?" Kathy began to ask, then stopped.

Uh oh, Alice thought. She suspects something. Alice strained to listen.

"We aren't sure if another cop set them up or what. Yes, they were dirty, and killing your dog was the least of it. I can't investigate, so I took myself off the case."

"You did? Why?"

"Because I'm involved with you now, and it wouldn't be ethical to be involved in the case."

Yeah, you're dating a suspect and my wife, Alice mentally added, listening hard through the soft rain. She looked and thought she saw Kathy nod.

"Are you okay?" she heard Kathy ask, but either the cop didn't answer, or she had gestured. Alice couldn't really tell.

"I hate to think we have a cop killer."

"They weren't cops any longer," Kathy pointed out.

"Once a cop, always a cop."

Alice was becoming very uneasy as they dissected the information. She knew Kathy could put two and two together and come up with more than the cop knew or even suspected.

"I'm sorry," she heard Kathy say.

"For what?"

"I know they weren't friends of yours, but a cop is a cop."

What the hell did that mean?

"Thanks, babe. I should go. You make the arrangements for this weekend, and we'll get away."

What? This weekend? She realized more than a make out session had taken place in the car. She really didn't enjoy seeing the goodbye kiss either.

"I'll do that, and I'll let you know," Kathy said softly.

They both watched as the cop drove down the driveway, and Alice watched as Kathy took another thoughtful look at the broken window and shook her head before going inside.

Alice waited a while before slipping into the house through the door that was jury-rigged to bypass the alarm system. For some reason, she felt compelled to check on Kathy. For a second as she slipped into the room, she thought Kathy was awake. Finally, whatever compulsion had made her worry about her wife dissipated, and she was able to leave.

She quickly circled the house and went to her parked car, soaked to the skin and shivering. She headed for the twenty-four-hour gym to wash up and change her clothes, working out until she was sweaty again and exhausted, so she could go to the house in the valley and sleep. She did her laundry at a laundromat the next morning before hopping on her laptop and checking on the videos she had missed.

Alice was thrilled when Linda's work forced her to cancel her and Kathy's plans for a weekend away. She'd heard Kathy make the reservations, and her heart had dropped knowing this was 'their' weekend and sex would be involved. Now that it was to be cancelled, she could have cheered.

When Kathy gave the weekend off to their nanny, she had been surprised but thought it a very nice gift, but even Alice couldn't have foreseen the unexpected result of Kathy's generous gift.

The nanny resigned after her weekend away. It was time though— the children had long outgrown the need for a nanny. That Kathy had kept her on for so many years when they didn't need her just attested to her loyalty to their long-standing employee. Now, she was leaving, and Alice felt the time was right.

Alice was thrilled to see Kit come home as they said goodbye to the woman. Apparently, Nan was engaged to be married. Alice would have liked to congratulate Nan herself. Instead, she continued to watch her family voyeuristically.

There was an unexpected benefit to Nan being gone. Now, there was one less set of eyes to watch out for, and Alice used her old bedroom to hide in from time to time, becoming more daring.

Alice was pleased when she overheard Kit say, "Emily is looking better." She had thought it was her imagination or wishful thinking. When Kathy agreed with her, Alice mentally cheered. It had looked like Emily was gaining a little weight, and she was not nearly as pasty as she had been. It had taken so long to see any results that Alice had begun to despair that the platelets she continued to donate weren't working. Dr. Wilkerson's admonishment to be patient had Alice wanting to floor him. He had also commented on Alice's weight, asking if she was okay. He'd secretly run tests on her blood to make sure she wouldn't transmit anything to Emily as that would have been fatal.

Listening in on the cameras, Alice was annoyed to hear Kit ask, "So, when do I get to meet Linda?"

Kathy's answer had Alice sitting up to listen. "Well, I don't know. Something is going on at work, and she has been putting in very long hours." She'd wondered why the cop and Kathy hadn't rescheduled after their ruined weekend and why she hadn't been around as much. Perhaps, Alice's extracurricular activities were being noticed? At least, she knew she hadn't been messy or lazy about the crime scenes.

"Well, something happened at work. She can't or won't discuss it. It ruined our weekend plans a couple weeks ago. In fact, I gave our reservation to Nan, which is when Connor proposed."

"So, you could say you led to the defection of our nanny?" Kit teased.

Kathy was annoyed when she called Linda and invited her to meet her oldest daughter, and Linda had said she would *try*. Alice considered bugging Kathy's phones. She wanted to hear what Linda had said that pissed Kathy off, but she didn't tell Kathy that as she retold the story.

"You don't sound very happy about that?" Kit asked.

"Well, you kids didn't need a nanny anymore."

"No, we haven't needed a nanny for a long time, but it was nice to have her around."

"Yeah, well, it's not like we couldn't afford her," Kathy answered. Alice had smiled listening to this. She could see Kathy was a little embarrassed about keeping a nanny when the children were in their teens, but she simply hadn't had the heart to let the woman go.

"I get it. You were sentimental," Kit joked and nudged her. Then she asked, "Why don't you go visit Linda?"

"You mean at her work?" Kathy asked, surprised.

"Well, why not? Or is it forbidden since she works in Internal Affairs?"

"I don't know that it's forbidden..." Kathy mused, looking thoughtful and then asking, "Want to go for a ride in my new car?"

Kit's smile lit up as she eagerly nodded. "Can I drive?"

"Heck, no!" Kathy laughed.

Alice was out in the valley on her laptop and couldn't very well drive down to Linda's work, so she had no idea what happened until she heard them talking about it in the house later. Unfortunately, they didn't talk fully about what happened, but Alice could see Kathy was worried about something. She also saw when the cop arrived at the house that night for dinner and met Kit. She turned up the volume to hear what Kathy and the cop had to say to each other when Kit left them alone.

"Well? What happened with him?" Kathy asked.

"He said you killed his brother," Linda stated, and she was watching Kathy very closely.

"Who was his brother?" Kathy asked, and Alice cheered about the lie her wife was telling. She could tell Kathy was agitated but the cop couldn't. She wondered about that briefly but continued to watch avidly.

"That locksmith?" Linda reminded her.

"Okay?" Kathy shrugged.

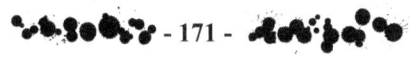

"What I'm about to tell you could get me fired if anyone else heard it, so what I tell you must remain confidential for now." Linda looked intently at Kathy to see if she could trust her with this information. Alice leaned into the computer as though that would help her see more clearly through the grainy video. She was frustrated that she wasn't there to listen to this exchange in person...she had been once or twice before.

"Okay?" Kathy's tone indicated a concerned interest.

Linda sighed, and Alice sensed she was about to confide something. "Remember that weekend two weeks ago when we had planned to go away together?" she waited for Kathy's nod before continuing. "We got a call about a loud, drunken party, and we had to go break it up. Nothing new about that, but it turned out to be a loud, drunken, *cop* party. Not only were they drunk, but a sex orgy had been going on. What we found was gruesome, and they all died from alcohol poisoning."

Alice smiled at the screen. She had wondered what happened with that bit of cleverness. She was strangely relieved too.

Linda wasn't done. "We arrived too late and got them to the hospital too late. The charcoal didn't work, and they all died." She looked ill even through the computer screen.

"I'm sorry, babe. Were they friends of yours?" Kathy asked and damned if she didn't sound sincere. Alice wasn't about to be that generous with those she had killed. They had deserved what they got, and she hoped it had been as painful as she had planned.

Linda looked at her in surprise. "No, they weren't friends of mine. You'll recognize the names though: Officer Ramirez, Officer Rogers, and Officer Green all died. Leskowitz got away before we got there. In fact, it was his house." She looked down for a moment. "What they did to Green was disgusting and filthy...those animals!" she shook her head as she began to shake. "We got him though. Today, we got Leskowitz!" she said it triumphantly. Alice wondered if that was what had happened at the police station that she had missed.

"Oh, my God. Are you okay?" Kathy asked, concerned. Alice could see that Kathy looked slightly worried. She supposed she might be worried that Linda would arrest her. Leskowitz would try to blame her.

"I'm okay, but no one deserves to die like that. And what they did to Green..." Alice watched as Linda shuddered, remembering.

Alice remembered adding a few drops to the alcohol. The bodies were still warm as she placed them carefully in grotesque poses that would have some of the cops puking their guts out. Some had been extra creative, depending on their crimes as listed in the dossier Alice had compiled. One or two had begun to come to as she worked on them, and their screams had nearly given Alice away. She had hoped anyone who heard them would just think the party had gotten out of hand and they were screams of ecstasy. She had been particularly pleased that she was able to pin everything on Leskowitz as it was his home the party was taking place in. Unfortunately, he had gotten away until Alice had tracked him down. Her tip, in an authentic Russian accent, had given away his location. She smiled as she heard Linda say, "We've got him now. He'll pay for what he did," she said adamantly.

Seeing Kathy take the cop in her arms and hold her, rocking her, annoyed Alice. She sneered at the screen, jealous for something she couldn't have…at least not yet.

"Thank you," Linda said after a while.

"For what?" Kathy asked. To Alice's ears, she sounded very cautious.

"For just being you," Linda said mushily, holding her tighter.

Alice was shocked as they went to the bedroom together. She hadn't put a camera over the bed but wished she had. The best she could hope for was that they just slept and didn't have sex, but the cop was still there in the morning. That didn't stop Alice from heading over to Palos Verdes, angry and ready to kill the cop if she had touched her wife. By the time she got there, the drive had cooled her anger, and she was very pleased to find the two women sleeping on top of the bed, a blanket covering them both. Body language said a lot, and the two of them had rolled far away from each other on the bed during the night. Alice stood watching them for a while. Alice froze when she thought she saw the cop wake up, but based on the pattern of her breathing, she went right back to sleep. When Alice sensed Kathy waking up, she quickly slipped from the room and the house.

That night, Alice called in a favor, startling the person on the other end of the phone and triggering him to call in a few favors of his own. With Alice Weaver alive in front of him and demanding he do as she asked, he immediately made the necessary arrangements. A cop was killed that night in jail, a dirty cop by the name of Leskowitz. It was made to look like a suicide. He was left alone for only a few minutes, and that was all it took. The perpetrator was pleased to so easily pay off his debt to someone so powerful. The person who arranged it for Alice was relieved to have the favor so easily taken care of.

Alice was pleased to see Emily getting a bit of color back in her face. She also appeared to be regaining some weight. Dr. Wilkerson had told Alice at her last donation that he was pleased with her daughter's progress. When she heard Kathy and Emily talking, she listened avidly, desperately wanting to make herself known. She suspected Kathy was beginning to realize she was alive. Too many things were going on that only Kathy would recognize. From the cop killings to the life-saving treatment for their daughter, only Alice had that signature, and only Kathy would be likely to spot it. Alice certainly hoped no one else would, but she believed only her wife knew her that intimately.

Dr. Wilkerson had told Alice that Emily wanted to go back to school, but he was recommending she wait another month to be certain the procedure was working. He didn't want to act prematurely, but he was almost certain it would be successful.

"I think your wife may be suspicious," he warned Alice.

"Why?"

"She knew the odds of finding a match for Emily's blood were incredible. I think I may have distracted her, implying it wasn't an exact match and was just something else we were trying. We did try a lot of things that didn't work," he reminded her.

Alice admitted, based on her surveillance, Emily was looking better every day.

Alice began to fret as the weeks and months went by. She was sure Kathy and Linda were going to take their relationship to the next level, and she wasn't ready for it. What was holding her back from making

herself known? She really couldn't say, but something in her gut was telling her this wasn't the time.

She had seen the two women making out and petting heavily, which was raising Alice's blood pressure, but so far, it had gone no further. She wondered about Linda. She knew she wouldn't have waited this long to put the final moves on Kathy.

"Don't you want me?" Linda asked her one day.

"Of course, I want you!" Kathy stated vehemently.

"We've never really talked about all our exes," Linda said, pulling Kathy down on the couch next to her and holding her hands. "Perhaps we should have, for transparency sake."

There were some things about Kathy's past Alice hoped she wouldn't share.

"Do you want to talk about it?" Linda asked her

"Well, you know I was kidnapped years ago–" she began hesitantly and squirmed.

Alice was chanting, hoping that Kathy wouldn't tell her anything. She was relieved when Linda interrupted.

"You don't have to talk about that if you don't want to," she said gently, her hands caressing Kathy's comfortingly.

"I don't want to, but beyond that, my experience has been limited."

"Okay. Before Alice, how many partners did you have?" Linda asked quietly.

"Well, my husband, of course," she began.

Linda chuckled. "No, I knew that, and Kit is a beautiful result of that. I meant before Alice, how many *women* had you been with?"

Kathy shook her head. "None," she said absently.

"Alice was your first? Your only?" she asked, shocked.

Kathy nodded. "Why? Is there something wrong with that?"

"No, not at all," Linda quickly assured her. "I'm just surprised..." she began.

"If you are talking about my captivity..." Kathy began again, sounding defensive.

"No, not at all," Linda said quickly, "I'm actually thrilled you don't have a past full of exes that are going to screw this relationship up." She smiled at Kathy, and Alice wanted to choke the woman. She knew where this was leading.

"If you want to wait...I'm a patient woman. I don't want to screw this up by rushing you."

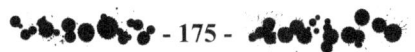

'Sure, you don't,' Alice thought. She even more annoyed when Kathy fell for it.

"No, you've been patient enough. I understand. Time and time again though, it seems we start to make plans or start to make love and it gets interrupted. Somehow, some way…."

"It does seem like that sometimes, doesn't it? It will happen in its own time."

Not if I have anything to say about it.

"Let's just take it day by day," Kathy answered. Alice could hear her the resignation in her voice.

Linda looked happy.

Alice heard an interesting fight between Emily and Kathy one day.

"But why can't I go back to school yet?" Emily practically whined.

"Knock it off, Emily. Until Dr. Wilkerson releases you, you aren't going back!" Kathy argued with her.

Alice could see the teen was bored. She needed the physical and emotional stimulation of social interactions. Skype and similar applications weren't stimulating enough with her friends for her. She was not only looking better, she was feeling better, she had more stamina, and she didn't sleep as much. She needed more than mental stimulation. She wanted and needed exercise as she began to gain back the weight she had lost. Her coordination was off a bit, and Dr. Wilkerson had suggested she start physical therapy to get herself back in shape.

After a month, Dr. Wilkerson cautiously allowed her to return to school but with certain limitations. She could not participate in school sports or activities until she had reached six months of physical therapy, which included water therapy and weight lifting. Those activities would help her young body regain its physical fitness, and he hoped she would once again become a 'normal' teen. He wasn't sure yet if she would continue to grow. She was still shorter than Kathy, but her growth might be stunted from the illness. He explained this to Alice when he reported to her.

When Alice asked about a specific scene she had witnessed, Kathy explained it for her.

"C'mon, Kathy. When?" Linda asked her as they came home from a delightful date. She had been trying to get Kathy into bed for months and now, and with Emily getting better every day, she could see no reason to put it off anymore. After their previous conversation, she had thought they would be intimate by now. She loved this woman. She found her intelligent, delightful, and frustrating.

"I'm sorry, Linda. I want it too," Kathy told her earnestly.

"You wouldn't know that from the way you keep avoiding me," Linda told her. She had never wanted a woman this badly before or waited this long for her.

"Well, Dr. Wilkerson wants to take Emily's catheter out next week. If everything's okay after that, let's you and I plan a romantic getaway. Okay?" she promised, reaching over to squeeze Linda's leg suggestively.

Linda felt a physical jolt at the sensation, which traveled right to her crotch. She couldn't wait to make love to Kathy. At the next stop light, Linda leaned over to catch Kathy in a deep kiss. It went on a bit too long and they both laughed as they sprang apart when the car horns began blaring behind them. What they didn't know was Alice was the third car behind them, and she was glaring at them. She wished she could hear what they were discussing but seeing the heated kiss, she could guess.

"Next week then," Linda agreed.

That night, Kathy took off her wedding band and engagement ring. Looking at them sadly, she put them in a special compartment of her jewelry box. Maybe, someday, Emily would like to wear them.

"Now, that makes sense," Alice nodded as she had watched on the computer when Kathy took them off and hid them in her jewelry box. It saddened her more than she would have thought possible. It wasn't the fact that Kathy thought her dead that saddened her, it was the fact that she was making a concerted effort to move on without her.

Kathy told her about what happened in the doctor's office the following week.

"That's it then," Dr. Wilkerson said as he removed the catheter after freezing Emily's chest.

"How is that possible?" Kathy asked, amazed and bewildered.

"The donor worked," he said, trying not to say too much as he cleaned up the spot where he had removed the catheter. "Now, this should heal with no scar," he assured the young woman, hoping to distract both the child and her mother from what he had unconsciously told them. He applied a bandage to the site before pulling her gown up and allowing her to adjust it.

"Dr. Wilkerson, could I see you a moment?" a head popped in to ask, and they recognized one of his nurses.

"Just a minute. I'll be right back," he assured Kathy and Emily.

"Who do you think was the donor?" Emily asked as she put her shirt and bra back on, turning her back to Kathy for modesty's sake.

"I don't know," Kathy replied. Just then, she spied Emily's chart and opened it. Reading quickly, she gasped one word…"ALICE!"

"Mom?" Emily asked in confusion.

Kathy wasn't sure if Emily was addressing her or referencing Alice.

"What did you say?" Emily asked as she came to look at her chart.

Kathy closed it quickly as she got up. "All ready?" she asked pleasantly to hide her agitation.

"What was in my chart?" Emily asked, reaching for the file folder.

Kathy held it out of the way and said instead, "C'mon, we have to get going. I have errands to run."

"But I want to see," Emily whined.

"Emily, we have to get going," Kathy said firmly, dropping the file behind her, putting her arm around her daughter, and steering her out of the room.

"All set?" Dr. Wilkerson came hurrying down the hall. He must have realized he had left the folder as he glanced anxiously behind them into the room.

They nodded in unison as Kathy asked, "We don't need any more treatments?"

"No. You are all finished, but I want you to come back in three months, so I can draw some blood for tests?" he asked anxiously. He was thrilled with the results so far and anxious to write up his findings.

He glanced uneasily into the room behind them at the chart sitting on the examination table. Was it in the same place he had left it? He couldn't recall.

"We will be here," Kathy reassured him. After the medical staff had saved Emily from certain death, she would walk on coals for them.

Everyone, from the technicians to the nurses, smiled and waved and wished them well as they made their way through the clinic. It wasn't set up like a regular doctor's office since they were an experimental clinic. Kathy and Emily waved, nodded, and accepted everyone's congratulations as they left.

"I think your wife may have read Emily's chart," Dr. Wilkerson told Alice when he reported to her that evening, telling her the catheter had been successfully removed.

"Is my name in there?" she asked, concerned.

"No," he shook his head. "You are, of course, listed as one of her mothers, but I did describe some characteristics of the donor that might be obvious to someone who knows you."

"Shit," she muttered as she left the doctor after receiving the good news about Emily. She sighed. The time was fast approaching when she would have to reveal herself to her wife. She was just cleaning up a few loose ends to ensure she couldn't be traced to the murders she had committed, especially since they were cops.

"I had remembered a conversation with Simone back in New York," Kathy interrupted again to muse. "She said, '*Don't count Alice dead until you see the body, and even then....*'"

Alice laughed. Simone was very astute. Back then, she'd been a good lover for a college woman. It seemed so long ago. Simone had also been a good friend in New York. She only hoped that nothing else had happened to end that friendship. "Is that when you really suspected I was alive?"

"I wasn't sure if the doctor hadn't somehow found a relative of yours somewhere. With Connie dead, I simply didn't know." Kathy did think she was going crazy and had been distracted a lot with thinking about Alice.

"I decided to check out the house in the Valley." Kathy had gotten the key from the gardener and caretaker, Raul and his wife. She didn't see how he hadn't spotted Alice. She must have been extremely careful. "I called to you in that house, but I think I would have been shocked if you had answered."

Alice smiled. She also wouldn't have been happy at that moment if Kathy had found her. She hadn't been quite ready at that point.

"I noticed the place didn't have dust on any surfaces," she said knowingly.

"Well, that would certainly give me away," she acknowledged.

"Where did you put the sleeping bag and air mattress you mentioned?"

"Those went into a pack and into my car whenever I left. I couldn't be sure that Raul, his wife, or you wouldn't come in. And see, I was right."

Kathy laughed now, trying to imagine what it would have been like if she had found Alice back then. She told of going down into the basement and calling to her again and getting no answer. She wasn't sure the stars hadn't been moved but couldn't remember exactly what position they had been in. Still, there was no dust. She looked around but couldn't find anything, and when someone knocked on the door upstairs, she was startled out of her thoughts and went to answer it. She hadn't quite gotten upstairs when the knock was repeated, a little more forcefully. She was shocked to see Special Agent Linda Miller on the doorstep.

"What in the world are you doing here?" Kathy asked after finally opening the door, which was sticky and hard to open due to age and lack of use.

"She followed you?" Alice asked, annoyed that 'the cop' knew about her house in the valley. It had been her hidey-hole for a long time.

"Yeah," Kathy answered. She had also been annoyed at the time. She continued telling Alice what had happened at the house, how defensive she felt, and how invasive it felt knowing Linda had followed her.

"Did you know she followed you other times too?"

"What?"

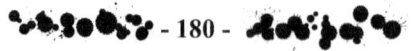

Alice nodded. "I was following you, and I had to be careful that she didn't see me too. It was tricky because she was watching you so closely. She must have been really paranoid about you."

"I wonder if she suspected something?"

Alice nodded again. "I think her cop instinct was at work and she probably did suspect something."

"It was that incident that made me check the cupboards. They were well-stocked, and that made me suspect you were staying there. Logically, I knew it was just wishful thinking that you were alive that made me think that."

"There were only canned or dry goods there," Alice pointed out.

"Yeah, nothing refrigerated," she added as she laughed over the observation. "Just the fact that the cupboards were stocked made me suspicious. I think that was the beginning of the end with Linda," she mused.

Alice was relieved. She had been thinking of bugging Kathy's phones and the cars, yet she also felt the extra cameras were an invasion of privacy. She had caught voyeuristic glimpses of her wife and children in various stages of undress, which she had fast-forwarded through, but just knowing her wife had moved on and was dating 'the cop' made her jealous, and she didn't like knowing that about herself. Alice recalled one incident where she'd watched Kathy masturbate in their bedroom. Because of the camera angle she hadn't been able to watch properly, and it had aroused her and annoyed her at the same time. She had hated that she was watching her wife in this way.

"I kept asking myself, if you were alive, why didn't you make yourself known?"

"You know why now."

"Yes, but even that doesn't completely make sense to me. You could have let me know you were alive sooner."

Alice had to admit Kathy was right, but at the time, it had had made sense to her. She hadn't been ready. She had to know what was going on in their lives first.

"Do you know how devastated I was to find out Linda had tried to get into the computers?"

Alice had watched the cop confidently roam through their house admiring the view and their possessions. She was certain Linda had also gone through the real estate listing. She clearly remembered the description of their house before they bought it:

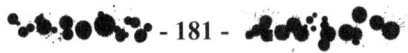

A private estate located in the prestigious Palos Verdes Estates offers resort-style living at its best! This secluded estate boasts sensational panoramic views of the Pacific Ocean from almost every room of the home. A total renovation was designed and completed by the famous architect Don Hendrickson during the last three years. This renovation is a perfect balance of refinement and resort-style living. This estate will exceed all your expectations, with its grand curb appeal, huge lobby to a spacious living room, formal dining room to a great master suite, gourmet kitchen, fantastic library, multi-function media/ family room, two staff quarters with their own kitchen/ laundry/ dining facilities, N/S tennis court with ocean views, wine/cigar cellar, fantastic semi-outdoor gym with its own bath and two separate garages with space for a total of nine cars! The park-like grounds are lavishly designed and surrounded by three sides of parkland. This is one of a very few contemporary styled architectural estates on the hill with big windows filled with sunlight and views! Please do not miss this grand estate, which has so much to offer!!!

Alice had watched as Linda roamed through the house. She did know what she was waiting for, but she was ready to pounce if necessary. She really resented how freely the cop moved around in her home, but she supposed Kathy had allowed it. She saw the kids watching TV and playing on their computers in their own rooms, both unaware that the cop was looking around. Watching as the cop wandered through the bedroom Alice had shared with Kathy, Alice wanted to hit her upside the head and make her body disappear. How dare she? What the hell did she need in there?

When the kids headed to the kitchen for snacks, Linda joined them. Then, after eating a quick snack, the kids returned to their rooms and Alice watched the cop head downstairs to the family room. Alice fidgeted where she was hiding in the extra bedroom. With Nan gone, she was at the house more frequently, but she didn't tell Kathy that as she relayed her story. Alice watched on the laptop as the cop hesitated outside the two staff bedrooms. She worried that she had made some noise to give herself away. Hidden in the closet of Nan's bedroom, she froze as the cop opened the door, looked around, and saw nothing. Alice was relieved when the cop closed the door. She relaxed, then watched on the live feed as Linda went into the office and sat down at *Alice's* desk. *What are you doing, cop? What do you think you are going to find?*

Alice sat up suddenly as she watched Linda turn on each of her computers, but she knew it wouldn't do her any good. Alice was the only one who could get into those computers. Even after all this time and all the changes in technology, these computers couldn't be accessed...Alice had made sure of that long ago. She laughed silently as the cop tried and tried to get into the various computers. After several attempts, the computers simply shut down as they had been programmed to do. Watching the frustration mount on the cop's face made Alice happy. Time and time again, she had tried to reboot the computers, and time and time again, they had shut down on her. Alice watched the cop's face as one computer burst into maniacal laughter, frustrating the cop even more. Smiling broadly, Alice wished she could share this with someone. She looked at her watch and when half an hour went by, she almost applauded the cop's tenacity. She smiled again when the cop finally turned off the computers, and she laughed as she watched the cop wipe them down to remove fingerprints. She shook her head. She already had video proof of the cop's attempts to break into the computers, and she made sure she had the correct times on the video feed.

She continued to watch as Linda went first, to their weight room and then, into the wine room. Alice was quite certain the cretin had no idea which wine to choose. She finally settled on a bottle, then went to sit and vegetate in front of the television. Alice shook her head at Kathy's choice of replacement for her. The woman was totally lacking in sophistication; she watched sports on the TV and fell asleep.

Alice watched as Kathy drove the Lexus into the garage. She approved of her wife's purchase to replace her totaled Porsche. It looked like fun, and she really admired the sporty convertible. She also liked the practical purchase of the RAV4, which she knew the kids would be driving before too long. Even replacing the old Volvo that Mrs. Fernandez drove had made sense. She realized now, or at least she surmised, that Kathy had been paranoid about the vehicles being searched and had gotten rid of the older ones. She understood, and after all, the money was no big deal. It was Kathy's money to do with as she wanted.

Alice listened as Emily complained to her mother about the mean girls at school, who had spread rumors about her weight loss and illness. She listened as Kathy tried to explain about wines to the cop and simply shook her head. Some people simply didn't want to improve themselves, and it was obvious the cop was outclassed by Kathy. She remembered when she had met Kathy years ago, saved her really. She hadn't known much then either, but she had wanted to learn, and she had learned...very well. The Kathy on the video before her now was much different than the Kathy who had needed her help so badly when they met. Confidence and familiarity alone had changed the woman. Alice laughed out loud as Sean broadly hinted that he needed a car. He hadn't gotten his driver's license yet, but he wanted a car?

She sat up as Kathy and Linda went skinny-dipping in the pool after dinner. She saw the cop sending looks to her wife. Alice hadn't put as many cameras outside and watching the scene from afar angered her because she couldn't clearly hear them or see them. She did see them embrace and could surmise a lot, knowing they were both naked. Seeing them play around in the pool, Alice groaned as her jealousy almost overcame her. She nearly cheered when Emily went outside to call her mother, the sound coming in loud and clear over one of the newer cameras she had planted. Seeing Kathy sprint out of the pool and into a towel, she realized the mother of three was shielding her equally naked girlfriend and distracting the teen at the same time. The robe Kathy was wearing hid her assets well. She watched dispassionately as the cop made her way to a bedroom and got dressed. She was fit, Alice would give her that, but other than that, she despised the cop.

Seeing Linda try, once again, to seduce Kathy before she left set Alice's teeth on edge. It was with delight and a bit of vengeance that Alice set up the scenario that would prove to be the cop's downfall. She listened with interest to the conversation Kathy had with their growing son and felt all warm and cozy when Kathy admitted to him that Alice had been the love of her life. Seeing him standing next to Kathy, now taller than her and so strong and healthy, she was proud of his maturity.

As Kathy locked up the house for the night, she found the desk light on and noticed the security program running on the computer. Alice could see her puzzlement since the security program wasn't on frequently, but this time, Alice had left it running deliberately. Kathy turned on another desk lamp as she sat down and watched what was before her, puzzling over it.

Alice smiled at the loop she had created, some of it on fast forward. It showed the kids getting home from school, then the fast forward showed them quickly exiting the cop's car with Linda and everyone going inside, their motions jerky and abrupt. Then, Kathy watched with interest as Linda started exploring the house. She had previously given her a tour, but now that she was alone, she was going through the house again. The scene skipped from camera to camera, and Kathy could feel a tiny kernel of resentment building at Linda's nerve. It suddenly occurred to Kathy that there were too many camera angles on the loop…she didn't remember there being that many cameras. Kathy didn't like that the woman went into her bedroom and bathroom.

Alice was pleased by the look on Kathy's face as she watched the video Alice had created for this moment.

Kathy watched on a different video as Linda passed out of one frame and into another when she went downstairs to fix herself a drink and then went to the basement. Linda checked out both employees' bedrooms and entered the office. Kathy was furious when she realized Linda had tried for half an hour to get into Alice's encrypted computers. She rewound the loop to make sure of the time stamps. She then watched as Linda got up and went to the wine cellar to choose the atrocious wine that had accompanied their meal. Kathy was trying to educate the cop on the various wines, but it was apparent she wasn't interested in learning. Kathy watched as the video showed her and the cop stripping and going to the pool. Remembering how anxious she had been to be with Linda at that moment, she was now ashamed and angry too. Knowing how easy it would have been at that moment to go all the way, she was glad they had been thwarted by Emily's interruption. The loop began again, and Kathy watched all the scenes once more, paying extra attention to the different angles, the cop's nosiness, and her attempts to get on Alice's computers. Kathy was royally angry by the time she finished watching everything for the second time.

Alice heard Kathy's voice on both the video she was watching and through her earpiece from the bedroom where she was hiding, "Oh, my God!" The expression on Kathy's face was just what Alice had hoped for. She was royally pissed. Alice had gotten up as Kathy daydreamed in the office, and thinking she was unobserved, had watched her looking around the office and out the window. She realized her mistake when she heard Kathy's gasp. Alice had momentarily been visible in the reflection of the darkened window, and as Kathy spun, she dropped silently to the floor and began to crawl away until she could rise and hide herself once again in the bedroom.

"You should have made yourself known right then," Kathy whispered, listening to Alice explain how she had protected her family by making that video loop. Her wife needed to see the cop's perfidy. She'd known then why she had been reluctant to sleep with Linda all along. Kathy didn't trust her, and while Linda did make her feel safe, she could never be completely honest with the cop. If she told her everything, she'd arrest her for murder.

Alice remembered watching the cameras again and her heart nearly breaking as Kathy looked around and whispered, "Alice?" into the darkness. There was such longing in her voice that Alice wanted to go to her, but she couldn't. The timing was all wrong, and Kathy had just found out about the cop.

The next day, Alice watched Kathy go through the many videos. There were more than when she had originally set up the system, and she watched the puzzlement on her wife's face as she viewed them all. She watched as Kathy's eyes narrowed over the ones Alice had edited. She had doctored the videos that showed Alice in plain view. Alice was good, she was very good, and Kathy didn't fall for all the edits but enough that she questioned herself. Only a few frames here and there were edited, and Alice hoped Kathy would merely think they were a glitch in the system…the vastly expanded system.

Listening to Kathy break up with Linda on the phone the next day, Alice only felt a tiny bit sorry for the cop. Hearing how enraged Kathy was at her invasion of privacy and at being followed, Alice wished she could have heard what the cop was saying too.

"You weren't sorry in the least, were you?" Kathy asked Alice.

"No," she admitted. The cop had become suspicious and was a danger to her family. Rather than kill her for something like that, which would have been excessive, she had merely presented the facts to her wife and let her make the decision. It was the right decision, and that was the reason the woman was alive to this day.

Listening to Kathy tell the children later that day that she had broken up with Linda bothered Alice a little, *very little*. Hearing a one-sided conversation between Kathy and who she assumed was either Portia or Andie, Kathy cried over the breakup, and that made Alice feel a little worse.

Whoever she was speaking to, Kathy admitted she had thought about getting rid of Alice's clothes. Alice had tried on a few of the outfits but wasn't back to her former weight. It was taking a tremendous amount of time to gain the weight back, and it bothered her that her nice clothes were hanging in her closet and going to waste. Hearing that Kathy had considered getting rid of her clothes had also bothered her.

Alice was alarmed when Portia showed up at the house the next day, and she and Kathy removed Alice's computers from the house and put them in the RAV4. What the heck was that about? She was relieved when she followed them to the office and they took the computers up there. Now, she would have to figure out the building's security system and break into the office too. She sighed. Kathy was making so much work for her, but she was confident it wouldn't be easy for anyone to break into the computers. Most of the security she had set up herself and the other parts she had learned from some of the best. Some of the security was extremely illegal, and it was the most sophisticated encryption programs her money could buy.

Alice felt good about the bug she had set up in the office that Andie, Portia, and Kathy had set up to handle Weaver investments. She laughed as she looked around at the many things she had handled single-handedly and effortlessly in the past, not needing the teams of people they were using to figure them out. They had turned a simple task into a gargantuan task. "Talk about making a mountain out of a mole hill," she murmured as she looked around. Many of the things she'd set up under various names had enabled Alice to hide money, hide her identity, and thwart the government's efforts to get much of her hard-earned dollars, deutschemarks, pounds, and now Euros. They got plenty from her as it was, and Alice wondered when it would become apparent to Andie, the accountant, how much had been hidden. She was certain they wouldn't find it all.

"I don't know who set up the programs on these computers, but they were brilliant. I can't get on them, and believe me, if I can't, no one can," one of the many computer 'experts' they had brought into the office told Kathy.

Alice smiled and cheered hearing that. Her ego had needed a boost, and she was pleased with the compliment as she listened in the house in the Valley. It was just the first of several comments Alice listened to as Kathy brought in experts to try and break into her computers. She had also gotten on the computers remotely a couple times and changed things, so these experts were foiled when trying to restart from their own previous attempts.

Andie even suggested, "Maybe you should try hiring a teenager? You know, one of those geniuses who fiddles with computers?"

"Yeah, but who knows what's on these things…a time bomb waiting to go off?" Portia teased.

Alice smiled evilly when one of the experts who claimed to have worked in the government couldn't even get into them.

Alice was not pleased to hear that Special Agent Linda Miller was trying to get more information out of Kathy regarding Detective Dewayne Leskowitz. She really didn't want to have to kill Agent Miller, who had done nothing to warrant it other than date Alice's wife.

From what she gleaned through the office and home bugs, Kathy was becoming paranoid about it too. She was sure, and rightly so, that she was being followed. Listening to Kathy's conversations, she knew Kathy wasn't stupid or paranoid, and she realized Kathy instinctively knew on a subconscious level that it was Alice in her bedroom and following her; they were just that in tune with each other. Alice was startled to have that fact spelled out for her. Kathy was beginning to connect the dots. Alice had left too many unique signatures that she wouldn't eventually figure things out.

She laughed when Andie asked if she thought there was a ghost in the house. She also enjoyed the byplay between the three friends. These two women were loyal and faithful, and they had been Kathy's friends since their college days. While they didn't understand Kathy's attraction to Alice, they were supportive of her.

Alice knew her time of anonymity was coming to an end. Twice, she thought Portia had caught glimpses of her, but her appearance had changed a lot, and she was used to coming and going with secrecy. Alice had to be extra careful. These women were not stupid, and they were beginning to share notes. Andie had contributed as well, and Alice was surprised that she also thought she saw someone that looked like Alice Weaver, but the woman had been much thinner and had short, spikey hair.

Looking at Alice now, Kathy could see that it had indeed been Alice that Andie had seen so long ago. Alice had been watching them all.

Alice was annoyed when a hidden alarm was tripped. She'd been careful, and she was very good, but she must be getting sloppy or the alarm wouldn't have almost caught her in the offices while trying to get into her own computers. She'd barely gotten out before security arrived. As the police followed, Alice made her escape. She wasn't the only one trying to get at those computers. Officer Smith, who Alice wasn't sure was even a real police officer, began to get very interested in them. It was time for Alice to make a move.

"I was shocked when the computers disappeared from the office," Kathy confided in Alice about the events after the break-in.

"Yes, I had to get the evidence out of the office. That cop, Smith, made a call that started the IRS investigation."

"You know about that?"

"Of course, I do."

"What do you mean, 'Of course, you do'?"

"If they can't get you on criminal charges, they seize your assets in a bogus IRS claim," she pointed out.

"I thought it was bogus too!" Kathy exclaimed, sitting up excitedly.

"Look, I did things that weren't honest—I'll admit that between you, me, and the lamppost—but Andie filed the correct paperwork to substantiate the other monies you found. It's on the up and up, but someone, somewhere, has started looking into it in a way that is punitive, which is why your assets have been frozen," she explained.

"But who?"

Alice shrugged. She hadn't figured that out yet. It was the reason she had come forward to help her wife. She had heard her stressing about having to pay her employees using cash instead of her accounts since everything was frozen and might remain frozen for months as the IRS made their investigation. It pained Alice to see her wife so upset, but it also pissed her off that the government had knowledge about assets she had hidden so well for so long. Andie had done her job correctly and still, it wasn't good enough.

She distinctly remembered the other night before she had told Kathy everything. She'd seen Kathy agitated and upset over the fact the IRS had seized everything. The little she had gleaned of what was going on from the bug in the office made her wish she had put in cameras too. On the one-sided telephone conversations from home, Kathy was very upset. It was time Alice helped her wife and that was why she had come out of hiding.

She'd watched Kathy lock up the doors and set the alarm that night. Mrs. Fernandez had asked for time off, which was a good thing since Kathy couldn't afford to pay her with her assets seized. She watched Kathy try to watch a movie. Alice hesitated to interrupt. She wanted to help, but she had also gotten used to shadowing them and not participating. Being alone for so long, even with all that had happened in Kazakhstan, had made Alice realize how much she liked being alone. She was a loner, but her family—this woman, she admitted as she watched Kathy—made her want to be with her. Her heart ached as she watched her daydream, thinking about Alice and grieving over her. She could see Kathy was hurting, and as always, she wanted to help her. Alice decided to make herself known as Kathy gave up watching the TV and sat in the office crying. She watched her wife standing in the office as she cried her heart out. She wanted to approach her, but she didn't want to frighten her.

Alice saw Kathy's face change when she finally noticed Alice standing there. She thought Alice was an aberration and just a reflection in the window.

She smiled at Alice weakly. "I wish you were real," she said.

"What if I were?" Alice had asked.

"I'd hug you and kiss you. I miss you, Alice," she answered mournfully.

"Then, why don't you turn around?" Alice asked.

Kathy blinked and hesitantly turned. Slowly, she realized what she had thought was her frazzled imagination was very real.

"You look so different," Kathy commented, playing with the short, spikey hair. "You've lost so much weight," she added.

"Well, my time in prison and in Russia wasn't conducive to three meals a day," she laughed.

"I really thought I'd finally gone crazy," Kathy admitted. The days of telling were over. They were here together, and as much as she wanted Alice and thought she had conjured her, she was just deeply grateful she was alive. She didn't have long to enjoy it though. They both spent the days looking at and feeling each other out as Alice told her abbreviated story. The kids had stayed away. They thought Kathy was working down in the office, and they were so self-absorbed in their own rooms with computers, TV, phones, and friends that they hadn't realized Kathy wasn't watching TV too. Avoiding Portia and Andie had been the hardest. The constant phone calls that went to voice mail, the children taking calls that Kathy avoided by saying, "Tell them I'll call them back. I'm busy," to hiding Alice until she knew the complete story.

"There were times I thought I had gone crazy too," Alice admitted, relieved that the telling was over. It had taken too long to get to this point.

"Mom? Who are you talking to?" Emily called down into the family room where they were sitting.

"Are you ready for this?" Kathy asked low, ready to hide Alice yet again.

Alice considered for only a fraction of an instant before she nodded. She was ready. It was time.

"Emily," Kathy called to her. "Ask Sean to come down here with you."

"Did we do something wrong?" Emily asked, sounding cautious and not willing to come downstairs if they *had* done something.

"Not at all. I have something to show you."

They both heard her calling up the stairs, "Sean. Mom wants to see you."

"I didn't do anything," he called back just as loudly, and Kathy and Alice grinned. Teenagers!

"She wants to see us both!" Despite being self-involved, they hadn't been completely unaware of how upset their mom had been the past few days. Something had happened. She had been working on something, and maybe now, she was about to tell them.

Alice got up and stood in the corner, so they wouldn't see her right away. Her stomach was strangely tied in knots at the prospect of seeing her children up close and personal after all this time.

"What are you going to tell them?" Kathy hissed, suddenly worried. They couldn't know the truth, that was a given, but at the same time, they shouldn't be lied to.

"I'll think of something," she admitted. She was good at thinking on her feet, and she knew what Kathy's question meant...she didn't want them to know the truth, but she didn't want Alice to lie either. Alice would improvise.

The two teens made their way slowly down the stairs, obviously reluctant about whatever Kathy had to show them or tell them.

"What?" Sean asked, teenage surliness evident in the tone of his question.

Struck by the size difference in the two teens, Alice could tell that the petite Emily was recovering from her illness. The meat on her bones was increasing, and the flush to her cheeks was attractive, but the always healthy Sean looked robust next to her. "Is that any way to talk to your mother?" Alice asked him from where she stood in the corner out of his sight.

Both teens whirled, and it was Emily who cried, "Mom?" Sean grinned widely and barely beat Emily, who flew into Alice's outstretched arms. They hugged tightly for a long time, Kathy looking on and crying with joy at seeing her family reunited. Alice gestured, and Kathy joined them for a group hug. Slowly, after quite a while, they let go. It was Sean who finally asked, "What happened to you?" He could see she had lost weight, her teeth were odd, and her hair was gone.

"You've been gone a long time," Emily contributed.

"Yes, I know. Let's sit down and I'll explain."

Kathy hoped not. It had taken days for Alice to explain to her. She didn't want a repeat of that...ever. Still, she followed them to the sofa and sat where she could watch Alice and see both children's expressions.

"I was kidnapped. It was a case of mistaken identity," she said, thinking on her feet.

"Kidnapped?"

"Why?"

"That Russian woman I was in business with? They thought I was her."

"But wasn't she missing too?"

There was no way to get things by these intelligent kids. With the internet, Alice was certain they had read a lot of articles about her disappearance. Sasha Brenhov had been one of the richest women in the world, and the press would have covered her disappearance extensively too. Alice reflected for only a second on the fact that people didn't know of Sasha's wealth, had only speculated, and how she was now much, much richer, they both were, thanks to Alice and her efforts.

"Yes, she was kidnapped too. They didn't know who was who, so they took us both. I've spent all this time getting back to you guys," she admitted, a genuine tear coming to her eye.

They wanted to know details, but she would only tell them it had been rough, and her captors had starved her and shaved her head. That explained her appearance and seemed to satisfy their need for details temporarily. Alice asked them what they had been doing, as if she didn't already know, and she heard about Emily's views on her illness and what Sean had to say about what he had been doing.

"Sean is planning on playing football," Kathy put in, smiling proudly at her son.

"Those guys are a bit stupid," the young man informed her, but he was anxious to show what he could do. "You can come to the games next fall," he suddenly sounded enthused.

Alice smiled and agreed, glad they were so easily distracted from her story. She shouldn't have to lie too much if she kept it simple. They were still kids and some of the details might slip out, so she would just have to be careful.

"Someone's here," Kathy said suddenly, hearing the beep of the security system. She got up to look at the monitors and Alice followed her.

"It's Portia," Emily said. "I knew she wasn't happy that I kept telling her you'd call her later. She didn't believe it."

"Now, you're in for it, Mom," Sean teased Kathy.

Kathy laughed.

"How about I handle this?" Alice asked with a conspiratorial grin, and they all laughed as they went upstairs to answer the door before Portia had a chance to ring the doorbell. They stood back, and when she rang the bell Alice opened the door.

"Hello, Portia...."

~The End~

❖ MARKED MALICE ❖

BOOK 24

Would you know how to bring someone back to life? Well, Alice is not just a killer...she once brought her wife back to life. And now, her wife has an opportunity to repay her. But can Alice keep fact and fiction straight while trying to avoid sharing the gruesome details of her recent adventures with her teenage children? What happens when one of the children learns some of what Alice has been through? And what happens when Alice and Kathy realize their children aren't the only ones aware of Alice's deeds during her time away? Join Kathy and Alice as they answer two vitally important questions: 'Who believes they have damning evidence that gives them the power to control Alice Weaver?' and 'Can these two women salvage their marriage...do they even want to?'

"Oh, my God! Alice, is that really you?" Portia asked, shocked to see Alice standing before her. Looking beyond her into the hall, Portia saw Kathy and the children beaming at her, so it must be true.

"Yes, it's me in the flesh, such as it is," she said in reference to the loss of her curves.

"I can see that," she murmured wonderingly.

"Why don't you come in?"

Portia entered the house, and Alice closed the door behind her. "It's good to see you, Portia," Alice said formally and then shocked everyone by pulling her in for a hug. Anyone who knew Alice Weaver knew she wasn't a huggy-kissy kind of person. "I am so grateful to you for taking such good care of Kathy all this time," Alice said as she pulled away, grinning at the look of shocked surprise on the lawyer's face.

"Where have you been? Did you just get back?"

"She was kidnapped," Emily said and quickly covered her mouth. Alice had asked that they not spread that around. They could tell people she was back, of course, but they should try not to give out too many details. Emily had been warned, and already, she was blurting things out. Alice fixed her with a stern look but inside she was laughing. She had known the children couldn't keep that information to themselves. It was part of being a teen, and Emily was impulsive. She would learn in time. Sean nudged her firmly to make his point.

"Kidnapped?" Portia repeated and then, looking at Alice and her thin appearance, she realized this was probably true. "Was that you I saw the other day outside the office building?"

Alice nodded. "I had to see what was going on with everyone before I made my presence known."

"We are going to have to file papers..." she left off as she looked at Kathy. "Is that why you asked about making someone alive again?" she asked, suspiciously.

"No, I didn't know Alice was alive then. I told you, I saw it on some TV show and wondered about it. Now, of course, we are going to have to do just that." She didn't tell the complete truth to her friend. She didn't want her to know how long Alice had been watching them all. She knew even she probably didn't know the whole truth. Alice couldn't possibly have told her everything. Realistically, she knew Alice would have tried to protect her. Alice would hide some facts for Kathy's own good and some she would hide believing it was for the benefit of them all. Alice couldn't help herself, and strangely, Kathy understood that. Kathy was just so grateful her wife was back and alive and now, apparently in their lives.

"Come on, let's sit you down, relax, and talk," Alice ushered everyone out of the hallway and into the living room. The children sat on both sides of their mother, not willing to let her out of their sight.

"So, what happened?" Portia asked, her lawyer mind already multitasking, thinking about what papers she would have to file to make Alice alive again.

"It's a long story, and believe me, I don't want to tell it again," Alice told her truthfully. "It was a case of mistaken identity. They were after Sasha and got me too."

"Is Sasha alive too?"

"Yes, and she's in Europe with her girlfriend the last I heard," Alice admitted another truth. She had to be careful. She had also been in Europe and hadn't told anyone about that except Kathy. She saw Emily looking at her, her eyes so much like her own. Emily was changing a little as the flesh continued to grow on her bony body after her illness.

It was obvious Portia had a lot of questions but would be unable to ask them with the children present. Portia was chafing at the bit, even Kathy could see it, and she grinned her enjoyment of the moment.

"I think you can probably contact Nia Toyomoto and coordinate the paperwork," Alice suggested.

"Nia?" Portia asked. She hadn't thought of that. Nia would have the resources of the large firm she worked for, and that would make more sense than Portia trying to handle it herself here in LA. Between the two of them they would be able to straighten out the mess Alice's death had created for everyone. "Did Kathy tell you–" Portia began and then stopped herself. She wasn't sure Kathy wanted the children to know about the tax problem.

"Kathy and I talked a lot," Alice reassured her, "but right now isn't the time," she warned. She put her arms around the children. "I am

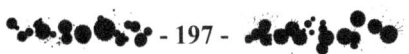

sorry to hear about Coco," she told them sincerely, not mentioning she had been there and seen their beloved pet's death.

"Yeah, that was really sad," Emily put in innocently.

"I heard those cops got theirs though." Sean sounded proud.

"Sean!" both Kathy and Alice admonished the teen, then looked at each other and laughed. It had been a long time since they disciplined their children together.

"Oh great, you gonna tag-team me now?" Sean asked, grinning to show he didn't mind. He leaned in to Alice's arm to give her a sideways hug. "I'm so glad you're home, Mom," he said, and Alice could hear the tightness in his manly voice. He was feeling emotional and she understood.

"Can we get another dog?" Emily asked, earning an eye roll from Kathy.

"That isn't up to me," Alice put in and glanced at Kathy. "I'm just back," she lied. "Your mother and I have a lot to straighten out and everything, especially making me alive again, is going to take some time." She glanced at Portia, who nodded unobtrusively. Alice could tell Portia wanted to ask a million questions and get into the meat of the IRS case against her estate, but Andie was going to have to be part of that conversation. "How is Andie?" she asked innocently, knowing full well that their third friend was fine.

"She's good," Portia admitted, looking at Alice critically. Despite the weight loss and punk hair she looked good. She didn't look as old as Portia thought she should, since she was older than her, Andie, and Kathy. There was always something about this woman that bothered her. She'd seen her take someone off her property a couple years ago and the person had disappeared. She didn't like that but she accepted it. Being an accessory to a crime didn't sit well with her; however, she knew she shouldn't question that incident. Still, she wished she could just figure out what it was about this woman that bothered her, what made her tick….

Alice was very aware of Portia's scrutiny, and she could probably even guess at some of her feelings. She'd known for a long time that the attorney didn't trust her, and rightly so. Alice knew what she was capable of, and she knew the attorney would be horrified if she knew even half of it. Alice smiled blandly and continued showering the children with attention until Kathy announced it was bedtime.

"Aww, Mom," they both complained in unison.

"You have school in the morning, and I don't want you thinking you can sleep in."

"But we should take the day off and spend it with Mom," Emily tried, hugging Alice harder.

"I'm not going anywhere. I'm here to stay," Alice told her, glancing at Kathy and wondering if that was true. Kathy really hadn't answered the question about whether she wanted their marriage to continue. Alice had taken note of that. "I'll be here when you get up in the morning," she promised as she kissed the teen on the cheek.

"It was you who donated the blood for Dr. Wilkerson, wasn't it?" Emily asked astutely.

Alice had to be careful. That put her supposed timeline in jeopardy if she didn't watch what she said. She nodded but added, "Yes, I couldn't come to see your mom and you guys right away though. I had some business to finish."

Portia watched closer, trying to see if Alice was lying. She should have known better. That woman could put up a wall when she wanted to hide what she was really thinking or saying.

"You'll be here in the morning?" the teen asked to be sure.

"I will."

"Can you take me to school?" she asked, excitedly.

"Apparently, I don't have a car anymore, or so your mom tells me." Alice squeaked out of that one. She had no desire to chauffer her daughter around.

"Yeah, she totaled that car," Sean put in with a small attempt at humor.

"There's nothing funny about that," Alice said sternly and saw he had the grace to blush.

Kathy shooed the children off to bed, and the two women heard her arguing with them upstairs.

"So, where were you really?" Portia asked quietly.

Alice nearly smiled at the direct question. She had known it was coming. Some people were so predictable, and she anticipated Andie would do the same. "I told you. I was kidnapped, and I've spent all this time trying to come back home."

"Yes, but where were you held?" she asked, wondering if Alice would tell her the truth. She knew this woman was adept at lying.

"I was in Central America in a prison cell," she admitted, surprising them both. "But I don't want the children to know that, and I don't

want you to repeat it." She looked directly at the attorney, unnerving her with the cat-like eyes that could change color and become threatening so easily. For now, they were just direct. She relaxed when the attorney nodded. "It's really an unpleasant part of my past I'd like to forget, but I suppose I'll have to make an official statement about it to a judge or some other party when we work to get me all legal again."

"How did you get back into the country without anyone knowing?"

Alice just stared at her, a kind of sardonic look that said a lot without her speaking. Portia started to fidget, realizing her mistake. Something about this woman....

"There, they're getting ready for bed. Emily has asked that you tuck her in," Kathy told Alice, coming back into the room and amused by the teen's demand.

Alice laughed as she got up. "Well, far be it from me to disappoint Lady Emily," she said in a playful voice. She headed up the stairs, knowing the two women were probably burning holes in her back with their eyes, both for very different reasons.

"You believe her?" Portia couldn't wait to ask.

"I believe her," Kathy said simply.

"Is she going to help with the taxes?"

"I don't know. I'm sure she can help us. We really didn't talk about that too much." They'd talked about a lot, but the taxes certainly hadn't come up in the majority of their conversations.

The conversation upstairs was quite different from what was being said in the living room as Alice reached up to pull her tall, strapping son down for a kiss. "Good night, Sean. See you in the morning?"

"Good night, Mom," he said, giving her a squeeze, surprised at how petite she really was. He had remembered her much differently, but maybe it was because she had always looked so healthy. The lack of weight on her thin bones and the haircut really altered her appearance. "See you in the morning," he confirmed before going into his room.

"Come in?" Emily asked when Alice knocked on her door. It was a typical young teen's room with posters of horses and the current teen heartthrob on the walls. *Its pink color would have to be changed soon*, Alice thought. She could see her daughter was growing up by the picture of the attractive young man she had pinned up.

"Hey, there. You wanted me to tuck you in?" she teased, knowing her daughter hadn't needed that in ages.

"Yeah, well, you know," she began shyly and then smiled. "I missed you, Mom," she said honestly.

"I missed you guys too. I'm sorry you were sick."

"I'm better now, and Dr. Wilkerson said I'm doing good." She looked momentarily sad.

"What is it?" Alice asked astutely.

"Oh, there's some girls at school who are saying mean things."

"There always seems to be someone who says things in school or at the office," she pointed out. She understood bullies well. To a degree, she could be one, but she tempered it by turning it into something productive...like killing people; however, she didn't tell her daughter that.

"I know, and Mom says to ignore them, but sometimes it's hard."

"Yep, I get that," Alice said, sitting down on the bed to tuck Emily in. "I hope I don't cause you any anxiety by being back."

"Oh, no. I always hoped the report of your death was wrong. When they couldn't find your body, I just hoped it was all a mistake," she said with the confidence of youth. She had no idea what Alice had been through. "Did you really kill all those people?" she asked, shocking them both.

"Pardon?" Alice asked, blinking, too shocked to think fast enough.

"I heard you the other night when you were talking about Kazakhstan," she admitted.

"And tonight, you just pretended it was the first time you knew I was home?" she asked, remembering the sound that she and Kathy had heard. Kathy had investigated and found nothing, but apparently, it hadn't been nothing.

"Well, that was for show. You know how it is? Some people need to see one thing even if you are another thing. I do that at school too."

Alice didn't know what to say. What else had the teen overheard? She wasn't going to take a chance. "You can never tell anyone what you overheard, not even your mother. She'd be horrified and afraid."

"I won't tell anyone. I promise," Emily said earnestly. "Is it true?"

"What do you think?" she asked, wondering if there was going to be a problem she hadn't anticipated. She wouldn't admit the killings, not if she could help it.

"I think you did whatever you needed to do to those bad people, so you could get home."

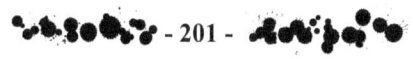

Alice was surprised at how amazingly astute her daughter was, but she was also surprised she could shrug off the lives her mother had taken. She wondered if it was the violence on TV and how desensitized their youth was becoming. "Well, I must have thought about you all a hundred times a day," she admitted. "Emily, I don't think you realize how important it is that you never repeat what you overheard."

"I know, Mom. I keep lots of secrets for my friends too. I think I know what to keep to myself." She suddenly sounded older than her years, and Alice watched the wise eyes that were growing in her daughter's youthful face. She'd been through a lot in her life.

"I would go away for a long prison term if they could prove what I did," Alice mentioned, trying not to make a big deal out of it but stressing her concern.

"Yeah, I thought of that. I don't ever want to lose you again."

"Well, in a few years, you will go off to college, and your mom and I will be waiting here whenever you want to visit," she teased with a grin, lightening things up. It had all been so intense for those few minutes. and she didn't want to scare her.

"That is a long way off," Emily admitted. "What if I don't want to go to college?"

"Hmmm, maybe we should send you off to boarding school?" she teased further. "Whatever you want, baby, is fine with us. First and foremost, I want you to be happy, but to get ahead in this life, you need education."

Emily agreed with her mom, but she knew she didn't have to worry. She was good at her studies and buckled down when a new challenge arose. She'd stayed at the top of her class despite the months of home-schooling when she had been ill. Now, she was back, and those bitches who kept spreading rumors that she was bulimic or anorexic could kiss her ass. She settled into her bed. "Good night, Mom. I'm so glad you are back."

"Good night, Em," Alice said as she turned out the light and left the room. Emily smiled. Hearing the familiar shortening of her name made her feel everything was going to be all right.

The paperwork to start the process of legally bringing Alice Weaver back to life was insane. The phone call to Nia Toyomoto alone took some doing just to get through to the partner of the law firm in New York. At first, they had thought it was a prank…until Portia got angry.

"Portia," Nia finally came on the phone. "You have a question about Alice Weaver's will?"

"No, Nia. I have another problem," Portia told her, smiling at Alice, who was listening in on the extension. "It isn't the will, it's the execution."

"What?" she asked. That had been presented in court over eighteen months ago. Nia was frowning at her end of the line, looking out her corner office windows at the New York skyline.

"Well, the problem is, Alice Weaver is alive," Portia told her, still grinning, imagining the attorney's reaction.

"Are you kidding me?"

"Nope. She's sitting right here listening to our conversation."

"Hello, Nia," Alice's distinct voice came through the line. "Hang on to your hat. Sasha Brenhov is alive too."

"What the hell, Alice! Where have you two *been*?"

"We were kidnapped, and it took us quite a while to escape." She had decided to stay with this simple story since eventually the word would get out.

"Kidnapped? By who?"

"Someone that wanted Sasha but wasn't sure who was who. They thought I was Sasha at one point, and since they couldn't be sure, they took us both." Alice had sent a message to a seldom used email address explaining this story to Sasha, who had remained hidden for a while, recovering from their ordeal. She had warned Sasha about the background story Alice was going to use, keeping it simple, so it would be easier to remember. What Sasha did on her end was her concern.

"Jesus Christ, Alice! You really know how to throw a monkey wrench in things. Do you know how many lawsuits I've fielded on both of your estates' behalf?"

"Well, now you can really earn your outrageous fees," Alice laughed, and Portia chuckled at that one. It was a good zinger because she was certain the New York attorney earned much more than she. "Look, I'm going to get off the phone and let you and Portia plan this out, but we are also going to have to do something about the IRS, who have frozen Kathy's accounts."

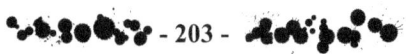

"That's the first I've heard of that. Yeah, let me hash this out with Portia. Alice, before you go, let me just say it's nice to know you are alive." Alice felt Nia was one of the few people who would actually mean that too. Nia had known Alice since college, and while she wasn't exactly sure of everything Alice had done during the years, she'd handled some things for the millionaire and Nia didn't wish to cross her either. There was something almost dangerous about the blonde, and she really wanted to make sure their friendship was intact. She wondered if their mutual friend, Simone knew Alice was alive?

"Thanks, Nia. Let's get this fixed soon. Kathy needs to pay some bills." She grinned as she said it. She had access to money and would go out later to get some cash for her wife, if she needed it. She hung up the extension to let Portia and Nia speak in lawyer talk as they worked out how to straighten out this mess.

"How are you doing?" Kathy asked Alice as she made a stack of sandwiches for them all. Andie was due there anytime. She'd stopped by the offices to gather some things as they fought the IRS. She thought Portia and Kathy were pulling her leg when they told her Alice was alive.

"Tell me exactly what happened with the agent who came to the office," Alice asked as she started nibbling at the fixings Kathy was using. She really wondered what was going to happen with Kathy. She hadn't slept with her wife last night. Instead, she'd been put up in the guest room, and that bothered her. Kathy said it was just until they fixed a few things in their marriage, and Alice, while she said she understood, really didn't. She hadn't expected Kathy to jump into her arms, but she had expected her to show more affection since it had been years since they had been intimate.

While she made a plate for them all to munch on, Kathy explained how she had come into the office only to have a black man with a badge identify himself as a member of the Internal Revenue Service. "They claimed they were doing a full-scale audit of our assets. I don't think they believe anything we filed is legitimate. He seems to believe we've been laundering money."

Alice froze only momentarily. She had enough legitimate businesses doing exactly that—laundering the millions of illegally-gotten gains she had deposited into their real accounts over the years—that she was an expert at hiding it. She had seen what Andie filed about the few discrepancies they had found. They didn't know the half of it, and she wasn't about to tell them.

"He said it was going to take months. He didn't look displeased about that either," Kathy lamented, sounding distressed again. Alice had observed that as she became aware of the problems. It was why she had refused to remain hidden any longer. Kathy *needed* her. Alice just wasn't sure that her wife *wanted* her. "I couldn't even use my credit card at the gas pump," she reminded her wife of what happened the other day. "They froze all the bank accounts. Checks are going to start bouncing."

Alice had heard of the IRS being used for punitive damages. Whose Cheerios had someone peed in that they were coming after all their money? She had hidden so much money over the years that she could simply walk away from all this and be fine for the rest of her life, but she didn't like the fact that their reputation as law-abiding citizens was being tarnished, especially as Kathy went on with her tale.

"He informed the media," she pointed out.

"So, this is about humiliation too," she mused as she nibbled on a carrot. "Did he leave a card?"

"Andie's bringing it. He wasn't too concerned about how I was going to eat or pay our bills. I asked that question, and he said, 'That isn't my concern.' He even made it sound like he was doing me a huge favor by *allowing* me to live in the house here."

Alice nodded. Yeah, that was a bit much. Who was out to get her and why? She hid her tracks well and assholes like that were old school. The IRS had stopped such heavy-handed tactics years ago when the public complained. It wasn't allowed, but that didn't mean it wasn't still happening.

"To put a lien on our real estate though?" Kathy questioned. "How much do you own?"

Alice shrugged. Whatever she had owned before her death was nothing compared with what she owned now, thanks to her travels in Russia. What hadn't been sold was now in various accounts around the world, untraceable, and the IRS would never get a dime of those funds. They knew about enough that she had paid taxes on, and she felt they should be satisfied with that. Even with the amendments Andie had filed, they should be good. Tax and penalties notwithstanding, someone was after more than the government's fair share.

Portia agreed that someone was trying to take them down, and with Alice showing up again, things might prove extremely interesting.

The doorbell rang, and Alice went to answer it. She was pleased to see the momentary look of startled surprise on Andie's face.

"Oh, my God! You *are* alive!" she said with a delighted laugh, pulling Alice in for a one-armed hug. Her other arm was filled with a box of paperwork she had brought from the office. "I'm glad you are, so you can help us clear up this shit." She hadn't ever been audited like this, and in just the last few days, she'd had to answer rapid-fire questions as the IRS went over things. They were building a case against Kathy that would leave her with nothing. That was how the IRS worked—they found something wrong, and using penalties and interest, they would wipe out the person they were targeting. Andie had heard the tales but had never been a party to it herself. After first, seeing all of Alice's known assets, and then, seeing a few unknown assets come to the forefront, she wasn't so sure the IRS was wrong. "I really thought they were pulling my leg when they said you were kidnapped and had finally made your way home," Andie said as she pulled back and looked at Alice. What a difference the spiky hair made. She could see Alice had lost weight too; it really changed her appearance.

They got down to work, and Alice didn't even need to refer to the little paperwork they still possessed. She was able to answer both Portia's and Andie's questions from memory.

"How do you remember all that?" they repeatedly asked.

"I just do," she said confidently. Finally, she told them, "Look, it doesn't matter if the agent confiscated all those files or not because I have copies."

"Where?"

Alice wouldn't answer that question. In fact, something about their conversations was beginning to bother her. Her multi-tasking mind was thinking of other things. It wasn't that she didn't trust the three women, but there was something...and then she made a gesture to them, her finger touching her lips in a shushing movement. "Eat. I'll be right back. I need to use the bathroom," she said meaningfully.

After Alice left the room to go upstairs to the bedroom she used to share with Kathy, the women remaining behind exchanged looks. "What's going on?" Andie asked Kathy, as though she should know.

"Maybe she isn't feeling well?" her wife guessed.

Portia's eyes narrowed. Any time a witness refused to answer questions fully and completely, she was suspicious, and Alice, while somewhat forthcoming that morning, had never completely answered the questions to Portia's satisfaction. Something was going on.

Alice returned after a long period of time. She was carrying a gadget with a weird, little antennae on top. It looked like a TV remote gone awry, and Alice shushed the women again before they could ask what it was. The gadget made a faint blipping noise, and Alice reached down to remove a small disc she discovered attached to the bottom of the couch. She made a 'come-hither' gesture to Kathy as she found another disc in the kitchen, two in the office, one in the family room, and one more in the exercise room. The women all followed Alice as she traveled between rooms.

"Wha–?" began Andie, and Alice shook her head, gesturing for silence as she put the little discs in a baggie and placed them in the freezer.

"Those are listening discs, and I'm sorry," she said to Kathy, "someone's been listening to us, possibly for *days*," she said meaningfully.

As Kathy thought about the implications of that statement, Portia pointed out they hadn't said anything that could get her into trouble by discussing her tax information.

"This isn't just about the taxes," Kathy realized and looked at Alice in growing horror. Whoever had put the discs around the house had done so with the hope of finding incriminating evidence. Other than an occasional visitor of the children's, no one had been in the house except....

"Who would do that?" Andie asked naively.

"It could have been put there months ago," Alice pointed out, speaking just to Kathy but answering their friend's question. "I'll bet there are listening devices at your office too."

"You're being paranoid," Portia pointed out, but she was shaken. "What is that device?"

"It's used to detect certain sound frequency waves. Whoever has been listening probably has recordings, and I'll bet I might not have gotten all the discs because this is an old receiver. Be careful what you say everywhere."

"Why would someone target Kathy?" Andie asked.

"Probably because she was married to me," Alice said succinctly.

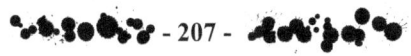

"But as far as anyone knew, you were dead."

"Yes, and my reappearance is just a bonus." She was thinking. She had been around for months and had put the video cameras in a while ago. She'd not seen anyone attaching those bugs, but given their locations, it was possible someone could have casually put them under furniture and no one would have noticed. At least, not anyone who wasn't specifically looking for them. Mrs. Fernandez' cleaning wouldn't have dislodged them as the adhesive had bonded them tightly to the various surfaces. Someone had been targeting Kathy, not Alice, but as a bonus, the past few days' confessions had given them enough information to put Alice away in a federal prison for life. Even though she hadn't given Kathy every single detail, the listener had a ton of information, and Alice wasn't foolish enough to believe they wouldn't either blackmail her or go to law enforcement with it.

"But who?" Portia asked and looked from Kathy to Alice in concern. The two exchanged a look that said, *Later.*

"How come you have such a gadget?" Andie asked almost simultaneously.

"Well, I like gadgets," Alice admitted. Only Kathy realized the depth of meaning in that statement.

They went back upstairs and continued discussing Alice's tax situation as well as the paperwork Portia and Nia would be filing to bring Alice back to life legally.

"I think that paperwork will affect this tax situation," Andie indicated some of the paperwork the IRS had served them and referenced the other legal paperwork.

"She was declared dead in absentia, so that is all legal," Portia pointed out.

They didn't notice that Alice and Kathy had now stopped contributing. Both women were exchanging looks as the other two women continued to pore over strategy and what little paperwork they had left.

"Alice? Alice!" Andie finally said, and the blonde looked up, distracted. She'd been lost in thought.

"Ah, yeah?"

"We're going to need any copies of the paperwork you can get me, so we can fight this in court when the IRS makes their case..." she droned on until Alice's eyes glazed over from the financial mumbo jumbo she and Portia were so keen on. Normally whip-smart regarding finances, Alice was more concerned about how upset Kathy was when she realized the importance of the listening devices, which the other two women seemed to have forgotten about. They were finally saved by the children's arrival.

"I think we can wrap this up for today," Kathy said brightly, seeing the children coming up the drive after hearing the security pad being accessed to open the gate.

"Oh, sure," Andie said, gathering her paperwork and putting everything back in the box she had brought. "I'm going to take this home and go over it some more. If you'll get me the paperwork I requested, I can investigate further," she directed that last statement at Alice, who nodded to acknowledge her request.

"As Nia said, we can have the paperwork filed by the end of the week and get that process going," Portia reiterated for at least the third time that day since she had gotten off the phone with the New York attorney. They were going to file jointly since Alice owned properties and lived in both states. It was very technical, and Nia would be handling most of the work at her end with her resources. Portia could see her services were no longer necessary with Alice's return, but she would make herself available if Kathy needed her. She wondered if the Kathy and Alice had decided to continue their marriage or dissolve it at this point. She hadn't had a chance to ask Kathy yet.

Alice was glad to see the lawyer and accountant leaving. She realized they were too small to handle the firepower the IRS and whoever else was involved were about to unleash on the Weavers. They needed a larger firm, and Alice had the resources to hire the best. Alice didn't like anyone knowing exactly how extensive her resources were, but with the listening devices she'd found, she realized they could have a good idea now. The monies she had taken from the Russian mafia players could be speculated on, and the IRS and whoever had been listening would want a cut, perhaps a large cut…they might even want it all. She wasn't foolish enough to think they wouldn't try to take it all. She remembered well that the punitive aspect of the IRS meant they would come at them with penalties and interest to the point where she would owe them everything and would be ruined financially. They didn't care if the Weavers were left destitute, and that was what angered Alice the most. Whoever had gotten this bee in their bonnet was vindictive and would throw her family into the streets if they could.

"What are we going to do?" Kathy breathed after they waved their friends off and the children stopped to talk to them for a moment.

"We are going to fight, and we are going to win. I need to get a newer one of these," she gestured to the bug finder in her hand, playing with it thoughtfully, "but I want something stronger that can destroy those buggers."

"The bugs or the people listening?" Kathy asked.

"First, I have to figure out who is listening. I mean, if it is the IRS, they set you up a while ago, and if it is…" she wanted to say 'the cops' but didn't want to hurt Kathy's feelings. Alice had been very careful to disguise her jealousy and contempt when she told Kathy of her observations while watching them.

"You aren't in this alone. I want to be included," Kathy said in a tone that surprised Alice. Just then, the kids came up.

"Hi, Mom!" they said, obviously delighted to see both women.

The two women were lost in the moment as the children demanded and got their attention for the next half hour. Kathy went off to call Kit and inform her of Alice's presence when Emily reminded her Kit hadn't been told yet.

Alice noticed Emily looking at what appeared to be a fancy card. "What's that?" she asked the teen.

"It's an invitation to a party, but I'm not sure I want to go."

"Why is that?"

"It's being given by some of those mean girls I told you about."

"Why would they invite you if they don't even like you?"

"That was my thought," Emily answered ruefully.

Alice watched her for a moment and then asked, "Do you want to go even though they have been nasty?"

Emily looked up and nodded. "All my friends are going, and they're really excited."

"Are you sure they are your friends?"

"Well, when we first heard about the party, we all felt left out. Then, when Michaela came around and specifically handed us each an invite, we felt honored. I didn't want it, and at the same time, I *really* wanted it." She looked at Alice in a beseeching manner. "Does that make sense?"

"Oh, yes," she admitted, nodding. Alice couldn't have cared less back in high school, but she remembered that clique kind of thing very

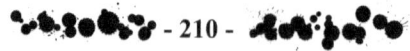

well. "You want to be included, and yet, you despise who is putting on the party?"

"Yeah, that's it. We don't want to be left out, so we really want to go," she sighed.

"You aren't still friends with that Susie chick, are you?"

"Susie? That was Kit's friend, and that was years ago," she said, frowning. "Don't you remember?"

Alice shrugged. She realized it had been years ago and Susie had been part of the lure to get Kit since those people had Kathy. Now, she remembered Kit had backed way the hell off from that friendship, and she had been relieved. "Sorry, I don't keep track of your friends," she laughed it off. There had been a time when Alice would have tracked the children's friends, and she wondered if she should be now.

"My friends, my *true* friends," she started, then seeing Alice's look she clarified, "the friends that stood by me through my illness," she waited for Alice to nod before continuing, "are thrilled to hear that you are alive and home. They want to see you again."

Alice smiled. "Invite them over. But first, let's check with your mom and see if it's okay with her. We could have a pizza party one Friday or Saturday?"

"Saturday is this party," she indicated the invitation.

"We're going to want to meet the parents," Alice told her.

"Oh, Mom. That's so old-fashioned," she whined slightly.

"And the rules still apply," she said firmly and smiled. "I'm sure your mom didn't let the rules slide just because I was gone?"

"No," the teen admitted sulkily.

Alice wanted to laugh and then, she saw Kathy walking up. "Kit wants to talk to you. What are you two up to?"

Alice could see Emily wasn't going to tell her. "Emily is invited to a party, and we were discussing that. She also would like her friends to come see me one day, and I suggested a pizza party, if that's okay with you? Why don't you two discuss the details, and I'll talk to Kit," she said as she took the phone Kathy held out and walked away.

"Hello, Kit," she said affectionately.

"Oh, God. Mom, it's great to hear your voice. Are you okay?" the young adult said excitedly into the phone. Not waiting for an answer, she continued, "When Mom told me you were alive, I didn't believe her. I guess I will have to believe her now. I want to come home this weekend, so I can see you. Is that okay?"

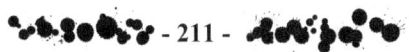

"I can't wait to see you," Alice answered, smiling at the excitement in her adopted daughter's voice. Kit would always hold a special spot in Alice's cold, little heart. Alice had seen Kit on the computer and thought she looked a lot like a younger version of Kathy. She'd loved Kit since she was a child. Kit was the first child Alice really had a lot to do with, and she had melted a portion of Alice's heart, making it easier for her to have children of her own with Kathy. Mother and daughter chatted for a while before Alice hung up. She agreed to send Kit a first-class plane ticket and pick her up at the airport Friday afternoon. Alice knew with Kathy's accounts frozen she would have to pay for the ticket in cash. She couldn't let the IRS know she had her own cards and accounts, or they would go after those as well. She cursed the listening devices they had found, wondering again who had planted them and now possessed all their information. She couldn't help thinking it was the good and honorable Special Agent Linda Miller. She knew Kathy was likely thinking the same thing. Who else had that kind of access to the house? They hadn't had a chance to talk about it yet. Alice wandered out to the pool with the device in her hand and found two more bugs that she placed in the baggie with the others in the freezer. She headed out to scan their garage and cars and found several more listening devices. She was just bagging those up when Kathy came up.

"Whatcha doin'?" Kathy asked, her hands in her pockets.

Alice held up the devices before throwing the bag on top of the ice in the automatic ice maker and closing the freezer door, so they would freeze faster.

"*More?*" she asked, aghast.

"These were in the garage. I found a couple around the pool, although I wonder if weather or wind are a factor. These aren't government issue, and I know they aren't very good. Whoever placed them–" she began but Kathy interrupted.

"You are thinking the same thing I am, that Linda put them around the place."

"I know you had feelings for the woman, but she was in internal affairs. She also tried to access my file and yours at the police department."

"How do you know that?"

Alice put her finger to her lips again and beckoned Kathy towards their back yard. Looking around, she realized someone could point a device and listen to them there too, but she hoped the winds coming up from the beach would hide or distort anything they had to say. "I know because I put certain controls in place to protect exactly what she was trying to access. A lot of things in those reports have been redacted and can't be seen by anyone anymore. She also put in a request for the files at the FBI," Alice informed her wife.

"How do you know that?" Kathy repeated, looking frightened.

"Those computers of mine aren't just computers, they have back doors inside of back doors. That's the reason I didn't want them in your offices, which turned out to be a good thing since the IRS raided there. If they had those computers now, it wouldn't be only the IRS after us. We'd also have the FBI and probably the CIA on my tail. I don't know…after this," she gestured to the device in her hand, "we may have a few other acronyms chasing us." She sounded amused at her own sally but also concerned.

"What are we going to do?"

"We aren't going to do anything. I'll get you out of this, I promise," Alice said, grabbing both of Kathy's arms in her desire to make her wife understand.

Kathy knocked Alice's hands aside, not wanting to be held like that. "We are in this *together*, aren't we? Or are you going back to that same secretive life you think I don't know about?"

"Kathy, some of the things I keep from you are for your own protection…" she began.

"Am I your wife or are we going to finish the divorce?"

"Is that what you want?" Alice's eyes narrowed dangerously

Kathy wasn't scared. Alice may be a killer, but she would never hurt her, of that she was certain. "What do you want?" she asked instead, her own eyes narrowing as she contemplated being free of this marriage, of being free of Alice.

"I spent two years trying to get back to you and the kids, and you can ask me that?"

"Did you spend two years trying to get back because of your sense of obligation to us or was it love?"

"You know I never stopped loving you," she began heatedly, wanting to shake Kathy.

"And I didn't stop loving you," Kathy returned just as heatedly.

"Then, why are we arguing?"

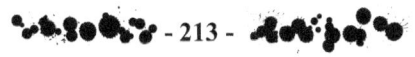

"Because we love each other but don't know *how* to love sometimes," she said, exasperated.

They started to laugh, one feeding off the other until they both had to wipe at the tears in their eyes. It was so frustrating.

"Seriously, Alice, I *do* love you," Kathy said earnestly. "But sometimes I can't love you because of what you do and what you are."

"I know," Alice acknowledged. She'd always known. She hadn't wanted Kathy to ever find out what she was.

"Do you think it's safe to talk outside like this? Can they hear us?"

"I have no idea," Alice admitted.

"That isn't like you."

"What?"

"To admit defeat," Kathy stated, alarmed a little. Alice had always been the one she could turn to in any crisis. This was unnerving Kathy.

"Oh, I'm not defeated," Alice admitted, a smile forming. "Let's go shopping," she said, taking Kathy's hand in hers and leading her back into the house.

"Have you forgotten they froze my assets the other day?"

"They didn't freeze mine," she countered. "We need a few *supplies*, and I want you to drive me in that beautiful car you bought."

Kathy smiled. This was a side of Alice she liked, loved even. They had been tiptoeing around things. Despite the fact Kathy hadn't let Alice sleep in her bed, Alice still tried to help them. She could see that Alice had been completely bored by Andie and Portia's meeting that day; it had gone on far too long, and Alice had other things to do. She was only grateful Alice was including her. "So, you like my car, do you?"

"Oh, yes. It's beautiful and classy like you," Alice said offhandedly. "I love the blue color too."

Kathy was blushing at the unexpected compliment.

"Kids, we're going out for a while," Alice called up the stairs, still holding Kathy's hand.

"Can we come?" Emily called back.

"Do you have your homework done?" Kathy called up. "That's almost a guarantee she can't come with us," she whispered to Alice.

"Yes," Emily said as she came to the top of the stairs.

"Well, to be honest, I would like some alone time with your mom. Is that okay?" Alice asked her.

Emily smiled ruefully. She couldn't deny her mothers' attempts to reconcile. She shrugged and nodded. "I'll babysit Sean," she answered.

"I heard that," he shouted from his room where the door was open.

"Good. Maybe you'll get your homework done?" Kathy teased. She had no worries there. They were good kids.

The two women headed down to the garage. Alice ran the device over the car once again but found nothing. She shrugged. That was one of the reasons they were going out, to get some new toys to make their home safe from whoever was monitoring them. She directed Kathy to a store.

"A spy store?" Kathy sputtered, laughing when she saw where they were going.

"What? They have legitimate purposes," Alice said as she got out of the beautiful Lexus. She'd admired it and loved how it felt to be the passenger, but she didn't dare ask to drive it. That reminded her, she had to go pick up the car she had been using.

"Yes, but a *spy* store?"

"Well, there are more *sophisticated* shops I know of, but I didn't really want to expose you that element," she admitted.

"Alice, when are you going to realize I know what you do? I may not know everything, and I know you don't want to tell me everything for my own safety, but I know who and what you are."

Alice looked at her for a moment. She did know. And she was right that Alice didn't tell her everything. She never had, and she wondered if she ever would. She trusted Kathy, she really did, but at the same time, she didn't trust that others wouldn't get the information and use it against them. Apparently, this had just happened, and she wasn't happy about it. She wanted to blame someone, and Kathy had been the one to let the cop into their family, but still, she couldn't blame Kathy. Kathy had been lonely, and the cop had seemed like a companion she could trust. Alice had to stop this line of thought. She didn't know for sure it was the cop who had planted the bugs.

Alice walked with Kathy into the store and waited until the salesman was alone to begin asking about sensors and other things she wanted for their house.

"Sounds like you are arming your place to fend off an invasion," he teased about her questions and the things she wanted to buy. He stopped when those curiously yellow eyes fixed themselves on him.

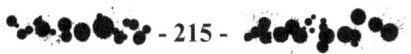

"Well, legally, we don't have that," he said, dropping his voice when she asked about a specific model and application.

"How about in the back?" Alice asked knowingly and held his stare until he dropped his eyes.

"Legally, that doesn't exist," he rephrased.

"I'm sure for the right price it exists. Why don't you ask someone?" She waited quietly until he left to go in the back.

"What are you doing?" Kathy asked in a whisper. She was concerned when Alice began acting a certain way. She wouldn't want to be on her wife's bad side at that point. Alice wasn't quite *there*, but Kathy could sense she was using her forceful personality on the young man.

"I'm getting what we need to combat this and…" she began whispering back, and then, the young man returned with an older man.

"I believe you are looking for the XR17?" he asked, looking her straight in the eye.

"No, not looking," she responded. "Buying." She knew this was a game, and she knew she could outplay them.

The man smiled, but no humor reached his eyes as he started to laugh. "That is the stuff of science fiction and spy magazines."

"Maybe," she agreed, smiling herself, "but the technology is out there, and I'd like to buy it. Name your price."

He hesitated. Her eyes had changed slightly. The humor hadn't reached her eyes either, and he studied her for a moment, trying to determine if he was being set up. He glanced down, and her hand made a rubbing motion, the thumb across the pads of the first two fingers. He glanced up at her again with a question in his eyes, and at her nod, he commanded the young man in Russian, "Go get her the item."

"Make sure it's nice and new and functional too," Alice said in English. Both men looked at her, unsure if she had understood what they said. She turned innocently to the older man. "I want these items too," she indicated what the younger man had set out on the counter.

He started ringing up her purchases, and the young man returned with a boxed item. Kathy went to open the box, but Alice stopped her with a little shake of her head and stretched her neck to indicate the other patrons in the store. She heard a little cracking sound as she stretched. Kathy got it. They weren't to open the box in the store because they never knew who was watching them. Alice slid a few hundred-dollar bills across the counter, then a few more, and finally after the third pass, he nodded that it was enough. Kathy's eyebrows shot up. She took the packages that had been put into bags for them, and they exited the store.

"That was an expensive trip," she commented.

"We've just begun," Alice admitted and proceeded to buy an array of computers and accessories that shocked Kathy. They hadn't gone to the big box stores to buy new computers. Rather, Alice had visited pawn shops all over town to find older computers that looked just like Alice's now outdated computers. They began to set it all up at the house, much to the eager delight of the children when they noticed one of the computers was newer and was a gaming computer with a keyboard that lit up in a rainbow of colors.

"We can use this?" Sean asked eagerly as he helped.

"Yes, but it's for all of us, and you are not to access it from your room or take it up there," Alice told him. He didn't realize it, but she was eager to play with him because it was also a way to communicate with other players that she wanted to find.

"What is all this?" Kathy asked as Alice turned on a shortwave type radio.

"This," she said quietly, so the children, who were playing with the gaming computer in the office wouldn't hear, "is a dispersal ban radio," she explained. "It will totally screw with anyone who tries to bug our house. And that," she indicated another computer, will also give off an erroneous signal when I get it hooked up. We'll do that tomorrow while they are at school," she said meaningfully. Kathy nodded.

"Come on," she said, pulling out the XR17 and opening the box. It looked like a sex toy. In fact, for just a second, Kathy looked startled, and Alice's eyes crinkled up in humor over what she had to be thinking. "This will find what this," she pointed at the other, older detector, "couldn't find." She started waving the wand, and it immediately sensed the other detector. Alice plugged in a set of earbuds, and after she handed one to Kathy, the two of them began walking around the house. They found a couple more different style bugs, and all were put in the freezer for the time being.

"They bugged our house," Kathy gasped, still not sure how or when.

"Some of these look old, but I wonder how old?" Alice murmured. She'd been gone more than two years, and she'd regularly been home and checked for such things, so they couldn't be more than two years old. "What has someone heard in the last couple years?" she murmured aloud.

Kathy looked at her wife, startled. She had never talked about Alice in a way that could give her away, but in the last week since Alice had started telling Kathy where'd she been while she was away, a lot of incriminating things had been said. "What can we do?"

"We seem to have gotten all of this type bug," Alice indicated the darker bugs the wand had located.

"Why didn't the other one detect them?"

"They are more sophisticated than the lighter ones," she mused aloud. They were making a second pass of the house after having checked the children's rooms. She was relieved not to find any bugs in there with the XR17. After all, they had expected that they could talk freely in the safety of their home. Whoever was bugging them had counted on that.

They found no more bugs, and Kathy asked, "Now what?"

"Now, we start playing it against them. We'll wait until the kids are at school."

"What about Portia and Andie?"

"Do you think you can keep them at the office instead of having them come here?"

"I want to be in on this," she demanded.

"I understand that, but I have work I must do, and setting this up will take time," she pointed out. "It won't be an overnight thing."

"But if those computers are to replace your others...?"

"No, those are decoys. I'm going to set up my computers in the basement of the house in the valley, but we must be careful there too. They know I have the sedan, and this," she indicated the XR17, "has to check that car as well as the valley house."

"Wait, you just spent thousands of dollars on decoys?" Kathy asked, aghast at the expense, especially while she was facing financial ruin.

Alice smiled. "They have to find something when they raid the house looking for computers and what they expect the computers to contain."

"Are you sure they are going to raid the house?"

"Well, they didn't find what they wanted in your offices. Go back with Andie and Portia and work in the office. I'll explain what I'm doing here and in the valley house on the nights when you are home."

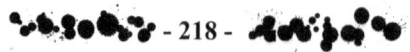

"I don't think you should set your computers up in the house there," Kathy objected.

"Why?"

"Because I think I added that house to the rolls of what you owned, and they are going to check that out."

Alice sighed. That made sense. She decided she needed another storage unit and fast. "I better check out the office too," she added, indicating the XR17.

Kathy looked startled at that but nodded. There was no telling what had been bugged. She was startled to realize how many there were.

The next day, Alice was busy setting up the new computers in their house and installing new software the computers hadn't come with. Some of it was older software because she was making it look like she was an investment trader again, something they would expect. Of course, she couldn't invest until the government legally brought her back to life, but in the meantime, this was all for appearances anyway. She put the dummy information from her other computers on the new equipment, and she moved her old computers from the house into a storage facility, which was wired for electricity. She rented two units, so she could park her sedan in the adjoining storage unit. The car was certified clean by the XR17. She could find no bugs anywhere on it. Alice took Kathy to the new storage facility on Friday morning. They had to be home in time to welcome Sean and Emily's guests and pick Kit up at the airport.

"Jeez," Kathy said as she realized how much the new setup looked like the one at the house. Alice was a creature of habit on one hand and surprisingly random on the other hand.

"Here, look through this and see if anything looks familiar. Do you sense a pattern?" Alice asked her, giving her a computer printout to look at on one screen.

"What am I looking for?"

"Repeated blips on the screen. If there are two identical blips, look for a third or more. Any two blips that are alike are suspicious at this point."

"This is going to take hours, maybe days," Kathy complained.

"I'll do it if you don't want—"

"No, I guess I just didn't realize how much preparation was required in advance of some of the things you do."

"We only have two hours," she reminded her wife, so they could get started. She'd run wires into the unit, so she could get a signal to use the internet, and she had already started going through her computers, copying some information she wanted to keep and deleting other material. Some of the data would appear meaningless to some people, and some of the evidence would have to disappear because it could and would be used against her.

"Here, do you see that?" Kathy said half an hour later, pointing to some slight rises in the pattern on the screen. Alice came over to examine what she had found, her eyes narrowing at what her wife pointed to. She was right next to Kathy when she felt a wave of desire for her wife. Ignoring what she had found on the screen, she looked at Kathy intently for a moment, glancing down the shirt that showed off her body. Then, gulping and closing her eyes slightly, she turned back to the screen.

"Yes, that's what I meant," she praised her wife.

Kathy wasn't unaware of Alice's closeness. She scented the vague perfume that was Alice. It was not the perfume she occasionally used; this was the scent that was so uniquely Alice. Kathy was pleased that she had been some help to her wife. She often felt useless when she was around Alice and her expertise.

Together, the two women assessed the peaks and valleys on the report and finally determined there was a pattern to it.

"But what does it mean?" Kathy asked as they drove in Alice's junky sedan, a far cry from the Porsche she had loved. They were heading back to where Kathy had parked the Lexus, so they could pick up Kit at the airport. They left the sedan in a carpool lot and got back in the Lexus. Alice closed her eyes almost reverently as she settled into the luxurious vehicle.

"It means we need to activate a couple of those bugs and then try to pinpoint who is listening and from where."

"You can do that?"

"With the setups we bought this week, certainly."

"Thank you for restocking the cupboards, by the way. Sean appreciates it," she added when she thought of it. The trip to the supermarket had been an experience. Alice hated shopping and had nearly gone into cart rage as other shoppers got in her way.

"Kathy, you know I would never let you go hungry, much less lose what we have."

"I know, but it was frightening how arrogant the IRS agent was when they raided the offices."

"Yes, I know," Alice agreed. She'd checked out the card that Andie handed her, and the guy was legitimately employed by the IRS. She had used the back doors her computers had into several official government sites including the FBI. If they ever found out she had those, she'd be locked away, but she rarely used them and tried not to leave a signature or a trail. She was very good at that. "That's what they count on. They want to frighten you into confessing, and whether you are guilty or not is irrelevant."

"What are you going to do if it's Linda?" she asked worriedly.

"What do you want me to do?"

"Oh, God. Alice, I don't want you to kill her. She's a nice and kind woman. She…" she began and then trailed off as she realized she was talking about her girlfriend with her wife…and it was Alice to boot, who handled things differently than a normal person.

"I know she is an honest person, and she has integrity, but she did snoop," Alice pointed out.

"Do you think she bugged our house?"

"Do you?"

"Stop doing that!" Kathy exclaimed as she maneuvered on the freeway towards the airport. LAX was always a nightmare of traffic. She was also used to Alice being the driver, the one who escorted her around, and this was unnerving.

"Doing what?" Alice asked innocently, but she knew what her wife meant. She really couldn't help it. It was automatic. Alice had been alone for a long time. Even while married, she'd been alone in her extracurricular activities. She wasn't used to sharing the responsibility or the activities. This was still new ground for her. Even last year with Sasha, Alice had taken the lead as the Russian woman hadn't been capable of being as dirty and deadly as was required. Sasha had learned, but it was only after she had the realization they had no other choice.

"Doing what? Turning my questions back on me. This isn't my decision alone. This affects you and the children."

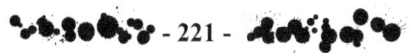

"I know, and I'm sorry," Alice apologized, truly feeling contrite. "Let's worry about it when we have conclusive evidence. We don't know for sure it is Linda yet."

"But you are thinking it is?"

"Who else had that kind of access? She did snoop, that we know, but did she also bug the house? Something must have made her suspicious."

"Being a cop, I think she was suspicious by nature."

Alice wanted to condemn her wife for getting involved with the cop, but really, who Kathy fell for wasn't her fault. Still, would they be in this mess if Kathy hadn't gotten tangled up with the cop? She really couldn't say anything about who her wife had chosen to date. As far as Kathy had been concerned, Alice was dead, and she was moving on. Alice just nodded in answer to Kathy's statement. She had to agree that some cops were suspicious by nature. Alice had dealt with some decent cops, and she had thought Linda was decent. But Alice had also dealt with a lot of dirty cops, and they had paid the ultimate price.

"Oh, God. I bet she heard me talk about Leskowitz," Kathy suddenly exclaimed as she thought over last week's confessions of what they had been doing.

"If she did, she'd have arrested you. Besides, we don't know conclusively that it's Linda," she pointed out, feeling strange to be defending the woman who had wanted to have sex with her wife. Alice wanted to be fair, she really did, but that didn't prevent her from wanting to kill the woman who had felt up her wife.

Kathy had to admit Alice was right, and she pulled off the freeway onto Century Boulevard. She checked the clock and thought they were going to be late, effortlessly accelerating to maneuver around slower vehicles.

"Careful. You don't want to get a ticket," Alice teased with a grin, trying to brighten her mood before seeing their daughter. Kit had been her daughter longer than she had been her father's, and Alice considered her as much her own as Sean and Emily.

They met Kit coming out of the terminal as she was looking around. To Alice it was like seeing a younger, college age version of Kathy, and in that instant, she remembered when Connie had been alive and was friends with the younger Kathy. It brought up unfamiliar, nostalgic feelings as Alice got out of the front seat of the Lexus and enveloped the taller, young woman in her arms.

"Wow! Alice, look at you," Kit said, hugging her back just as hard.

"Alice?" she asked, her eyebrow raising slightly.

"Sorry, Mom. You look so different." Kit played with the spikey, short hair, her fingers mussing it up only to have it immediately spring back into place. It was a far cry from the neat and orderly long hair Alice had sported in the past.

"I've really missed you," Alice admitted, grabbing her daughter's bag.

"Hey, Mom," Kit greeted her biological mother with a kiss as she leaned across to hug her.

"Hurry up and get in. We're in the red zone," Alice kidded, getting in the back seat with her daughter, holding her hand and smiling at the young woman. She left the bag in the front seat.

They talked a mile a minute, including Kathy in the family reunion as she headed the car home to Palos Verdes. Alice warned Kit about talking with anyone about her return or the fact that they were under investigation by the IRS.

"I don't think my friends will care," the young woman pointed out.

"I know, but these people are insidious. Your friends might not realize that a casual comment could really come back to haunt us, and I just don't want you hurt."

Kit nodded, not used to this type of clandestine conversation. She'd been in some weird situations over the years with her parents, but she'd been striking out and growing up at college. In fact, she had wanted to talk to her parents about getting an apartment instead of living in the dorms. Now, with Kathy's assets frozen, she knew the time wasn't right.

They got home and quickly set things up for the party. An anxious Emily was already stressing out, and at first, Sean was no help, but Alice got him setting things up with the threat that she was going to start pulling out baby pictures to show his friends. "I do have them all on a projector someplace," she said musingly, looking around as though considering where to set it up.

"Okay, okay, I'll help," he answered grudgingly. Still, he was thrilled to have Alice home and didn't mind the threat of public humiliation.

Alice and Kathy took turns answering the door, leaving the security gate open, so they didn't have to keep opening it for the cars that were arriving. Alice had to ask one of the kids to please get their Ferrari off

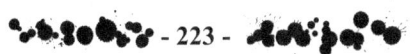

her lawn and park on the blacktop like everyone else, but other than that, the kids were all being respectful.

"Hi, Mrs. Weaver. These are my parents, Sandi and Richard Pasternack," a girl whose name Alice had already forgotten introduced them to her parents. Alice never turned a hair at the name, but she recognized it instantly. She examined both people intensely, looking for any familiarity that might be found there. After all, many others in the world had the same last name. She wondered if they recognized *her*?

"It's a pleasure to meet you," Alice said politely. She and Kathy had met many of the children's parents as they dropped them off. Some allowed their kids to drive to the party and others had walked over with them.

"We live three doors down," Sandi explained, pointing down the block, which was quite far away, what with the sizes of the estates out here.

"Oh, that lovely Tudor style home," Alice answered, sounding knowledgeable.

"Yes. You noticed," Sandi said, sounding pleased.

Alice saw Kathy walking up and introduced her. "This is my wife, Kathy. Kathy, this is Sandi and Richard Pasternack. They live in that lovely Tudor home down the block." She knew she sounded like a parody of some television program but was playing her part to the hilt for the children's sake.

"How do you do?" they said, shaking Kathy's outstretched hand. Alice saw a momentary flash of dislike in Richard, his eyes betraying his homophobia. She wondered if he was aware of it? But it was Sandi's eyes that bothered Alice more. Looking in Sandi's eyes, she recognized something immediately. Like knew like, and in Sandi's eyes Alice saw a killer. It was a startling find. She'd rarely seen another. It was an odd realization, especially in this atmosphere where teenagers were hanging out playing games on the computer and eating pizza in Sean's room with the soda flowing. She wondered if Sandi was self-aware?

"I hope you don't mind that we came with Carmen to meet her little friend's parents?" Sandi said, also startled to see the speculative look in Alice's eye. She didn't recognize the look, but it made her cautious about the woman.

"Oh, absolutely. It's nice to meet you," Kathy answered, unsure why this woman made her uncomfortable. Richard also had an aura about him, which she was responding to. "I don't think I have seen you around the neighborhood?"

"We moved here about a year and a half ago," Sandi informed her as they let some of the kids go by.

"Would you like to stay? Parents are welcome," Kathy said.

"We wouldn't want to intrude, and you have other guests," she said politely.

"I've got the door, Mom," Kit said, popping up.

"This is our other daughter, Kit. This is Mr. and Mrs. Pasternack," Alice introduced her daughter proudly, her arm going around the taller young woman. Alice looked positively small next to her grown daughter. The Pasternacks looked from Alice to Kit as they greeted her and determined she took after Kathy, which was true, but they couldn't know that for a fact. Emily, who they had already met, looked a lot like Alice in the face, especially in the eyes, but the rest of her looked like Kathy. Sandi, for one, was curious how that was possible.

"Would you like to come in?" Kathy repeated. "We can sit on the patio and avoid the teen noises," she joked, having already told Sean to turn down the music on the awful video games he and his buddies were playing. Alice had hooked up the big screen to the computer and allowed the gaming computer to be taken out of the office and put in the living room for the duration of the party. Sean had brought down his computer games and TV, and several screens were going at once. Emily and her friends were going from the games to the kitchen and giggling over the older guys.

"No, we are going to walk back to our place. We just wanted to meet you both and say hello," Sandi said, excusing themselves. Sandi wanted to talk to Richard now that they had met the Weavers. The gossip in the neighborhood was already rampant about Alice's return, and there was that small news article in the paper about the Weavers' assets being frozen. Sandi wanted to see if they could somehow benefit.

"I was going to escape, and since Kit has volunteered to watch the door, I'm going to take that walk. Did you want to come?" Alice put in, unexpectedly holding out her hand to Kathy. "We'd be happy to walk you back, if you don't mind the company?" she asked the couple as Kathy caught onto the fact that something was up and took her wife's hand at the unexpected invitation.

Not wanting to look like jerks, the Pasternacks accepted, and the two couples walked down the steps to the driveway where kids were still arriving for the impromptu party. They walked down the driveway past expensive cars, which were all parked to one side. The big turnout was mostly because of Sean; Emily did not have that many friends.

"So, what do you two do?" Alice began casually, hating the inane conversation starter.

"Dickie is in banking, and I'm a nurse," Sandi admitted, warming to the innocent question.

"Oh, that's nice," Alice answered and squeezed Kathy's hand to try and get her to say something. The name Dickie, a shortened version of Richard or Dick, had her biting her tongue because she wanted to say something rude. Kathy was puzzled and didn't know the reason for the hand squeeze. She glanced at Alice, trying to read her. "You say you only moved here a year and a half ago?"

"Yes, I got a transfer out here from New York, and fortunately, Sandi was able to get a job with a hospice service in LA."

They nodded as they continued the conversation while walking down the driveway and out onto the road. Alice glanced at the cars parked along the road, something that didn't happen often, and realized the small party was going to get very big. She was anxious to get back but having agreed to accompany the couple, almost forcing themselves on the couple, she had to see it through. Leaving the Pasternacks at the end of their drive, Alice and Kathy waved and headed back towards their place.

"What was that all about?" Kathy asked, still holding Alice's hand and enjoying it.

"There's just something about them, and the Pasternack house is where Emily will be partying tomorrow," Alice mentioned.

"You figured that out already?" Kathy asked, surprised. She hadn't realized.

"I remembered the name, but I hadn't seen Emily's invitation until she showed me. I recognized the name but not for that reason," Alice admitted as she slowed to go around a car that was coming down the street. The lights of the car highlighted some people in parked cars, and Alice's eyes narrowed in on one of the parked vehicles. She examined it closely as they approached, then as they passed, she casually looked in the car and made a hair-trigger decision.

"What reason?" Kathy asked, becoming confused when Alice swooped down and picked up a rock the size of her fist. "What's going on?" she asked as Alice let go of her hand and returned to the car they had just passed.

Alice knocked on the window of the car. Startled, the female cop looked up to see their quarry standing there. "Hi, there," Alice said with an innocent smile and wave before revealing her other hand holding the rock. She abruptly smashed the rock through the window into the cop's face, knocking her out. Alice quickly reached into the car and under the woman's jacket to pull her semi-automatic from its holster. The cop's passenger soon found herself staring into the barrel of the gun. "I do NOT like to be followed," Alice said conversationally. She gestured with the gun, "Let's see what you've got."

The other woman slowly pulled out her own gun and held it by the butt with two fingers.

Alice gestured again, "Throw it in the back." She watched as the woman threw it towards the backseat of the unmarked squad car, she heard a satisfying clump as it hit the cushion and fell to floor. She gestured again with the cop's gun, "As I said, I don't *like* to be followed." She glanced at the first cop one more time, saw that she was already starting to come around, then turned and walked away rapidly. She pushed the button to release the clip on the gun and threw the clip as far away as possible. Next, she pulled the barrel forward and unhinged it, so the gun began to pull apart in her hand, ready for cleaning. Instead, Alice threw the pieces as far as she could in multiple directions. By the time the other cop retrieved her gun from the back of the car, Alice had returned to the shadows with Kathy and was gone.

"What the hell was that about?" Kathy asked, alarmed.

"I would say the games have begun," she said as she pulled her wife along as fast as she could in the shadows.

"Yes, but what?" she asked, confused.

"I realized something was up when we were walking with the Pasternacks and the passengers in that car both kind of slouched down." She indicated the unmarked cop car. "I pretended not to see them. I saw that you didn't notice."

"No, I wouldn't have. Should I?"

Alice chuckled. Kathy didn't have it in her to be the serial killer Alice was, but she had killed before. Kathy didn't have the instincts, and even under Alice's tutelage, she would never develop them. It was okay though. Alice loved her wife as she was. She did love her, and she stopped before they got to their driveway. "No, you don't need to spot those things. Just try to be aware, so you don't get hurt. I don't know what the hell is going on or what we're involved in here, but we will figure things out, and I'll get to the bottom of this one way or the other. I'm sure those people there," she gestured back to the cops she had upset, "are just a small part of what is happening. I have to wonder if we have something on our computers now?"

"The ones at the house?"

"No. Like I said, those are decoys. I'm talking about the computers at the storage place," she answered, whispering. It was getting distracting. Alice had her mouth by Kathy's ear and could smell her personal scent. She desperately wanted to kiss her wife. Alice stopped what she was saying to give into the impulse and kissed Kathy gently on her lips. When she sensed Kathy responding, she deepened the kiss, enjoying it. Kathy put her arms around Alice, holding her and equally relishing the kiss.

"I thought we'd never get here," she murmured as she kissed Alice again.

"I'm sorry," Alice told her as she kissed back, bringing her tongue into play.

"For what?" Kathy breathed, feeling herself becoming aroused as only Alice could make her feel.

"For everything," Alice breathed in return before taking her wife firmly in her strong arms and kissing her hard, deeply, and with so much emotion she could have wept. Only the beeping horn, their silhouettes caught in the headlights, and the ribald comments of the teens parking their car stopped their passionate embrace. Smiling wryly, Alice started walking with her wife again, their hands entwined and Kathy leaning her head on Alice's firm shoulder.

"I've missed you so much," she said sadly.

"About half as much as I missed you," Alice said in return as they turned up their driveway.

"Yes, but you knew I was alive. I didn't know you were alive," Kathy pointed out.

"Okay, you win," Alice teased.

"What do I win?"

"Me," she promised, and they began walking up the drive.

"I don't think these kids are all friends of our children's," Alice pointed out unnecessarily, seeing the party was getting out of control and all the kids heading for the front door.

"Yeah, I'd say these are friends of friends and they heard the word *party* and took it a little too far," Kathy said angrily, pulling ahead slightly.

"We'll handle it," Alice promised, then did. Upon entering the house, they noticed kids seemed to be everywhere in the short time while they had taken their walk. Alice looked and saw someone dispensing beer and what looked like whiskey. "That's it. You can leave," she told the kid.

"I just got here," he said in protest, grabbing at the alcohol.

Alice swiped it off the counter and said, "Then leave *now*."

"That's my–" he began to protest, but Alice gave him a shove across the kitchen.

"It's forfeited," she said as she escorted him to the front door that Kit was once again manning. "Where were you?"

"I had to pee. Sorry," the young woman answered, frowning at the kid Alice was kicking out.

"He's not allowed back in," Alice told Kit and then re-entered the fray.

"Out! OUT!" Kathy was shouting at the kids who had jumped fully clothed into the pool. "You there! Get your clothes back on! That isn't even an attractive bra," she told the girl, who had stripped down to her underwear, obviously unaware that her pubic hair was clearly visible through the panties.

Alice glanced towards the pool and saw Kathy had it clearly in hand, so she picked up the beer and whiskey and locked it securely in a cupboard. Seeing another guy drinking surreptitiously from a flask, she slapped it from his hand. It fell with a clatter to the kitchen floor.

"Hey!" he shouted, looking down on the small woman who had attacked him. "That's prime–."

"Were you invited to this party?" Alice interrupted.

"Yeah," he challenged her, not in the least intimidated by the petite woman. A couple of his buddies started grinning, showing their support.

"Are you twenty-one?"

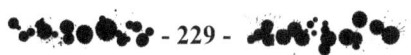

"No. So? Everyone does it."

"You're a jock, aren't you?"

"So?" He put such utter contempt in the word that Alice could feel herself becoming deadly cold. Still, he was young and stupid.

Alice didn't bother with the niceties. He was obviously not going to respond to them. Instead, she took his hand, which had been thrown up in a gesture towards her to show his contempt, and she grabbed the thumb. Spinning him slightly, she had him on his knees in record time and screaming from the pain she exerted on his thumb. "Have you ever broken your thumb, Jock Boy?" she asked conversationally.

"Noooo...n...n...noooo," he stuttered, obviously in excruciating pain. A couple of his friends guffawed at him being downed so easily by a woman half his size.

"It isn't a good feeling," she told him. "It messes with your ability to do so much...like pulling it out of your ass when you're being one." She knew her conversation was probably going over his head.

Kathy came in through the patio, a couple of kids following her. "Go around the house and go home," she ordered them. She turned to Alice and said warningly, "Careful, Alice."

"What's your name, boy?" she asked him.

"I'm eighteen. I'm a man!" he said, objecting to her verbiage.

"A man doesn't talk to a woman the way you just did. We've established you aren't twenty-one yet, so you're a boy." She twisted his thumb a smidge for emphasis.

"What the fuck?" he roared.

Alice slapped him with her other hand. "We don't talk that way in this house. What's your name, boy?"

"That's Josh McCullen," Sean spoke up, the only one in the room under the age of nineteen, who wasn't afraid of Alice at that moment. "He's on the LA Charger's team," he mentioned, hoping his mother wouldn't break the guy's thumb.

"High school, right?" she clarified, glancing up at her son, who was looking at her meaningfully. She got the gist. At least he wasn't from Sean's high school. This incident could seriously cramp Sean's high school years. At his nod, she asked the downed football player, "Were you invited to this party by my son, Sean, over there?" When Josh didn't answer right away because he was starting to cry at the pain and humiliation, she twisted his thumb ever so slightly.

"N...n...no," he stammered, the tears coursing down his cheeks now.

"No, what?" she asked and saw Kathy look away, rubbing her thumb and forefinger along her mouth to keep from laughing.

"What?" he asked through the pain, looking up at her and amazed to see she was holding him with just one hand. A look came over him as he had a thought. He'd worked through pain before on the field....

"Don't do it. You'll break your thumb, and it won't be from anything I did," she told him. "In this house, we value manners, so I'll ask you again... No, what?"

It took him a moment to understand what she meant. "No, ma'am," he said in a greatly different tone of voice.

"So, you weren't invited, and you brought alcohol. Have you been drinking, Josh?"

They both knew she had slapped the flask out of his hand, but the question was asked for the benefit of the crowd that had formed. Someone had alerted Sean that his mother was humiliating Josh McCullen in the kitchen, and he had sprinted upstairs to see what was going on. The guy was a bully, and Sean would never have invited him to a party at his house.

"Yes," he answered.

Alice increased the pressure slightly and asked, "Yes, what, Josh?"

"Y...ye...yes, ma'am," he tried to breathe through the pain in his hand, which was radiating up his arm and into his shoulder and brain. It was excruciating. The tears were pouring down his cheeks.

"We didn't invite you, you brought alcohol, and you were rude to your host's mother. Is that how people behave in your neck of the woods?"

"No, ma'am," he said respectfully. His friends had stopped smiling and egging him on, no longer thinking he'd get out of this with his smart mouth and look all cool while doing it. Several friends were looking on with pity now. A couple had drifted away and left the party already.

"Did you drive here, Josh?"

"Yes, ma'am."

"What do you drive?"

"A Charger."

"Of course, you do," she said using the same contemptuous tone he had used on her earlier. She whipped him down on his face, let go of

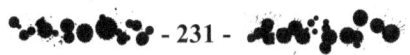

his thumb, and reached into his front pocket where she saw the bulge of his keys. She fished the keys out. "You will have to pick up your car tomorrow, Josh. Leave my home now." She looked up at the gathered crowd. "If you aren't a friend of my son or daughter, I suggest you leave. This is not a free-for-all, and no one mentioned alcohol." She watched as kids exchanged looks, and then, at her clear, firm, "NOW!" they began to file out of the house. She let Josh up. He was rubbing his hand and stumbling to the front door, a couple of his buddies helping him.

"Wow, Mom. You are going to make me look like the biggest geek in town," Sean complained.

"Yeah, but you are going to be the geek who's not drinking and driving like those idiots," she pointed to where the other people like Josh had left. "Your friends," she smiled at a couple that she recognized, "are welcome here anytime, so long as they remain respectful." God, those kids had grown in the years she had been gone.

"Thank you, Mrs. Weaver," a couple of them mumbled, embarrassed, before returning to play their video games. They were geeks and had been flattered that some of the jocks from neighboring schools had come to the party, but it had quickly gotten out of hand.

"I didn't invite them," Sean stated.

"I know you didn't, but people will judge you by the company you keep, so bear that in mind." He nodded, still unhappy at what had just happened as he turned to join his friends. He could still hear some of the partiers turning around in the driveway. He hoped none of them burned rubber or his mom would be furious.

Alice waited until the kids had gone before turning to Kathy, "Did I go overboard?"

"Hell, no! I would have been scared to take on that big kid."

"I didn't hurt him, but he might have hurt me if he'd been given the chance. I don't want that kind of shit in our home."

"Amen," Kathy agreed as they began to clean up the kitchen.

"Mom?" Emily came around the corner carrying some things she had cleaned up from the living room. "I just want you to know I had nothing to do with those apes that came to the party."

"I know, sweetie. Word spreads when there is a party. That's why you should trust your friends and even then, just use your head."

Emily grinned wryly. Carmen was standing right there listening to them, and Emily asked her, "Do you want something to drink? We have soda."

"Sounds good. Let's get soda for everyone and some of that pizza if there's any left after those jocks grazed."

Emily laughed and agreed. They made another pizza in the pizza maker and got out some soda. While they were waiting for the pizza buzzer to go off, they helped Alice and Kathy straighten up the kitchen and living room, and a couple of the other girls and Kit joined them to help.

"Why don't the guys help us?" Emily wondered aloud as they finished up.

"Guys don't think like girls," Alice answered for her daughter's friends. "It's a patriarchal thing."

"My brother cleans up," Carmen put in.

A couple of the girls agreed. "My brother would never get away with not cleaning up," one commented.

"Should I have pulled Sean away from his friends to help?" Kathy asked with a grin.

They decided that *this* time it was okay that he didn't help, but in the morning, he would have to empty the dishwasher. They all chuckled over that.

The doorbell rang, and Alice went to answer it. It was a police officer. She checked the sleeve to make sure they were with Palos Verdes and not the Los Angeles Police Department. "Can I help you, officer?" she asked respectfully, wondering if it was about the rock through the window. Kathy came out of the kitchen to see who was at the door, thinking it was another partygoer. She tensed when she saw the police were there. Kit, seeing Kathy freeze up, went to see what was up, and one by one, the girls drifted out of the kitchen to see who had arrived.

"Yes, we have a complaint about a party going on here?" the first officer stated in the form of a question.

"Yes, we do have a gathering here, but as you can see, there is no party." She was thankful she had shut everything down not half an hour ago and the boys hadn't put the volume up on the games they were playing once again.

"We have a complaint about the noise," the second officer put in.

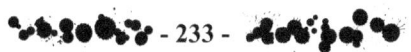

"Noise?" she asked. It hadn't been that noisy even when everyone was there. She also lived on acreage and was quite a distance from her neighbors, who also had acreage. They probably couldn't have heard the music that Sean had turned down earlier. "What noise?"

"Ma'am, I'm sure you understand we have to investigate when we have a complaint."

"Yes, officer, I do understand, but as you can see, we are not having a party. We have a small gathering of my children's friends, and it's relatively quiet." Just then, she heard the dinger of the pizza oven going off in the kitchen and turned to see everyone watching. She frowned at them and several girls scurried back to the kitchen. "Are you waiting for an invitation to eat pizza and drink soda?" she asked, trying to lighten the moment.

"Is there alcohol on the premises?" one of the officers asked.

"Of course, there is, and it's locked up." She was starting to become annoyed, but cops usually had that effect on her; they just rubbed her the wrong way.

"Are you the homeowner?" the second cop asked.

"Yes, I'm Alice Weaver, and this is my wife, Kathy," she said, introducing them. "I've explained we are having a gathering. There is no noise, as you can clearly hear, and we are not having a party. Is there anything else, officers?"

"Are you serving alcohol to minors?"

"No," she answered, her voice justifiably becoming angry. "We don't do things like that." She realized that sounded prissy, but she didn't care. These cops were annoying her.

"May we come in and look around?"

"Do you have a warrant?" she asked in return, her anger causing her to suddenly become belligerent. She wasn't going to be pushed around, and she sincerely doubted the cops whose window she had broken were with these bozos. Something or someone was afoot, and she was angry enough to let it show.

"You are refusing to let us look around?" he countered.

"You are being refused entry to my home because you don't have a search warrant. You don't have probable cause to enter the premises, and I'm refusing to allow you to enter. Good night, gentlemen. Have a good evening," and with that, she closed the door on their surprised faces. She watched as they turned and went back down the stairs to their patrol car. After they had left, she pushed the button to close the gate. She wouldn't be leaving it open any longer. She looked down the driveway at the Charger parked to the side and wondered if it was killing the grass. She sighed.

"What the heck?" Kathy asked. She'd listened to every word of that exchange.

"Let the harassment begin," Alice murmured. This wasn't an isolated incident. She was sure there was more than one thing going on.

That night after the kids had all gone home, Alice locked up and turned to go to the guest room where she had been staying. Kathy was there, having done a walk-through to make sure they had cleaned up all the snacks and dishes, and she said, "Why don't you sleep in our room? This is silly. We both need to move on from the past and look towards our future, don't you think?"

"I'm willing," Alice whispered with a smile and put her arm around her wife as they walked together to the master bedroom. Emily, who had just come from the bathroom, finished closing her door and smiled. She didn't understand all that she had overheard from her mother last week but seeing them together and seeing how Alice had kicked ass that night at the party, Emily felt better about having her other mom home. Maybe they would finally have a normal life?

"Why do I feel like this is the first time?" Kathy asked as she turned to Alice after shutting and locking the door.

"Because it's been so long for both of us?"

"You didn't…while you were away…you didn't…?"

"No! How could I, Kathy? I love you, and even though we were separated, I knew I was coming back to you. To *you*!"

Kathy didn't understand that kind of love, not really. Sometimes, she didn't feel she deserved Alice, and then Alice made her feel so safe. Even in the few weeks she had known Alice was back and alive, she had felt safer. What was it about this woman that inspired that kind of confidence? She should be afraid of her, but she wasn't. She wanted her, and she wanted her *now*. Kathy leaned in to kiss her wife.

Alice immediately took control. It had been too long, and the desire she felt for her *wife* was not going to be assuaged by mere kissing.

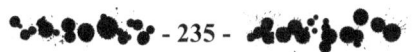

Sure, she could have had causal encounters when she was away, but she hadn't. She had remained faithful because it was part of her own code of conduct. She wouldn't cheat on Kathy, and she was certain Kathy hadn't been unfaithful, even with the cop. She pushed aside thoughts of the cop feeling her wife up and concentrated on Kathy. Pulling her wife into her arms, she held her as she ravished her mouth, showing her need for her and only her.

Kathy relished the feel of Alice against her and immediately started pulling at her clothes. She wanted to be naked against Alice. She wanted to see the changes up close that she had noticed in her body. She simply wanted...Alice.

Quickly, they removed each other's clothes while continuing the kisses that were arousing them. Hands caressed bared skin and fingers dug in to pull one body against the other. This wasn't going to be pretty. There wasn't going to be a lot of finesse when both hungered so badly for the other. Alice slowly dropped to her knees in front of Kathy and took her lower lips in her mouth. Kathy looked down at the submissive posture of her wife before her and melted. Her juices flowed copiously from her body in response to the stimulation. She began grinding against Alice's upturned face. Alice plunged her fingers inside her wife, wanting to fuck her hard and furious, to show her that she owned her, and at the same time, to show by her position that she was also owned by her wife. Kathy nearly lost her footing as her knees weakened. Alice lifted one of her wife's legs and put it over her shoulder, further unbalancing Kathy, who was forced to grab the wall. With her hand flat against the wall, she ground down.

"Uh, uh, uh," she grunted, seeking to come against her wife and her administrations.

"Come for me, baby," Alice whispered as her tongue laved attention on Kathy's erect clit. She swirled it around on her tongue, sucking it in along with the slick folds that dripped their juices down her chin and onto her chest. She increased the pace of her fingers inside Kathy and felt the shudders beginning inside her. Her wife's body stiffened as the orgasm ripped through her. Alice looked up in time to see Kathy's head back and her teeth biting her lips. It was a turn-on like nothing else, and Alice could feel her own juices dripping down her legs. She slowed her fingers as she kissed her way up Kathy's overheated body. Her fingers were soused, and she let Kathy's leg slip slowly to the floor, which nearly unbalanced her again as the foot hit the floor. Alice rubbed her body against her wife's and whispered, "Did you like it?"

"Wha—?" she breathed, unsure what the hell had just happened.

Alice took Kathy and spun her to the bed, removing her hand with a loud, splattering pop. She kissed Kathy's mouth before burying her lips hard in Kathy's neck. Alice climbed on top of her wife immediately, warming her cold body against Kathy's heated body. The violence of her lovemaking showed as she continued to rub her body against her wife's. One at a time, she gently took the erect and aroused nipples in her mouth, pinching one before going to the other. Back and forth she continued as Kathy gasped at the pleasure-pain.

"Oh, God. Love me! Love me!" Kathy pleaded, unable to believe she was finally here with Alice. She tried to get the upper hand and failed, but she didn't mind. Then, as she was about to give in, she got an idea. Her body arched in a second orgasm, Alice's almost violent lovemaking achieving this in a relatively short period of time. Quickly, she rolled Alice onto her back and tried to hold her down.

Alice had always been the stronger of the two women, so she was surprised to find she wasn't as strong as she had once been. She vowed to begin working out again as she held her wife to her and Kathy began to make love to her with the same intensity she had shown. Alice closed her eyes and enjoyed the feelings this woman engendered. She let her body relax, and no matter what Kathy did, her body responded to it immediately.

Half their night was spent making mad and passionate love. On the edge of violence much of the time, it eventually dissipated into loving tenderness and the enjoyment of just knowing each was alive. Finally sated for a while, Kathy examined Alice from head to toe. She nearly cried over the new scars she saw and the loss of not only the curves but the muscle tone that had once been there.

"You've been through so much," Kathy lamented, circling Alice's nipple with her fingertips.

"I had to get back to you," Alice told her, holding her head with the palm of her hand and looking up at those brown eyes she adored.

"And then, you come back to this mess," she added.

"We'll clear it up," Alice promised. She waited a moment and said, "We better open the windows and take a bath."

"This late?" she asked. She agreed the windows needed to be opened. The room reeked of the passionate sex, and she knew she'd have to change the sheets the following day since there was more than one wet spot. Maybe pulling the covers back would allow them time to dry until she could throw them in the washer?

"Come on, I've dreamed of bathing in that large tub with you for a long time," she grinned as she got up from their bed, pulling the covers back.

Kathy pulled the covers way back to air the sheets as Alice opened the window and headed to the bathroom to start filling the tub. They spent a good hour in the tub, playing, touching, and getting to know each other again. Both were relieved they had found their way back to each other.

"Mrs. Fernandez, I am so happy to see you are still taking care of my family," Alice said, greeting the older woman, who had been with the family for years.

"I wasn't sure you would have me back when I saw the newspapers," the woman admitted.

"Well, you are going to get your pay in cash for a while," she mentioned. Kathy had worried about paying her. "But as long as we have a receipt, everything will be fine until we are able to straighten this matter out."

The woman nodded appreciatively, knowing Alice had always been good to her and not worried about anything. She had never pried, not wanting to know her employers' personal details, but seeing the article about Kathy's assets being seized, she had worried she would be out of a job. Seeing Ms. Alice there once again, she knew that whatever was happening, it would be handled. She just wanted to do her job.

Kathy already had the laundry going. Their sheets needed a good cleaning after their night together. Even with the party they'd had, the house was fairly clean, but the housekeeper would make sure it was spotless.

Alice and Kathy had errands to run in the morning. They drove the Lexus to the carpool lot to fetch the sedan and drive to the storage unit. After driving it inside the unit and closing the door, they hurried to the computers to see what they could find.

"I no longer think Linda is involved in this. I think this is something else," Alice said, pointing at the triangulation the radio receivers had done the previous night. With the gathering at their home, they thought it would be a perfect time for whoever was listening to have their moment. She had taken some of the bugs out of the freezer and put them in the room with the most activity, which was the family room. She'd chosen some of both types of bugs in the hopes that her equipment could track the perpetrators. There had been two signals, and looking at a map online, neither of them went to the precinct Linda was in.

Kathy was relieved. She had hoped Linda was clear. Kathy knew if Linda had been dirty or involved in any way that eventually, Alice might have to kill her. The thought wasn't pleasant.

"Now, how do we find out who they are?"

"Well, we know this is a police station here," she said, pointing to the map, and then she looked closer, enlarging the other map. "I have no idea who that is," she admitted.

"Should we do a drive-by?" Kathy asked, wondering if she sounded foolish or naive.

"I think we should," Alice agreed. She printed out the location and then sent a few things to the computer, executing commands on the first signal. She smiled as data began to come up.

"What are you doing?"

"I'm transmitting a virus to the first signal," she explained.

"Can you do that with a radio signal?"

"Oh, yes. I'm duplicating the signal from the house where they were listening, and it will go to the computer where they are recording the audio, or at least *think* they are recording the audio. Once the virus gets into a computer, I've got them, and I can get into their computer system to see what they have recorded and determine if they've made copies, even if they electronically transmitted them elsewhere."

"Jesus, Alice. Where did you learn how to do this?"

"You don't really want to know, Kathy. Do you?"

She admitted she didn't. She shouldn't be amazed by what Alice knew anymore.

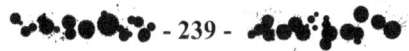

Alice stretched and got up, hugging Kathy just because she could…she finally could. They exchanged smiles. Both were a little tired today but had been anxious to get this data. Suddenly, Alice frowned at the spike in signal that was coming from their home.

"What?"

"Someone is listening at the house again," she said and typing rapidly, she quickly turned on the sound and shoved a cord into the plug, so they could listen. Alice didn't want anything to come over the speakers in case any other renters could overhear from their storage units.

"Where did Mom and Mom go?" they heard Sean's voice.

"They had errands. They probably needed some time alone," Kit answered.

Kathy looked at Alice in wonderment that the sound came in so clear. Alice pointed at the wires she had run to the unobtrusive antennae on the roof.

"Sick of you guys already?" Kit teased to get a rise out of her brother.

"They didn't need to go on errands until you got home," he gave as good as he got.

"Oh, yeah?" Kit challenged him, laughing. They were probably tussling on the couch. "No tickling!" Kit yelled.

"What's going on?" they heard Emily's voice.

"Stop him. Get him, Em. Get him!" Kit ordered as she tried hard not to laugh. They could hear the laughter as the children roughhoused.

"Hey, what do you think is really going on?" Sean asked after they had calmed down. Alice and Kathy exchanged looks.

"The IRS raided the office and took all of Mom's records," Emily told them.

"I heard that. Duh," Sean added.

"Wait. What?" Kit asked, not in on the latest happenings while at school.

They explained what they had overhead and gleaned from pieces of information. "Mom looked pissed," Sean added.

"Which mom?" Kit asked.

He started chuckling. It had been confusing all their lives. At one time, one was Mom and one was Mum, but it had merged over time until now, they were both Mom. "Momma A," he sing-songed, making it sound effeminate. The lisp coming through had them all giggling.

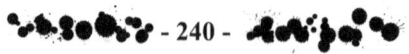

"God, I'm glad she's back. Did you see how happy Mom is now?" Alice looked at Kathy with a grin, touching her wife's arm with her finger affectionately.

"She was happy dating Linda," Kit pointed out.

"Yeah, but it wasn't the same. Linda wasn't Mom."

Kit must have nodded as she didn't say anything, and then they missed something as static came over the line. Alice played with something on the computer, changing channels, and Kathy asked softly, almost as though their children could hear her, "What?"

"Someone's trying to figure out where we are. They are running something to try and triangulate our signal here. I'm putting out another signal that will make the chances of them finding us about one in five hundred thousand."

"That exact number?" she asked, surprised.

"It might be more," she admitted, grinning as the children's voices came back into focus through the static.

"Well, I hope she's home to stay. I'm sick of losing our parents," Em was saying.

"Don't you have a party to go to tonight?" Sean asked.

"Yeah, I better lay out what I'm going to wear."

"Aren't those the girls you used to call 'mean girls'?" he asked.

"Yeah, but they're the in-crowd, and I really want to go," she said, sounding very young. The two moms exchanged a look of understanding. They knew she just wanted to fit in.

"Are they the ones that called you bulimic and anorexic?" Kit clarified.

"Yeah, but they've stopped that now," she excused them.

"I wouldn't want to go," Kit admitted.

"It's different from when you were in middle school."

"Not much different. They're still jerks, from what I've heard."

They didn't hear anything else worth listening to and finally, turning it off, Alice cut the signal.

"Do you think anyone can find this place?"

"Eventually," she shrugged, already thinking ahead to other locations and other setups. She had taken what she wanted off these computers and kept the backups separate. She'd laid the dummies on the computers at home. Now, all they had to do was wait: wait for the IRS to get a warrant to confiscate the files at the house and wait the

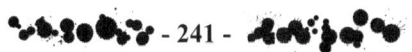

weeks, possibly months, it would take for Alice to legally be brought back to life. They just had to *wait*.

They weren't left to wait in peace though. Both Portia and Andie were strategizing. Alice had provided them with electronic copies of the paperwork that was confiscated, and they were working on that. The waiting bored Alice to no end, and Kathy frequently was shanghaied to attend their endless meetings. Alice and Kathy couldn't pretend they weren't interested. It was important to them, but in the weeks while the IRS was dragging its feet, they would have gone bankrupt and starved if Alice didn't have access to cash and credit. No one asked where she got the funds, although everyone suspected, given how many aliases they had found and how many they suspected they would never find.

Alice used this time to have a dentist work on her teeth. She hated the sounds of drills but worried more about the anesthetics as some work required her to be put under. She wouldn't have done that work without Kathy there to watch over her. She let the dentist and his staff think she was simply scared of dental work, but it wasn't that. She was more worried what they might do or what she might do under the influence of anesthesia. She came out of it fine. Her new, white teeth looked almost natural, but the work took quite a while, and she was frazzled by all the work in her mouth.

Alice and Kathy were sick of Em's new 'best friend,' Carmen. Carmen's parents had invited Alice and Kathy over for dinner several times in the weeks following the party, now that their children were friends. The conversation had been stilted, but the two women had gone for their daughter's sake. Alice hadn't changed her opinion of either of the Pasternacks and had, in her spare time, begun to investigate them. It was difficult for Alice to get to the storage unit and use the real computers since Kathy was with her a lot. The two girls and a select few of their friends, mostly Carmen's friends, were in and out of each other's houses, and it was driving the two moms crazy. If Alice hadn't seen that some of Em's older friends were also included, she would have believed that Carmen had been specifically instructed to befriend Em.

"Look at this," Alice told Kathy while running several programs simultaneously. Whoever it was at the police department that bugged their house, they hadn't passed on the information. Alice was slowly mining the information. Her heart had been in her throat several times as she discovered there was a great deal of information they had gotten from her surprise return home. Alice was going slow because whoever it was hadn't signed the report he or she was compiling on Alice and Kathy Weaver. They were trying to get it all down, and if they were successful, it would really sink Alice. She already had little microprograms in place that would make it seem that whoever compiled the report had downloaded spyware from a porn site. She was just waiting....

"Holy shit! They got all that transcribed?" Kathy said, looking at what she was reading. It was worse reading it again than it had been hearing Alice tell what she had done in Kazakhstan. All those bodies...she shook her head over the carnage Alice had admitted to.

"Yeah, I think it's time to try and discover who this person is," Alice said as she delved further into the police officer's computer, trying to avoid triggering any alarms that would allow the police to trace it back to Alice's computers. If she were suddenly unplugged, the bots would automatically begin wiping the officer's files, the police department's files, and the backups she had found. She was prepared to be quite thorough. "Why does the name Smith sound familiar?"

"It's a name commonly used on the North American continent?" Kathy tried to contribute without laughing.

"Thanks, hun. No, seriously. That name was used recently. Someone..." she began trying to figure it out. "Where's that card from the IRS agent? You know, the guy you said smirked when you protested?"

"That was Smith," Kathy said, having an 'aha' moment. "Is he involved with the police on this?"

"No, but look here," she said, pointing to the report. "They know we are being audited, and he suggested they coordinate with Smith. I bet that's the guy at the IRS."

There was a slight flutter on the screen, and Alice looked on in alarm. "Uh oh. I think it's time to pull the plug," she said as she watched. "They know someone is on the system," she murmured as she enacted a couple commands and watched the screen begin to form the number one and the number zero, then begin to fade out. "Someone in Los Angeles is going to be very unhappy shortly," she stated, wishing she had found out more.

"That's it? That's all erased?" Kathy asked, obviously alarmed.

"Yeah, and from what we saw, he had the tapes on the computer and it was voice to text transcription. That's quite faulty, and of course, once it's on a computer..." she smiled at the fading numbers on her screen.

"What if he has the original recordings though?"

"That one notation said everything was on the computer. I'm hoping they put it all on the computer thinking that was safer, including the audio tapes," she admitted as she analyzed the work they had done in the weeks since they learned they were being bugged.

"Remember that one notation that said there was a lot of static on the recording and they lost a segment?" Kathy asked. "Do you think they erased it and used it over and over?"

"If it's a digital recording, they may have, but they never run out of room on a computer for things like that. This," she slapped at the commands she had just enacted, "just erased all the files regarding us and also everything that was transcribed, and it is now working its way up the chain. Those bots are in their system now and will cause a type of blackout. It's also in the backups," she repeated what she had said earlier to emphasize their previous discussion.

Alice had another thought. "I'm sorry to ask, babe," she began and noticed Kathy tensed slightly. "Do you think since Linda was personally involved with you that she maybe had someone else investigate you when she became nosy or suspicious?"

Kathy wasn't insulted. She'd thought about that too. "I don't know who she trusted. I met a few of her friends and colleagues when we went out, of course, but she never mentioned if Leskowitz had a chance to confess." Kathy had never asked about that particular incident, but she assumed Alice had somehow gotten the man to commit suicide in jail. Alice had told her about the other cops but not Leskowitz. Maybe that omission had saved them from being arrested, but they would never know.

Alice turned off the computers since their primary function had been completed. Once they signed out of the computers and shut them down, they couldn't be logged into again without her various protocols. She wasn't day trading anymore, and she kind of missed it. She had enough money to last her family several lifetimes but had to wait until the IRS thing was straightened out before she started bringing it into the country. She'd heard from both Portia and Nia that the paperwork had been filed and was progressing, so she was stuck here...waiting. Patience wasn't one of Alice's virtues.

The two women headed out in the sedan, locking up the storage unit behind them, then going to the lot where the Lexus was parked and getting in. As they pulled into their own driveway, they saw several cop cars and plainclothes officers.

"What the hell?" Kathy asked, alarmed, her mind immediately thinking of the computers they had destroyed that day. "Do you think they know?"

"No. Just keep cool, and if you think you are going to panic, stay quiet. Silence can't be held against you," she said as they stopped their car behind the various cars parked by their garage. They couldn't even pull into their own garage because there were so many cars. "What's going on here?" Alice asked as she got out of the Lexus.

"Are you the homeowner?" an officious-looking man approached them.

"I am, and this is my wife, Kathy. I'm Alice Weaver."

"This is an order to confiscate your computers for evidence," he said as he handed her the paperwork.

Alice opened it and read it rapidly. They had known it was coming, but it had taken much longer than she expected for them to execute the order. She wondered if they had confiscated anything more from the offices, although she knew there wasn't much there anymore. Alice glanced up as a black man came rapidly down the steps. She wondered if that was the Smith Kathy had told her about? Men and women were hauling the old computers out of the house, and she could hear Sean protesting as they took not only the new gaming computer but also his personal computer from his room. An officer stopped him.

"Let go of the boy," Alice told him in a menacing voice.

"Who the hell are you?" the black man asked.

"Who the hell are you?" she parroted back, not liking his attitude. She could feel the old fighting Alice rising in her, and she didn't like it. She had just wanted to come home and regain her health and happiness. She glanced at Kathy, who nodded slightly to confirm it was the man they had just talked about not even an hour before.

"I'm Mr. Smith," he said with a little grin that Alice instantly hated. "We have a warrant–" he started to say, and when Alice held it up, he

nodded. "Yes, that's it. I'm with the IRS, and we have a warrant to check your computers."

"Check them or confiscate them?" she asked. These computers didn't have the sophisticated software of her original computers and wouldn't keep these people out, but then, they weren't supposed to. She wanted them to break into the computers. She'd tried to make it just hard enough for them to get in that they wouldn't suspect a thing, at least she hoped they wouldn't. Meanwhile, she had a game to play, and these people didn't know she played the game better than most. She eyed the man and felt he was enjoying this a little too much. Alice wasn't happy with cocky sons of bitches like that.

"Well, we need them for evidence," he qualified, again with the little smirk.

Alice returned the smirk, her eyes narrowing slightly, and she was pleased with the fact that he took an involuntary step backwards as a predatory look came into her eyes.

Shaking his head, sure he had just imagined the look, he returned to his usual cocky, self-assured attitude. "We'll let you know what we find." He glanced up at the house they had purchased many years ago. What was the price all those years ago? Maybe ten million dollars? He'd find a way to confiscate the house in penalties, and he was certain it was worth much more now. He looked down at the blonde woman before him. She didn't look like she was worth that much money. In fact, she looked like a has-been punk rocker. He also wasn't afraid of the money she supposedly had with her wife. The wife wasn't going to win this. They had these women by the short hairs, and he was going to make them pay. He'd make an example of these rich bitch lesbians. He really didn't care that they were lesbians. He only cared that they had thwarted the law and avoided paying their fair share of taxes.

Alice couldn't read his mind but people like him gave off unconscious cues. It was just like when she recognized Sandi Pasternack for what she was. Body language told the hunter in her what they were, if they were aggressive, if they were passive, and sometimes it also told her what they were about to do. "Let my son go," she ordered the big man smirking before her and the officer who had grabbed Sean's arm.

"And if I don't?" he challenged, feeling he had the upper hand in this situation with his badge and not willing to just let it go.

"Then the child will be suing your office for excessive force, assault, and anything else my lawyers can find."

Having met Portia Spiros, he wasn't worried. Still, he was also aware of the New York law firm that was involved in getting Alice's paperwork in order. Already, there had been inquiries about why the investigation was taking so long. Weeks had gone by as they perused the paperwork. His excuse that they needed the computers at the persons' home had eventually led to this warrant. He was very proud of that. He had played them until his superiors had given in to what he sensed would be a bonanza. "There's no need for that," he signaled to his officer, and he let the kid go.

Alice went to Sean and asked, "Are you okay?"

"They came in and took everything," he nearly sobbed. His computer games were extensive, and they had just taken everything.

"It's okay. Deep breaths," she advised. She turned to watch them take out the old computers and place them none too gently in the back of a van. She exchanged a look with Kathy, who had gone up and was talking to Emily. She saw that Carmen was there again, so she supposed that the Pasternacks would soon know of this incident. She sighed. It was time to end this, whatever *this* was. She just wanted her peace and quiet.

Alice got another business card, this time from another agent assigned to their case. The agent, a Sophie Wickert, assured Alice she would be happy to answer any questions they might have. Assessing Sophie as she introduced herself, Alice wasn't certain the woman could do anything, and Mr. Smith seemed to be relishing the thought of finding something on their taxes with which to penalize them.

The long line of cars was leaving as Portia arrived at the gate. She waited until they were gone before driving her own Porsche up the drive. Both she and Andie got out and ran up the stairs to where Kathy and Alice were waiting. The children had gone back inside but not before Alice had noticed Carmen looking at them speculatively. She tried to dismiss the feeling, but she couldn't be certain she wasn't just being paranoid and seeing conspiracies everywhere around them.

"What the heck is going on?" Portia asked at the same time Andie asked, "Was that the IRS?"

Alice nodded as Kathy said, "Well, we were expecting this, weren't we?"

Both her friends nodded in agreement. But with all the time that had gone by, they had begun to hope that it might not happen. Watching that many cars leave, it had struck home. They realized the authorities were in the driver's seat, not the Weavers.

"Why do you think they are coming at you so hard?" Portia mused as they went into the house.

"It can't be that you're the one percent?" Andie asked.

"Have you hired the other firm as I asked you?" Kathy asked. They needed more manpower on this, and Alice had suggested the other firm to Kathy. Kathy had been surprised because Alice usually did most everything by herself, only using accountants to prepare the documents that were submitted to the IRS annually.

Andie nodded. It was a good firm, very prestigious, and they were accustomed to dealing with the IRS and these kinds of situations. They had tax attorneys on staff, and Portia and she had already met with them.

"Let's forget about all this shit for the day and have a barbeque," Alice suggested. She was tired of it all. It was all a giant chess game, and she wanted a break from the constant worry and the outmaneuvering. It was ridiculous, and she knew it wasn't going to end with the confiscation of the computers. They wanted something from her and Kathy, and Alice just had to wait for them to ask at their leisure. The next step was likely going to be the two women being asked to come in and answer questions. They would probably be subpoenaed to do so. The stress was going to be horrendous.

"Can you afford–?" a worried Andie began, and then, seeing Alice's amused look, she shrugged and went inside to enjoy herself.

"Where are you getting the money?" Portia worried. "Should I be prepared to bail you out?"

Alice looked at Portia in amusement. She knew Portia had seen a couple things she shouldn't over the years. The extent of the company they had set up to handle Alice's assets had proven that things in Alice's world weren't all on the up and up, but she had covered her tracks well. Portia knew she was damned clever. "They haven't even begun to chip at the tip of the iceberg," Alice admitted as she flipped the burgers frying on the grill. The kids were playing in the pool, and while she wasn't happy to see Carmen still there, she couldn't find a reason to throw the kid out, even subtly. She didn't trust Carmen, and she was sure the girl told her parents everything she observed in the

Weaver household. She didn't want to tell 'Em not to trust Carmen. At the same time, she wanted to warn Em not to tell her anything, but she knew if she kept doing that to her young daughter, Emily was going to crack under the stress of what she had overhead and couldn't ever share or discuss.

"I figured that but even an iceberg can melt," Portia commented, wryly taking a sip of the beer she was drinking.

Alice smiled, enjoying the exchange of quips. Portia and Andie had been her sister's friends, never really hers. They had also been her wife's best friends, and she would never think of denying them access to her wife, but she didn't really consider them *her* friends. Still, she supposed they might think they were friends because she was married to Kathy and had been helping her with the estate. She just would never trust them as she trusted Kathy. "What should I do, Portia? Go into the IRS office and throw myself on the mercy of the US government? You know what they are doing to us; it's punitive, straight and simple."

Portia nodded. Even the outside firms they had hired told her that. Someone had it in for the Weavers, and they intended to make them pay. That little article in the paper had been a clear declaration of war.

"Let me show you something," Alice said. Then, as Sean walked by, she asked him, "Sean, will you watch the burgers and corn for a moment?" He immediately took the flipper and tongs from her. "No playing with the fire," she teased as she left him doing exactly that and headed into the kitchen. She opened the freezer and pulled out the baggie containing the bugs to show Portia.

"What are they?" Portia asked, looking at the little things in different shades of white.

"They're bugs."

"Really, what kind of bugs are–. Oh," she realized how stupid what she had been about to ask would sound. "They bugged your house? Are these different from the ones you found before?"

Alice nodded, seeing Kathy come in with Andie. "Yes, but I am not certain it was the IRS."

"How did you find those?" Andie asked.

"I have a gadget that finds them. They give off a rather unique signal."

"Yes, but why would you have such a gadget?"

Alice stared at her for a moment, pondering how to answer that. "I like gadgets," she answered lamely.

"It doesn't matter why she has one. The fact is, they bugged our house." Kathy was feeling defensive.

"Who is *they*?" Andie asked, looking concerned and wondering what the hell was going on in this house. First the IRS raids and now further bugging?

"We aren't sure," Kathy admitted and glanced at Alice. She'd let her take the lead on this, so their skirting of the truth didn't conflict.

"I'm betting it's the police," Alice put in.

"The police, as in Leskowitz and that situation?" Portia asked, alarmed.

"Or is it something to do with Linda?" Andie asked.

Both women looked at Kathy and then Alice, to see if she reacted. "It's okay. I know about Linda," Alice confessed. She'd let them think that Kathy had told her, not confessing that she had anything to do with it. She didn't want a smart cookie like Portia figuring out that the deaths of those police officers coincided with Alice's return. Portia tended to think like the lawyer she was, and Alice knew better than to give her too much information. She didn't want Kathy defenseless though, and by telling their friends, she hoped to prevent anything further that might happen. She didn't know what yet, but something was in the air.

"So, you think the police are out to get you?" Portia asked, now beginning to think they were paranoid.

"Yes. Who put these in our home?" she indicated the baggie as she threw it back in the freezer. She'd have to get back the few they took out and replanted and put them back on ice once again too.

"You attract trouble like a magnet, don't you?" Portia asked, shaking her head.

"Yes, I do," Alice admitted, although the attorney didn't know the half of it. Remembering the iceberg analogy they had shared just a few minutes ago, Alice had the urge to laugh but knew no one would understand her humor.

"What are you going to do? What are *we* going to do?" Andie asked.

"We are going to continue doing what we have been doing," Alice told her. "When the IRS asks us to go in and submit to their questions, you are going with us," she gestured to both women, "along with the firms you hired on our behalf. We will show a united front and see if we can bluff our way out of this. If we can't, I have other means of preserving my lifestyle and my family's."

"If you are talking about bringing illegally-gotten gains into this country, I can't have any part in that…" Andie began.

"Who says any of it was illegally-gotten? I've earned every dime of that money," she said emphatically. She knew some of it was over the top, but she had earned it in one way or another. "I used their loopholes to write it off on my taxes, and we did nothing illegal."

Andie, listening intently to Alice, believed her in that moment; however, there were too many pseudonyms for everything to be legitimate. They'd found too many other companies, and those were just the ones they found. She knew Alice was wealthy, but wealth like this was suspicious, which was probably exactly why the authorities were after her so harshly.

That night, they dined on hot dogs and hamburgers and fresh, sweet corn with plenty of butter, chasing it down with beer, wine, or soda as they enjoyed their little, extended family. Kit had gone back to school, and she intended to find a summer internship, so she could stay in the San Francisco area. For now, Alice contented herself that this was the best it was going to get for a while.

Alice didn't know what was more tedious, meeting with a team of lawyers or meeting with a team of accountants and going over the paperwork the IRS had confiscated. There were many different personalities too: some were a bit confident, some were a bit condescending, and a few she wondered if she should fire on the spot. Still, Portia and Andie were convinced these were good people. One of them, the partner in the firm of tax lawyers, knew Alice from before.

"Your memorial service was just lovely," he said by way of greeting, holding out a hand for her to shake.

Alice chuckled, imagining it had been. "It's good to see you again," she said politely and introduced her wife.

"Ah, yes. We met at the memorial service, but I bet you don't remember me."

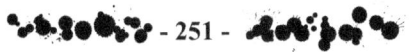

"No, I'm afraid I don't. There were just so many people," she said, remembering that sad time. With Alice standing next to her, it seemed like a bad dream.

"Well, hopefully we don't go to another one any time soon, eh?" he teased. "We'll have to get this straightened out quickly," he promised, sounding optimistic. "What have you been up to, Alice, you naughty woman, you?" he continued in a jocular manner, shaking a finger warningly at her but smiling.

Alice smiled, already annoyed, but willing to play her part while they attempted to defend her.

"Why do you think they are coming at you so hard?" one of the attorneys asked.

Alice hated that they were all staring at her and Kathy. Where they attempting to break them or get them to confess? She had to remember these people worked for her or she'd tell them off and take her family out of the country. They could live in a non-extradition country the rest of their lives, if she wanted. Hell, they could start over under one of the many aliases their lawyers hadn't found yet. "I think someone has a point to prove," she answered calmly. If she mentioned her belief that there was a vendetta, they'd think she was paranoid. She already knew that Portia and Andie were each suspicious in their own ways. Kathy had told her they were worried that Alice's return had just made things worse.

The lawyers grilled the women for hours, then the accountants got their turn. Alice answered as truthfully as she could, knowing down to the dollar in some cases exactly where the money had come from and gone to, and she was able to reference that.

Still, the IRS didn't request they come in, and this, more than anything else, worried both firms. Andie and Portia were trying to coordinate with both firms, and they were beginning to feel left out of the loop.

"We have nothing to do, and we certainly aren't earning our salaries," Andie complained to Kathy.

"You already earned them, and you'll continue to receive them in arrears when we clear this up."

"What if we don't? I can't live on my savings indefinitely," she pointed out.

"Andie, if you need to move on, we certainly wouldn't keep you from whatever you want to do." Alice knew Kathy's friend had given up her previous job in order to help them when Alice was thought to have died.

"You're firing me?" she asked, incredulous.

"Not at all. But if you want to leave, we won't force you to stay. You are welcome to stay for as long as you want."

Andie sighed. This whole mess was making her nervous. There was too much money for anyone to believe it was legitimate, and she wondered where Alice was getting the money for them to survive on. Sure, they had let all their employees go, but the IRS hadn't released any of their assets yet, and Alice still had money. That alone would surely make someone suspicious at some point, if it didn't already.

"See, there," Alice said, showing Kathy the worms that were wiggling through the IRS computers and were 'breaking' into her computers. They hadn't been able to get into a couple of the computers but only because Alice designed it that way. Finding computers similar to her old setup had been the hard part. Buying the computers at pawn shops had relieved the shops of some crap equipment that was too old to get them much money anyway. Still, Alice had been persistent and now, their fishing expedition was paying off. By opening or 'breaking into' their computer, it had given the IRS a bonanza of past trades and financial information. The funny part to Alice was, all that information was contained in the paperwork they had already confiscated. It was legitimate and could be traced.

"What are they doing?"

"Hooking them into their computers. Now, we'll have a back door to go through, and I can snoop around in their computers," she said with a smile, showing an almost predator-like glee at the task at hand.

"You're enjoying this, aren't you?" Kathy asked her, seeing how excited she seemed.

"Look, they are the ones playing hardball. We haven't been contacted, and our requests for the return of our assets and paperwork have been ignored," she indicated the computers she was following. They are running out of time and will be compelled to return them shortly, but I'm already done with their attitudes. Who the hell do they think they are to punish American citizens, who pay their taxes?"

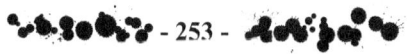

"Yes, but did you pay *all* your taxes?" Kathy asked, now amused at Alice's phrasing.

"That's beside the point," she said prissily, and then they both had a good laugh. Alice started nosing around, wanting to see what they were looking for. They were going to make something up, and she was certain it wouldn't be good, but it would be big. It would be something high in taxes, penalties, and interest.

"You know, you could have handled this differently," Assistant District Attorney Lenora Quinn was speaking to Special Agent Linda Miller, who was standing in her office at that moment. "Now, the damn virus in the LAPD computers is spreading, and there are a lot of unhappy people.

"I turned it over to the correct authorities, and now, with Alice Weaver's return, there is even more to be suspicious about. I believe Kathy Weaver may have been involved in the suicide of Detective Dewayne Leskowitz."

"You know this sounds like sour grapes, and had you gone through your own station house, they would have dismissed your suppositions. Instead, you went to Palos Verdes, and not only have they lost their entire computer system, but it's spreading through Los Angeles and the valley. They can't find the virus to stop it!"

"You don't know if that is my fault in the least!" she contested hotly.

"You dated the bitch–"

"She isn't a bitch!"

Quinn continued as though Miller hadn't interrupted, "She was targeted by those dirty cops and you protected her because you were hoping to get in her pants."

"Look, I had evidence that would have put her wife away for a long time."

"Prove it then!"

"I can't. It was all on the computer. If you had read everything I read, you wouldn't be asking me this shit. You would have demanded we arrest them." She had been horrified to read the transcripts of the bugs she had planted, using some old contraband from their evidence

locker along with some of their new equipment as she became suspicious of Kathy. Yes, she had wanted her, and she had hoped to have a long-lasting relationship with her, but this was not about sour grapes. This was about putting people like her and her murderous wife behind bars. Apparently, something had happened with the transcripts, and the virus had spread from there. Anyone who had been sent a copy of the transcript, or had received an email, or whose computer was connected with that investigation, had their computer infected when they opened their email. Computers were shutting down all over. It was like a tidal wave, and it was alarming a lot of people. Even worse, the bugs she had planted had apparently all expired or been found; she was getting nothing from them anymore. In reality, they had been grilled that day out at the fire. Alice and Kathy had ceremoniously dumped them in the fire and then waited for the plastic to burn away before making marshmallows and smores.

"Then, we don't have anything, and it's hearsay."

"Surely, we can find something?"

"If you are willing to go that route and make things up, then sure, we can find something," Lenora said sarcastically and meaningfully. "Look, is the Weaver family dirty? Probably. Anyone with that much money must be. They are being investigated by the IRS, and that was a stroke of luck. Smith is determined to catch them. I can't get involved with it beyond that."

"If you weren't fucking him, I bet he wouldn't have done jack," Linda sneered, angry at being thwarted.

"Damned right he wouldn't, but he's a good lay and an honest agent. He isn't going after them for nothing!"

"I'm going to stir the pot a little."

"It's your hide and your badge," the attorney warned. "I'd be careful. I don't know why all that information was redacted, but from what I read, Alice Weaver is not someone you want to screw with."

"I didn't want to screw *her*," Linda quipped, still angry and frustrated.

"Yeah, and that's going to be your downfall," the attorney told her and watched as the agent walked out of her office. She shook her head. Linda was a good cop, had always been a good cop, but getting involved in the Weaver case had been bad news all around for her. Not only professionally, since she was already in internal affairs, but emotionally and personally as well. Something about that Weaver family was bad news, and the little she had seen in the files warned her to stay the hell away from them.

"Mom?" Emily called down to the pool where Alice and Kathy were floating on pool lounge chairs in the heated water of the pool. They were holding hands, so the wind couldn't blow them apart in the middle of the pool as they lazed and tanned in the hot Southern California sun.

"Yes?" they answered in unison and chuckled.

"You have a visitor."

"Send them down," Alice called, wondering if it was Portia or Andie coming to complain some more. Those two worried more than the whole team they had hired, and it was stressing the women out. It simply wasn't healthy. She had been about to insist that Kathy tell them to take a break. They already had a team of accountants and lawyers that were going to cost them an absolute fortune to extricate them from this situation. They didn't really need the two of them, but they were friends, so they couldn't just fire them. Alice didn't want to move. She was enjoying the sun worshipping, the random lovemaking with Kathy, and the lazing about. This was what she had craved when she was freezing her ass off in Russia and Kazakhstan.

It was less than five minutes later when they heard Special Agent Linda Miller's voice say, "Hello, Kathy."

Both Kathy and Alice looked up at their visitor, shading their eyes from the sun's glare with their arms. Kathy immediately looked uncomfortable laying there in her swimsuit.

"Linda!"

"Surprised to see me?" she asked, examining her 'competition' for the first time and seeing how thin Alice still was. She didn't look like much. Her pictures had made her look prettier. Still, she was able to wear a bikini at her age and that said something.

"Yes, I am," she replied and then glanced at Alice.

Alice was examining the cop for the first time, face to face, her eyes hidden behind her sunglasses. She had known who Linda was as soon as she heard her voice. She now wondered if this was an official visit or a personal visit.

"This is my wife, Alice Weaver. Alice, this is–."

"I know who it is," Alice said in chorus with Linda.

Linda looked startled at first, then looked speculatively at Alice, who hadn't done anything but sit up in the lounge chair. Her expression was evident to both Kathy and Alice.

"To what do we owe the honor of your visit, Agent Miller?" Alice asked casually.

"I need to talk to you both," she began.

"Well, we're right here," Kathy answered, wondering the same things Alice was.

"Are you going to come out of the water?" Linda asked, impatient to get a few things off her chest.

"Is it that important?" Alice asked, being deliberately annoying.

"Well, we could do this the hard way, or we could do it the easy way…" she began.

"What's the hard way?" Alice asked insolently. She wished she had a drink in her cup holder. Now would be a good time to slurp on the bottom of a drink with a straw; it would further irritate the cop. Kathy squeezed Alice's hand warningly and let go to propel her chair through the water to the steps.

"The hard way is, I arrest you and take you downtown for questioning."

"On what charge?" Alice asked in a bored tone that told the cop nothing.

She's one cool cucumber, the agent thought. She knows I don't have anything on her and is going to bluff it out. "For one, cyber sabotage," she began, trying her own bluff. She'd thought a lot on her way over here.

"Hmm, that sounds serious. You have any proof of that?" Alice now sounded a little insolent as she stared through her sunglasses at her former competition. She had thought Linda was not involved with the bugging of their home, but now, with that one statement, she realized Linda must know the computers containing the information on Alice were destroyed. The only way that could lead back to Alice was if you assumed that since the information was about Alice, she must have destroyed them. Alice briefly wondered how far her bots had gotten and what they had damaged.

"Oh, yes," Linda breathed, and then, Kathy was out of the pool and wrapping a terry cloth towel around herself.

"Come on, Linda. What the heck are you talking about?" Kathy tried to lie.

"You know, Kathy, you never told me your wife was a killer," she said conversationally, trying to get a reaction out of her.

Kathy froze, and Alice glanced at her, willing her to say nothing.

"Now, that's an interesting allegation," Alice put in, bringing the agent's attention back to her. Linda had just further confirmed she had read those transcripts. She hoped Kathy was figuring that out too.

"My mom is not a killer. She's a hero," Emily suddenly put in, proving she was eavesdropping.

"Emily, go to your room," Kathy gasped, shocked to see her daughter on the patio above the pool.

"No, Emily. Please come on down," Linda invited, suddenly pouncing on the idea and waving the teen down. If Emily knew something, maybe she could exploit it.

Suddenly, seeing the weak link, Alice was genuinely afraid. She could take the harassment, but not her family, and especially not her children. She hopped out of the chair and started to walk through the water towards the steps. "Emily, go in the house," Alice called, part warning and part command. Alice hoped she could avert what she saw the cop was angling for.

"Emily, why do you think your mother is a hero? My information says she's a killer," Linda taunted, her voice not betraying the triumph she was feeling.

"She is not!" the young teen contradicted.

"Emily! GO IN THE HOUSE!" Alice ordered, and glaring, she got out of the pool to confront the cop, who was taller and more physically fit than Alice.

Kathy slipped by Linda to head Emily off in case she disobeyed Alice. They didn't need this headache, and she could see Linda was on to something. It wouldn't matter if they had destroyed all the evidence if Linda had read something or seen something and could get Emily to testify against them without even arresting her. In that event, she could and would be able to make a case against Alice.

"I think you better leave, Agent Miller," Alice said cordially, but the tone in her voice brooked no interference.

Agent Miller looked down at the petite and still emaciated woman and glared her contempt. She'd taken off her glasses when she rang the gate bell and Emily had let her in. Trying to see through Alice's sunglasses was difficult. She couldn't tell what the woman was thinking. "No, I came here for answers, and I intend to get them."

"Do you really want to do this?" Alice asked, and the menace began to slip into her voice; she couldn't help it.

"Alice," Kathy warned. She knew Linda better than Alice did, or so she thought.

"Kathy, don't think you'll get off scot-free," Linda added, looking up at her former girlfriend. "After all, being an accessory to the crime or an accessory after the fact is still punishable by prison."

"What do you want?" Alice asked, sick of Linda's comments.

"I want you to turn yourself in for the murder of six cops that we know of and for the cyber crimes against the Palos Verdes Police Department, the Los Angeles Police Department, and the Pasadena Police Department."

Palos Verdes made sense since their home was within its jurisdiction, but Pasadena? Then it hit her. There were crime labs that centralized out of Pasadena. The bots must have been sent to them in an email and were eating away at their computers too.

"Again, I will ask if you have any proof of these allegations?"

"I'll get Emily into protective custody and force her to testify," Linda threatened.

"Okay, that's it! You obviously have no proof, and you are going to have to leave. I won't have you threatening my family anymore. If you don't leave, I'll throw you out of here," Alice promised.

"Alice," Kathy warned, but she was also furious at Linda's threats. She well remembered the thought that if something had happened to her back when Kit was young her daughter might have ended up in foster care. Protective custody, indeed!

"Oh, should I add assaulting a police officer to the list?" Linda taunted.

"Oh, hiding behind your badge now, Agent Miller?" Alice taunted back. She was furious, coldly and deadly furious, and she was doing her best to restrain herself from striking the woman standing before her. She well remembered when this woman had felt her wife up, *her* wife, and she recalled how it had felt watching her make out with Kathy.

Linda smiled. She welcomed the thought of beating the shit out of this plucky, little blonde. She had lived with the memory of this woman when she was dating Kathy. She had been led on for months, only to find that Kathy preferred a killer and thief to an honest, hard-working police officer. "No, I'm not hiding behind the badge at all. Maybe you should record this statement, Kathy. Go on. Use my phone and record that I'm not hiding behind my badge." She waited as Kathy turned on the camera as she was asked. "I'm not hiding behind my badge at all," she repeated for the record. "I'm just a common citizen, and anything that happens in the next half hour is between two civilians." She turned back to look at Alice and removed her jacket, folding it neatly over a chair. It revealed her shoulder holster, gun, and the badge on her belt.

"Alice," Kathy warned, knowing full well how dangerous her wife was. She wished that Alice would take off her sunglasses, so she could see those eyes.

"Are you serious?" Alice asked, eager for this confrontation. For too many months, she had let this woman get away with things that she normally wouldn't have let anyone do. She'd had no choice then, and now, the woman was being presented to her on a silver platter. She watched as the badge came off and was put in the jacket pocket along with the gun. "Really?" she smiled delightedly.

"Oh yes, I've been looking forward to meeting you for a long time," Linda replied, unbuttoning her sleeves and beginning to roll them up.

"Alice, no," Kathy called, starting to come forward, but Linda held up her hand to stop her.

"Kathy, if you don't want to see this, maybe you better call an ambulance for the agent. After all, she asked for this, and it would be rude of me to decline the invitation."

Just the cocky tone of Alice's voice was setting Linda's teeth on edge. She knew behaviors like this were deliberate, intended to make the person lose their cool, but something about this woman simply pissed her off. Reading the transcripts hadn't helped either. She hadn't gotten that far into them, but what she read had horrified her. The fact that Kathy would help someone like that, a killer, an admitted killer, angered her more. Linda took a swipe at Alice to test her. She was taller, her reach longer, but she didn't know Alice, who was grinning unrepentantly at this opportunity.

Kathy turned off the phone at Linda's first swipe. "Alice, please don't kill her," Kathy called, horrified at what was happening before her.

"Do you still care for her, Kathy?" Alice asked, suddenly willing to give it all up if that was the case. She was watching Linda, who took another half-hearted swipe.

"No, nothing more than as a friend, I swear."

To Alice it sounded sincere, but to Linda it sounded trite and pitying. With that, Linda's anger bubbled over and she took a real swipe at Alice, knocking her glasses to the ground. Alice responded instinctively. She pointed her fingers as she dodged Linda's blow once again, brushing it aside with one arm as her stiff fingers punched into Linda's windpipe, which was suddenly crushed, even momentarily. Linda was gagging and grasping at her neck. She fell to her knees.

"Oh, shit," Alice swore when she realized what she had done. She eased the cop onto her back and yelled to Kathy, "Get me a knife and a hollow straw or pen, something stiff." As Kathy nodded, horrified at what she had witnessed, she dropped Linda's phone and turned to run into the house to get the items Alice had requested. Alice yelled after her, "Bandages too and rubbing alcohol!" She knew where she had struck, and it wasn't good for the cop. She'd also been off balance and coming in, so the blow was probably harder than Alice had intended. She knelt over the choking cop and said, "Don't you dare die on me, or Kathy will never forgive me for killing you!" She tilted the woman's head back to stretch the muscles in her neck, trying to get the damaged trachea to stretch, so the woman could breathe. Linda fought Alice's hands, looking into those strange cat-like eyes. Finally, after panicking and losing too much oxygen, she began to black out. Alice held down one of her hands with her knee and then tried to administer CPR. There was no air going into her lungs when she tried holding Linda's nose shut and forcing air through her mouth. Alice thought briefly about the fact that these same lips had kissed her wife and continued administering CPR to the woman.

"Here," Kathy said, running back with the items Alice had requested. "She's blue!" she gasped.

"Call an ambulance," Alice ordered as she grabbed the knife Kathy had brought. Fortunately, it was a sharp steak knife. Alice poured the rubbing alcohol on the knife and across Linda's neck, then made a cut above the hollow in the woman's neck. It immediately began to bleed.

Alice cut deeper and deeper until she met with resistance. Praying to the spirits, since she wasn't sure she believed in a God, she pushed the knife through the resistance. Alice couldn't see with all the blood, and she wasn't sure the cut had worked. She grabbed the pen and cut off the end where it tapered. After pouring rubbing alcohol on it, she carefully inserted the piece of pen into the bleeding hole she had made in Linda's neck. Strangely, Alice was shaking as she did it. As she poured more alcohol over the wound to wash away the blood, she worried if she pushed hard enough it might pierce an artery or something. She decided not to do that and searched for the resistance, hoping the pen would go through the hole she had made.

Alice pulled the tissue back on both sides of the hole with her fingertips, making it bleed faster and making her ability to see anything even more impossible. She felt her way through the resistance and saw a bubble gurgle up the pen. Pinching the flesh on either side of the pen to close the wound, she watched the end of the pen. There were more bubbles, and she leaned down to suck on the pen, spitting the blood onto the tiles and blowing air in once she had removed all the blood. Alice pulled back for a second to push on Linda's chest and then blew into the pen again, then continued repeating that procedure. She kept going until Linda was breathing on her own, and then, using the rubbing alcohol again, she washed the blood away from around the pen again. She was finally able to look around, and she was shocked to see her wife on the cordless phone and her children staring at her with wide eyes.

"How long?" she gasped, spitting out more of Linda's blood from her mouth. She briefly wondered if the woman had any blood diseases that would infect her and then dismissed the thought.

"What?" Sean asked, blinking.

"How long have you been standing there?" she gasped out, trying to draw breath into her lungs. She really wanted to know how long Linda had been unconscious, how long it had taken for her to begin breathing again but she didn't know how to ask in that moment.

"I have no idea," he answered truthfully.

"Do we have any bandages? Rags?"

Sean pulled his t-shirt off. "Here, this is clean. I just put it on half an hour ago," he said, handing it to his mother. Alice grabbed the knife to cut the shirt into thick strips and pack it around the pen that she was holding carefully. She had to stop the blood. She realized she was still kneeling on Linda's hand and got up, so the blood could flow back into the hand.

Alice suddenly felt exhausted. She knew it was an adrenalin rush and she needed electrolytes. "Emily, could you get me a red Gatorade?"

"But you don't like Gatorade," Emily protested, sure her mother was just trying to get rid of her, so she didn't see the blood.

"That's right. I don't like it, but I *need* one. Would you please get me one? A small one, if we have it?"

Reluctantly, the teen left and climbed the stairs to the balcony. She was still unsure if Alice had just given her busy work to get rid of her.

"Alice, an ambulance is on the way, and the 911 operator is asking for information."

"Well, she's breathing. Barely," Alice said, still panting a little as she held the pen in place and listened to the wheezing. She felt Linda waking and looked in her startled eyes as she became aware of her situation. "Don't move, not even a little, if you want to live," Alice warned her. "You have a crushed trachea, and I had to cut into your neck, so you could breathe."

The eyes looked on in alarm as awareness returned. She went to move her hand, and Alice warned her again. "If you move even a fraction, you could kill yourself. I did the best I could, and you're alive for now, but I would hate for all my hard work to be for naught."

As Linda became more aware, she couldn't believe that this…this killer literally held her life in her hands. She looked into the strangely colored eyes, wondering at the odd shape. She'd never seen anything like them. They all heard as the sirens approached, and Kathy said to Sean, "Go open the gate for them." He took off from where he had been watching the drama, fascinated by the life-saving pen his mother had shoved in the cop's neck.

"Here is your Gatorade, Mom," Emily said as she returned with the bottle.

"Could you open it for me? My hands are kind of full," she teased, trying to crack a smile and failing. She was glad to see Linda had closed her eyes. Maybe she had passed out again. She checked to see if she was breathing and was strangely relieved when she saw she was.

"Back here! Back here!" Kathy was calling, redirecting the EMTs from the front door to the gate of the pool that she had unlocked. She

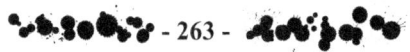

led them to the side of the pool where Alice was crouching over the prone body of the police officer.

"What do we have here?" one of them asked Alice.

"She has a collapsed trachea. I've punched a hole through her neck, so she can breathe," Alice answered, pulling back the shirt strips to show him where the pen had gone in. "We're going to have to tape that in place. I've been holding it for quite a while. I don't know exactly how long," she admitted, stretching her neck and longing for that cold Gatorade Emily was holding. She might not like the taste, but right now, she was severely thirsty.

The EMTs asked a few more questions as they taped off the wound, securing the pen in place, then strapped Linda to a board, taping her head down because Alice told them Linda had regained consciousness and tried to feel her neck. They strapped her hands down as well. After removing the t-shirt strips, they replaced them with sterile gauze and soon had her on the stretcher, ready to be rushed to the hospital. Alice had gotten up, her spot now taken over by the EMT, and she was sipping at the Gatorade gratefully. She hadn't realized she was totally covered in blood.

"Ma'am?" an officer got her attention. "Could you tell me what happened?"

Alice looked away as they were strapping Linda down to the board, and she began answering the officer's questions. She sent Emily a look when she tried to interrupt.

"So, she wanted to fight you?" he asked, curious when they came to that part of the story.

"She was in some weird mood. I think she was jealous because my wife had broken up with her some time ago."

"Your wife was dating her?" he asked, confused, as he wrote furiously.

"Yes, you see I was missing for quite a while, and they thought I was dead," she explained.

"Wait! You're Alice Weaver?" he asked.

"Yesss," she answered cautiously.

"I read about you in the paper," he admitted, sounding shy and blushing. "I think it's terrible that no one will be prosecuted for your kidnapping."

"Well, I'm home with my family, and that's all that matters," she sounded sincere.

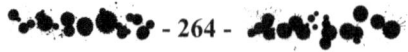

"You think she wanted to challenge you over your wife?"

"No, I think she wanted to prove she could beat me. She took three swings at me. I ducked two of them and brushed off the third, but she was moving in as I was returning the third punch, and I'm afraid I hit her in the neck. Her trachea collapsed, and she couldn't breathe."

"You cut into her neck to help her?"

Alice nodded, looking concerned as they put Linda on a gurney. She was unconscious but at least she was still breathing.

"She collapsed on the ground and I could tell she was choking and gagging. I called to Kathy, my wife," she said, identifying her, "and asked her to get me a knife, a pen, some bandages, and rubbing alcohol."

"I heard you yelling," Emily put in, sounding concerned.

"It's okay now. Thank you for this," she said, holding up the Gatorade bottle she had been sipping as she talked with the police officer. "You've been wonderful," she told her daughter, her eyes sending out warning signals. She hoped the teen wouldn't contribute anything further to the conversation.

"You heard your mother call for those things?" the officer asked the teen.

Emily suddenly seemed frightened about saying the wrong thing. She now realized it was her defense of her mother that had made things worse. She understood a little better why Alice had warned her not to say anything. "Yes, I heard her yell for those things and my mom ran and got them. Then, Mom called 911. Is Linda going to be okay?" Emily asked as the EMTs wheeled her away.

"I don't know," the officer admitted as he too watched them wheel her away.

"These are her things," Alice distracted him to show him the gun and the jacket. "She put her badge in the pocket."

"You saw her do that?" he asked, puzzled. He thought perhaps he had missed something.

"She said she wanted to challenge me, and I made a comment about her hiding behind her badge. She took off her badge and gun, and she told my wife this had nothing to do with her being a cop and this was just between her and me."

"And you tried to avoid the fight? You hit her in self-defense?"

"Yes, sir," she answered respectfully, looking him straight in the eye while trying to look innocent.

He believed her, partly because she was still covered in the cop's blood and partly because she had saved the woman and didn't appear to mean the woman any harm. He couldn't believe she would harm the woman and then waste time trying to save her. "Okay, I think I have what I need. I'll take Agent Miller's things with me to the hospital. If I need anything more from you, I will contact you, but I think I have all I need," he said as he handed her his card. Alice narrowed her eyes a little. Still, she thanked the officer and watched him go.

"What?" Kathy breathed after he had gone, and the children were talking between themselves.

"He called her Agent Miller. How did he know she was an agent?"

"You called her that," Kathy said, looking at Alice strangely.

"No, I never did," she pointed out.

"Sure, you did," she tried to argue.

"No, Kathy, you don't seem to understand...I never did."

"Do we have bugs out here?" she whispered, looking around in alarm.

"No, we checked. Remember?"

"What does that mean?"

"I don't know," Alice admitted, and then, looking down at the card thoughtfully, she put it on the table and jumped into the pool to wash off the blood.

Two days later, Alice was on a private jet heading for Washington D.C. She hadn't told her wife or her children where she was going. She walked, not into the offices of the Federal Bureau of Investigation, but into the building and across the seal of the Central Intelligence Agency.

"Can I help you, Ma'am?" the guard at the desk asked respectfully.

"Yes, my name is Alice Weaver, and I'd like to make a deal."

~The End~

❧ MANDATING MALICE ❧

BOOK 25

Who is Alice Weaver? The CIA believes they are about to find out...but are they? Do they really want to meet the real Alice Weaver? Perhaps, some things are better left hidden. Some agents think they already know who Alice is. After all, they have a file on her and so does the FBI. But what they know is only what Alice wants them to know. When Alice Weaver shares information with those in authority, they will be left scrambling for cover!

"A deal, ma'am?" he asked respectfully and cautiously. They got a lot of crazies in here thinking they had valuable information on UFOs or neighbors who must be spies from another country because of their accents. People didn't realize exactly what the CIA did, but since so much of it was covert, people assumed the agency would want to learn their secrets. As the first line of defense in this building, he had to screen everyone.

"Yes. Is Madelyn Korbel in?" she asked pleasantly.

The man looked at her, relaxing marginally. She was dressed nicely, and that alone had him judging her as *not* one of the crazies. Plus, she was asking for a senior person within the hierarchy that made up the agency, so she either knew something, or someone had given her the name to help her get past this first level of security. "Your name?" he asked officiously.

"Alice Weaver," she told him and had her identification ready. It was the new card issued by the state of California. It was brand spanking new and shiny. It had only recently been reissued when they confirmed she was indeed alive. They had reinstated her driver's license with a horrible picture showing her emaciated face and punk rock hairstyle. She had frequently thought the identification she had forged or had forged for her over the years was better than anything the state issued. She'd even started to round out a little since this picture was taken.

"Wait here, ma'am?" he said as he scanned her ID and handed it back to her, looking at her inquiringly and watching her behavior surreptitiously as he reached for a phone.

Alice nodded, looking curiously about as people came and went within the large atrium. It looked like everyone was conducting important business from all the suits she could see. She kept herself quiet and breathed slowly to still her hammering heart. Was she anxious? Yes, that must be it. She wasn't anxious for what she was about to reveal but for her family and what could happen to them. She was taking a gamble, but she had gambled all her life. Mostly, she had won, but occasionally, she had failed, and that wasn't an option she took lightly.

"Someone is asking for Madelyn Korbel? By *name?*" a voice asked into the phone, shocked and becoming concerned. No one asked for her anymore. He listened for a moment before nodding and hanging up the phone after saying, "I'll be right there." As soon as his phone disconnected, he made another phone call, going up the chain of command. When his call was answered, he said, "Someone is in the lobby asking for Madelyn Korbel." He listened, nodded a couple of times as though the speaker could see him, and said, "Yes, sir. I'll see what I can find out."

Alice was superficially aware when someone exited the elevators at the far end of the atrium. Another suit. He hurried up to the reception desk where several uniformed guards were busily doing their jobs, but he specifically approached the guard she had spoken with. By body language alone, it seemed obvious they were trying to talk about her without giving themselves away. They failed. Alice was very aware she was under surveillance. Anyone who entered this establishment was watched, and the name she had so innocently asked about was one she knew would produce results. She glanced at the obvious cameras in the lobby trained on this guard station. She wondered idly how many cameras there were that she couldn't see.

"Ms. Weaver?" the man approached her, and Alice pretended to turn in surprise. She'd watched them out of the corners of her amazing eyes, very aware of her surroundings.

He was holding out his hand to shake hers, and she took it, noting that it was soft, so he must not do much manual labor. The handshake was firm, and she responded in kind, assessing the man now that he was up close. "I'm Stewart Commons," he told her. "You were asking for Madelyn Korbel?"

"Yes, I was. Is she available?" she answered pleasantly, releasing his hand. She was pleased that his palm hadn't been damp or his hold on her hand too long.

"I'm sorry, Madelyn Korbel has retired. Is there something I could help you with?" He was assessing her just as the security officer had. She was dressed nicely, not too corporate, but she looked…powerful was the only word he could think to express himself, but that word was inadequate. There was something about her he couldn't put his finger on, something he sensed due to his training over the years. He'd think more about it later.

"Are you her replacement?" she asked, surprised to find that Madelyn had retired. Alice thought that woman would have died at her desk before she left. Then she had a thought, *Either Madelyn was testing her, feeling her out to see what she really wanted, or they had forcibly retired her.* That sounded plausible. The woman was a legend.

Stewart chuckled and shook his head. "No one could replace Madelyn. What was it you wanted to see her about?"

"Mr. Commons," she said, and her tone suggested she didn't believe that was his real name, "Let's not play the social niceties game. Neither of us has the time. By now, my name is raising certain flags within your agency. It will raise further flags in the FBI databases you share. The redactions in my file alone should tell you and your people that I don't just drop in for tea or a friendly visit with an old friend. Let's get Madelyn or her replacement, and let's see if the information I have is useful to you and your people, shall we?" her voice was cordial, polite even, but at the same time, it was commanding, and he found himself compelled to do exactly what she asked but stopped himself.

"Ms...Weaver, I have to know what you are here to see Madelyn about before we can proceed."

"Ah, I see. You are going to play the games associated with your level of clearance, which you seem destined to remain at," she said, exasperated already and not willing to be too polite with this hireling. This really was a matter of some urgency. She sighed. "I have information regarding arms shipments in Kazakhstan and Russia, and I'm certain that anyone who pulls up my files will see I'm not bluffing. Your obviously inadequate security clearance makes it impossible for me to divulge further information, so trot back to your superiors and tell them I would like to make a deal. And if you can't produce Madclyn, I suggest her replacement or a superior be coughed up pretty quickly, because my patience is going to run out if I'm only given subordinates to deal with."

He was shocked and surprised to be referred to as a subordinate and insulted that his security clearance wasn't high enough to deal with this. His eyes betrayed his annoyance, but Alice wasn't perturbed in the least. She tended to rub people the wrong way...often deliberately. People in this line of work judged on appearances. She was aware of that and had picked out this pantsuit accordingly. It fit her better than any of her older clothes, which would have hung on her reduced frame. At least, this one appeared fitted for her. She felt confident in it, which would help her maintain her cool through what she was certain would be a long day or two.

Without saying a word to her, he nodded stiffly and walked away, murmuring to security to, "Watch her," which they would have done anyway. Alice made herself comfortable on a bench. She knew the wait wouldn't be too long, but she wanted to watch the atrium while she sat. She knew there had to be dozens of cameras trained on anyone entering the building, but she was certain several would now be analyzing her, making sure she matched whatever outdated photographs they had on her.

Two days ago, Alice had been answering the officer's questions about the nearly fatal encounter with Special Agent Linda Miller. This officer had been at the scene for what had been the first of three questionings their family had been put through. After the first session, Alice had called Portia, not only to get her perspective on the situation but to hand her Linda's phone and download the files on it. Breaking the phone's security code had been a simple matter of learning Linda's birthdate and entering it backwards. Not too concerned with security on her personal phone, it had taken a mere half hour for Alice to figure out the code, so they could download the files to Portia's computer. Since Alice's household computers and her children's personal computers had been confiscated by the IRS, she couldn't use any of the fancy programs she normally had access to. After finding the most important file on the agent's phone—her recording that proved she was not hiding behind her badge—Alice sent it to herself in the form of an email. The remaining files she placed into a file she created on Portia's computer to use in her defense because she knew this wasn't over, not by a long shot. The call history, Linda's contacts, even her photos and text message screen captures, were sent to Alice's email address but only when Portia wasn't looking. Alice quickly erased the history on Portia's email and computer, so she wouldn't be aware of what Alice had done, hoping if Portia's computer were compromised, it might not show up easily. She wished she had her own computers, so she could overwrite her actions and prevent whoever was investigating her from discovering what she'd done, several times if necessary.

The second interview with a lieutenant from Linda's precinct didn't go as smoothly as the first. He was a little suspicious, perhaps also a little homophobic, and he took in the expensive Palos Verdes estate with distaste. Officially giving him Linda's phone, which they claimed to have found after the other officer had taken away Linda's badge, gun, and jacket, didn't seem to faze him the same way.

"Have you seen what is on here?" he asked suspiciously, holding up the cell phone.

"As you can see, it's locked," Alice replied and saw from the corner of her eye when Portia shifted uncomfortably. It was a telltale sign to Alice, but the lawyer was out of the officer's line of sight and only listening in to protect her client's interests, just in case. Alice gave the appearance she was answering his questions but was doing her best not to.

"Were you aware of Agent Miller's interest in your wife?" he asked.

"Of course. My wife was free to date when she thought me deceased, and she informed me when I returned." *I also watched the entire failed courtship*, she felt like adding but refrained.

"You weren't jealous? You didn't want revenge?"

"Of course, I was jealous. I love my wife. However, the logical side of me," she nearly laughed at this statement but refrained from making the situation worse, "says she didn't know I was alive and was free to pursue other arrangements."

"You were getting a divorce before you disappeared?"

"We were estranged when I disappeared but hadn't started divorce proceedings," she corrected tightly, the only sign of her annoyance as his questions became increasingly personal. They continued like this for half an hour, and Portia only interjected twice: once, when he asked about the IRS, which was none of his business and had nothing to do with his investigation into the behavior of his agent, and the second time, when he warned Alice not to go anywhere.

"Are you saying my client is under suspicion of something?"

"Well, we do have to get Agent Miller's side of things," he tried to say reasonably but forcefully, and Alice deliberately looked at the lawyer. Was this guy in on whatever Linda had been looking into? Was he aware of her extra-curricular activities?

"You'll let us know?" Portia asked dismissively, a cue for the lieutenant to leave.

"Of course," he said charmingly while rising. "If you think of anything else, please let me know," he added as he dropped his card on the coffee table.

"Think you'll get the recording off that?" Alice asked innocently, gesturing at the mobile phone.

"I'm sure we will," he assured her as he slipped it in his pocket.

"Wanna bet that phone disappears?" Alice murmured to Portia as he drove away.

"You think he'd tamper with evidence?" she asked, shocked.

Alice looked at their family friend. She had known this woman for decades, and it still amazed her how naive the attorney could be. She didn't answer, her sardonic look and raised eyebrow saying it all.

Alice looked at her cell phone to check the time. They'd kept her waiting an hour already. There were several calls from Kathy on her phone, but she hadn't heard them because she'd turned off the sound. She glanced at security and saw them watching her to see if she was going to use her phone, so they could either report her or ask her to put it away. She had no intention of answering Kathy or anyone else's calls right now. She had a specific agenda, and the time spent here had been allotted in her carefully-made plans. She thought back to what had happened the day after she sent Linda to the hospital....

The IRS had turned up at the end of their driveway, flashing badges and demanding they be let into the estate. They had officially *served* Alice and Kathy Weaver for bank fraud, tax fraud, and failing to report a foreign bank account as well as tax evasion, grand larceny, and finally, criminal liability. The document implied they could stay in their home for the time being but that was pending as the case wound through the court system. The clear threat was they were about to be arrested, and yet, they didn't arrest them, which was suspicious given the charges being leveled. Alice was genuinely surprised they weren't being evicted based on the charges before them; however, the good ole American system of justice made the IRS comply, and they would have to wend their way through the courts. The family's eviction and the selling of their estate, which the IRS would confiscate for unpaid taxes, was the ultimate goal and would come in time.

"Oh, my God, Alice! What are we going to do?" Kathy asked, panicked as she read through the charges.

"I'll handle it," she tried to reassure her wife.

"But what can you do? They seem pretty sure they have a case." Kathy sounded like she was going to cry, and it irked Alice that her wife didn't have more faith in her abilities. Just then, the phone rang, and Kathy went to answer it. Apparently, Andi and Portia had been served at their office at the same time. They would learn a while later that their accountant and tax firms had been served as well.

"Someone seems to have a hard-on for us," Alice murmured thoughtfully as she began to formulate her plan of action. This two-pronged attack that *seemed* unrelated was too unrelated not to *be* related.

"Where are you going?" Kathy asked as Alice put on a jacket.

"You don't mind if I drive your Lexus, do you?" Alice asked as she grabbed the keys off the hook.

"Don't you think I should go with you?"

"The kids are going to be frightened if those bozos come back," she pointed out, not being clear if she meant the IRS agents who had tacked official notices at the end of their driveway on the gate as well as on the front door or the police investigating Linda's accident at their house. Alice had torn the notices down, seeing no need to advertise their personal business to their neighbors.

The third police interview had been rather tense when the lieutenant returned with another officer, this one from the Palos Verdes police department. Alice now knew who had been on the other end of the tapes that had been transcribed; she recognized the name from her computer files. And so did Kathy, whose poker face could use some work. "I need to check the computers," she said in a low voice, so only Kathy could hear. "I want to check them," she lied cheerfully, knowing Kathy wanted to be in on this as a true and equal partner. Kathy didn't like that she couldn't know everything, and Alice had already started working out a plan to leave her family in peace.

Alice shook her tail after getting on the freeway, backtracking enough to ensure she was no longer being followed. She parked at the car park and got into her sedan, first checking in on the computers as she had told her wife and then heading to a rental counter where she rented a Porsche. She sighed in relief to be driving one of the familiar, expensive sports cars again. It further helped to disguise her when she stopped to buy some clothes. She got several outfits that fit her better than her old clothes and were even better than the things she had purchased in Dubai.

She approached a house in the expensive Los Angeles suburb of Trousdale Estates, located in an exclusive Beverly Hills' community in the foothills of the Santa Monica mountains. She looked up at those mountains, feeling the cold and wondering if they would get snow on them this year. Was it colder today, or was that just her imagination? She had been in their heated pool just yesterday. *Wow! Yesterday seemed a lifetime ago*, she thought as she pressed the button at the gate, her Porsche being scrutinized by the security camera.

"Can I help you?" the voice came through the tin box.

"I'm here to see Sebastian."

"Who are you?"

"Alice Weaver."

There was a delay of several moments before the voice continued with, "Alice Weaver is dead."

"I assure you, I am not," she replied, wanting to laugh.

"Sebastian can't see you," the voice answered with finality.

Alice sighed. Did Sebastian not want to see her, or was this a ploy? She knew she scared him as well as excited him. This was one of several homes he owned, which she had found over the years, and she knew he hated that she was so easily able to find him. However, he had given up long ago trying to figure out how she found him. His enemies couldn't find him, so how could Alice?

Well, she had tried the diplomatic approach. Now, she was going to have to get dirty, and that wasn't something she relished. She backed the Porsche away from the gate and considered ramming it—after all, she had taken out some rather expensive insurance on the over-priced sports car—but she reconsidered. She didn't want to start with hostilities, and those around Sebastian tended to have automatic machine guns. She parked the Porsche in the next neighborhood, which was saying something about the distance, with these little estates. It reminded her of her own Palos Verdes estate, but her view was better as she looked onto the ocean instead of Los Angeles.

She slid off her impractical but stylish shoes, replacing them with black sports shoes. She zipped up a matching, black sports jacket and slicked her fingers through her spiky hair, wondering if it would grow faster someday, although she did like the ease of caring for it these days. She walked down the street, appearing to the casual observer as a lonely jogger on a midday run. She searched for and figured out which were the walls to Sebastian's estate. Noting that one of his neighbors was leaving as she approached the gate, she slipped between it before it could close, so she could follow his wall and leap up to swing over the eight-foot fence using a branch to facilitate her boost. It had been a scramble, and she was grateful there was no razor wire or broken glass on the top to keep out intruders. She looked over the area for a while, saw where the guards and cameras were, and ascertained a blind spot which she didn't hesitate to use, slipping into it to get within feet of the house before she had to duck and pry open a window. The window creaked from disuse, but she got inside. Breathing hard, she wondered if she would ever get back in the shape she had been. Kazakhstan, Russia, and Central America, while she'd been on the go and active, had been the culmination of a lot of hard times, and her body was still recovering slowly, from that emaciation.

Haltingly, she moved through the unfamiliar house, looking for alarms or triggers that would give away her presence. She saw the library and was headed for it but veered away when a well-dressed man headed upstairs with a tray. Curious, she slipped from the shadows, watching for laser lights that would have set off any alarms and rapidly following his footsteps up the stairs in time to see him slip into a double-doored room. She slipped into the room next door to it and looked around. She saw it was empty and put her ear to the wall first, and then against a door. She was hearing a rumbling of voices, one of which she thought she recognized as Sebastian's, but it had been so long and perhaps she was mistaken. Something about what she was hearing felt off, and this disturbed her. She waited until she heard the door in the next room open and shut, then let a little time pass before she left the room she was hiding in and headed for what she was sure was the master bedroom.

"Sebastian?" she asked, shocked to see the condition her old friend was in. He was lying in bed and looked just as emaciated as she had been, only he also had a flushed face and his customarily impeccably trimmed beard was looking unkempt. The normally large, robust man was a fraction of what he had been. She looked around the darkened room with its drapes drawn and saw the medicines on the side tables and the tray of food across his lap.

He stared hard at her, not believing his own eyes. She was dead! If Alice was coming to take him on to Valhalla though, he couldn't have asked for a better escort. Damn, she was thin. What happened to those amazing breasts and the curves he had often lusted after? "Alice?" he asked in a slightly raspy voice, unsure. He wasn't sure he shouldn't be terrified. She had meant death to many people over the years.

She smiled, showing even and very white teeth. Was it his imagination, or were the eye teeth a little longer than necessary? Was she now a vampire? Surely, it was his imagination. Yes, that was it, the medications were off. "I come to visit my old friend only to find him in bed. Are you ill?" she asked, knowing the answer before he even answered. Her eyes didn't lie.

"Cancer," he growled, sounding winded.

"Damn!" she exclaimed. "I am sorry, my friend. I won't bother you. I hope you get better and soon."

"Wait, don't leave!" he stopped her with his request. "You can't possibly know what this visit means to me, my friend. When I heard you were dead..." he began and then thought again. "I went to your memorial and gave my regards to your widow. I should have known...no corpse, no Alice," he chuckled at his sally. "What can I do for you?"

"Sebastian, really. I wouldn't think of asking for a favor..." she began, knowing he wasn't up to the task she had intended to ask.

"I am still in charge," he insisted, sounding a little like the Sebastian of old. "Dammit, don't write me off yet. Those bastards are already thinking they can divvy up my belongings," he lamented angrily, gesturing out the bedroom door and towards the downstairs. "At least, you bring some excitement. There is an honesty I cannot compare. No one is like the great Alice Weaver. I can see your death was greatly exaggerated, although, you didn't come away unscathed." At her nod, he smiled, but it was a mere caricature of the former man. "I believe I am still in your debt for some diamonds you left with me. What can I do for you, my friend?"

"I would like to hire some of your men and women. I need them to be invisible, and I want some of your best weaponless fighters."

"Of course. You have a job that needs this expertise?" he asked, sounding excited at the prospect of ordering his people around.

She nodded. "I need them to guard my family," she said simply.

His eyes took on a speculative look. "You won't be there?"

"Your people can disappear *if* I return home."

"If?"

She nodded, not going into details. She waited. He waited. When the waiting became unbearable, he cleared his throat and nodded. "I can let you have four. Will that be enough?"

"Thank you, Sebastian. You must let me pay you...."

He shook his head. The hair on his head had thinned to an alarming degree, its blackness making it look stringy, and were those grey hairs? "No, Alice. This may be my last order, but I give it gladly. You have made my life interesting a few times," he laughed, ending in a coughing fit that caused him to hock up something in a fine, linen napkin from the tray. He hadn't eaten much; he wasn't that hungry.

Alice waited respectfully, waiting for him to get his breath back. She admired the art above his fireplace mantle, the room warm and cozy and not in need of a fire.

"Need I ask how you found this hideout of mine?" he asked finally. She always found him, even when he didn't want to be found.

Alice turned back, a grin on her face. Her eyes were glittering, and he laughed again as he shook his head. "You'd be a better bloodhound than my enemies. I wish..." he began but left off. They both knew what he wished. He had tried to recruit Alice years ago. It hadn't gone well. He had not only tried to recruit her but also seduce her. She broke all his limbs for his impertinence and persistence, and he'd been laid up for months. She had visited him faithfully every week, feeding him chocolates and bringing him sweet and exotic-smelling oils that could be rubbed on his aching limbs until they healed. He had been in one of their safe houses, locked from the inside, and still, she managed to appear frequently, in a different spot in the house or sometimes, a different house. They never did figure out how she had done that. It was then, he determined she was a better friend than an enemy. It had been a very profitable friendship over the years.

His mind, usually wandering because of his illness, medications, and boredom, remembered when someone had asked if she had special

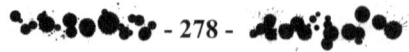

training and he attempted to find out. The men he had sent to find this information for him had come up missing. The fourth one had appeared in his bed with blood leaking from every orifice. There was no sign of struggle, and it had been a definite warning. He'd been in another safe house that time too.

Alice was one amazing woman, and he had regrets, but he had been younger and in the prime of his life. He had never thought his strength would fail him, but the cancer had been insidious. He wasn't sure going out in a blaze of gunfire wouldn't have been a better option. The pain was...well, it was more than he had expected. He cleared his throat and asked, "How is your family? The kids okay?"

She smiled again, looking proud. "The younger ones are teenagers now."

He winced, realizing the passage of time. He'd remembered Alice when she was single and with no sign of marriage in sight. He wouldn't have thought someone like her would have dared because it made her vulnerable. With her skills, he would have thought she'd...still, she looked happy. He envied her that since he had missed finding happiness in his own life. "Anyone in particular coming after them?" he asked suddenly, all business again.

"IRS and apparently, the cops."

"You want us to shoot it out with them?"

She immediately shook her head. "No, but if it looks like they are going to take the house, I want you to get my family out. Get them onto a private plane south of the border with enough gas to get them to South America. Kathy will know where to go from there. Just make sure she has a few thousand cash to play with."

He nodded. Kathy would have every luxury, if he had to do it himself, and he would. It might kill him to do so, but for Alice Weaver he'd do it. "Anything else?"

She shook her head. "Anything I can do for you?" she asked, then turned as the door opened and a man and a woman entered. She stepped back into the shadows but not before she was seen. Dammit! She should have heard them coming. Sebastian's carpets were rich and deep, and she'd been concerned for her friend, so she'd missed the sound of their approach.

The man reached for a gun, and that was his mistake. Alice took him down, almost reflexively, and when he tried to fight her, she broke his arm. The exertion was a bit much for her, much to her surprise, but she triumphed, and she froze when she was confronted by the woman.

"No," a now weak Sebastian tried to stop the inevitable violence. The man, his bodyguard, had been taken unawares, and it was natural that he reached for a gun, but he didn't know Alice Weaver. Sebastian was shocked when Alice stood there, just staring at the woman. "Do you know each other?" he asked, breaking the silence as both women seemed equally startled to find the other there.

"She's my neighbor," the woman told him, suddenly shaking slightly.

"That's right," Alice said, not sure she could lie her way out of this one. Since Sandi had found her in Sebastian's bedroom, it was fair to assume she was involved in something illegal, and then Alice remembered that Sandi was a hospice nurse. She glanced at Sebastian. Maybe her presence was legitimate; he did not look well.

"Alice is a business acquaintance. She used to invest money for me and came by to see how I was doing."

"Ugh," the man on the floor was moaning, holding his broken arm.

"I suggest you go get that fixed," Alice told him conversationally. "And I'd leave that gun alone or I'll shove it up your–" she started to add but glancing at Sandi, rethought it. Nothing like impressing the neighbors.

Two other men, having heard the commotion, came running into the room. Seeing Alice, they went for her. She crouched, preparing for their attack, but Sebastian croaked, "No!" Holding up his hand, he pointed and added, "Take him out of here, and see to his arm. You can go too, Sandi."

"You need your meds now that you have eaten," she contradicted.

"I have not eaten. I've been discussing old times with Alice. I'll call you when I'm done," he said meaningfully, "so you can tell me which meds I need."

Sandi took the hint, glancing curiously at Alice Weaver. She would have never thought to find her here. She hesitated only a moment, used to arguing with this difficult patient and not wishing to lose the upper hand. Then, seeing Alice watching her, those disturbing cat-like eyes on her, she decided to leave. She left the door open, and Alice followed to make sure no one was outside the door before gently closing it and returning to stand near Sebastian as he gestured from his bed.

"She's killing me," he stated boldly.

"Are you sure?" It confirmed something Alice had seen in the woman's eyes the first time she met her.

He nodded. "I think she gets joy from it, but I'm not sure what she's using. I'm dying by degrees, and I don't know how to tell. She's a sadist."

Alice added to the mental file she had started on Sandi and Richard Pasternack. "Let me guess…someone in Russia recommended her?"

"How in the world did you know that?" He was astounded by the things she just seemed to *know*. She was always miles ahead of everyone else.

Something clicked for Alice. She didn't answer Sebastian. "Is Richard handling your portfolio or banking for you?"

He nodded warily, wondering what she knew.

"You can bet you won't live to see your ill-gotten gains, and those moneys are probably back in Russia now. Do you have a will?"

He nodded but looked entirely floored by her knowledge of his finances and personnel.

"It's not going to mean diddly when they get done with you. There won't be anything left. Want me to do you a favor?" she asked, feeling the old impulses rising through her pores.

"No," he said, surprising her. "I transferred the funds a long time ago. I have no children, and the aunts and uncles who benefited got that benefit long ago. I sold most of my assets, but they don't know that. When the doctor gave me my terminal diagnosis and recommended hospice care, I took his recommendation, and the Pasternacks came into my life. The little they have seen and have handled isn't nearly as much as they think I have. Convenient, eh?"

She nodded, wondering at this new mystery but knowing the result would be the same.

He started to cough again, took a sip of water from the glass on his side table, and began again. "I see it in her eyes. She's enjoying the pain I'm in and what she is doing to me."

Alice nodded again. It confirmed once again what she herself had seen in Sandi's eyes. Someday, she'd do something about that, but right now, she had other things to take care of. "Is she causing you additional pain?" she asked. Had he been standing up, he would have taken a step back, but as it was, he cringed slightly at the look on her face…those eyes!

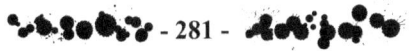

"No, no pain from her, but she enjoys making me feel helpless, and these drugs…" his hands took in the many medications, "some have no effect until I wake many hours or maybe days later. She's killing me slowly and enjoying every minute of it. I thought you were a ghost come to take me to Valhalla when I saw you," he laughed, making an odd sound as he gasped for breath. This was the most he had spoken in a while as he waited to die. He wanted to die in his own bed in comfort. The thought of going out in a blaze of bullets was a young man's bravado.

"Wouldn't be a bad way to go, eh?" she asked softly, knowing of his attraction for her for so many years.

"We've both gotten older. Well, you got better, and I just got old," he acknowledged. He leaned over and pressed a button on the side table. "I pay my debts," he promised.

Alice stood by as the same two men returned to the room, looking at her curiously.

"This woman needs your expertise. She needs four people to watch her home in shifts. *Quietly*. No guns and no violence unless necessary. You pick the four," he said, addressing the older of the two men. "I want absolute discretion." Alice fidgeted, and Sebastian saw it. "Something to add?"

"They should look like they belong in Palos Verdes," she added, seeing the younger man wearing a sports track suit that looked like it belonged at a Good Guy's reunion with its zipper down the front. It screamed mafia wannabe.

Sebastian nodded, and the older man he was addressing nodded. "Where?"

Alice gave him the address and added, "It's my wife and kids. The IRS and the Palos Verdes' cops are watching. I'm going to rattle some cages, and I don't know who might come for them. If that happens, I want you to get them out of there. They can't see your people–"

Sebastian interrupted, "Have my jet gassed and ready in case it's needed to take them to South America. Mrs. Weaver, Kathy, will tell you where to take her when the time is right…if it comes to that." He knew with the order coming from him, his men wouldn't dare deviate from the plan. "Got that?" he asked, commandingly. He was holding back a spate of coughing, manfully swallowing the built-up phlegm.

"Yes, sir," the man said, and the younger man looked curiously at Alice, wondering who she was to command them or ask the old man for a favor. It was quite an ask.

Alice saw the young man eyeing her and stared him down, making him extremely uncomfortable. He turned his attention back to the old man.

"You don't deviate or improvise unless necessary. If I must repeat any of that, there will be hell to pay!" he threatened, again swallowing against the need to cough and ruin the ominous feel of his commands. "Four of your best, and they better look the part. *No weapons*," he stressed, knowing the man would get the implications.

"Got it," the man promised, giving a little bow and backing from the room until the two of them were alone again.

"Alice, I'll say goodbye for now," he hinted broadly, hoping to hold back the coughing spate that was due.

"Are you sure I can't take care of something for you?" Her head tilted back towards the door where they both knew the hospice nurse would soon be coming through.

"After I'm gone, do what you will. For now, she relieves *some* of the pain. I'd have played with her if I was younger."

"And made her pay," Alice added with a grin. She reached out to the frail man's equally frail hand and clasped it for a moment. "I'm sorry, my friend. See you in the next life?"

"I'll reserve a mansion for you and yours," he promised with a grin. A tear was forming in his eye. He was feeling emotional and not from his medications. He would never see the likes of an Alice Weaver again. He wouldn't want to, but she was something special. He missed the added curves. Her body was a lot different now, but he also liked the punk rock look.

Alice walked out of the room, shutting the door behind her carefully and leaning against it for a moment. Out of the corner of her eye, Alice saw movement down the hall and pretended she didn't see Sandi as she deliberately turned the other way and headed for the stairs. This time, she didn't bother with a window but walked boldly out the front door and down the steps. The man Sebastian had commanded was standing there with the sports track-suited guy, staring curiously and intimidatingly. As she walked out the front door, several guards looked at her curiously as she walked down the drive, obviously having been made aware of her presence inside the mansion. She needed to release some of her nervous energy. She wanted to jog and use the suit she was wearing, but she knew they would think that a sign of fear. She passed through the gate, which magically opened as she approached it, proving she was being watched by the many cameras.

She made her way around the block and back to the Porsche, lamenting the fact that some of the old friends she had made over the years were passing. Sebastian wouldn't be the first or the last. Still, it was like passing a torch. She sighed. Her body wasn't what it once was either. The time in Kazakhstan had really taken a toll. Then she thought about how old she was and shrugged, there was nothing she could do about getting older.

Unbeknownst to Alice, Sebastian had one more conversation after she left and before the pills Sandi supplied him came into effect. He could feel the taste in his mouth that told him he would be drifting soon. The triumph in Sandi's eyes as she administered the liquid meds through the tube in his arm told its own tales. She reluctantly left the room as the man Sebastian had commanded came into the room.

"Artum close the door," Sebastian rasped, waving Sandi away.

Artum waited until Sandi started down the hallway and then stuck his head out to make sure she was gone. He could see her curiosity and knew it was unhealthy. If what he thought was really happening, he would kill her, but someone had asked a favor, and Sebastian had employed the nurse. Artum didn't trust her for some reason. It was in his nature not to trust strangers, regardless of their associates or nationality. Closing the door, he turned back to Sebastian. He was sad to see his uncle looking so frail. He'd always been a man to look up to, but now, he was a shadow of his former self. "Yes, Uncle?" he asked, prompting him. He could see he was going to fall asleep soon.

"No one is to ever touch Alice Weaver and her family. Is that understood?"

"Yes, Uncle, I'll pass the word. Is she one of us?" he asked, wondering at her connection to this Russian-American mobster.

"No, she's outside the system. She's a system to herself. If anyone makes that mistake, there will be hell to pay, and she's died more than once." He started coughing, alarmed that there was blood on the tissue this time. That couldn't be good.

Artum thought perhaps his uncle was exaggerating. How did someone die more than once? "No one touches the Weaver family. I understand."

His uncle grasped his hand, his grip amazingly strong for a moment as he tried to make himself understood. "Artum I'm serious. She will destroy everything I ever built if she feels we betrayed her. She has resources we could only dream of and wouldn't hesitate to take us out. Every...one...of...us." He was fading, and he knew it, but he had to get his point across. There was fear in his voice that Artum dismissed as the ramblings of an old man. Still, she had taken down one of their men and broken his arm, and she was an interesting-looking woman. He could bet she was hot in her younger days.

"I'll keep that in mind, Uncle."

Sebastian began to mumble, trying to tell his great-nephew what Alice had been like twenty years ago, but the drugs were too powerful and too insidious, and he stopped midway through his speech, dozing off. Artum watched to be sure the old man was asleep before he tucked him in respectfully and left him.

"Mrs. Weaver?" a voice woke Alice from her daydream. She glanced at the woman standing before her, her body tensing as though ready to spring up. The woman saw the narrowing of the eyes and was momentarily startled at their color...were they orange? "I'm sorry. Did I startle you?" the woman asked ingenuously.

"Yes, I'm sorry," she excused herself, having not heard the woman approach. That wasn't like her. Thinking again about Sebastian, she had lost herself in memories. Maybe she was getting old. Still, she had taken that bodyguard down and broken his arm. Those were not the actions of someone who was old. The man had been young and virile, and surprise had been on her side. Secretly, she was proud of herself, even if her body said, *"You're stiffening up from that."* She'd eased the stiffness on the flight back with a little alcohol, something she hadn't indulged in much in her life. That was last night, and now, she had to deal with whatever was before her.

"If you'll come this way, please?" the woman said kindly, indicating that Alice should follow her across the large atrium. The security guards were still surreptitiously watching her, just in case.

She got up, still a little stiff from the activities of a couple days before. She'd slept well the previous night in the hotel, but she was still tired. As they passed security, the woman held out a hand and was given a guest pass. She handed the pass to Alice before the small, blonde woman went through the metal detector. For once, Alice was glad she had left her special, metal belt back in the hotel room with her other clothes. Alice followed the woman into the elevator where she pressed five, and the car rapidly rose. Alice was escorted to a room, not an interrogation room as she'd thought, but to what looked like an office. She didn't miss the one-way mirror. That must be standard issue. She didn't sit down right away. Instead, she looked out the window at the Virginia countryside. Whoever occupied this office enjoyed a nice view.

"Someone will be with you momentarily," the woman informed her as she indicated the seats across from a bare wooden desk.

Alice wondered at the treatment she was receiving. Why wasn't she in an interrogation room? What was the purpose of this? She saw several things she could use to defend herself if necessary, including bookshelves made of wood, scissors, and even a ruler. Was this really someone's office?

"Ms. Weaver?" a voice interrupted her perusal of the relatively bare room and the view outside the window. Alice turned to the man standing in the doorway, who smiled and indicated a seat as he came into the room. "You were asking for Madelyn Korbel?"

She nodded, not saying anything as she sat down.

"She's retired."

"I heard."

He waited, hoping she would say more. When she didn't, he asked, "You have information about Kazakhstan and arms shipments?"

She nodded and waited, examining him as he had her.

He was surprised how close her scrutiny of him was. He had been trained to look for signs from people he interviewed, watching for things that would give away whether they were lying. She didn't give off any of these signs. She just waited. It was almost...predatory.

"Who are you?" Alice asked, tired of waiting.

"I'm sorry. I'm Albert Miller. I worked with Madelyn when she was here."

"Did she retire voluntarily?"

He smiled slightly. She obviously had known Madelyn and her work ethics well. Madelyn had been obsessed with the job and had risen quite high in its ranks...for a woman. The intel she had collected had been very beneficial to her career. "I'm not at liberty to give out that information. Can you tell me how you knew her?"

"By now, my file should have been pulled, and you will see I supplied her with information from time to time. I now have information that I wish to trade." She folded her arms across her chest, leaned back in the chair with her legs out before her, and looked absolutely relaxed. He wasn't fooled. She was not relaxed in the least. He was quite sure she could spring up and defend herself if needed. He had read some of her file although there wasn't enough time to read it all. Plenty of it had been redacted, and he wondered at that. Who was Alice Weaver that she could uncover information that someone like Madelyn would have used?

"I've read some of your file," he admitted. "Quite a lot has been redacted."

She nodded to acknowledge that but didn't offer an explanation or additional information.

"About Kazakhstan?" he prompted, wondering if this was a dead end, and she was here for some sort of glory. From the little he'd read, he doubted an online trader and investment broker, would have much information that was helpful for the country. He had read the newspaper articles about her disappearance, death, and reappearance. She had claimed she'd been kidnapped, but nothing in their system supported that information. He wondered at that. Authorities should have interviewed her and pursued that lead.

"Nuh uh. I'll give you the information when I'm assured that my family and I will no longer be the victims of the IRS and police witch hunts. When we have an agreement in writing to that effect, I'll give you enough information that the trail to the billions exchanging hands will keep quite a few of you spooks busy for a long time."

He blinked, surprised at her statement. Surely, she was kidding. "I can't make the IRS or the police stop investigating...."

"Yes, you can," she said simply and stopped talking, waiting.

"Ms. Weaver surely you can't think you can walk in here and make demands like that–" he began officiously.

Alice knew she was being jerked around, and it pissed her off. She interrupted him, waving off whatever he had been about to say, "Look, you have a limited window of opportunity to gain my cooperation. Had you really read my entire file, you would know I don't jerk people around, and I don't appreciate having my time wasted. There is a time limit here–"

"Are you threatening me?"

Alice smiled slightly. "Yes, I am, and don't interrupt me again. In fact, I think you should consult Madelyn to see if I'm kidding. There is a short time limit before this information goes public…worldwide."

He blinked again, wondering if she was bluffing and not appreciating the threat. But he could sense she wasn't kidding. His glance took in the mirror at the end of the room, and that simple act alone gave him away.

"I'll wait here if you want to consult with someone in a position of authority, but the clock is ticking. I've set it up so this information will go public shortly. I'd rather give it to you all in exchange for a dismissal of all charges against me and mine."

"If you are guilty of tax fraud–" he began, getting angry, but Alice cut him off.

"You've interrupted me again!" she said, interrupting him. "I am telling you about the time limit, so you don't make the mistake of thinking I won't follow through. I assure you, I don't play those games, and I don't have to bluff. Read my file again. Oh, and you just gave yourself away there," she informed him helpfully. "If you knew nothing about the charges being brought against me and my estate, then you wouldn't have mentioned tax fraud." Pointing that out gave her immense satisfaction, but it proved they had looked her up and were gathering information. "Run along and get this sorted," she said to him as though talking to a child. "Find someone in a position of authority." When he made no move to get up and do as she told him, she turned away, looked right into the mirror, and grinned. Her smile looked great with the new teeth. "I'm not kidding," she informed the mirror before getting up, putting her hands into the pockets of her pants suit, and looking out at the view again.

"Ms. Weaver, Alice…" he began heatedly, annoyed that she was turning this interview into a travesty. "You can't come in and threaten the CIA."

Alice whirled, amazingly gracefully but so fast it surprised him into silence. "I did not give you permission to call me by my first name, *Mr.* Miller. Learn the courtesies, and you'll go a lot further. Even Psychology 101 classes teach that." She turned back to look out the window and spoke to it, knowing the man was still trying to outwait her. "If you are thinking you can hold me indefinitely, you are right. Only a couple people know where I am, but they are going to blow the whistle if I don't make an appearance or contact them in a period of time. You are wasting my time, Mr. Miller." She went silent, and the questions he tried to fire at her were not answered as she stood there, looking out. Alice Weaver had the patience, and the eyes, of a cat.

He finally looked exasperatedly at the mirror, rose, and left the office. Alice heard the lock engage and laughed. It wouldn't matter if they locked her into a jail cell. Nothing could be worse than what she had gone through in Central America, Russia, or Kazakhstan.

It took another half hour before a woman came in to try using the same tactics and the same questions, and Alice stopped repeating herself. "That's it! Contact Madelyn Korbel, or we're done!"

"Ms. Weaver, I assure you we can detain you and your family for–"

That was when Alice unleashed some of her inner self. She leaned across the desk and breathed into the woman's face, "Touch my family, and I'll make sure the people who have this information make fools of the CIA, the FBI, and even the Secret Service. This will embarrass many powerful politicians in this country and several other countries. What do you think will happen to *your* job...*all* your jobs, if that happens?"

"What is the information you have that you think will affect us all so greatly?" she asked, but Alice was done. They had threatened her family, as she had known they would. She wouldn't speak to them again unless they brought her Madelyn, and she told them so.

They left her waiting for two days in that office without food and water, and she ended up squatting in a corner and peeing because she had no facilities either. Their wood floor was no longer pristine. She made no move to break up the room, either sitting angled in the chair, so the mirror had her back or laying on the desk as she dozed. Already sleep-deprived, she knew what they were doing. She could handle it, and this office was more comfortable than some of the cells she had been in. She was disgusted by the lack of facilities and almost wished for a jail cell, so she could use the toilet. Her own fastidious nature didn't appreciate the situation in the least.

The cars turned one by one into the long drive in the Connecticut countryside, perfectly in sync. They were like puppets on a string, all of them black with blackened windows. Madelyn saw them before they stopped before her circular drive. Only feds traveled in packs like that, so she wasn't surprised to see Clifford Wolf step from one of the black Suburbans. She met him at the front door, saying sardonically before he could open his mouth, "Whatever it is, no. I'm retired."

Cliff laughed, knowing she wouldn't have answered a mere phone call, but they needed her. The file on Alice Weaver had frightened a few people who knew more than they admitted as they read through portions of it. The woman had been instrumental in several things they weren't allowed to discuss without the proper clearance. If Ms. Weaver had information on arms shipments, and her threats indicated she did, they needed Madelyn to at least clue them in on how to deal with her. They were one step away from imprisoning Alice and her family, if necessary. Some of the gist of what they had been able to get out of her had been verified, and they needed the details.

"Don't even try the *'let's be friends'* tactic, Director Kolby. I'm serious. I'm retired!" She went to close her door, but he grabbed it.

"What about national security?" he began, but she waved her hand dismissively.

"I've given my life for the CIA. Don't start that crap," she said angrily.

"What if we give–?"

"No matter what you give me, it isn't enough. I've given my all, and I'm retired, dammit!"

"Alice Weaver," he said, watching her closely and seeing her blanch. "What do you know of her?"

"Did you arrest her?" she gasped out, looking genuinely frightened. Her hand came up to the top of her blouse, worrying the fabric there as she waited for his answer.

"No, she came in voluntarily. She's asking for a deal." He watched her curiously, wondering why that name had caused such an extreme reaction in this normally unperturbable woman.

"She came in voluntarily? She's where? Langley?" She sounded incredulous.

He nodded. "She walked in of her own accord two days ago. We're holding her for information."

"You haven't escalated your interrogation tactics, have you?"

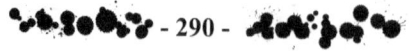

"You think we should?"

She immediately shook her head. "No, I wouldn't suggest that at all."

"May I come in?" he asked, growing weary of standing on her doorstep.

Madelyn made a gesture. It wasn't really a welcome, but it certainly indicated he could come in. She saw the others standing by the vehicles and looking about. That was going to make an impression with her neighbors, if they could see the men and women in black suits wearing sunglasses. If that didn't scream CIA or some other secret service, she didn't know what did. She sighed at the inconvenience. She was *retired*, dammit!

"Ms. Weaver, I'm sure we can make a deal," Mr. Miller tried interrogating her again, telling her these things as another woman, a cleaning lady from the look of her, cleaned up the corner Alice had squatted in. "If you do not cooperate, you must realize we can't help you with the tax lien. The IRS will forfeit your bank accounts, the insurance policies, all your real estate, as well as your children's trust funds."

Alice didn't react. She knew they were finally doing their homework on her. His stating all these things made it more obvious to her that they believed her when she said she had information regarding the arms shipments.

"The IRS is alleging that you defrauded the government of tens of millions of dollars that you didn't pay taxes on. We can't offer you a deal unless you tell us more. And part of making that up will clearly be you handing over your ill-gotten gains. Tell us the things you did to attain those monies and the real estate involved."

Alice nearly smiled; she had anticipated this. It was why she had exchanged cash for the real estate that Sasha now owned outright. She didn't want her name on any of it. The government of the United States, much less Russia, would never find the monies. She glanced at the woman finishing up in the corner, who had stiffened at the man's words, unconsciously acknowledging that she was listening. Alice didn't believe she was a cleaning woman and wondered who she was.

"You paid, what, ten million for your Palos Altos' property? I bet it's worth a whole helluva lot more all these years later," he commented.

Alice finally looked at him in a bored fashion, but he swallowed as he realized her odd eyes weren't the shade of yellow he had become accustomed to. They were listed as brown in her file, but right now, they were decidedly orange. "Are you going to produce Madelyn Korbel or not?" she asked, her voice also sounding bored.

"You've been informed that Madelyn Korbel has retired," he told her, trying to imply with his tone of voice that she wasn't too bright.

"But she's not dead," Alice said in a murmur and turned to look out the window again.

He tried to go back to his agenda of intimidating her. "The analysis of your assets, the sum the IRS expects to recover, nearly covers the estimated costs of the investigation to date."

Alice laughed. It was a genuine laugh, and this puzzled him. He couldn't figure her out. He glanced at the mirror and shrugged slightly. He didn't know how to interrogate such a witness. She could sense that they had ascertained she wasn't intimidated, and she hadn't given them anything really, and then....

"Vashti Baltizar, Leonid Baltizar, Alexander or Xander Baltizar, the Bogomolov family, Filipov, Kozlov," she chanted, ticking off the names that were indelibly inscribed in her mind. She would remember them forever.

"Who are these people?" he asked.

Alice turned her orange eyes on the idiot interrogator. "You really are a novice at this, aren't you? Why are you the one chosen to talk to me? You don't know how to do this," she gestured across the table, indicating the ill-fated interrogation. "I give you the names of some of the most notorious mobsters on the planet and you ask me who they are. They really scraped the barrel with you and your skills, didn't they? Let me guess...last in your class?" She smiled slightly, enjoying the fact that she was making him squirm. And, he *was* squirming, a sure sign her questions and statements were making him uncomfortable.

"Furthermore, the IRS hasn't gone through due process. Do you know what the term due process means?" she asked him as though he were a child, and she had to explain things to him. She was using his own tone of voice from earlier against him, taking delight in humiliating him. "Due process refers to the general principal that the United States government can't take away a person's rights or property without a legal proceeding. I haven't been given due process. Instead, someone's vendetta is getting the best of them, and they are using the IRS as a punitive measure. I just gave you the names of mobsters that I will give the CIA further information on. In exchange, I want a clean slate. I want the investigations by the IRS and police stopped, and I want this vendetta stopped," she gestured again, "and I want you to give me the names of those who instigated this vendetta!." She stopped, staring him in the eyes as he squirmed further, before she swung to the mirror, staring through it at the people behind its reflection, or so they felt, before turning and looking out the window again. She wouldn't say anything further.

This silence, which was stretching out to days, and their further investigations into Alice Weaver, as well as the names she had given them, had them scurrying to find out where Madelyn Korbel lived.

"Director Kolby I am not at liberty to tell you anything about Alice Weaver other than what you can find in her files," she gestured to the thick files of mostly redacted information that he had pulled from his briefcase. She nearly laughed as one file, at least four-inches thick and heavy, flipped open and nearly every other line was blacked out.

"I am the director of the CIA. I can assure you I have clearance," he chuckled, sitting back and waiting, glancing around the comfortable and sophisticated living room they were sitting in. The furniture was as elegant as the woman before him. "Who is Alice Weaver, and why haven't I heard about her before?"

Madelyn fidgeted slightly, wondering if she should even say anything. She could refuse. She wasn't in that game anymore. Politics had forced her out, but she had been surprised to learn how relieved she was to be out of the spy game. The information in her head alone was invaluable. She glanced at the files, nearly laughing at how little information on Alice Weaver was contained there. "You could subpoena the original records."

"Apparently, there is no *time*," he said exasperatedly, sighing loudly.

"Why don't you tell me what you do know?" she asked instead of volunteering anything.

"Why don't you tell me what you know?" he countered, wondering why she was so reluctant to assist on this.

Madelyn smiled but shook her head. She gestured at the files. "You have what you need there."

"Alice Weaver is requesting that you interview her."

Madelyn's heart leapt into her throat, nearly choking her as she shook her head. "I'm retired," she repeated.

"I've heard that somewhere," he smiled, showing he wasn't about to let her off the hook so easily. "She's named a number of Russian mobsters, oligarchs some call them."

"And?" she asked, intrigued despite herself. How had Alice Weaver gotten involved with Russian oligarchs?

"All dead. Some by mysterious circumstances. The whole family in some situations. The pictures we were able to obtain are rather gruesome."

She blanched at this news and then quipped, "Well, isn't that law enforcement's problem then?"

"What is the connection? Why would Alice Weaver know these people, and who is she?" He gestured at the file. "What would a stockbroker or a day trader know of these people?"

"You'll have to ask her."

"Believe me, we've tried."

"Man or woman?"

"Huh?"

"Did you send a man or a woman to interrogate her?"

"A man. Why? Would she respond better to a woman?"

"Did he insult her? Was he condescending in any way?"

He laughed. Madelyn obviously knew this Alice Weaver well. "She called him a novice. She accused him of being last in his class."

Madelyn sat back on her couch, laughing despite herself. "Then there you have it. You won't get anything else from her. She's the most...stubborn individual," she understated, "I have ever had the misfortune to come across."

"What exactly was your relationship with her?"

"Exactly that," she indicated the file. Her eyes gave nothing away as she stared directly into his. "Occasionally, she had information we could use."

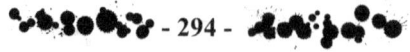

"And how did this come about...occasionally? Files this thick didn't come about with random interrogations or information.

"It's all there, if you care to read," she hedged, but it was a weak hedge, and they both knew it.

"Why don't you come back and interview her?" he asked.

"What makes you think I would come back after all this. I'm *retired*," she reiterated meaningfully.

"We both know you got the shaft on that, and you'd have had my job if the administration wasn't what it is. Politics are the bane of our existence, and it sucks."

"What makes you think Alice Weaver has anything you can use?" she asked, wondering what they had gotten out of her other than Russian oligarchs. What had Alice dangled before them? What shiny lure was she using to catch them?

"There are...*rumors*," he said, hedging himself, "that the media may have gotten hold of some rather embarrassing information. We need to confirm, but they are being amazingly tight-lipped about the information and their sources, citing the First Amendment. Alice mentioned arms shipments in Kazakhstan and Russia."

Madelyn's eyes suddenly became so focused it was alarming. Her slate gray eyes were sharp, and she was listening intently. "Will I be put back on the payroll at the same grade and clearance?" she asked suddenly.

Surprised at the sudden change, he looked at her in alarm. Which part of that had triggered her? "When exactly did you change your mind?"

"If Alice Weaver says she has information on arms shipments in Kazakhstan and Russia, you can bet she has something to back that up. I want my same clearance, so I can cut a deal with her, and we can get this information before the media releases it. I assure you, the panic that would ensue wouldn't be worth our jobs."

"Tell me," he ordered, but she shook her head.

"This was on a "need to know," Director Wolf, and you really don't want to know," she assured him. "I am not authorized to ever release this information. Do what you have to do," she said, gesturing to his phone and getting up from the couch. "I'll go pack."

He sat there a moment before he reached for his phone. Whatever Madelyn Korbel knew, he wanted to know too. Whatever or whoever Alice Weaver was, he wanted answers.

Langley was the name of the McLean neighborhood where the CIA was located. Supposedly, the Central Intelligence Agency was a civilian foreign intelligence service of the United States' federal government. Tasked with gathering, processing, and analyzing national security information from around the world, too often politicians and world leaders mistook its mandate as something they could use for their own benefit and not for the United States. As one of the principal members of the U.S. Intelligence Community, which included the Federal Bureau of Investigation (FBI), they reported to the Director of National Intelligence. This information was then passed through those offices to the president and the cabinet, so they could make informed decisions regarding both foreign and domestic policy.

Unlike the FBI, which was supposed to be a domestic security service, the CIA has no law enforcement function. Their only mandate is to gather overseas intelligence and limited domestic intelligence. They are also the only agency in the intelligence community authorized to carry out covert action at the behest of the president. If Alice Weaver, a civilian, had the information she implied, the CIA should know about it, so they could act on it.

With one of the largest budgets of all the Intelligence Community (IC), the CIA was authorized to carry out covert actions and influence foreign politics. The CIA had expanded its role over the years to include covert paramilitary operations, counter-terrorism activities, and cyber operations.

Madelyn looked through the information they had on Alice Weaver, laughing as she filled in the blanks of the blacked out or redacted information on the woman. She knew a lot more than she could ever say. If Alice Weaver said she had this information, Madelyn, for one, believed her.

She looked at what the IRS had on Alice Weaver: bank and tax fraud for failing to file a foreign bank account under an assumed name, tax evasion, grand larceny, criminal liability, but she realized there weren't enough specifics, which the IRS would need to make these charges stick. The allegations were vaguely worded, and Madelyn knew the agency was coming down hard on the citizen in the hope she would fold and implicate herself. They didn't know Alice Weaver.

In 1970, the Racketeer Influenced and Corrupt Organizations Act (RICO) federal law was enacted to combat organized crime in the United States. It allowed prosecution and civil penalties for racketeering activities. She could see what the IRS was trying to build here against Alice, but she could also see from the tax forms Alice had filed that most of the money was legitimate. It was only after Alice had been reported dead that someone, a Portia Spiros and an Andie Wilson, had found additional information and filed the appropriate paperwork. The IRS had seized on that instead of just imposing taxes and penalties for the 'oversight.' Nothing Alice had done, and nothing indicated here, was a RICO violation. There was no racketeering and nothing criminal, but the IRS was trying to make a case of it and prove there was. Why? Madelyn looked up from her seat in the SUV transporting her. She was going through all the current paperwork, so she would be up to snuff before she saw Alice Weaver once again after all these years.

As she started in on the police investigation, she was disappointed to find opinions and speculation but few hard facts. Someone had a bee in their bonnet from what she could see. They had gone to Alice's home and initiated a hell of a search. The yard had been dug up in the last few days. They were looking for money that was supposedly buried in her yard. They were also looking for a safe, and they found two in her office. They were able to open one safe, and the other had been opened by the homeowner, Kathy Weaver. So, Alice had married. That was interesting. It also made Alice vulnerable. She saw where the interrogator had threatened Alice, not very bright on the interrogator's part, and her response was that he had made an enemy for life.

She read the transcript of a phone conversation as she listened to the recording they had given her, since Alice Weaver's phones were now tapped.

"Mrs. Weaver, we'd like you to come down to the police department for an interview," the voice on the phone informed her.

"I never applied for a position in your department," Alice responded blandly. Madelyn nearly laughed at the dry reply. She also knew that going to a police department without her lawyer would be foolish. They would question her, and anything she said could and would be used against her in a court of law. Alice wouldn't make this easy for them, not if she could help it. Alice was far too smart to fall for their ploy.

"Do you find this amusing?"

"No. Do you?" Alice played with her prey a little more before she let them off the hook. "If you have any further questions, you will have to talk to my lawyer."

"Which one?"

Alice laughed into the phone before she hung up, and Madelyn smiled. That woman wasn't going to fall for anything.

She looked curiously at the inventory of the house, a joint effort of the IRS and the police at this point. She knew that would piss off any homeowner. Strangely, they were allowing Kathy and their children to stay in the house. Children? Hmmm, another vulnerability on Alice's part. Very interesting. She wondered if this wife of Alice's knew where she was.

Kathy didn't know where Alice was, and this, more than anything else over the past few days, pissed her off. Alice had left a note that Kathy was certain she wasn't expected to find right away, but the police and the IRS, who had obtained a federal search warrant, had leapt upon it immediately.

"Where has your wife gone?"

"Did she know this warrant was coming?"

"Has she left you to face this alone?"

The questions came fast and furious. They were all accusatory, and Kathy simply didn't know the answers. Everything was making her question Alice and her intentions since she had been left out of the loop once again. Fortunately, after being married to Alice all these years, she was smart enough to know not to respond to the many questions.

The backhoes and front-end loaders that dug up the landscaping and the lawns were frightening, and they made a general mess of the yard, but it was the officers going through the house that managed to completely unnerve Kathy. She had been tempted to just let them find the safe with the bear trap on their own. As it was, it was a near thing because when she disclosed its location, they wanted the combination to get into it. She asked that she be allowed to disarm it first. Seeing the look on the officers' and agents' faces when they realized that someone's hand or arm would have been impaled on the spikes of the trap gave her a note of satisfaction. She could see that the children, who she wouldn't let out of her sight with all these intimidating strangers in her home, were shocked about the second safe as well. The whole family had known about the wall safe, but only Alice and Kathy and a few now dead individuals knew about the floor safe.

They found the hidden panel in the master bedroom, but Alice must have foreseen that possibility and emptied it. Kathy was relieved since it had contained cash money that she couldn't readily explain as well as various passports in different names. When the authorities found their real passports, they were confiscated.

The meticulous inventory of all the items in the house took forever, and Kathy was losing her patience as she helplessly watched the officers going through their things. They were prying boards off the floor and walls looking for more hidden devices, and they were pulling apart the furniture, turning everything upside down, looking for hidden pockets and going through everyone's dresser drawers, clothes, and personal effects. They were also trying to question the children which Kathy wouldn't allow. Finally, a phone call came in that stopped all their searching. Whoever was on the other end of the phone had Mr. Smith standing at attention. He was trying to argue but ultimately conceded.

"That's it. Let's go!" he said to the men and women staring at him. "We're done here...*for now*," he added ominously, glaring at Kathy accusatorily.

Slowly, everyone filed out of the Palos Verdes house, tracking dirt on its beautiful floors as they left. No one apologized. Few, if any, looked contrite. Kathy looked out to make sure they had all left and saw some of the neighbors gathered at the end of the driveway. They were looking on and discussing what was going on behind the wide-open gates. She saw the Pasternack family and Em's little friend, Carmen, staring before she closed the door to their curious looks. Kathy was left there, her children in her arms, although Sean was angry enough for all of them.

"Why did they behave that way, Mom?" Emily asked, sounding frightened.

"I don't know, honey. I don't know," Kathy answered, watching as the many cars, the heavy-duty equipment, and the SUVs left the property. It was a mess, and it would cost tens of thousands of dollars to get the lawns and landscaping back in order.

"Do you think Mom knows?" Sean asked, sounding belligerent. He had been ready to fight the agents and the police for access to his room. Kathy had gotten him away but not before a few of his insults had landed home, and as a result, his room had been tossed a little more frantically than the others.

"I don't know," Kathy admitted, angry that Alice wasn't here to witness this. She knew the final humiliation would come when they ordered her to leave their home with her children. She jumped a foot when the doorbell rang.

"They're back!" Emily squawked, sounding frightened.

"They wouldn't have rung the doorbell, stupid," Sean said, still sounding angry.

"Sean!" Kathy's tone warning him about calling his sister names. It was something she had always discouraged her children from doing, but without Alice here to back her up, it was sometimes hard, especially with teenagers. She pulled him back from the door, going to answer it herself.

"Yes?" she said to the men standing there intimidatingly. She looked between the dark-haired men, wondering who and what they were. They were dressed in leather coats and had a distinctive aura about them. They looked dangerous from what she could see.

"Mrs. Weaver?" the man in front asked, trying to soften his facial expression and be courteous. "Ms. Alice asked that I stop by."

"Alice?" she asked, confused. Alice's note had said she had gone to stop this madness. Apparently, she had been mistaken as she glanced past the men at the destruction to their yard. There were piles of sod and dirt, and flowers were strewn haphazardly where they had dug up the entire lawn and gardens.

"Yes, I'm Sebastian's nephew, Artum. He and Alice spoke the other day and arranged that I stop by. I didn't think it prudent to butt in while the agents were here," he told her, trying to sound kind.

"Alice arranged...?" she asked, confused. It was obvious they had seen the ransacking of her yard and home.

"Yes, ma'am. Is there somewhere we can talk privately?" he asked, glancing at the teenagers looking on.

"Um, yeah, I guess," she said, holding the door wide and stepping aside, so the two men could enter. She glanced at the teens, who were staring wide-eyed. Sean looked belligerent. "You two start cleaning up your rooms."

"We didn't make the mess," Sean pointed out.

"I know, but you will feel better when things are straightened out. I don't think those officers are going to come back and clean it up for you, so please get started."

Sean looked like he was going to argue but after looking at their guests and then back at his mother, he shrugged angrily and stomped up the stairs.

Emily stared at the men for a moment before she left without a word but glanced back repeatedly, gauging how frightened her mom was. She didn't know why Alice had left them alone to handle all this, but she was certain it was for their own good. What Alice could have done, she didn't know, but she had the utmost faith in her mom.

"I'd ask you to sit down," Kathy gestured to the living room where the cushions were all off the furniture and there was a tear in the couch, which had cost them well over five grand. That couch had survived the children growing up and a dog, yet the officers had felt obliged to tear it open. "But as you can see..." she left off, gesturing helplessly and feeling embarrassed. "You said Sebastian sent you?"

"Yes, Alice came to see him, and they worked out an arrangement. I am to take you to our plane, which is standing by, and get you out of the country."

Kathy was stunned. Alice thought things were bad enough that they should leave the country?

"I was to come get you if the IRS or the police were about to pounce, but I had some bad information about that," he said, glancing at the other man, who was looking about and had the good grace to blush at this statement.

"Wait! You and Alice knew that they might do this?"

"Yes, ma'am," he said, wanting to just put her in their car and take off, so he could get her to the plane that was ready and waiting for her.

"Where is Alice?" she asked, suddenly wary of going with anyone she didn't know.

"I don't know," he admitted, glancing up the stairs where he could see the teenagers were listening. He nearly smiled, knowing it was something he would have done if he had been in their shoes.

"Well, I'm not going. I'm not leaving my home and my children's home. I don't know what Alice was thinking. If we leave, we look guilty!" she said, outraged.

"I don't know about that, ma'am," he said respectfully. "All I know is I was instructed to get you out before they did this, and I failed. I have a plane standing by to take you to South America, and Ms. Alice stated you would know where to go from there. I have cash for you to live on–" he began, but Kathy silenced him with a raised hand.

"I don't know you. I don't know Sebastian. Apparently, I don't really know my wife," she answered, sounding tired and angry. "I won't be going anywhere, so you can save your breath."

"I was to get you out," he began, reverting to his old ways when someone didn't obey his commands. "We were to get you out," he said ominously.

"What are you going to do? Pick me up physically and haul me out of my own home?" she asked, trying not to sound nervous.

"I was told…" he began, but Sean appeared just then, carrying an aluminum baseball bat.

"You gentlemen had better leave," he said, holding the bat up in a way that showed he could easily bring it into play.

The man with Artum made a move as though to grab something out of his waistband.

"If you move any farther, I'm going to bash in your head or break your arm," Sean said conversationally, trying to sound like one of his heroes on TV. Inside his heart was beating hard.

"Yeah, and I'll shove this up your dick," Emily said crudely, coming up behind Sean with a wooden baseball bat.

"Emily!" Kathy castigated her, sounding horrified. "Give me that," she said, wrenching the bat out of her daughter's hands. She looked up at the amused Artum. "I think you and your associate had better leave. Apparently, we aren't going anywhere."

He nodded tightly, knowing Sebastian would be furious. Alice hadn't said what to do if her wife refused to leave. He wanted to just rush the helpless woman and her children, sure they could overwhelm them, but he was amused that they would try to defend themselves with baseball bats. He eyed Kathy. Maybe she wasn't as helpless as she appeared. "I will check back in case you change your mind," he said respectfully, nodding coldly to the young man and smiling charmingly at the skinny girl. The man with him followed resentfully behind, glaring at the teens.

"Did you see that house? Even tossed there are some nice things," he said as they got in the Cadillac.

"Sebastian said they weren't to be touched. Keep your greedy eyes off them," Artum warned, wondering what he was going to report to Sebastian. He only hoped Sebastian would be asleep when he got back to the safe house.

Alice was hungry. It had been three days, and they hadn't fed her. Her belligerent peeing in their corner had finally forced them to produce a bucket she could use but nothing better. At least, they could have put her in an office or an interrogation room that had a toilet, but then, they wouldn't have the benefit of the two-way mirror.

Alice had the fortitude to outwait them. She'd been hungry before, and she'd been interrogated before, and she wasn't about to budge. She was, however, wondering if some of the safeguards she had put in place were failing at this point or what was going on. She wished she knew, and these morons they had sent to interrogate her weren't giving away much.

"You realize that lying to the CIA is a crime?" the current one asked.

"Yes, and so is lying to the FBI," she returned agreeably, amusing herself as she surprised them both by answering. Her silence had been *unnerving* to those who had tried to question her.

"How did you get the information on these men?" he tried again, indicating the names she had given them.

"What men?" she returned, sounding innocent and infuriating those less inclined to play the games they were playing.

"The names you gave us!"

"What names?" she asked.

"Would it help if I played back the tape?"

"That would only prove that I am being taped. Did I consent to being taped? Isn't it a crime to tape someone without their consent or knowledge? It's a crime in many states not to have it posted," she

pointed out, looking around as though searching for such a post, which they both knew was preposterous.

They tried tag-teaming her, proving they had delved further into her FBI, CIA, and possibly police-related files. "So, what are you, some kind of hacker or something?"

Alice's lips moved into a semblance of a smile as she turned to face her accuser. "Yeah, okay. We will go with that."

The less-experienced interrogators allowed themselves to be overheard. Alice knew they sometimes did that on purpose, but as her patience was wearing thin and time was running out, she didn't rise to their bait.

Finally, on the fourth day, the most delicious aroma of steak and potatoes preceded her interrogator into the room. Alice looked up, her head practically snapping to attention as she looked in the eyes of Madelyn Korbel. She smiled, pleased to see the woman and noting the grey hairs that hadn't been there the last time she had seen her so long ago.

"Ms. Korbel it has been a long time," she greeted her, watching as Madelyn put a covered plate in front of her and placed an identical plate at her own seat as she sat down.

"We weren't–" began the young interrogator, gesturing towards the food.

"To feed her?" Madelyn finished for him. "Run along, Johnny," she said, making shooing gestures. "You're in the big leagues now, and it's against the Geneva Convention to withhold basic human necessities. Furthermore, Ms. Weaver is not a prisoner." She smiled at Alice, sharing a glimmer of humor with her as the young man practically ran out of the room to report to his superior. He didn't know who this woman was, but she had been let into the room. Madelyn looked at Alice. "Hungry?" she asked.

"Thirsty," Alice acknowledged, and she watched as Madelyn approached the cart that had rolled the wonderful smelling food into the room. She saw it also contained an ice-cold pitcher of water, and the condensation dripped down the outside as Madelyn poured them both a full glass.

"You don't drink alcohol, if I remember correctly," Madelyn began conversationally.

"Not often, no," Alice admitted as she sipped slowly at the water. She knew drinking too fast would cause her stomach to clench after all

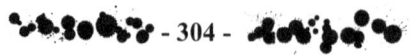

these days deprived of water. "Thank you. That hit the spot," she said, saluting the CIA woman with her glass.

"Please, help yourself. I hadn't eaten either, so I had them make us both steak and potatoes," Madelyn told her, gesturing to the covered plates. Alice removed her cover and found they also had onions and carrots on the plate. She saw the steak was deliciously well done as she cut into it.

"You *remembered*," she stated, flattered.

"I did. Well done because you don't like your cows to moo when you cut into them," Madelyn said, sitting down across from Alice and lifting her own lid. The steak on her plate was only done on the outside. She lifted her silverware, put her napkin across her lap, and then cut into her own steak. "Ketchup?" she offered Alice, taking steak sauce for her own.

"Thank you," Alice answered. They were both quiet while they ate as much as they could. Alice's stomach had shrunk, so she couldn't eat as much as she would have liked, and she wisely stopped when she realized she was full.

"Was it good?" Madelyn asked, seeing how much her guest had left on her plate.

"Delicious," Alice agreed, wiping her lips delicately with the napkin.

"Would you like to take a walk?" Madelyn asked, glancing at the mirror where she knew there were a bevy of agents that had just watched them eat.

Alice was amused. "How do you know I won't run off?"

Madelyn grinned. "I think you have some information you wish to trade?"

"I do," she agreed, nodding.

"Then, I think some exercise is order, so we can walk off this excellent meal and get down to business," she stated, rising and stretching slightly. She was pleased to note that Alice checked her out.

Alice rose too and cracked her neck. She would be pleased to get out of this room and knew without a doubt they would be followed.

Madelyn didn't say anything as she escorted Alice out of the office, to the bank of elevators, down to the lobby, and out the front door. The grounds were extensive, and they walked for a while, enjoying the cool, fresh air of Virginia.

"You know they found your storage unit?"

"They did?" Alice asked, sounding surprised, but with a glimmer of humor in her eyes. She had known they would, but they wouldn't find anything other than her completely outdated computers. All the information she wanted from the computers was gone including the programs and whatever she had found using them. The computers were mere shells of what they had once been.

"Shouldn't you be asking which storage unit?" Madelyn asked, knowing Alice was playing with her.

"Okay…" she hesitated for a moment, "Which one?"

"Do you have more than one?" Madelyn asked.

The humor increased in Alice's sparkling eyes, but the irises were changing. Madelyn thought she saw them turning a shade of orange. That must be a trick of the light, right? Then, remembering a previous experience years ago, she realized that orange wasn't a good sign. She'd prefer Alice Weaver's eyes to remain their normal brown. Even yellow wasn't too bad, but orange was positively dangerous.

"You tell me?" Alice asked patiently, willing to play the game. She cocked her head sideways, waiting for an answer.

"You could do this all day, couldn't you?"

"Do what?" she asked innocently, a ripple of a smile twitching her lips. Her eyes were dancing, and they were most definitely turning yellow.

She didn't know what it was about this woman's eyes that entranced her so. They also made her decidedly uncomfortable, but so long as Alice was smiling….

"What do you want, Alice?" she asked, using her first name since they were alone.

"I want a letter of apology from Mr. Smith on behalf of the IRS. I want all inquiries into my finances to be dropped by the IRS, and I want my funds released. I want the police to stop their inquiry as well, and I want the name of whoever started all these actions."

"You think the CIA can stop an IRS audit?" Madelyn asked, amused. It seemed such a small request for someone of Alice's…*expertise* to come all this way.

"Yes, you can do that…and more. What I offer in exchange is ties to organized crime in Russia."

"You gave us those names," Madelyn mentioned.

"I have more: dates, times, and locations as well," she told the woman.

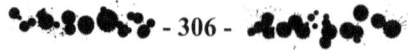

Madelyn had thought there would be more. Alice was the best poker player out there where lives were concerned. She wouldn't have been here if she merely wanted the IRS inquiries dropped. It wasn't an even exchange, and she wondered how much of that information Alice was really going to give them.

"Okay, you give us—" she began, but Alice was already shaking her head.

"I want the letter of apology from Smith, another from the IRS, and an official letter stating that all these inquiries were a bureaucratic mistake and will be dropped. I want the same assurances from the police. I want *immunity*," she stated.

"Now, you are asking for more—" she began, mentally going over the police report she had read about the woman Alice had nearly killed and yet saved.

"Yes, and I will continue upping the ante as you continue delaying. You see, the media is in possession of all this information. They are just waiting for the password to access the many drives I sent them containing everything I am offering to tell you. Imagine if it were to go public that the CIA was giving guns and other things to the public in Russia, as well as to the mobsters, gangsters, and organized crime. You all are going to have a big, black eye," Alice pointed out matter-of-factly.

"How do I know you really have all that?" Madelyn asked, her training forcing her to hedge in order to buy her some time to think.

Alice had been anticipating that and merely smiled, halting their walk to look up at the taller woman. "When have you ever known me to lie over important things such as this? You know I'm not bluffing."

Madelyn did know, and she knew that if someone in the CIA was directing this, Alice and her family were as good as dead. It had been clever and just like the Alice she knew to hedge her bets with the media. She didn't doubt for a moment that they had such drives in their possession. "So, if I get this letter of apology and the immunity, you will give me the drive?"

"Of course," Alice responded, sounding insulted.

"And the password?" she verified, knowing her simple tricks.

Alice laughed, glancing at the many agents that were following them and almost surrounding them. They didn't realize it, but she could have gotten away despite their numbers. They were very good, but she was better. She also didn't want to have to do that. "Yes, the password too," she agreed with a grin.

Madelyn relaxed slightly. She knew that nothing was at all what it seemed with Alice. She knew this probably wasn't all the woman had for them, but she would take what she could get. "Let's get you comfortable while I see what I can get for you. How much time do I have?"

"Not enough. They wasted a lot of time bringing you in."

"I was *retired*," she told the blonde, reiterating something she had said time and again to various people.

"What? Were you holed up in a cabin deep in the woods somewhere?" Alice teased. They shared a laugh. Neither of them was really the outdoorsy types.

"Let's just say I was reluctant," she told her instead.

"Did you retire, or were you forced out?" Alice asked as they turned back towards the buildings, their followers trying to remain unobtrusive and failing, at least to Alice's sharp eyes.

Madelyn sighed. She too saw their followers. It was like old times. She'd have to talk to a few people about better surveillance techniques. These were sloppy. "Let's just say the latter and leave it at that," she told Alice.

Alice nodded knowingly. She wouldn't ask further. They were too close to the building, and she was certain there were listening devices. She hadn't considered that Madelyn might be wearing a wire and maybe she should have. "Mind letting me use the bathroom?" she asked.

Madelyn sighed again. "Your peeing in that room didn't go over well," she told her as she led her past security, nodding to one of the older guards she recognized who remembered her from back in the day. She headed to a public restroom.

"Then they should have provided better accommodations," Alice told her, starting to feel uncomfortable from the food they had eaten, which was going right through her. She was relieved to have a toilet and toilet paper available to her, even if it was one ply...the cheap bastards!

Madelyn, who had waited for Alice, had also signaled a couple officers and given instructions to make accommodations available for their guest. Alice was not a prisoner, and she made that clear to them.

As Alice washed her hands a while later, she glanced up to exchange a look in the mirror with Madelyn. The CIA operative glanced down the length of the bathroom and back at Alice, letting her know they were being observed even here. Alice didn't flicker an eyelash to indicate she understood the woman. She dried her hands and followed her out of the bathroom and back towards the bank of elevators. They went to the third floor this time and entered a room with a bed and a full bathroom. Clothes were laid out on the bed.

"Give me a few hours to see what I can get going on our end," Madelyn told her as she showed her the room. "If you need me, they'll let me know," she indicated the guards outside Alice's room.

Alice nodded, pleased there were no two-way mirrors, but she was certain the room was bugged and was determined she wouldn't say anything. She waited for Madelyn to leave the room in order to strip, shower, and change into the rather nice clothing they had supplied her. It even fit, which surprised her. They had confiscated her identification and hotel room key, so she had nothing to transfer from the old clothes. She sat and dozed off on the bed as she waited. She wondered how much time she had left…how much time *they* had left.

"What are you going to offer her?" Director Wolf asked Madelyn when she returned to the office they had given her. She had gone straight to her phone and looked up, startled, as he entered her office without knocking.

Replacing the phone in its cradle, she swallowed her annoyance. "I'm going to give her exactly what she asked for," she responded, and before he could interrupt, she added, "after I verify a couple things."

"How do you know her?" he asked again and was annoyed when she wouldn't answer him. "You do know I'm your supervisor, right?"

"Yes, sir," she said patiently, waiting for him to leave as she glanced pointedly at the phone.

He sighed. Somedays he hated his job. Secrets within secrets; that was the job. He had to trust her. This woman had been a valuable asset, and he had been sorry to lose her to politics a couple years ago. He'd had to pull a few strings to get her reinstated and had been surprised that she would even condescend to come back. Whoever

Alice Weaver was, he was grateful that her presence had brought this woman back. He nodded stiffly as he waved and left the office.

Madelyn made several calls, working up the chain of command at the Palos Verdes and Los Angles police stations and getting information that wasn't on the computer yet. She was amused to learn that both departments were experiencing computer malfunctions that had spread to Pasadena and several other stations including the FBI but had been stopped at their firewall. Later, she discovered the FBI was experiencing their own version of the virus. It was slowly spreading through their system, which didn't really have outside access. Something or someone from within had to have planted it. She thought about that as she was on hold with the powers that be at the IRS, getting information she would need in order to proceed with Alice Weaver. She glanced at her computer and saw their *guest* was sleeping on the bed in her room.

"Do you really think what this civilian has to offer is of such great value that we can simply dismiss the charges the IRS has on her, much less disregard what the police suspect?" she was challenged by one of the agents in the meeting she attended later that day.

"Yes, I do. I've checked with my media contacts, and it is confirmed that a drive was delivered to each of their stations, and they are awaiting the key code to open it and retrieve the promised information. I don't know that the drive is from Ms. Weaver, but if she says she has information that will be embarrassing for us if we don't comply, I believe her."

"You realize this is blackmail?" one of the men pointed out, sounding angry.

"Yes, it is, and we deal with that every day of the week," Madelyn countered. "Think of it as tit for tat. She has information she is willing to give us, if we can get the charges dropped and stop this IRS audit. It isn't a normal audit," she informed them, glancing among them to see who might be playing both sides of this game. Her people, who she had asked for based on her previous time at the agency, as well as the new ones assigned to her had uncovered some really interesting things, and she could now go in and negotiate with Alice from a position of power. "Whoever is behind this has powerful friends and is out to make Alice Weaver pay."

"Do you know who is behind this?" Director Wolf asked speculatively. He was wondering, not for the first time over the past few days, who the hell Alice Weaver was and why she was so important. It would take weeks, possibly months to get copies of the reports that weren't redacted.

"No, sir. Not yet," she said respectfully, wondering if he knew and wasn't telling her. She trusted Director Wolf. After all, she was working for him. But in this business, it didn't pay to trust anyone completely. It wouldn't be the first time someone in the intelligence community went rogue.

"She'll have to give up her illegally-gotten gains," mentioned one of the agents who had looked at what the IRS had compiled.

"No, that's part of the agreement. She keeps what they are after. They have no proof those gains are illegally gotten, and I think with the alias she used, and they found, she will agree to pay the penalties. That, at least, is something for the IRS to salvage their pride on. This Mr. Smith, who is so gung-ho and has a hard-on for the Weavers, will be losing his job over this snafu he created."

"Why?" several people wanted to know.

Madelyn told of the backhoes and the search that had gone on at the Weaver estate. When Alice found out, she was going to be wild. In the meantime, Kathy Weaver and their teenaged children were probably frightened and upset. Alice Weaver with children…Madelyn had shaken her head over that. She had never thought she'd see that day.

"So, you are just going to give in to all her demands?" someone asked, wondering at this position.

"No, not all. We will negotiate with her, but we want to get that information before the media puts it out there."

"I say lock her up until she gives us all of it," the young agent Alice had verbally torn apart put in, sounding like he was laughing about the situation.

"Do you know what would happen if Alice Weaver was locked up?" Madelyn rounded on the young twit. She waited for him to shake his head. "We would never get one iota of the information we are seeking. The news—TV, paper, and radio—would spread this story far and wide, and the credibility of the United States would be ruined. We don't know what stations have the information or who is waiting for the

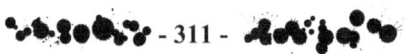

password, and it might be worldwide for all we know. Based on the names she gave us and what information we now have on them, this could be extremely embarrassing for us."

He looked uncomfortable, but he wasn't down and out. Instead, he foolishly answered with, "There are ways of making people like that talk."

"Get out," Madelyn said, glancing at the man she suspected was the twit's supervisor. "Such talk is foolish! Alice Weaver is a citizen of the United States, and if you read her file," she indicated the thick redacted file they all had copies of, the CliffsNotes version as it were, "you would know she would never give it up. She is bargaining in good faith, and I say we give her what she is asking for. We need this intel to determine how to proceed." She waited as the man left the room, closing the door with a sullen look back at the woman who had embarrassed him.

"You have such faith in her," Director Wolf stated, eyeing Madelyn speculatively and wondering about her relationship with someone he suspected was a criminal. "How do you know that she won't stiff us once we do as she asked? Why can't she give us the information first?"

"This woman was one of the most brilliant minds at Harvard. She didn't even have to go to classes half the time," Madelyn had ascertained over the years. "She has helped us time and again, and yes, I do have faith in what she says. She's always been honest with us, and she's always cooperated," she indicated the files again. "Would you give up your cards before you got what you wanted? What kind of bargaining chip would she have then?" she asked everyone at the table. She saw several heads nod.

"Then, we arrest her for espionage, conspiracy, and fraud when this is all done?" someone else asked, and Madelyn looked up angrily.

"I don't think you people understand. What she is going to give us won't be all she knows. It's probably the tip of the iceberg, but it will be enough to sink our teeth into and help our investigations. Hell, the names she has already given up have provided you all with plenty to research," she indicated the stacks that were already piling up. "We deal in good faith, and eventually, she might even give us more...*for free*." A couple of the more senior men and women nodded sagely, hoping that the younger staff would learn from this. You don't go after someone who is providing you with intel you don't have and couldn't have gotten any other way, and you certainly don't go after someone who might have more intel that you desperately need.

"How did she obtain this information?" someone asked, and that led to endless debates about what she might have based only on the names she had given them. Finally, Director Wolf put an end to the speculation, pointing out that they could debate it after they saw what information Alice Weaver had for them. They would decide on a course of action later.

It took many hours, and Alice finally got a good night's sleep. When a disheveled-looking Madelyn knocked and was granted entry into her room, she brought breakfast with her. Over bacon and eggs, she told Alice what she had done.

"Okay, here is a faxed letter of apology from Mr. Smith," she said, holding out the paper for Alice to read. "This is a letter of apology from the IRS, which is forgiving your debt to them, indicating there was a bureaucratic error," she shared a smile with Alice over that wording, "and halting the investigation. There is one penalty," she said apologetically. She showed Alice the one alias that Portia and Andie found that had triggered the red flags with the IRS. "You will have to forfeit that one," she said, sounding sincerely sorry for the blonde. She was uncomfortable immediately as the blonde's eyes glowed yellow. Damn, that again? What was with the lights in this place? She looked up to be sure they were the same fluorescent lights as elsewhere in the building.

"The district attorney in Palos Verdes will be dropping all charges," she said, indicating another fax. "And this gives you immunity from all criminal prosecution, if the data you have for us proves sufficient," she added, knowing her superiors were listening to this conversation and had insisted on that addition.

Alice nodded as she munched on her toast. She waited for Madelyn to finish, swallowed, took a swig of the orange juice, and said, "I want the originals in my hands before I give you what you want."

"Now, wait a minute. These faxes–" Madelyn began.

"Aren't the originals," Alice finished for her, scooping up some eggs with her fork and picking up a piece of bacon.

Sighing, Madelyn knew better than to argue. "How much time do I have left?"

Alice had no idea what date it was as they had kept her isolated, so she asked.

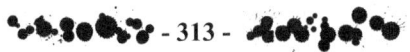

Madelyn was surprised. Alice was usually so on top of such things. Still, it had been a lot of years. She told her the date and the time, and Alice's usually cat-like eyes opened wide in surprise. She glanced out the window. She had lost a day. "I'd say this evening's news is going to be *very* interesting," she answered blandly, sounding genuinely sad.

"*What?*" Madelyn asked, getting up from her chair in alarm and nearly knocking it over.

Alice shrugged. "I did try to tell your fellow agents that there was a time limit, but they chose to ignore me. By the way, how is my wife?"

Madelyn blinked at the rapid change in conversation. "Your wife is fine. Why?" Did Alice somehow know about the raid on her estate in Palos Verdes?

Alice shrugged again. "I have had a lot of time to think in here," she gestured at the room with its unmade bed.

"It's a lot better than the office they had you in," the CIA operative pointed out.

"It's still not freedom," Alice pointed out in return, and for further emphasis, she pointed to the paperwork. "You also forgot a name."

"A name?"

"Who instigated that?" she indicated the IRS paper.

"Your alias–" she began, but Alice was on to her in an instant.

"Bullshit," she said blandly, and Madelyn smiled, moving in the way of the camera she knew was on them both and putting her back to it, so no one would see her facial expression.

"I'll get back to you," Madelyn promised, giving Alice a look and leaving her own unfinished breakfast to hurry out of the room. Alice's voice stopped her at the door.

"I want you to fax those originals to my lawyers in both New York and Los Angeles, and I want you to show me the printout verifying the faxes," Alice called.

Madelyn nodded to show she had heard. She was surprised Alice hadn't mentioned that tidbit sooner. It made sense. Even if she had the originals in her possession, it wouldn't mean anything if someone else hadn't seen them.

"Cool cucumber, isn't she?" Director Wolf asked from where he had been monitoring the conversation.

"You don't know the half of it," she understated. "We better give her the originals as soon as possible," she suggested, hinting broadly to her superior. She looked pointedly at the clock.

"And if we don't?" he asked, feeling a bit peeved that this Alice, this *nobody,* was basically holding the CIA hostage. He wasn't sure he didn't agree with that young twit about torturing the information out of the woman. There was something here, something *criminal,* and the redacted files alone told him she wasn't someone to be fully trusted. How did she have information on all those Russian criminals?

"Then, sir, you will be responsible for the biggest embarrassment the CIA, and who knows what other government agencies, have suffered in recorded history. This is all going to blow up in your faces."

"You are part of this now," he pointed out angrily.

"Yes, I am *now,* but I have deniability. I haven't been here in years."

"If it tarnishes me and the other agents, it tarnishes you."

Madelyn just smiled, and he wondered what else she was holding back from him, knowing he couldn't ask. He was determined to get Alice Weaver's unaltered file from the archives. "You realize if this gets out there," he gestured beyond the building for emphasis, "she doesn't have a leg to stand on. There will be no deal, and we will hold her until we figure out what she knows on those names."

"Sir, I wouldn't suggest that. You can bet what little she gave us, and you have to admit it is just names at this point, means bupkiss."

"I don't care. She has information we need, and she's blackmailing us to get it."

"You don't know what information she has or doesn't have. She walked in here of her own accord. You can bet someone somewhere knows something about that. She's probably one of the most brilliant women I have ever met."

"I don't care if she's a genius. Something is off with that woman," he responded, feeling uncomfortable for some reason.

"Probably," she agreed, "but she also has information we need and is willing to work out a deal," she wouldn't use the word blackmail as it seemed to feed his fervor in this, "and I say we get the deal brokered for her."

He just smiled slightly, and she knew he wouldn't let this go. "Oh, and by the way, the police asked one more favor. They wonder if somehow, we could stop the virus that is spreading through their computers? Apparently, it's shutting down key systems now, and no one can figure out how to stop it. They can't afford to bring in a whole new system."

"Are you suggesting the CIA step in and stop it?"

"I already have some of our best programmers on it. It's a worm and very sneaky," he answered, sounding annoyed.

Madelyn glanced at the door where Alice Weaver was sitting, and she glanced at the monitor where she saw Alice munching happily on her breakfast...actually, she realized Alice was eating what had been left of her breakfast. Alice's stomach must have returned to normal. That petite woman could *eat*! "Are you suggesting that Ms. Weaver can fix the worm?" she asked, putting as much incredulity as she could manage into the question.

"Well, did she upload it? Cyber sabotage is a crime too, you know," he reminded her angrily. "If we can prove that...."

"You have supposition, innuendo, and speculation...no hard facts," she pointed out to him, feeling defensive about it. She didn't like being put in the position of having to defend Alice Weaver. They had both read the police file and found nothing to substantiate the officer's outrageous claims. No matter what Alice Weaver had done in the past or in the present, she did have information they needed. Now, they *wanted* the previously unknown information. Those few Russians she had mentioned were powerful men and women, who were now dead, and Madelyn and others wanted to know why and how they died. Accusing Alice without evidence was not something she was prepared to do.

Director Wolf sighed. Getting angry at Madelyn wasn't going to solve the problems and headaches that had arrived with Alice Weaver. There was just too much that wasn't known about the woman. The police chiefs he had spoken with on Madelyn's behalf hadn't been pleased to drop their investigations. One officer had been up in arms about it Special Agent Linda Miller raved about the things she had heard and transcribed, but all that was moot since there was no proof. Apparently, her evidence had disappeared with the virus. With no tapes, no transcriptions, and only the agent's word, they didn't have anything to arrest Alice Weaver for. Since Agent Miller was just home from the hospital, and it was Alice Weaver that had put the officer in the hospital, it looked like her allegations were simply revenge on the cop's part. "Do you think Alice would help us with the computer worm?" he asked, wondering how much Madelyn really knew about this woman that she wasn't saying.

"Actually, I don't think you want her anywhere near our computers," she put in and then dropped it, not willing to say more.

"Why?"

She shrugged and looked away. Her suspicions, well founded as they were, wouldn't help them anyway. She didn't have the *proof* they required to charge someone like Alice Weaver.

"Madelyn, tell me why?"

"I wouldn't put it past someone to bug our computers. You know the FBI is apparently having problems over on their system, and we share a lot of information with them. We don't want our computers having problems too." The FBI had a *closed system*, which no one on the outside could hack into. The fact that the computers were dealing with something *internal* alarmed many people.

"Are you saying we can't trust Alice Weaver?" he asked, suddenly feeling as though the rug had been pulled out from under his feet after everything they had been going through the past few days.

"I'm saying I wouldn't trust a civilian in our systems," she answered and went silent, waiting for his decisions.

"I have the originals of the faxes in my office," he finally gave in. "Do you think this drive she has will have a bug on it too?"

Madelyn shrugged, but she knew their firewalls and computer people would be watching for it. Just the suggestion of a potential threat would have started alarm bells ringing in their small intelligence community. She went to find the fax numbers for Alice's lawyers, sending the fax copies and all the papers Alice had refused off to New York first, then to Los Angeles. She didn't know that the paperwork sent to New York would have Nia Toyomoto and several senior partners boarding the fastest private jet that could get them to Langley. For Alice's sake, Madelyn also sent the letters to her office where she now knew Portia Spiros worked, and then, she sent them to Alice's home. She hoped Alice's wife would see everything. She picked up the acknowledgements of the faxes, which would confirm to Alice the receiving fax number, the time, and the number of pages sent.

"Nia Toyomoto to see Alice Weaver," she said as she held up her driver's license to confirm her identity.

"Who?" the security officer asked, taking the license and scanning it into their computer. He was hedging for time by asking her question.

"My client is being held upstairs. Director Wolf and an agent..." she checked one of the faxes to be sure of the name, "Madelyn Korbel...should know what this is about. They will want to see us," she indicated the New York lawyers standing behind her with their identification in their hands. Some didn't have driver's licenses and were using passports.

"And you are?" he asked, reaching for the other IDs to scan them in. At least, they would have a record of who was coming into the building. What security did with the information was beyond his pay grade.

"We're her lawyers," Nia told him quietly, amused at their delay tactics, which seemed so obvious to her.

He glanced at the well-dressed men accompanying their spokeswoman. She was a good-looking woman and was also well-dressed. He would bet their outfits cost more than his monthly salary. "I'll call upstairs and see what I can find out," he promised, reaching for the phone as he continued to scan in the information and hand back the various IDs to the high-powered attorneys. "Please wait over there," he said, indicating a bank of sofas that looked unused.

"Think they are going to deny she is here?" Stewart Dunham, one of the senior attorneys accompanying her asked. He was due to retire soon but had jumped on this situation once Nia had brought it to the other partners' attention. Alice Weaver was one of their most important clients, and it was imperative that they keep her from being imprisoned for any information the CIA thought she had.

"I don't know. I bet they keep us waiting though," she quipped, wondering how long the wait would be. She had been impressed that the other partners joined her but knew it was mostly because Alice Weaver and the business she had brought their firm through Sasha Brenhov, one of the richest women in the world, was so important to all their well-being. Nia had done most of the legwork in bringing Alice back to life, but that didn't mean the other partners didn't take credit for having her in the firm. Her name, and Sasha Brenhov's name, brought in other business from equally important people. Nia knew one of the only reasons Alice was with their firm was because she had known Alice back in college. She settled down for the wait as the other partners stood or sat, talking quietly as they waited while looking impatiently at their smart phones, which had stopped working properly as they came into this secure building.

"Ms. Toyomoto if you would accompany me?" a lower-level agent finally came to them after a very long while. The lawyers knew their identification had been thoroughly checked to see who they were. They hoped their most impressive credentials would ensure they were treated well, but when the other partners got up to follow, the agent waved them back. "I'm sorry, only Ms. Toyomoto may come up," he told them over their protests and arguments. Security looked up and would have converged if the agent hadn't waved them back. "Only Ms. Toyomoto," he repeated several times, ignoring the impassioned speeches by the other partners.

"Why only me?" Nia asked curiously as they got on the elevator. She could see her partners, most of them her seniors in the firm, were angry that she was the only one allowed to see their valuable client. They wanted in on this, so they could use their expertise and perhaps earn brownie points for having rushed to Alice's aid. They didn't want Alice Weaver to forget that their firm was there for her onehundred percent. Nia knew that several of these men still thought her much too young and inexperienced to be handling the Weaver and Brenhov files. She shared information and used their expertise when warranted, but Nia was both women's 'go to' lawyer before the cases that came their way, and she earned the firm a lot of money, which was then handed off to the various lawyers and departments within the firm.

"I don't know. I was instructed that you, and *only* you, were to be escorted up," he replied, having no idea why. He followed directions and didn't ask too many questions. It was better that way.

Nia looked about curiously as she was escorted into a private office and introduced to Director Wolf and Madelyn Korbel.

When Director Wolf went with Madelyn to hand Alice the original, signed paperwork, Alice was surprised and pleased to see Nia Toyomoto accompanying them.

"Hello, Nia," she said with a smile.

"Well, Alice, as I live and breathe. Nice to know you are really alive and not just on the paperwork I filed," Nia said with a smile, having handled the intricate and delicate wording of bringing Alice back to life in previous months. "What have you gotten yourself into that requires you to have immunity?" she asked, sitting down and indicating the papers.

"Is it all in order?" Alice asked blandly, amused with her lawyer. She knew Nia was now an important partner of the law firm in New York. At Nia's nod, she looked them over, folded them neatly, and sat back, her arms crossed. She glanced at the fax acknowledgements and the various numbers they had been sent to, nodding coldly to Madelyn and waiting.

"Is there no way you would have done this simply as a citizen and out of the goodness of your heart?" the director asked as he looked at Alice Weaver. He detested her hair, which was sticking up all over, messed up further by her fingers running through it as it dried after her shower. He could mentally see her in grunge clothing, something he abhorred. His own impeccable suit was like a uniform, and he was judging her on her appearance. Nia and Madelyn both knew that was a mistake.

"Oh, but I assure you, Director, I am a good citizen," Alice informed him, glancing at Nia, who had stiffened at the tone he used on her client. She hadn't liked the short meeting in his office. He was an arrogant ass, and she knew Alice enjoyed deflating such people. This didn't bode well, and she only hoped her firm's expertise would get her client out of this mess.

"Well, then where is the information you promised me?"

"You? It's for the American people," she corrected, antagonizing him and seeing Madelyn turning aside slightly, almost as though to hide her laughter. Nia grinned, not caring if the man saw it. She too could appreciate the hairs Alice was splitting. Whatever Alice had done, Nia would defend her with her dying breath. "And when I get everything I asked–" she began, but he interrupted.

"We gave you everything you asked for!" he thundered. "Where the hell is our information? We gave you that," he slapped at the paperwork, "in good faith. Where is your good faith?"

Alice deliberately looked at his watch, surprised that anyone wore a watch anymore with the proliferation of cell phones. "Tick tock, Director. The evening news will need some time to process it, but I wonder how many of the stations will really vet that information before broadcasting it?"

He leaned over the table in front of her, trying to intimidate her. "If one word of that information gets out, I'll throw you in prison and throw away the key."

"You aren't trying to intimidate my client, are you?" Nia put in, but it was too late.

Alice rose abruptly, the top of her head hitting his jutting jaw and closing it painfully as they collided. "If you knew where I'd been the past few years, you would know nothing you can do to me could be worse than that," she spat defiantly in his face where he was already nursing a painful jaw.

"Then we will go after your–"

"Don't finish that sentence, Director. Trust me, you don't want to finish it," Madelyn interrupted loudly enough to drown out what he had been about to say. She could see the lawyer was ready to do battle. "Ms. Weaver has complied, and we have complied," she indicated the paperwork. "I promise to get you that name," she looked earnestly in Alice's glowing, orange eyes. She realized the color wasn't a trick of the light, and Alice's eyes were orange. This woman was very dangerous. She had had her suspicions about this woman before based on some of the reports she had read over the years, but she felt the current information and accusations of Special Agent Linda Miller plus other suspicions confirmed it. Madelyn's training instinctively told her the look in this woman's eye meant Alice Weaver was a killer. She would have taken a step back if she wasn't preparing to defend her superior. He had no idea the mine field he had been about to step into.

Alice looked at Madelyn, glanced at Nia, and calmed down. She was very, very angry, and she was tired of being held here. She nodded slightly, agreeing to Madelyn's terms. She trusted that the agent's word was her bond, and Madelyn would get the information or pay Alice's price. She rubbed the top of her head where it had collided with the director's jaw, then she used her fingernail to slit the skin on the webbing between her thumb and forefinger, peeling it back.

Madelyn, Nia, and the director stared in fascinated horror as she removed a bloody microchip that looked amazingly like a slimmed down, smaller SIM card that could be found in any cell phone. She held it up between her nails. As the director went to take it from her, she pulled her hand back, looked at him angrily, and handed the microchip deliberately to Madelyn.

"I'll expect that information from you shortly," Alice told her as she watched the agent close her fingers on the chip. She appreciated the tissue the agent handed her to staunch the flow of blood from her hand and used it to clean her fingernail as well.

"You understand, I have to review this?" she said, indicating the chip in her fist.

"Of course. You have…" she looked again at the director's watch, "two hours."

"Can't you stop it?" she asked, worried that they wouldn't have enough time.

Alice smiled, and it looked rather sinister. "Not unless I'm released from here. I must have time to get back to my hotel."

"We've already–" began the director before he caught himself.

Alice turned her smile on the man, her orange eyes glowing. She didn't say a word as Madelyn hurried out.

Hearing her leave, the director turned and left the room. "Watch her," he said unnecessarily in a low aside to the pair of armed guards outside the door. He looked back at Alice, who was still smiling, before he hurried away, and the door shut.

"Care to explain what is going on?" Nia asked, watching as Alice sat back and refused to answer her. She sighed. Apparently, Alice didn't *need* her. She knew the other partners would begrudge her the time alone with this woman. Alice Weaver was a significant and profitable client and had brought them Sasha Brenhov, one of the richest women, if not the richest women, in the world. Their business had increased exponentially since these two women had used the services of their firm. Would the partners mind that they had come here to Virginia for nothing? Probably not.

"We should arrest her now," he mumbled as he hurried to the tech room where Madelyn had run off to. And she had run, despite her high heels.

"You'll have a hard time arresting her with that letter she has in her hands," Madelyn mumbled as she heard him enter the room. She knew the reputation of the firm Nia Toyomoto worked for and knew she could make real trouble for the authorities if her client wasn't released. The various partners that had accompanied the woman had ties to some very powerful people worldwide. The politicians alone that these men and women knew could and would create headaches that reminded her of her own political ousting years ago.

"I have a chip, and I need the information off it immediately," she called out, watching as the nerds and geeks, who loved this part of their job, clamored for the odd little chip.

"We're going to need a password," one of the techs announced.

"Shit!" Director Wolf ejaculated under his breath.

"I'll be right back," Madelyn said as she quickly left the room and ran up the stairs that separated it from an observation platform that ran around the entire room. She could see the director was angry with Alice's behavior, but she really didn't blame the woman. The CIA wasn't known to be trustworthy, and he would have double-crossed Alice if he could…he still would.

"Get a tap on the hotel room where Alice Weaver is staying," he ordered once Madelyn was out of the room.

"Won't we need–" began one of the newer techs, but he was shushed by a look from another tech, who immediately got on the order, reaching for his computer. If the director ordered it, they wouldn't need any other authorization.

Of course, Alice's room had already been tossed for information that could be used against her. She had planned for that. She was just lying in the room they had provided her, waiting for someone to come for the password. They hadn't asked for the password, and she hadn't volunteered that information. She didn't care. She had her get out of jail free cards in the forms they had given her. She looked at the fax acknowledgements and recognized her home number and her office numbers. She could only speculate that the numbers following the Los Angeles and New York area codes belonged to her lawyers' offices. If they really had copies of the forms that were now in her possession, she had corroborating evidence. She knew Nia must have gotten her copy, or she wouldn't have been here. Still, she didn't say a word to the Eurasian woman who stood patiently looking out the window from the very same spot Alice had stood in not so long ago. Nia was enjoying the view of the beautiful Virginia countryside outside the window.

A knock on the door had her looking up and over as it opened. Madelyn stuck her head in. "Password?" she asked without preamble, giving Alice a look that had them both trying to keep from laughing.

"Kazakhstan," she answered. "Good luck spelling it; it's a bugger." Alice laughed, knowing they had already gotten the chip inserted into their computers. She wondered when the worm that was in it would make itself known. *Worms*, she corrected herself.

Madelyn hurried back to the tech room and announced, "Kazakhstan," as she entered and saw the techs working on the card. The amount of information this tiny card could hold amazed and alarmed them as they began to print it out and analyze it. Madelyn called her team in to help, separating out various documents as they came up.

"We've got a bug," someone called. They had been expecting it as per the director's orders.

"See? We can't *trust* her," Director Wolf angrily aimed that one at Madelyn.

"Of course, we can. She gave us all this. You couldn't expect her not to try the bug," she reasoned as she looked at some particularly interesting pictures of the military equipment that had to be in Kazakhstan. What did this equipment have to do with the dead men and women who had been part of the Russian mafia?

"Another password," the tech announced as they started trying variations of the original password, deliberate misspellings, and even Alice's name.

"Try Russia," Madelyn suggested as she looked at the stack of intel they already had before them. This information more than paid for Alice's freedom. She moved to go and tell her, and Director Wolf stopped her.

"Where are you going?" he asked, looking up from some of the bloody pictures he now had in his possession, along with Russian newspaper articles that told of these people's deaths. They would have to bring in some of their bilingual people to interpret the Russian script.

"I'm going to release Alice Weaver, so she can call off the press before *this*," she gestured at the mound of paperwork stacking up, some of it very sensitive information, "gets out there."

He really badly wanted to stop her, but he felt his hands were tied. Alice Weaver had delivered. How she had obtained all this information, including financial information, he did not know. He learned from her file that she claimed to have been kidnapped last year with Sasha Brenhov, and he assumed it had to do with her. They would need to have more conversations. He needed to know more, despite their agreement. Private citizen or no, he must see her redacted file. He felt it was bullshit how she had been accorded special privileges! It was obvious she knew a lot more than she was telling.

"Ms. Weaver can go," Madelyn told the guards, who nodded. She opened the door and saw Alice gazing out the window with Nia. The two of them were laughing together as they chatted. "I have your clothes here," she said, looking down at the small pile of Alice's laundered clothes in her hands. "Shall I arrange to have a car out front to take you to your hotel?"

"Thank you," Alice said, glancing around and wondering what time it was. She glanced at Nia, who had been reminiscing with her.

"You still have half an hour," Madelyn told her as she put the clothes down and started to leave.

"Madelyn," Alice stopped her. When the older woman turned to look at the blonde, she said, "We both know this won't be the end of it. He will want more."

Madelyn nodded. "All I can do is try to rein him in. I hope he will be satisfied with what you gave us."

"He won't be," Alice said as she began to pull off her shoes and socks, stepping down on the heels of both to pull them off.

Madelyn nodded again, turned, and left the room. She knew Alice was right, and Director Wolf would want more. He would want to drain all knowledge from Alice until she was dry, and even then, he wouldn't believe that she had given him everything.

"Will you give them more?" Nia asked, turning to give Alice her back and some privacy.

"I have no idea," Alice admitted.

The decoy worm was easily killed in the system, but the other worm, rather *worms* that lay dormant within the layers of data they were going through were eager to work their way through the system in a less obvious fashion. They would pass the most comprehensive scans the super tech computers could throw at them. Even the most in-depth and destructive scans designed specifically to search for worms such as this would miss many of them because they weren't active. They would be activated...in time. They would be triggered by the actual scans searching for them, some in months and others perhaps not for years.

"Holy shit!" the analysts said time and again as they looked over the information Alice Weaver had provided the CIA.

"Do you have someone tailing her?" Director Wolf asked one of his men when he saw that Agent Korbel was perusing the stack of intel they had gotten off the disk.

"No need. Madelyn had a car take her back to the hotel."

"On that tap?" he asked another agent, who assured him it was in place.

Alice didn't *go* to her room. Her hotel had a payphone in the lobby, something that wasn't seen too often these days. She went to the payphone instead, and using a credit card she had memorized, she punched in a phone number, waited for an answer, and began typing in numbers, deliberately typing too fast for the men watching her as she also shifted from side to side to block her hand from their view. She paused, listened, then hung up the phone and went to her room where she began to pick up the mess the agents had left in the room. Nia followed her. Having given her the privacy she needed for her phone call she didn't ask any questions. The other partners had wanted to question Alice and let her know they were there for her, but she had gotten in Madelyn's car with Nia *only* and had left the rest of them to their own devices. Nia had waved her cell phone, a silent promise that she would be in contact. Taking a cab to the airport, Alice was able to get a ride on a private jet service back to Los Angeles, and Nia met up with the partners and headed back to New York. The lawyer was feeling particularly useless but had been pleased to see her old friend alive and well, even if she was up to something that Nia might have difficulty extracting her from. The other partners were particularly miffed that they hadn't been allowed to question their client. The flight back to New York was quite uncomfortable for Nia.

Alice's junker was parked in the carpark she and Kathy had been using to throw off would-be followers, so she headed directly there. She was shocked when she recognized Kathy's Lexus exactly where she had left it. She searched to find where she had hidden the key, found it, and got in to head for Palos Verdes, all the while wondering at her reception.

"I want you out! This is *it*, Alice; *this* is my limit. I want a divorce, and this time I'm not screwing around. I told Portia just today that I was done."

Alice was shocked when Kathy met her in the garage with this edict. "Didn't Portia get the fax? Didn't you?"

"Yes, I saw that you stopped the investigations. I even saw the apologies. I checked and confirmed all the accounts are unfrozen, but that doesn't mean anything to me. I want you out and gone. I can't deal with this shit anymore…it's never-ending. No matter what we have done or what you have said, it just keeps coming at us. I want the divorce, and I want out of this." Kathy was waving her arms passionately.

Alice looked at her sadly for a moment, contemplating, and then she nodded. The hair sticking up on the top of her hair made her look even more intense. "All right, Kathy, whatever you want," she told her wearily. "I still love you, you know?"

"I know, Alice," Kathy told her sadly, surprised at her easy acquiescence. "I love you too, but it's not enough. I can't keep going through these dramas forever."

Alice already knew that the house was probably in sad shape because she'd seen the state of the yard. She was furious and would lodge a complaint demanding that whoever was responsible should pay for the damage. In the meantime, she would pay to have her home and yard restored, at least for the children's sake. "May I get my clothes?"

"I've already packed for you. Do you want me to call a cab or an uber?"

"Call a cab. May I see the kids?"

"I won't ever keep you from our children," Kathy vowed in a small, sad voice, feeling her heart breaking. It wasn't the first time. This woman had broken her heart many times, and there wasn't much left unbroken.

"Mom!" Emily greeted her enthusiastically. "I thought you had gone forever," she said dramatically, throwing herself into Alice's arms.

"Naw, I had to go get this crap with the IRS straightened out," she told her, giving her as enthusiastic a hug as the teen gave her. She was pleased that her little girl was filling out after her long illness. It was even possible the teen was growing taller.

"It really sucked; those cops were really mean," Sean told her, following her into the master bedroom that Kathy had cleaned up in the days since the raid.

"Some are like that but not all of them," Alice told him, unable to be a cop hater despite what they had done. She picked up the cases Kathy had packed for her.

"Are you going somewhere?" Emily asked.

"Mom has asked me for a divorce, so I'm going to have to find a place to live. Now, not like that," she said, silencing the teen's argument. "I've put your mom through a lot, and it's not fair to any of us. I just want to know you guys are safe and happy. You can come visit me when I find a place," she promised. "At least we all know I'm alive," she joked, holding up the cell phone she had turned back on, only to find dozens of texts from her family. Some of the message had become increasingly hostile as Kathy got angrier.

"She shouldn't treat you like that," Emily said, defending Alice.

"Em, your mother and I love each other," Alice started, seeing beyond the two teens to where Kathy was unashamedly listening in the hallway outside the room.

"Then you'll get back together?" she asked hopefully.

Alice shrugged and shook her head regretfully. "I don't think so, baby. I think this time she's had enough. We both love you guys." She glanced up at their much taller son and smiled to include him. "You have to understand that sometimes relationships simply do not work out, and it's no one's fault. I will always love your mom. I'm certain she loves me too. I love you guys, and that will never change."

"I don't want you to leave," Em insisted. She was too old to stamp her foot, but she felt like doing it.

"And I don't want to leave you, baby but think how much fun it will be to shop for another place," she said, her words sounding weak to both their ears. Sean grinned but it was half-hearted at best. "You'll visit?" Alice asked the growing teen.

Sean nodded, sniffing suspiciously.

Alice picked up her bags, slinging one around her neck. Sean leaned over and carried several out for her, and Em grabbed a couple too. Kathy quickly ducked down the stairs, so the teens wouldn't see her. She'd already ordered a taxi for Alice. She wanted her gone. She and Mrs. Fernandez, along with Portia and Andie, had spent days getting the house in livable order. There were things that needed repair, and Portia had told her to keep the receipts. Already, they were closing the office. They no longer needed it since Alice had stopped the investigations and was here to take the reins of her business. Portia was sending out inquiries to law firms in Los Angeles, and Andie was thinking of moving out of state and looking for a position elsewhere.

The kids helped tuck Alice into her cab, and she ordered the driver to take her to the Ritz-Carlton where she was able to get a room. She looked sadly about the luxurious room, her luggage piled forlornly in the closet, waiting to be unpacked. She wasn't happy to be separated from Kathy and her children again. She sighed. Kathy was right; they had been through a lot. She was tired too. She wondered why Sebastian's men hadn't gotten her family out as planned?

The next day, Alice shopped for and bought herself a car but not the Porsche she had always favored. She decided to splurge a bit. After all, it was time to get a decent car, and the old junker certainly wouldn't do. She donated the junker to a charity, and they picked it up, not even realizing the name on the title was someone else's as they took it away. She was thrilled as she test-drove and enjoyed the feel of the Ferrari 488 that she eventually purchased. She knew her children would be thrilled, especially Sean, who was always looking at expensive sports cars. She had known she could remain unobtrusive with her Porsche. After all, they were much more common in Los Angeles than the Ferrari, but she felt justified. It was a similar blue to Kathy's own

Lexus. She loved the convertible and eagerly drove it, making sure to stay within the speed limit despite the temptation to push it.

"Mrs. Weaver I'm so glad you called!" Charlotte, the realtor, told her when she arrived at her office a few days later. It was the same realtor who had sold them the property in Palos Verdes, and she was anxious to accommodate this client again. Alice had told her she was about to become single and needed a place of her own. She didn't want one by the marina as she had been there when she and Kathy first married, and no, she wouldn't be selling the house in Palos Verdes. That house would go to Kathy for the children. Alice didn't need the money.

With all the listings Charlotte showed her, Alice was quickly on the way to owning a nice, small house on the beach in Malibu. It was a little ways from Palos Verdes—they had to cross Manhattan Beach and Santa Monica—but Alice loved the feel of the place. When she eventually showed her new house and car to her children, they were ecstatic. There had been a beach where they could walk down from the bluffs around the house in Palos Verdes, but it wasn't really a user-friendly beach, and this one was fantastic. When they found out which stars lived along this stretch of Alice's beach, they were thrilled.

"Spending a lot of money these days, aren't you?" Kathy asked when Alice came to retrieve the computers the police had returned. Sean was happy to get the gaming computer back, but Alice told him it should go to Malibu, so he had something to play there too. He was reluctant to let it go until she promised she would get another computer for him to set up at the Palos Verdes house, and she promised he could go with her to pick it out. She didn't tell him why she wanted his gaming computer for now.

"You know, for once in my life, I'm going to indulge," Alice told her. "There's plenty for you. I've already told my lawyers to give you the house and all the money in the bank accounts."

"You know I don't want your money," Kathy said, hurt as she watched Sean carefully pack the computer into the Ferrari. There wasn't a lot of cargo space in the low-slung vehicle.

"Yes, Kathy, I know that," Alice said sadly. She wanted to caution Kathy about saying anything but knew that would only piss her off. She could trust Kathy not to say anything.

"Linda contacted me," Kathy told her, looking at Alice. She was feeling bad about instigating the divorce Portia had already filed on her behalf. Alice was being beyond generous and beyond reasonable, giving her more than the fifty percent of the assets she was due, and that annoyed her more than if Alice had fought the divorce.

"Yeah? What'd she want?"

"She was going to sue, but Portia sent a copy of the video over to her lawyers and threatened something about illegal prosecution…those papers you faxed us?"

Alice nodded but didn't say a word. It was better to let the past remain there. She was done. Her marriage to this woman was over. "Well, I've got to go. You should come and see the house sometime."

"I'll let Sean drive the car, and he can bring Emily," Kathy compromised. She didn't want to see Alice's new house. The children raving about the new house hurt her for some reason. She did appreciate that Alice had sent landscapers over to restore their yard. It had taken weeks, but already, the new sod was taking root. Some of the flowers would take years to recover.

Alice understood. Making a break like this was hard, but it was necessary. She waved as she went down the stairs, the older computers in her car would have to go to someone who could recycle the parts. The gaming computer would go in her new den. She had some messages she had waited weeks to send, and she could only send them through that computer. She knew the police hadn't been able to find anything, but that was only because they hadn't thought about the fact that people could send messages through the games. They hadn't thought that someone like Alice would even *play* such games. Alice played games alright…just not the kind that were contained on a mere computer.

Alice was surprised to find Kathy on her doorstep a week later. "Someone killed Linda Miller!" she accused, looking at Alice with hard eyes.

~The End~

∽ About the Author ∽

K'Anne Meinel is the BEST-SELLING author of LAWYERED, REPRESENTED, SAPPHIC SURFER, DOCTORED, AND VEIL OF SILENCE as well as several other books including her first, SHIPS which was written in 2003 over the course of two weeks. She then played with it for several years before publishing it as an e-book and then was approached to publish it in book form. After that it was published on other sites as an e-book. In the meantime, she published some 50 short stories, novellas, and novels of various genres. Originally from Wisconsin, many of her stories have taken on locations from and around the state. A gypsy at heart, she has lived in many locations and plans to continue roaming. Videos of several of her books are available on YouTube outlining some of the locations of her books and telling a little bit more...giving the readers insight into her mind as she created these wonderful stories.

If you have enjoyed **MALICE MASTERPIECES 5**
please look for K'Anne Meinel's novel **FLIGHT** from
Shadoe Publishing:
We have a chapter here for your enjoyment.

A tragic explosion results in the death of over 200 airplane passengers. Was the explosion caused by pilot error, or was it a conspiracy?

Pilot Cathalene (Lena) Penn, accused by the airline of being a smuggler, died in the tragedy, and her wife, Jessica is desperate to clear Lena's good name.

When Jessica travels to Belgium, her wife's home away from home, she discovers diamonds, a second family, and a mystery...

Sometimes, choosing between what is safe and what is right isn't easy, and running away is always an option...Flight!

CHAPTER ONE

Bam! Bam! Bam! The banging woke Jessica from a sound sleep. At first, she blinked, thinking she had dreamt the noise. Then, it was repeated a second and a third time. Her heart began thumping in fear when she realized she wasn't dreaming, and the noise that had woken her was someone beating a tattoo on her front door. Her first instinct was to get up, run, and hide, but then logical thought took over. Slowly, she rose from the bed, grasping for her robe lying at the end. She covered her nakedness, but before she had the robe completely on, she heard the incessant beating on the front door start up once again. If whoever that was left marks on her lovely wood door, she'd give them an earful. Jessica glanced at the clock, noting it read 3:10 a.m. She glanced out the window at the solid darkness of the early morning. Sighing, she reached for the handle of the bedroom door and heard the tattooing on the front door erupt once again. Gawd, someone was persistent. She flipped on the hall light as she went out, and the pounding, which had been coming in spates of three, immediately stopped between the second and third knock. Slowly, she squinted into the dark, trying to see who was there. She knew for sure an intruder wouldn't knock so persistently. Jessica headed cautiously down the curving staircase towards the front door.

Making sure the chain was latched, she turned on the outside light in order to see better. Slowly, she unlocked the door, in no hurry as she saw a man in a coat, a suit visible beneath its unbuttoned opening. Her heart was beating as hard as he had been pounding on the door, a static tattoo with missed beats that she knew didn't signal anything good.

She wasn't sure the beats weren't a precursor of a tearing wrench that was about to come.

"Hello?" she asked when she got the door ajar.

"Mrs. Penn?" he asked, peering at her through the door. The light from the porch barely lit her face and everything behind her was in darkness.

Seeing the captain's wings on his collar, she realized what this visit must mean and asked simply, "When?"

"May I come in, Mrs. Penn?" he asked, ignoring her question.

Gulping, she nodded and closed the door to remove the chain. She pulled the door open slightly, turned away, and walked a few paces to the newel post on the stairs. Her back was to her guest, who let himself in. She asked again, "When?"

"One a.m. local time," he answered, knowing she had guessed the reason for his visit.

Jess' hand spasmodically squeezed the post in response. Clutching it slightly for its stability, she took a deep breath before releasing both the post and the breath and heading down the hall along the stairs. She could hear by the steps behind her that the man was following her. She went through the swinging door to the kitchen, flipping the switch to turn on the light. Sitting at the breakfast bar, she stared numbly, seeing nothing as she waited. She was superficially aware as the man rummaged in her cupboards for a cup and poured her some water from the tap.

"Here, drink this," he offered kindly, watching her face closely.

She took the cup and drank from it, not aware that she was thirsty, or the liquid in the cup was merely water. "Were there any survivors?" She was grasping at straws, any hope, maybe they were just bracing her for the reality of the damage.

He shook his head. He waited. They were both quiet a long time, then a slight noise from upstairs made them both jump. He glanced up, but Jess didn't budge.

"She'll go back to bed," she stated to no one in particular. In fact, they heard the squeak of the floorboards once more a few minutes later before silence overcame the house once again. Finally, Jess looked up at the man, gazing in surprise to find him there as memories had assailed her. "Who are you?" she finally asked.

"I'm with the union. I'm here...to help," he explained, feeling helpless. The devastation written on her face was worse than he had expected, although he hadn't really known quite what to expect.

"Are they finding..." she gulped before continuing, "any bodies?"

"They are already on the scene investigating and looking for anything."

She glanced at him sharply. "There are no survivors?"

He shook his head, denying her that last false hope.

She took a deep breath, letting it out slowly and wanting it to sound normal. She wanted to sob, to cry, to rail at the fates, but for now, she was going to hold herself up stoically. "Now, what?"

"There will be an investigation–" he began and then her phone rang. Without hesitation, he answered it for her. She watched in surprise as he said, "Hello?" He paused to listen. "No, no comment. No comment....No, no comment." He must have said 'no comment' at least half a dozen times before he hung up the phone.

"You don't want me to talk to the media?" she asked, staring at the water in her cup as she realized who must have been on the phone.

"It would be better if you didn't," he advised.

She nodded to show she understood. The phone rang again. She glanced up as he answered it again. This time, he seemed to know the person on the other end.

"Yeah?" A long while seemed to pass as he listened. "I've got it handled," he told the unknown caller and then hung up.

"You said you are from the union?" she asked, becoming more aware, wakening from what had been an almost dream-like state.

"I'm sorry. I didn't properly introduce myself. I'm Andy Warhowicz."

"You're a pilot too?" she asked, glancing at his wings again.

He nodded, realizing how observant she was.

"Do they know what happened yet?"

"I don't know," he admitted, still watching her.

She pierced him with a look. "You knew enough to come to my home."

He nodded, admitting she was right. "They wanted me here before the media arrived and surprised you."

She nodded, grateful for the consideration, but it didn't change the dilemma she found herself in.

"Is there any chance that she...?" she began, seeking out all options.

"All we do know is, there was some type of explosion."

She looked up again, this time staring at the ceiling as if seeking answers there. "How many were on board?"

"Two hundred," he told her sorrowfully.

Oh, gawd. Two hundred souls plus the crew all gone! "Where were they?"

"They were beginning their descent into Belgium," he explained.

"Land or sea?"

"Excuse me?"

"Did the crash occur over land or sea?"

"In the sea."

She nodded, realizing most would have frozen in those deep waters even if they had survived the explosion. She swallowed the sob that wanted to leak out. "You will have to excuse me," she told him. "Help yourself to anything in the kitchen," she offered, pointing to the cereal and coffee maker as she turned.

He watched as she shuffled off towards the stairs. He could already hear the sobs she had been trying so valiantly to hold back. Shrugging off his trench coat, he revealed his suit with the captain's wings on his lapel, which showed that he too was a full-fledged pilot. Laying his coat on the counter, he looked around, then following her steps to the stairwell, he glanced up. He heard her climbing the stairs and heard the already familiar creaking of the floor above his head before silence once again descended on the remote house. He no longer heard her muffled cries, the ones she wouldn't release in front of him, and now, the house was dark. Searching, he found a light panel and flipped a couple switches. Lights went on in both the living room and what looked like a den across the hall. He chose to look in the den, curious about this couple.

The den was decorated warmly with maple wood and matching leather couches and chairs. A desk stood in one corner, facing out of the room with a leather chair behind it. The leather of the desk chair matched the couches and chairs. It was all tastefully done. He remembered the dossier on this pilot said her wife was a decorator. He approved. The room was very inviting. He looked at the shelves, admiring the hardbacks and the pictures showing two women. The woman whose life he had just turned upside down, a brunette, and the other, a dark blonde whose death had shattered their seemingly picture-perfect life. Standing between the women in one picture was a little

girl, obviously the daughter of both women with her red-brown hair and a nose that matched the dead woman's facial features. He sat down on the couch next to an end table with a phone, wondering about the two women's lives together as he fielded calls and repeated, "No comment," at least one-hundred times that night.

~End Sample Chapter of FLIGHT~
For more go to www.Shadoepublishing.com to purchase
the complete book or for many other delightful offerings.

~ Because a publisher should stand behind their authors~

Discovering that you don't have everything you thought you wanted is a surprise. Getting a promotion, finding new friends, learning you are attracted to women....

Nia Toyomoto has worked hard all her life to prove she was the best; she graduated early from high school, college, and got the dream job in Manhattan. Becoming a partner at the tender age of thirty she thought she had it all until the law firm made demands about her personal appearance and a few other things that made her change her life for the promotion. Then she realizes having everything isn't all that it is cracked up to be without someone to share it with...

A successful lawyer in the big city, choices have to be made, sacrifices and surprises await this beautiful and talented woman...does she make the right ones though?

~ Because a publisher should stand behind their authors~

What do you do when you meet someone who changes everything you know about love and passion?

Paige Harlow is a good girl. She's always known where she was going in life: top grades, an ivy league school, a medical degree, regular church attendance, and a happy marriage to a man. Falling in love with her gorgeous roommate and best friend Alyssa Torres is no small crisis. Alyssa is chasing demons of her own, a medical condition that makes her an outcast and a family dysfunctional to the point of disintegration make her a questionable choice for any stable relationship. But Paige's heart is no longer her own. She must now battle the prejudices of her family, friends, and church and come to peace with her new sexuality before she can hope to win the affections of the woman of her dreams. But will love be enough?

www.shadoepublishing.com

~ Because a publisher should stand behind their authors~

Coming out is hard. Coming out in the public eye is even harder. People think they own a piece of you, your work, and your life, they feel they have the right to judge you. You lose not only friends but fans and ultimately, possibly, your career…or your life.

Cassie Summers is a Southern Rock Star; she came out so that she could feel true to herself. Her family including her band and those important to her support her but there are others that feel she betrayed them, they have revenge on their minds…

Karin Myers is a Rock Star in her own right; she is one of those new super promoters: Manager, go-to gal, agent, public relations expert, and hand-holder all in one. Her name is synonymous with getting someone recognized, promoted, and making money. She only handles particular clients though; she's choosy…for some very specific reasons.

Meeting Cassie at a party there is a definite attraction. She does not however wish to represent her despite her excellent reputation. She fights it tooth and nail until she is contractually required to do so. In nearly costs them more than either of them anticipated….their lives.

www.shadoepublishing.com

~ Because a publisher should stand behind their authors~

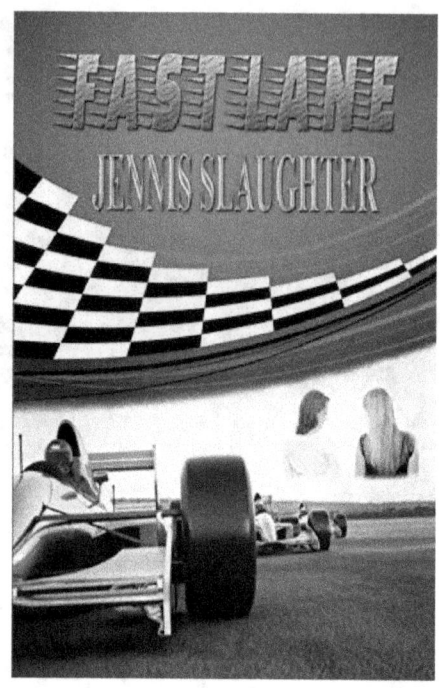

In the male dominated sport of Formula 1 racing, Samantha 'Sam' Dupree is struggling to make her mark against the boys. She hears about a driver who is making a name for herself in NASCAR and goes to check her out. Little does she know that she's in for the race of her heart.

Addison McCloud wants nothing more than to drive. She doesn't care about fame or fortune; she just wants to be fast enough to get herself and her family away from her abusive father. Meeting Sam, changes her world and revs her life into overdrive.

When the two women meet, sparks flies like the race cars that they drive. Will they be able to steer their relationship into something more and win the race, or will their families make them crash and burn. The boys of Formula 1 are going to learn that Southern girls are a force to be reckoned with.

~ Because a publisher should stand behind their authors~

Carrie flees from the demons of her present, trying to protect the ones she loves.

Frankie hides from the demons of her past, and the memory of loved ones she failed to protect.

A modern day princess thrown to the wolves, Carrie's only hope is the rancher who had spent the better part of a decade in self imposed, near total, isolation. Frankie's history of losing those she tries to save haunts her, but this madman threatens her home, her livestock, her sanctuary. She knows she can't do it alone, has she still got enough support from her oldest friends?

www.shadoepublishing.com

~ Because a publisher should stand behind their authors~

Amelia Gittens had the credit of being the first and only woman thus far in the United States military of being a sniper in combat, made possible by being in the Military Police unit of the crack 10th Mountain Infantry Division. After retirement she joins the City of New York Police Department, and suddenly finds herself involved in a suspect shooting incident which soon encroaches upon her entire life. In order to protect her therapist who has been targeted as a revenge killing, Amelia takes on the responsibility as if she was still in the Army, treating it as a tactical maneuver.

www.shadoepublishing.com

www.ingramcontent.com/pod-product-compliance
Lightning Source LLC
Chambersburg PA
CBHW071516260626
47170CB00002B/391